Thomas Hardy

AN IMAGINATIVE WOMAN
and other stories

Selected by MELVYN BRAGG

PHŒNIX

A PHOENIX PAPERBACK

First published in 1998
by Phoenix, a division of Orion Books Ltd
Orion House, 5 Upper St Martin's Lane, London WC2H 9EA

A CIP catalogue record for this book
is available from the British Library.

ISBN 0 75380 445 X

Typeset by Deltatype Ltd, Birkenhead, Merseyside
Printed in Great Britain by
The Guernsey Press Co. Ltd., Guernsey, C. I.

Contents

Note on the Author

THOMAS HARDY was born in Higher Bockhampton near Dorchester in 1840, the first of four children. His father was a stonemason and builder. At sixteen he trained as an architect and at twenty-two went to work in London. He returned home in 1867. He wrote poetry but failed to get it or his first novel *The Poor Man and the Lady* (1868) published.

Working on the restoration of a church in Cornwall, he met Emma Gifford and they married in 1874. He lost money on his self-financed novel *Desperate Remedies* (1871). *Under the Greenwood Tree* (1872) and *A Pair of Blue Eyes* (1873) followed. *Far From the Madding Crowd* (1874) was his first real success. Settling in Dorchester, he moved into Max Gate, the house he designed, in 1885. He wrote *The Hand of Ethelberta* (1876), *The Return of the Native* (1878) and *The Trumpet-Major* (1880). *A Laodicean* (1881) and *Two on a Tower* (1882) were followed by *The Mayor of Casterbridge* (1886) and *The Woodlanders* (1887). His first collection of short stories, *Wessex Tales* appeared in 1888; three further collections were published between 1891 and 1913. *Tess of the d'Urbervilles* (1891) brought fame, although its hostile reception in some quarters, and the further scandal accompanying the publication of *Jude the Obscure* (1895) led him to abandon fiction (except *The Well-Beloved*, 1897) and devote himself to poetry.

His first book of verse was *Wessex Poems* (1898), followed by seven further volumes. *The Dynasts*, an epic drama, was published 1904–8. In 1910 he was awarded the Order of Merit. His wife's death in 1912 inspired some of his greatest poems. He married Florence Dugdale in 1914 and died in 1928.

MELVYN BRAGG is an author and broadcaster. His novels include *The Hired Man*, *The Maid of Buttermere* and, most recently, *Credo*. He edits the South Bank Show on ITV and writes and presents Start-the-Week on Radio 4.

Introduction

Hardy sought to be immortal. His 'Wessex' was not only an invocation of a deeply ancient part of Britain, it was also, as he explained, near enough the size and population of even more ancient Greece, whose heroes and stories and dramas stretched across 3,000 years. In Hardy's novels and here in his short stories, he is often at pains to point out features of language, social customs, architecture or landscape which have changed in the few decades between the setting of a particular story and the time in which he was writing. He does this with the whisper of a sigh. Like most people, to Hardy the childhood world was golden and ever since, from that Eden, there had been a fall. If the old ways were not necessarily the best ways, they were certainly to this author, the best–loved ways. He wanted to make his past as enduring as the land and landscapes of Homer and because of that he, as it were, sealed it up in fiction.

It might strike Hardy, master of the ironic, steeped as all his work is in life's little and big ironies, as supremely ironic that it is the very strength of his association with the past that makes his work most poignant and on the surface most fragile. I believe he would have relished this. How many times is true love balked in his work? How many essential meetings are marred by an ironic encounter or damned by an ironic coincidence or undermined by an ironic echo from the past? Irony is one of Hardy's greatest dramatic devices and he has no qualms about over–using it, to great effect, time and again.

And so it bears repeating that as the old British countryside is now eroded by the year, as agricultural ways and sayings and metaphors which link us to Biblical times inevitably fade away in the great revolutionary swing from land to city which is one of the massive divides between ourselves and all previous centuries and cultures, Hardy's deep, landlocked Wessex looks increasingly isolated. It has gone forever. Those days when a heath in the South of England could be regarded as being of oceanic vastness and uncertainty are gone. Gone from our countryside too is the presence of innumerable crafts and skills passed on down the generations. Gone too the wide familiarity with nature, with the naming of trees and birds and flowers, the understanding of the seasons, the superstitions, the customs and the lore. If they are preserved, they are preserved by minorities sensing that they are holding onto something and not part of it.

The inextricably cross-hatched communities known to Chaucer and Shakespeare, to Fielding and George Eliot, have been swept away by industry and technology and the land which once sustained a vast majority of our people is now run by a computerized rump, inhabited by various categories of commuters, reinvented in dormitory suburbs and only here and there sprinkled with reaches where the old songs can still be heard.

This, to me, gives Hardy's short stories an even greater interest and intensity. It has always been a pleasure to read him for his robust story–telling, his unego-serving narrative force, his bluntness and yet his nicety of description which takes you into the character so immediately. These skills seem to be temporarily underestimated and Hardy's surehandedness – especially in an area of such traditional importance, the telling of the tale – is deeply refreshing. That will never go away for as long as we are intrigued by stories and he made himself a fine story–teller.

But the abandonment of the countryside and all that it means – perhaps it will take generations for the full effects to wear through – mean that Hardy can be treasured and appreciated on yet another level. He has become one of the prime historians of the way we once lived. The way so many of our ancestors existed over such a stretch of barely shifting, barely changing times is cocooned in his prose.

In Hardy you read of a silence in the countryside scarcely available today. The balance of sounds has changed, but here in these stories, again and again, we can sense the quality of a profound country silence, interrupted, yes, by animals and the force of the winds, but nevertheless a silence that can cover the world like an eggshell. And a different sense of time is here too. The time taken to move from place to place, the time to send and to answer messages marks the character, so that the sense of the unhurried – a Constable painting – takes us to a foreign, even exotic land which was commonplace a mere half a dozen generations ago.

Then there is the quaintness and direct and visible relationship with the past which a motorway world has largely overlaid. And the language of course, both Hardy's beloved dialect and his own high Tory English which remind us of a rooted almost instinctive way of life and a culture of lofty purpose – both of which are gone.

Like all truly great writers Thomas Hardy created his own fictional world. He could not have known how swiftly the real world on which it was moulded would disappear. In these stories we have not only the strongest insight into Hardy's fictional world, but also a map of a time that was ours and is lost.

AN IMAGINATIVE WOMAN
and other stories

The Three Strangers

Among the few features of agricultural England which retain an appearance but little modified by the lapse of centuries, may be reckoned the long, grassy and furzy downs, coombs, or ewe-leases, as they are called according to their kind, that fill a large area of certain counties in the south and south-west. If any mark of human occupation is met with hereon, it usually takes the form of the solitary cottage of some shepherd.

Fifty years ago such a lonely cottage stood on such a down, and may possibly be standing there now. In spite of its loneliness, however, the spot, by actual measurement, was not three miles from a county-town. Yet that affected it little. Three miles of irregular upland, during the long inimical seasons, with their sleets, snows, rains, and mists, afford withdrawing space enough to isolate a Timon or a Nebuchadnezzar; much less, in fair weather, to please that less repellent tribe, the poets, philosophers, artists, and others who 'conceive and meditate of pleasant things'.

Some old earthen camp or barrow, some clump of trees; at least some starved fragment of ancient hedge is usually taken advantage of in the erection of these forlorn dwellings. But, in the present case, such a kind of shelter had been disregarded. Higher Crowstairs, as the house was called, stood quite detached and undefended. The only reason for its precise situation seemed to be the crossing of two footpaths at right angles hard by, which may have crossed there and thus for a good five hundred years. Hence the house was exposed to the elements on all sides. But, though the wind up here blew unmistakably when it did blow, and the rain hit hard whenever it fell, the various weathers of the winter season were not quite so formidable on the down as they were imagined to be by dwellers on low ground. The raw rimes were not so pernicious as in the hollows, and the frosts were scarcely so severe. When the shepherd and his family who tenanted the house were pitied for their sufferings from the exposure, they said that upon the whole they were less inconvenienced by 'wuzzes and flames' (hoarses and phlegms) than when they had lived by the stream of a snug neighbouring valley.

The night of March 28, 182-, was precisely one of the nights that were wont to call forth these expressions of commiseration. The level rainstorm smote walls, slopes, and hedges like the clothyard shafts of Senlac and Crecy. Such sheep and outdoor animals as had no shelter stood with their buttocks to the winds; while the tails of little birds trying to roost on some scraggy thorn were blown inside-out like umbrellas. The gable-end of the cottage was stained with wet, and the eavesdroppings flapped against the wall. Yet never was commiseration for the shepherd more misplaced. For that cheerful rustic was entertaining a large party in glorification of the christening of his second girl.

The guests had arrived before the rain began to fall, and they were all now assembled in the chief or living room of the dwelling. A glance into the apartment at eight o'clock on this eventful evening would have resulted in the opinion that it was as cosy and comfortable a nook as could be wished for in boisterous weather. The calling of its inhabitant was proclaimed by a number of highly-polished sheep-crooks without stems that were hung ornamentally over the fireplace, the curl of each shining crook varying from the antiquated type engraved in the patriarchal pictures of old family Bibles to the most approved fashion of the last local sheep-fair. The room was lighted by half-a-dozen candles, having wicks only a trifle smaller than the grease which enveloped them, in candlesticks that were never used but at high-days, holy-days, and family feasts. The lights were scattered about the room, two of them standing on the chimney-piece. This position of candles was in itself significant. Candles on the chimney-piece always meant a party.

On the hearth, in front of a back-brand to give substance, blazed a fire of thorns, that crackled 'like the laughter of the fool'.

Nineteen persons were gathered here. Of these, five women, wearing gowns of various bright hues, sat in chairs along the wall; girls shy and not shy filled the window-bench; four men, including Charley Jake the hedge-carpenter, Elijah New the parish-clerk, and John Pitcher, a neighbouring dairyman, the shepherd's father-in-law, lolled in the settle; a young man and maid, who were blushing over tentative *pourparlers* on a life-companionship, sat beneath the corner-cupboard; and an elderly engaged man of fifty or upward moved restlessly about from spots where his betrothed was not to the spot where she was. Enjoyment was pretty general, and so much the more prevailed in being unhampered by conventional restrictions. Absolute confidence in each other's good opinion begat perfect ease, while the finishing stroke of manner, amounting to a truly princely serenity, was lent to the majority by the absence of any expression or trait denoting that they wished to get on in the world, enlarge their minds, or do any eclipsing thing whatever – which nowadays so generally nips the bloom and *bonhomie* of all except the two extremes of the social scale.

Shepherd Fennel had married well, his wife being a dairyman's daughter from a vale at a distance, who brought fifty guineas in her pocket – and kept them there, till they should be required for ministering to the needs of a coming family. This frugal woman had been somewhat exercised as to the character that should be given to the gathering. A sit-still party had its advantages; but an undisturbed position of ease in chairs and settles was apt to lead on the men to such an unconscionable deal of toping that they would sometimes fairly drink the house dry. A dancing-party was the alternative; but this, while avoiding the foregoing objection on the score of good drink, had a counterbalancing disadvantage in the matter of good victuals; the ravenous appetites engendered by the exercise causing immense havoc in the buttery. Shepherd-ess Fennel fell back upon the intermediate plan of mingling short dances with short periods of talk and singing, so as to hinder any ungovernable rage in either. But this scheme was entirely confined to her own gentle mind: the shepherd himself was in the mood to exhibit the most reckless phases of hospitality.

The fiddler was a boy of those parts, about twelve years of age, who had a wonderful dexterity in jigs and reels, though his fingers were so small and short as to necessitate a constant shifting for the high notes, from which he scrambled back to the first position with sounds not of unmixed purity of tone. At seven the shrill tweedle-dee of this youngster had begun, accompanied by a booming ground-bass from Elijah New, the parish-clerk, who had thoughtfully brought with him his favourite musical instrument, the serpent. Dancing was instantaneous, Mrs Fennel privately enjoining the players on no account to let the dance exceed the length of a quarter of an hour.

But Elijah and the boy in the excitement of their position quite forgot the injunction. Moreover, Oliver Giles, a man of seventeen, one of the dancers, who was enamoured of his partner, a fair girl of thirty-three rolling years, had recklessly handed a new crown-piece to the musicians, as a bribe to keep going as long as they had muscle and wind. Mrs Fennel, seeing the steam begin to generate on the countenances of her guests, crossed over and touched the fiddler's elbow and put her hand on the serpent's mouth. But they took no notice, and fearing she might lose her character of genial hostess if she were to interfere too markedly, she retired and sat down helpless. And so the dance whizzed on with cumulative fury, the performers moving in their planet-like courses, direct and retrograde, from apogee to perigee, till the hand of the well-kicked clock at the bottom of the room had travelled over the circumference of an hour.

While these cheerful events were in course of enactment within Fennel's pastoral dwelling an incident having consider-able bearing on the party had occurred in the gloomy night without. Mrs Fennel's concern about the growing fierceness of the dance corresponded in point of time with the ascent of a human figure to the solitary hill of Higher Crowstairs from the direction of the distant town. This personage strode on through the rain without a pause, following the little-worn path which, further on in its course, skirted the shepherd's cottage.

It was nearly the time of full moon, and on this account, though the sky was lined with a uniform sheet of dripping cloud, ordinary objects out of doors were readily visible. The sad wan light revealed the lonely pedestrian to be a man of supple frame; his gait suggested that he had somewhat passed the period of perfect and instinctive agility, though not so far as to be otherwise than rapid of motion when occasion required. At a rough guess, he might have been about forty years of age. He appeared tall, but a recruiting sergeant, or other person accus-tomed to the judging of men's heights by the eye, would have discerned that this was chiefly owing to his gauntness, and that he was not more than five-feet-eight or nine.

Notwithstanding the regularity of his tread there was caution in it, as in that of one who mentally feels his way; and despite the fact that it was not a black coat nor a dark garment of any sort that he wore, there was something about him which suggested that he naturally belonged to the black-coated tribes of men. His clothes were of fustian, and his boots hobnailed, yet in his progress he showed not the mud-accustomed bearing of hobnailed and fustianed peasantry.

By the time that he had arrived abreast of the shepherd's premises the rain came down, or rather came along, with yet more determined violence. The outskirts of the little settlement partially broke the force of wind and rain, and this induced him to stand still. The most salient of the shepherd's domestic erections was an empty sty at the forward corner of his hedgeless garden, for in these latitudes the principle of masking the homelier features of your establishment by a conventional frontage was unknown. The traveller's eye was attracted to this small building by the pallid shine of the wet slates that covered it. He turned aside, and, finding it empty, stood under the pent-roof for shelter.

While he stood the boom of the serpent within the adjacent house, and the lesser strains of the fiddler, reached the spot as an accompaniment to the surging hiss of the flying rain on the sod, its louder beating on the cabbage-leaves of the garden, on the straw hackles of eight or ten beehives just discernible by the path, and its dripping from the eaves into a row of buckets and pans that had been placed under the walls of the cottage. For at Higher Crowstairs, as at all such elevated domiciles, the grand difficulty of housekeeping was an insufficiency of water; and a casual rainfall was utilized by turning out, as catchers, every utensil that the house contained. Some queer stories might be told of the contrivances for economy in suds and dish-waters that are absolutely necessitated in upland habitations during the droughts of summer. But at this season there were no such exigencies; a mere acceptance of what the skies bestowed was sufficient for an abundant store.

At last the notes of the serpent ceased and the house was silent. This cessation of activity aroused the solitary pedestrian from the reverie into which he had lapsed, and, emerging from the shed, with an apparently new intention, he walked up the path to the house-door. Arrived here, his first act was to kneel down on a large stone beside the row of vessels, and to drink a copious draught from one of them. Having quenched his thirst he rose and lifted his hand to knock, but paused with his eye upon

the panel. Since the dark surface of the wood revealed absolutely
nothing, it was evident that he must be mentally looking through
the door, as if he wished to measure thereby all the possibilities
that a house of this sort might include, and how they might bear
upon the question of his entry.

In his indecision he turned and surveyed the scene around.
Not a soul was anywhere visible. The garden-path stretched
downward from his feet, gleaming like the track of a snail; the
roof of the little well (mostly dry), the well-cover, the top rail of
the garden gate, were varnished with the same dull liquid glaze;
while, far away in the vale, a faint whiteness of more than usual
extent showed that the rivers were high in the meads. Beyond all
this winked a few bleared lamplights through the beating drops –
lights that denoted the situation of the county-town from which
he had appeared to come. The absence of all notes of life in that
direction seemed to clinch his intentions, and he knocked at the
door.

Within, a desultory chat had taken the place of movement and
musical sound. The hedge-carpenter was suggesting a song to the
company, which nobody just then was inclined to undertake, so
that the knock afforded a not unwelcome diversion.

'Walk in!' said the shepherd promptly.

The latch clicked upward, and out of the night our pedestrian
appeared upon the door-mat. The shepherd arose, snuffed two of
the nearest candles, and turned to look at him.

Their light disclosed that the stranger was dark in complexion
and not unprepossessing as to feature. His hat, which for a
moment he did not remove, hung low over his eyes, without
concealing that they were large, open, and determined, moving
with a flash rather than a glance round the room. He seemed
pleased with his survey, and, baring his shaggy head, said, in a
rich deep voice, 'The rain is so heavy, friends, that I ask leave to
come in and rest awhile.'

'To be sure, stranger,' said the shepherd. 'And faith, you've
been lucky in choosing your time, for we are having a bit of a
fling for a glad cause – though, to be sure, a man could hardly
wish that glad cause to happen more than once a year.'

'Nor less,' spoke up a woman. 'For 'tis best to get your family
over and done with, as soon as you can, so as to be all the earlier
out of the fag o't.'

'And what may be this glad cause?' asked the stranger.

'A birth and christening,' said the shepherd.

The stranger hoped his host might not be made unhappy either by too many or too few of such episodes, and being invited by a gesture to a pull at the mug, he readily acquiesced. His manner, which, before entering, had been so dubious, was now altogether that of a careless and candid man.

'Late to be traipsing athwart this coomb – hey?' said the engaged man of fifty.

'Late it is, master, as you say. – I'll take a seat in the chimney-corner, if you have nothing to urge against it, ma'am; for I am a little moist on the side that was next the rain.'

Mrs Shepherd Fennel assented, and made room for the self-invited comer, who, having got completely inside the chimney-corner, stretched out his legs and his arms with the expansiveness of a person quite at home.

'Yes, I am rather cracked in the vamp,' he said freely, seeing that the eyes of the shepherd's wife fell upon his boots, 'and I am not well fitted either. I have had some rough times lately, and have been forced to pick up what I can get in the way of wearing, but I must find a suit better fit for working-days when I reach home.'

'One of hereabouts?' she inquired.

'Not quite that – further up the country.'

'I thought so. And so be I; and by your tongue you come from my neighbourhood.'

'But you would hardly have heard of me,' he said quickly. 'My time would be long before yours, ma'am, you see.'

This testimony to the youthfulness of his hostess had the effect of stopping her cross-examination.

'There is only one thing more wanted to make me happy,' continued the new-comer. 'And that is a little baccy, which I am sorry to say I am out of.'

'I'll fill your pipe,' said the shepherd.

'I must ask you to lend me a pipe likewise.'

'A smoker, and no pipe about 'ee?'

'I have dropped it somewhere on the road.'

The shepherd filled and handed him a new clay pipe, saying, as he did so, 'Hand me your baccy-box – I'll fill that too, now I am about it.'

The man went through the movement of searching his pockets.

'Lost that too?' said his entertainer, with some surprise.

'I am afraid so,' said the man with some confusion. 'Give it to me in a screw of paper.' Lighting his pipe at the candle with a suction that drew the whole flame into the bowl, he resettled himself in the corner and bent his looks upon the faint steam from his damp legs, as if he wished to say no more.

Meanwhile the general body of guests had been taking little notice of this visitor by reason of an absorbing discussion in which they were engaged with the band about a tune for the next dance. The matter being settled, they were about to stand up when an interruption came in the shape of another knock at the door.

At sound of the same the man in the chimney-corner took up the poker and began stirring the brands as if doing it thoroughly were the one aim of his existence; and a second time the shepherd said, 'Walk in!' In a moment another man stood upon the straw-woven door-mat. He too was a stranger.

This individual was one of a type radically different from the first. There was more of the commonplace in his manner, and a certain jovial cosmopolitanism sat upon his features. He was several years older than the first arrival, his hair being slightly frosted, his eyebrows bristly, and his whiskers cut back from his cheeks. His face was rather full and flabby, and yet it was not altogether a face without power. A few grog-blossoms marked the neighbourhood of his nose. He flung back his long drab greatcoat, revealing that beneath it he wore a suit of cinder-grey shade throughout, large heavy seals, of some metal or other that would take a polish, dangling from his fob as his only personal ornament. Shaking the water-drops from his low-crowned glazed hat, he said, 'I must ask for a few minutes' shelter, comrades, or I shall be wetted to my skin before I get to Casterbridge.'

'Make yourself at home, master,' said the shepherd, perhaps a trifle less heartily than on the first occasion. Not that Fennel had the least tinge of niggardliness in his composition; but the room was far from large, spare chairs were not numerous, and damp companions were not altogether desirable at close quarters for the women and girls in their bright-coloured gowns.

However, the second comer, after taking off his greatcoat, and hanging his hat on a nail in one of the ceiling-beams as if he had been specially invited to put it there, advanced and sat down at the table. This had been pushed so closely into the chimney-corner, to give all available room to the dancers, that its inner edge grazed the elbow of the man who had ensconced himself by the fire; and thus the two strangers were brought into close companionship. They nodded to each other by way of breaking the ice of unacquaintance, and the first stranger handed his neighbour the family mug – a huge vessel of brown ware, having its upper edge worn away like a threshold by the rub of whole generations of thirsty lips that had gone the way of all flesh, and bearing the following inscription burnt upon its rotund side in yellow letters: –

> THERE IS NO FUN
> UNTiLL i CUM.

The other man, nothing loth, raised the mug to his lips, and drank on, and on, and on – till a curious blueness overspread the countenance of the shepherd's wife, who had regarded with no little surprise the first stranger's free offer to the second of what did not belong to him to dispense.

'I knew it!' said the toper to the shepherd with much satisfaction. 'When I walked up your garden before coming in, and saw the hives all of a row, I said to myself, "Where there's bees there's honey, and where there's honey there's mead." But mead of such a truly comfortable sort as this I really didn't expect to meet in my older days.' He took yet another pull at the mug, till it assumed an ominous elevation.

'Glad you enjoy it!' said the shepherd warmly.

'It is goodish mead,' assented Mrs Fennel, with an absence of enthusiasm which seemed to say that it was possible to buy praise for one's cellar at too heavy a price. 'It is trouble enough to make – and really I hardly think we shall make any more. For honey sells well, and we ourselves can make shift with a drop o' small mead and metheglin for common use from the comb-washings.'

'O, but you'll never have the heart!' reproachfully cried the stranger in cinder-grey, after taking up the mug a third time and setting it down empty. 'I love mead, when 'tis old like this, as I love to go to church o' Sundays, or to relieve the needy any day of the week.'

'Ha, ha, ha!' said the man in the chimney-corner, who, in spite of the taciturnity induced by the pipe of tobacco, could not or would not refrain from this slight testimony to his comrade's humour.

Now the old mead of those days, brewed of the purest first-year or maiden honey, four pounds to the gallon – with its due complement of white of eggs, cinnamon, ginger, cloves, mace, rosemary, yeast, and processes of working, bottling, and cellaring – tasted remarkably strong; but it did not taste so strong as it actually was. Hence, presently, the stranger in cinder-grey at the table, moved by its creeping influence, unbuttoned his waistcoat, threw himself back in his chair, spread his legs, and made his presence felt in various ways.

'Well, well, as I say,' he resumed, 'I am going to Casterbridge, and to Casterbridge I must go. I should have been almost there by this time; but the rain drove me into your dwelling, and I'm not sorry for it.'

'You don't live in Casterbridge?' said the shepherd.

'Not as yet; though I shortly mean to move there.'

'Going to set up in trade, perhaps?'

'No, no,' said the shepherd's wife. 'It is easy to see that the gentleman is rich, and don't want to work at anything.'

The cinder-grey stranger paused, as if to consider whether he would accept that definition of himself. He presently rejected it by answering, 'Rich is not quite the word for me, dame. I do work, and I must work. And even if I only get to Casterbridge by midnight I must begin work there at eight tomorrow morning. Yes, het or wet, blow or snow, famine or sword, my day's work tomorrow must be done.'

'Poor man! Then, in spite o' seeming, you be worse off than we?' replied the shepherd's wife.

''Tis the nature of my trade, men and maidens. 'Tis the nature of my trade more than my poverty.... But really and truly I must up and off, or I shan't get a lodging in the town.' However, the speaker did not move, and directly added, 'There's time for one more draught of friendship before I go; and I'd perform it at once if the mug were not dry.'

'Here's a mug o' small,' said Mrs Fennel. 'Small, we call it, though to be sure 'tis only the first wash o' the combs.'

'No,' said the stranger disdainfully. 'I won't spoil your first kindness by partaking o' your second.'

'Certainly not,' broke in Fennel. 'We don't increase and multiply every day, and I'll fill the mug again.' He went away to the dark place under the stairs where the barrel stood. The shepherdess followed him.

'Why should you do this?' she said reproachfully, as soon as they were alone. 'He's emptied it once, though it held enough for ten people; and now he's not contented wi' the small, but must needs call for more o' the strong! And a stranger unbeknown to any of us. For my part, I don't like the look o' the man at all.'

'But he's in the house, my honey; and 'tis a wet night, and a christening. Daze it, what's a cup of mead more or less? There'll be plenty more next bee-burning.'

'Very well – this time, then,' she answered, looking wistfully at the barrel. 'But what is the man's calling, and where is he one of, that he should come in and join us like this?'

'I don't know. I'll ask him again.'

The catastrophe of having the mug drained dry at one pull by the stranger in cinder-grey was effectually guarded against this time by Mrs Fennel. She poured out his allowance in a small cup, keeping the large one at a discreet distance from him. When he had tossed off his portion the shepherd renewed his inquiry about the stranger's occupation.

The latter did not immediately reply, and the man in the chimney-corner, with sudden demonstrativeness, said, 'Anybody may know my trade – I'm a wheelwright.'

'A very good trade for these parts,' said the shepherd.

'And anybody may know mine – if they've the sense to find it out,' said the stranger in cinder-grey.

'You may generally tell what a man is by his claws,' observed the hedge-carpenter, looking at his own hands, 'My fingers be as full of thorns as an old pin-cushion is of pins.'

The hands of the man in the chimney-corner instinctively sought the shade, and he gazed into the fire as he resumed his pipe. The man at the table took up the hedge-carpenter's remark, and added smartly, 'True; but the oddity of my trade is that, instead of setting a mark upon me, it sets a mark upon my customers.'

No observation being offered by anybody in elucidation of this enigma the shepherd's wife once more called for a song. The same obstacles presented themselves as at the former time – one had no voice, another had forgotten the first verse. The stranger at the table, whose soul had now risen to a good working temperature, relieved the difficulty by exclaiming that, to start the company, he would sing himself. Thrusting one thumb into the arm-hole of his waistcoat, he waved the other hand in the air, and, with an extemporizing gaze at the shining sheep-crooks above the mantelpiece, began: –

> O my trade it is the rarest one,
>> Simple shepherds all –
>> My trade is a sight to see;
> For my customers I tie, and take them up on high,
>> And waft 'em to a far countree!

The room was silent when he had finished the verse – with one exception, that of the man in the chimney-corner, who, at the singer's word, 'Chorus!' joined him in a deep bass voice of musical relish –

>> And waft 'em to a far countree!

Oliver Giles, John Pitcher the dairyman, the parish-clerk, the engaged man of fifty, the row of young women against the wall, seemed lost in thought not of the gayest kind. The shepherd looked meditatively on the ground, the shepherdess gazed keenly at the singer, and with some suspicion; she was doubting whether this stranger were merely singing an old song from recollection, or was composing one there and then for the occasion. All were as perplexed at the obscure revelation as the guests at Belshazzar's Feast, except the man in the chimney-corner, who quietly said, 'Second verse, stranger,' and smoked on.

The singer thoroughly moistened himself from his lips inwards, and went on with the next stanza as requested: –

> My tools are but common ones,
>> Simple shepherds all –

My tools are no sight to see:
A little hempen string, and a post whereon to swing,
Are implementents enough for me!

Shepherd Fennel glanced round. There was no longer any doubt
that the stranger was answering his question rhythmically. The
guests one and all started back with suppressed exclamations.
The young woman engaged to the man of fifty fainted half-way,
and would have proceeded, but finding him wanting in alacrity
for catching her she sat down trembling.

'O, he's the – ' whispered the people in the background,
mentioning the name of an ominous public officer. 'He's come to
do it! 'Tis to be at Casterbridge jail tomorrow – the man for sheep-
stealing – the poor clock-maker we heard of, who used to live
away at Shottsford and had no work to do – Timothy Summers,
whose family were a-starving, and so he went out of Shottsford
by the high-road, and took a sheep in open daylight, defying the
farmer and the farmer's wife and the farmer's lad, and every man
jack among 'em. He' (and they nodded towards the stranger of
the deadly trade) 'is come from up the country to do it because
there's not enough to do in his own county-town, and he's got
the place here now our own county man's dead; he's going to
live in the same cottage under the prison wall.'

The stranger in cinder-grey took no notice of this whispered
string of observations, but again wetted his lips. Seeing that his
friend in the chimney-corner was the only one who reciprocated
his joviality in any way, he held out his cup towards that
appreciative comrade, who also held out his own. They clinked
together, the eyes of the rest of the room hanging upon the
singer's actions. He parted his lips for the third verse; but at that
moment another knock was audible upon the door. This time the
knock was faint and hesitating.

The company seemed scared; the shepherd looked with
consternation towards the entrance, and it was with some effort
that he resisted his alarmed wife's deprecatory glance, and
uttered for the third time the welcoming words, 'Walk in!'

The door was gently opened, and another man stood upon the
mat. He, like those who had preceded him, was a stranger. This
time it was a short, small personage, of fair complexion, and
dressed in a decent suit of dark clothes.

'Can you tell me the way to – ?' he began: when, gazing round the room to observe the nature of the company amongst whom he had fallen, his eyes lighted on the stranger in cinder-grey. It was just at the instant when the latter, who had thrown his mind into his song with such a will that he scarcely heeded the interruption, silenced all whispers and inquiries by bursting into his third verse: –

> Tomorrow is my working day,
>> Simple shepherds all –
> Tomorrow is a working day for me:
> For the farmer's sheep is slain, and the lad who did it ta'en,
>> And on his soul may God ha' merc-y!

The stranger in the chimney-corner, waving cups with the singer so heartily that his mead splashed over on the hearth, repeated in his bass voice as before: –

> And on his soul may God ha' merc-y!

All this time the third stranger had been standing in the doorway. Finding now that he did not come forward or go on speaking, the guests particularly regarded him. They noticed to their surprise that he stood before them the picture of abject terror – his knees trembling, his hand shaking so violently that the door-latch by which he supported himself rattled audibly: his white lips were parted, and his eyes fixed on the merry officer of justice in the middle of the room. A moment more and he had turned, closed the door, and fled.

'What a man can it be?' said the shepherd.

The rest, between the awfulness of their late discovery and the odd conduct of this third visitor, looked as if they knew not what to think, and said nothing. Instinctively they withdrew further and further from the grim gentleman in their midst, whom some of them seemed to take for the Prince of Darkness himself, till they formed a remote circle, an empty space of floor being left between them and him –

> ... circulus, cujus centrum diabolus.

The room was so silent – though there were more than twenty people in it – that nothing could be heard but the patter of the

rain against the window-shutters, accompanied by the occasional hiss of a stray drop that fell down the chimney into the fire,
and the steady puffing of the man in the corner, who had now
resumed his pipe of long clay.

The stillness was unexpectedly broken. The distant sound of a
gun reverberated through the air – apparently from the direction
of the county-town.

'Be jiggered!' cried the stranger who had sung the song,
jumping up.

'What does that mean?' asked several.

'A prisoner escaped from the jail – that's what it means.'

All listened. The sound was repeated, and none of them spoke
but the man in the chimney-corner, who said quietly, 'I've often
been told that in this county they fire a gun at such times; but I
never heard it till now.'

'I wonder if it is *my* man?' murmured the personage in cinder-
grey.

'Surely it is!' said the shepherd involuntarily. 'And surely
we've zeed him! That little man who looked in at the door by
now, and quivered like a leaf when he zeed ye and heard your
song!'

'His teeth chattered, and the breath went out of his body,' said
the dairyman.

'And his heart seemed to sink within him like a stone,' said
Oliver Giles.

'And he bolted as if he'd been shot at,' said the hedge-
carpenter.

'True – his teeth chattered, and his heart seemed to sink; and
he bolted as if he'd been shot at,' slowly summed up the man in
the chimney-corner.

'I didn't notice it,' remarked the hangman.

'We were all a-wondering what made him run off in such a
fright,' faltered one of the women against the wall, 'and now 'tis
explained!'

The firing of the alarm-gun went on at intervals, low and
sullenly, and their suspicions became a certainty. The sinister
gentleman in cinder-grey roused himself. 'Is there a constable
here?' he asked, in thick tones. 'If so, let him step forward.'

The engaged man of fifty stepped quavering out from the wall,
his betrothed beginning to sob on the back of the chair.

'You are a sworn constable?'

'I be, sir.'

'Then pursue the criminal at once, with assistance, and bring him back here. He can't have gone far.'

'I will, sir, I will – when I've got my staff. I'll go home and get it, and come sharp here, and start in a body.'

'Staff! – never mind your staff; the man'll be gone!'

'But I can't do nothing without my staff – can I, William, and John, and Charles Jake? No; for there's the king's royal crown a painted on en in yaller and gold, and the lion and the unicorn, so as when I raise en up and hit my prisoner, 'tis made a lawful blow thereby. I wouldn't 'tempt to take up a man without my staff – no, not I. If I hadn't the law to gie me courage, why, instead o' my taking up him he might take up me!'

'Now, I'm a king's man myself, and can give you authority enough for this,' said the formidable officer in grey. 'Now then, all of ye, be ready. Have ye any lanterns?'

'Yes – have ye any lanterns? – I demand it!' said the constable.

'And the rest of you able-bodied – '

'Able-bodied men – yes – the rest of ye!' said the constable.

'Have you some good stout staves and pitchforks – '

'Staves and pitchforks – in the name o' the law! And take 'em in yer hands and go in quest, and do as we in authority tell ye!'

Thus aroused, the men prepared to give chase. The evidence was, indeed, though circumstantial, so convincing, that but little argument was needed to show the shepherd's guests that after what they had seen it would look very much like connivance if they did not instantly pursue the unhappy third stranger, who could not as yet have gone more than a few hundred yards over such uneven country.

A shepherd is always well provided with lanterns; and, lighting these hastily, and with hurdle-staves in their hands, they poured out of the door, taking a direction along the crest of the hill, away from the town, the rain having fortunately a little abated.

Disturbed by the noise, or possibly by unpleasant dreams of her baptism, the child who had been christened began to cry heart-brokenly in the room overhead. These notes of grief came down through the chinks of the floor to the ears of the women below, who jumped up one by one, and seemed glad of the excuse to ascend and comfort the baby, for the incidents of the last half-hour greatly oppressed them. Thus in the space of two or three minutes the room on the ground-floor was deserted quite.

But it was not for long. Hardly had the sound of footsteps died away when a man returned round the corner of the house from the direction the pursuers had taken. Peeping in at the door, and seeing nobody there, he entered leisurely. It was the stranger of the chimney-corner, who had gone out with the rest. The motive of his return was shown by his helping himself to a cut piece of skimmer-cake that lay on a ledge beside where he had sat, and which he had apparently forgotten to take with him. He also poured out half a cup more mead from the quantity that remained, ravenously eating and drinking these as he stood. He had not finished when another figure came in just as quietly – his friend in cinder-grey.

'O – you here?' said the latter, smiling. 'I thought you had gone to help in the capture.' And this speaker also revealed the object of his return by looking solicitously round for the fascinating mug of old mead.

'And I thought you had gone,' said the other, continuing his skimmer-cake with some effort.

'Well, on second thoughts, I felt there were enough without me,' said the first confidentially, 'and such a night as it is, too. Besides, 'tis the business o' the Government to take care of its criminals – not mine.'

'True; so it is. And I felt as you did, that there were enough without me.'

'I don't want to break my limbs running over the humps and hollows of this wild country.'

'Nor I neither, between you and me.'

'These shepherd-people are used to it – simple-minded souls, you know, stirred up to anything in a moment. They'll have him ready for me before the morning, and no trouble to me at all.'

'They'll have him, and we shall have saved ourselves all labour in the matter.'

'True, true. Well, my way is to Casterbridge; and 'tis as much as my legs will do to take me that far. Going the same way?'

'No, I am sorry to say! I have to get home over there' (he nodded indefinitely to the right), 'and I feel as you do, that it is quite enough for my legs to do before bedtime.'

The other had by this time finished the mead in the mug, after which, shaking hands heartily at the door, and wishing each other well, they went their several ways.

In the meantime the company of pursuers had reached the end of the hog's-back elevation which dominated this part of the down. They had decided on no particular plan of action; and, finding that the man of the baleful trade was no longer in their company, they seemed quite unable to form any such plan now. They descended in all directions down the hill, and straightway several of the party fell into the snare set by Nature for all misguided midnight ramblers over this part of the cretaceous formation. The 'lanchets', or flint slopes, which belted the escarpment at intervals of a dozen yards, took the less cautious ones unawares, and losing their footing on the rubbly steep they slid sharply downwards, the lanterns rolling from their hands to the bottom, and there lying on their sides till the horn was scorched through.

When they had again gathered themselves together the shepherd, as the man who knew the country best, took the lead, and guided them round these treacherous inclines. The lanterns, which seemed rather to dazzle their eyes and warn the fugitive than to assist them in the exploration, were extinguished, due silence was observed; and in this more rational order they plunged into the vale. It was a grassy, briery, moist defile, affording some shelter to any person who had sought it; but the party perambulated it in vain, and ascended on the other side. Here they wandered apart, and after an interval closed together again to report progress. At the second time of closing in they found themselves near a lonely ash, the single tree on this part of the coomb, probably sown there by a passing bird some fifty years before. And here, standing a little to one side of the trunk, as motionless as the trunk itself, appeared the man they were in quest of, his outline being well defined against the sky beyond. The band noiselessly drew up and faced him.

'Your money or your life!' said the constable sternly to the still figure.

'No, no,' whispered John Pitcher. ''Tisn't our side ought to say that. That's the doctrine of vagabonds like him, and we be on the side of the law.'

'Well, well,' replied the constable impatiently; 'I must say something, mustn't I? and if you had all the weight o' this undertaking upon your mind, perhaps you'd say the wrong thing too! – Prisoner at the bar, surrender, in the name of the Father – the Crown, I mane!'

The man under the tree seemed now to notice them for the first time, and, giving them no opportunity whatever for exhibiting their courage, he strolled slowly towards them. He was, indeed, the little man, the third stranger; but his trepidation had in a great measure gone.

'Well, travellers,' he said, 'did I hear ye speak to me?'

'You did: you've got to come and be our prisoner at once!' said the constable. 'We arrest 'ee on the charge of not biding in Casterbridge jail in a decent proper manner to be hung tomorrow morning. Neighbours, do your duty, and seize the culpet!'

On hearing the charge the man seemed enlightened, and, saying not another word, resigned himself with preternatural civility to the search-party, who, with their staves in their hands, surrounded him on all sides, and marched him back towards the shepherd's cottage.

It was eleven o'clock by the time they arrived. The light shining from the open door, a sound of men's voices within, proclaimed to them as they approached the house that some new events had arisen in their absence. On entering they discovered the shepherd's living-room to be invaded by two officers from Casterbridge jail, and a well-known magistrate who lived at the nearest country-seat, intelligence of the escape having become generally circulated.

'Gentlemen,' said the constable, 'I have brought back your man – not without risk and danger; but every one must do his duty! He is inside this circle of able-bodied persons, who have lent me useful aid, considering their ignorance of Crown work. Men, bring forward your prisoner!' And the third stranger was led to the light.

'Who is this?' said one of the officials.

'The man,' said the constable.

'Certainly not,' said the turnkey; and the first corroborated his statement.

'But how can it be otherwise?' asked the constable. 'Or why was he so terrified at sight o' the singing instrument of the law who sat there?' Here he related the strange behaviour of the third stranger on entering the house during the hangman's song.

'Can't understand it,' said the officer coolly. 'All I know is that it is not the condemned man. He's quite a different character from this one; a gauntish fellow, with dark hair and eyes, rather good-looking, and with a musical bass voice that if you heard it once you'd never mistake as long as you lived.'

'Why, souls – 'twas the man in the chimney-corner!'

'Hey – what?' said the magistrate, coming forward after inquiring particulars from the shepherd in the background. 'Haven't you got the man after all?'

'Well, sir,' said the constable, 'he's the man we were in search of, that's true; and yet he's not the man we were in search of. For the man we were in search of was not the man we wanted, sir, if you understand my every-day way; for 'twas the man in the chimney-corner!'

'A pretty kettle of fish altogether!' said the magistrate. 'You had better start for the other man at once.'

The prisoner now spoke for the first time. The mention of the man in the chimney-corner seemed to have moved him as nothing else could do. 'Sir,' he said, stepping forward to the magistrate, 'take no more trouble about me. The time is come when I may as well speak. I have done nothing; my crime is that the condemned man is my brother. Early this afternoon I left home at Shottsford to tramp it all the way to Casterbridge jail to bid him farewell. I was benighted, and called here to rest and ask the way. When I opened the door I saw before me the very man, my brother, that I thought to see in the condemned cell at Casterbridge. He was in this chimney-corner; and jammed close to him, so that he could not have got out if he had tried, was the executioner who'd come to take his life, singing a song about it and not knowing that it was his victim who was close by, joining in to save appearances. My brother threw a glance of agony at me, and I knew he meant, "Don't reveal what you see; my life depends on it." I was so terror-struck that I could hardly stand, and, not knowing what I did, I turned and hurried away.'

The narrator's manner and tone had the stamp of truth, and his story made a great impression on all around. 'And do you know where your brother is at the present time?' asked the magistrate.

'I do not. I have never seen him since I closed this door.'

'I can testify to that, for we've been between ye ever since,' said the constable.

'Where does he think to fly to? – what is his occupation?'

'He's a watch- and clock-maker, sir.'

''A said 'a was a wheelwright – a wicked rogue,' said the constable.

'The wheels of clocks and watches he meant, no doubt,' said Shepherd Fennel. 'I thought his hands were palish for's trade.'

'Well, it appears to me that nothing can be gained by retaining this poor man in custody,' said the magistrate; 'your business lies with the other, unquestionably.'

And so the little man was released off-hand; but he looked nothing the less sad on that account, it being beyond the power of magistrate or constable to raze out the written troubles in his brain, for they concerned another whom he regarded with more solicitude than himself. When this was done, and the man had gone his way, the night was found to be so far advanced that it was deemed useless to renew the search before the next morning.

Next day, accordingly, the quest for the clever sheep-stealer became general and keen, to all appearance at least. But the intended punishment was cruelly disproportioned to the trans-gression, and the sympathy of a great many country-folk in that district was strongly on the side of the fugitive. Moreover, his marvellous coolness and daring in hob-and-nobbing with the hangman, under the unprecedented circumstances of the shep-herd's party, won their admiration. So that it may be questioned if all those who ostensibly made themselves so busy in exploring woods and fields and lanes were quite so thorough when it came to the private examination of their own lofts and outhouses. Stories were afloat of a mysterious figure being occasionally seen in some old overgrown trackway or other, remote from turn-pike-roads; but when a search was instituted in any of these suspected quarters nobody was found. Thus the days and weeks passed without tidings.

In brief, the bass-voiced man of the chimney-corner was never recaptured. Some said that he went across the sea, others that he did not, but buried himself in the depths of a populous city. At any rate, the gentleman in cinder-grey never did his morning's work at Casterbridge, nor met anywhere at all, for business purposes, the genial comrade with whom he had passed an hour of relaxation in the lonely house on the slope of the coomb.

The grass has long been green on the graves of Shepherd Fennel and his frugal wife; the guests who made up the christening party have mainly followed their entertainers to the tomb; the baby in whose honour they all had met is a matron in the sere and yellow leaf. But the arrival of the three strangers at the shepherd's that night, and the details connected therewith, is a story as well known as ever in the country about Higher Crowstairs.

The Son's Veto

To the eyes of a man viewing it from behind, the nut-brown hair was a wonder and a mystery. Under the black beaver hat surmounted by its tuft of black feathers, the long locks, braided and twisted and coiled like the rushes of a basket, composed a rare, if somewhat barbaric, example of ingenious art. One could understand such weavings and coilings being wrought to last intact for a year, or even a calendar month; but that they should be all demolished regularly at bedtime, after a single day of permanence, seemed a reckless waste of successful fabrication.

And she had done it all herself, poor thing. She had no maid, and it was almost the only accomplishment she could boast of. Hence the unstinted pains.

She was a young invalid lady – not so very much of an invalid – sitting in a wheeled chair, which had been pulled up in the front part of a green enclosure, close to a bandstand where a concert was going on, during a warm June afternoon. It had place in one of the minor parks or private gardens that are to be found in the suburbs of London, and was the effort of a local association to raise money for some charity. There are worlds within worlds in the great city, and though nobody outside the immediate district had ever heard of the charity, or the band, or the garden, the enclosure was filled with an interested audience sufficiently informed on all these.

As the strains proceeded many of the listeners observed the chaired lady, whose back hair, by reason of her prominent position, so challenged inspection. Her face was not easily discernible, but the aforesaid cunning tress-weavings, the white ear and poll, and the curve of a cheek which was neither flaccid nor sallow, were signals that led to the expectation of good beauty in front. Such expectations are not infrequently disappointed as soon as the disclosure comes; and in the present case, when the lady, by a turn of the head, at length revealed herself, she was not so handsome as the people behind her had supposed, and even hoped – they did not know why.

For one thing (alas! the commonness of this complaint), she was less young than they had fancied her to be. Yet attractive her face unquestionably was, and not at all sickly. The revelation of its details came each time she turned to talk to a boy of twelve or thirteen who stood beside her, and the shape of whose hat and jacket implied that he belonged to a well-known public school. The immediate bystanders could hear that he called her 'Mother'.

When the end of the recital was reached, and the audience withdrew, many chose to find their way out by passing at her elbow. Almost all turned their heads to take a full and near look at the interesting woman, who remained stationary in the chair till the way should be clear enough for her to be wheeled out without obstruction. As if she expected their glances, and did not mind gratifying their curiosity, she met the eyes of several of her observers by lifting her own, showing these to be soft, brown, and affectionate orbs, a little plaintive in their regard.

She was conducted out of the gardens, and passed along the pavement till she disappeared from view, the schoolboy walking beside her. To inquiries made by some persons who watched her away, the answer came that she was the second wife of the incumbent of a neighbouring parish, and that she was lame. She was generally believed to be a woman with a story – an innocent one, but a story of some sort or other.

In conversing with her on their way home the boy who walked at her elbow said that he hoped his father had not missed them.

'He have been so comfortable these last few hours that I am sure he cannot have missed us,' she replied.

'*Has*, dear mother – not *have*!' exclaimed the public-school boy, with an impatient fastidiousness that was almost harsh. 'Surely you know that by this time!'

His mother hastily adopted the correction, and did not resent his making it, or retaliate, as she might well have done, by bidding him to wipe that crumby mouth of his, whose condition had been caused by surreptitious attempts to eat a piece of cake without taking it out of the pocket wherein it lay concealed. After this the pretty woman and the boy went onward in silence.

That question of grammar bore upon her history, and she fell into reverie, of a somewhat sad kind to all appearance. It might have been assumed that she was wondering if she had done

wisely in shaping her life as she had shaped it, to bring out such a
result as this.

In a remote nook in North Wessex, forty miles from London,
near the thriving county-town of Aldbrickham, there stood a
pretty village with its church and parsonage, which she knew
well enough, but her son had never seen. It was her native
village, Gaymead, and the first event bearing upon her present
situation had occurred at that place when she was only a girl of
nineteen.

How well she remembered it, that first act in her little tragi-
comedy, the death of her reverend husband's first wife. It
happened on a spring evening, and she who now and for many
years had filled that first wife's place was then parlour-maid in
the parson's house.

When everything had been done that could be done, and the
death was announced, she had gone out in the dusk to visit her
parents, who were living in the same village, to tell them the sad
news. As she opened the white swing-gate and looked towards
the trees which rose westward, shutting out the pale light of the
evening sky, she discerned, without much surprise, the figure of a
man standing in the hedge, though she roguishly exclaimed as a
matter of form, 'O, Sam, how you frightened me!'

He was a young gardener of her acquaintance. She told him
the particulars of the late event, and they stood silent, these two
young people, in that elevated, calmly philosophic mind which is
engendered when a tragedy has happened close at hand, and has
not happened to the philosophers themselves. But it had its
bearing upon their relations.

'And will you stay on now at the Vicarage, just the same?'
asked he.

She had hardly thought of that. 'O yes – I suppose!' she said.
'Everything will be just as usual, I imagine?'

He walked beside her towards her mother's. Presently his arm
stole round her waist. She gently removed it; but he placed it
there again, and she yielded the point. 'You see, dear Sophy, you
don't know that you'll stay on; you may want a home; and I
shall be ready to offer one some day, though I may not be ready
just yet.'

'Why, Sam, how can you be so fast! I've never even said I liked
'ee; and it is all your own doing, coming after me!'

'Still, it is nonsense to say I am not to have a try at you like the rest.' He stooped to kiss her a farewell, for they had reached her mother's door.

'No, Sam; you shan't!' she cried, putting her hand over his mouth. 'You ought to be more serious on such a night as this.' And she bade him adieu without allowing him to kiss her or to come indoors.

The vicar just left a widower was at this time a man about forty years of age, of good family, and childless. He had led a secluded existence in this college living, partly because there were no resident landowners; and his loss now intensified his habit of withdrawal from outward observation. He was seen still less than heretofore, kept himself still less in time with the rhythm and racket of the movements called progress in the world without. For many months after his wife's decease the economy of his household remained as before; the cook, the housemaid, the parlour-maid, and the man out-of-doors performed their duties or left them undone, just as Nature prompted them – the vicar knew not which. It was then represented to him that his servants seemed to have nothing to do in his small family of one. He was struck with the truth of this representation, and decided to cut down his establishment. But he was forestalled by Sophy, the parlour-maid, who said one evening that she wished to leave him.

'And why?' said the parson.

'Sam Hobson has asked me to marry him, sir.'

'Well – do you want to marry?'

'Not much. But it would be a home for me. And we have heard that one of us will have to leave.'

A day or two after she said: 'I don't want to leave just yet, sir, if you don't wish it. Sam and I have quarrelled.'

He looked up at her. He had hardly ever observed her before, though he had been frequently conscious of her soft presence in the room. What a kitten-like, flexuous, tender creature she was! She was the only one of the servants with whom he came into immediate and continuous relation. What should he do if Sophy were gone?

Sophy did not go, but one of the others did, and things went on quietly again.

When Mr Twycott, the vicar, was ill, Sophy brought up his

meals to him, and she had no sooner left the room one day than he heard a noise on the stairs. She had slipped down with the tray, and so twisted her foot that she could not stand. The village surgeon was called in; the vicar got better, but Sophy was incapacitated for a long time; and she was informed that she must never again walk much or engage in any occupation which required her to stand long on her feet. As soon as she was comparatively well she spoke to him alone. Since she was forbidden to walk and bustle about, and, indeed, could not do so, it became her duty to leave. She could very well work at something sitting down, and she had an aunt a seamstress.

The parson had been very greatly moved by what she had suffered on his account, and he exclaimed, 'No, Sophy; lame or not lame, I cannot let you go. You must never leave me again!'

He came close to her, and, though she could never exactly tell how it happened, she became conscious of his lips upon her cheek. He then asked her to marry him. Sophy did not exactly love him, but she had a respect for him which almost amounted to veneration. Even if she had wished to get away from him she hardly dared refuse a personage so reverend and august in her eyes, and she assented forthwith to be his wife.

Thus it happened that one fine morning, when the doors of the church were naturally open for ventilation, and the singing birds fluttered in and alighted on the tie-beams of the roof, there was a marriage-service at the communion-rails, which hardly a soul knew of. The parson and a neighbouring curate had entered at one door, and Sophy at another, followed by two necessary persons, whereupon in a short time there emerged a newly-made husband and wife.

Mr Twycott knew perfectly well that he had committed social suicide by this step, despite Sophy's spotless character, and he had taken his measures accordingly. An exchange of livings had been arranged with an acquaintance who was incumbent of a church in the south of London, and as soon as possible the couple removed thither, abandoning their pretty country home, with trees and shrubs and glebe, for a narrow, dusty house in a long, straight street, and their fine peal of bells for the wretchedest one-tongued clangour that ever tortured mortal ears. It was all on her account. They were, however, away from every one who had known her former position; and also under less observation from without than they would have had to put up with in any country parish.

Sophy the woman was as charming a partner as a man could possess, though Sophy the lady had her deficiencies. She showed a natural aptitude for little domestic refinements, so far as related to things and manners; but in what is called culture she was less intuitive. She had now been married more than fourteen years, and her husband had taken much trouble with her education; but she still held confused ideas on the use of 'was' and 'were', which did not beget a respect for her among the few acquaintances she made. Her great grief in this relation was that her only child, on whose education no expense had been and would be spared, was now old enough to perceive these deficiencies in his mother, and not only to see them but to feel irritated at their existence.

Thus she lived on in the city, and wasted hours in braiding her beautiful hair, till her once apple cheeks waned to pink of the very faintest. Her foot had never regained its natural strength after the accident, and she was mostly obliged to avoid walking altogether. Her husband had grown to like London for its freedom and its domestic privacy; but he was twenty years his Sophy's senior, and had latterly been seized with a serious illness. On this day, however, he had seemed to be well enough to justify her accompanying her son Randolph to the concert.

The next time we get a glimpse of her is when she appears in the mournful attire of a widow.

Mr Twycott had never rallied, and now lay in a well-packed cemetery to the south of the great city, where, if all the dead it contained had stood erect and alive, not one would have known him or recognized his name. The boy had dutifully followed him to the grave, and was now again at school.

Throughout these changes Sophy had been treated like the child she was in nature though not in years. She was left with no control over anything that had been her husband's beyond her modest personal income. In his anxiety lest her inexperience should be overreached he had safeguarded with trustees all he possibly could. The completion of the boy's course at the public school, to be followed in due time by Oxford and ordination, had been all previsioned and arranged, and she really had nothing to occupy her in the world but to eat and drink, and make a business of indolence, and go on weaving and coiling the nut-brown hair, merely keeping a home open for the son whenever he came to her during vacations.

Foreseeing his probable decease long years before her, her husband in his lifetime had purchased for her use a semi-detached villa in the same long, straight road whereon the church and parsonage faced, which was to be hers as long as she chose to live in it. Here she now resided, looking out upon the fragment of lawn in front, and through the railings at the ever-flowing traffic; or, bending forward over the window-sill on the first floor, stretching her eyes far up and down the vista of sooty trees, hazy air, and drab house-façades, along which echoed the noises common to a suburban main thoroughfare.

Somehow, her boy, with his aristocratic school-knowledge, his grammars, and his aversions, was losing those wide infantine sympathies, extending as far as to the sun and moon themselves, with which he, like other children, had been born, and which his mother, a child of nature herself, had loved in him; he was reducing their compass to a population of a few thousand wealthy and titled people, the mere veneer of a thousand million or so of others who did not interest him at all. He drifted further and further away from her. Sophy's *milieu* being a suburb of minor tradesmen and under-clerks, and her almost only companions the two servants of her own house, it was not surprising that after her husband's death she soon lost the little artificial tastes she had acquired from him, and became – in her son's eyes – a mother whose mistakes and origin it was his painful lot as a gentleman to blush for. As yet he was far from being man enough – if he ever would be – to rate these sins of hers at their true infinitesimal value beside the yearning fondness that welled up and remained penned in her heart till it should be more fully accepted by him, or by some other person or thing. If he had lived at home with her he would have had all of it; but he seemed to require so very little in present circumstances, and it remained stored.

Her life became insupportably dreary; she could not take walks, and had no interest in going for drives, or, indeed, in travelling anywhere. Nearly two years passed without an event, and still she looked on that suburban road, thinking of the village in which she had been born, and whither she would have gone back – O how gladly! – even to work in the fields.

Taking no exercise she often could not sleep, and would rise in the night or early morning to look out upon the then vacant thoroughfare, where the lamps stood like sentinels waiting for some procession to go by. An approximation to such a procession was indeed made early every morning about one o'clock, when the country vehicles passed up with loads of vegetables for Covent Garden market. She often saw them creeping along at this silent and dusky hour – waggon after waggon, bearing green bastions of cabbages nodding to their fall, yet never falling, walls of baskets enclosing masses of beans and peas, pyramids of snow-white turnips, swaying howdahs of mixed produce – creeping along behind aged night-horses, who seemed ever patiently wondering between their hollow coughs why they had always to work at that still hour when all other sentient creatures were privileged to rest. Wrapped in a cloak, it was soothing to watch and sympathize with them when depression and nervousness hindered sleep, and to see how the fresh green-stuff brightened to life as it came opposite the lamp, and how the sweating animals steamed and shone with their miles of travel.

They had an interest, almost a charm, for Sophy, these semirural people and vehicles moving in an urban atmosphere, leading a life quite distinct from that of the daytime toilers on the same road. One morning a man who accompanied a waggon-load of potatoes gazed rather hard at the house-fronts as he passed, and with a curious emotion she thought his form was familiar to her. She looked out for him again. His being an old-fashioned conveyance, with a yellow front, it was easily recognizable, and on the third night after she saw it a second time. The man alongside was, as she had fancied, Sam Hobson, formerly gardener at Gaymead, who would at one time have married her.

She had occasionally thought of him, and wondered if life in a cottage with him would not have been a happier lot than the life she had accepted. She had not thought of him passionately, but her now dismal situation lent an interest to his resurrection – a tender interest which it is impossible to exaggerate. She went back to bed, and began thinking. When did these market-gardeners, who travelled up to town so regularly at one or two in the morning, come back? She dimly recollected seeing their empty waggons, hardly noticeable amid the ordinary day-traffic, passing down at some hour before noon.

It was only April, but that morning, after breakfast, she had the window opened, and sat looking out, the feeble sun shining full upon her. She affected to sew, but her eyes never left the street. Between ten and eleven the desired waggon, now unladen, reappeared on its return journey. But Sam was not looking round him then, and drove on in a reverie.

'Sam!' cried she.

Turning with a start, his face lighted up. He called to him a little boy to hold the horse, alighted, and came and stood under the window.

'I can't come down easily, Sam, or I would!' she said. 'Did you know I lived here?'

'Well, Mrs Twycott, I knew you lived along here somewhere. I have often looked out for 'ee.'

He briefly explained his own presence on the scene. He had long since given up his gardening in the village near Aldbrick-ham, and was now manager at a market-gardener's on the south side of London, it being part of his duty to go up to Covent Garden with waggon-loads of produce two or three times a week. In answer to her curious inquiry, he admitted that he had come to this particular district because he had seen in the Aldbrickham paper, a year or two before, the announcement of the death in South London of the aforetime vicar of Gaymead, which had revived an interest in her dwelling-place that he could not extinguish, leading him to hover about the locality till his present post had been secured.

They spoke of their native village in dear old North Wessex, the spots in which they had played together as children. She tried to feel that she was a dignified personage now, that she must not be too confidential with Sam. But she could not keep it up, and the tears hanging in her eyes were indicated in her voice.

'You are not happy, Mrs Twycott, I'm afraid?' he said.

'O, of course not! I lost my husband only the year before last.'

'Ah! I meant in another way. You'd like to be home again?'

'This is my home – for life. The house belongs to me. But I understand – ' She let it out then. 'Yes, Sam. I long for home – *our* home! I *should* like to be there, and never leave it, and die there.' But she remembered herself. 'That's only a momentary feeling. I have a son, you know, a dear boy. He's at school now.'

'Somewhere handy, I suppose? I see there's lots on 'em along this road.'

'O no! Not in one of these wretched holes! At a public school – one of the most distinguished in England.'

'Chok' it all! of course! I forget, ma'am, that you've been a lady for so many years.'

'No, I am not a lady,' she said sadly. 'I never shall be. But he's a gentleman, and that – makes it – O how difficult for me!'

The acquaintance thus oddly reopened proceeded apace. She often looked out to get a few words with him, by night or by day. Her sorrow was that she could not accompany her one old friend on foot a little way, and talk more freely than she could do while he paused before the house. One night, at the beginning of June, when she was again on the watch after an absence of some days from the window, he entered the gate and said softly, 'Now, wouldn't some air do you good? I've only half a load this morning. Why not ride up to Covent Garden with me? There's a nice seat on the cabbages, where I've spread a sack. You can be home again in a cab before anybody is up.'

She refused at first, and then, trembling with excitement, hastily finished her dressing, and wrapped herself up in cloak and veil, afterwards sidling downstairs by the aid of the hand-rail, in a way she could adopt on an emergency. When she had opened the door she found Sam on the step, and he lifted her bodily on his strong arm across the little forecourt into his vehicle. Not a soul was visible or audible in the infinite length of the straight, flat highway, with its ever-waiting lamps converging to points in each direction. The air was fresh as country air at this hour, and the stars shone, except to the north-eastward, where there was a whitish light – the dawn. Sam carefully placed her in the seat, and drove on.

They talked as they had talked in old days, Sam pulling himself up now and then, when he thought himself too familiar. More than once she said with misgiving that she wondered if she ought to have indulged in the freak. 'But I am so lonely in my house,' she added, 'and this makes me so happy!'

'You must come again, dear Mrs Twycott. There is no time o' day for taking the air like this.'

It grew lighter and lighter. The sparrows became busy in the streets, and the city waxed denser around them. When they approached the river it was day, and on the bridge they beheld the full blaze of morning sunlight in the direction of St Paul's, the river glistening towards it, and not a craft stirring.

Near Covent Garden he put her into a cab, and they parted, looking into each other's faces like the very old friends they were. She reached home without adventure, limped to the door, and let herself in with her latch-key unseen.

The air and Sam's presence had revived her: her cheeks were quite pink – almost beautiful. She had something to live for in addition to her son. A woman of pure instincts, she knew there had been nothing really wrong in the journey, but supposed it conventionally to be very wrong indeed.

Soon, however, she gave way to the temptation of going with him again, and on this occasion their conversation was distinctly tender, and Sam said he never should forget her, notwithstanding that she had served him rather badly at one time. After much hesitation he told her of a plan it was in his power to carry out, and one he should like to take in hand, since he did not care for London work: it was to set up as a master greengrocer down at Aldbrickham, the county-town of their native place. He knew of an opening – a shop kept by aged people who wished to retire.

'And why don't you do it, then, Sam?' she asked with a slight heartsinking.

'Because I'm not sure if – you'd join me. I know you wouldn't – couldn't! Such a lady as ye've been so long, you couldn't be a wife to a man like me.'

'I hardly suppose I could!' she assented, also frightened at the idea.

'If you could,' he said eagerly, 'you'd on'y have to sit in the back parlour and look through the glass partition when I was away sometimes – just to keep an eye on things. The lameness wouldn't hinder that.... I'd keep you as genteel as ever I could, dear Sophy – if I might think of it!' he pleaded.

'Sam, I'll be frank,' she said, putting her hand on his. 'If it were only myself I would do it, and gladly, though everything I possess would be lost to me by marrying again.'

'I don't mind that! It's more independent.'

'That's good of you, dear, dear Sam. But there's something else. I have a son.... I almost fancy when I am miserable sometimes that he is not really mine, but one I hold in trust for my late husband. He seems to belong so little to me personally, so entirely to his dead father. He is so much educated and I so little that I do not feel dignified enough to be his mother.... Well, he would have to be told.'

'Yes. Unquestionably.' Sam saw her thought and her fear. 'Still, you can do as you like, Sophy – Mrs Twycott,' he added. 'It is not you who are the child, but he.'

'Ah, you don't know! Sam, if I could, I would marry you, some day. But you must wait a while, and let me think.'

It was enough for him, and he was blithe at their parting. Not so she. To tell Randolph seemed impossible. She could wait till he had gone up to Oxford, when what she did would affect his life but little. But would he ever tolerate the idea? And if not, could she defy him?

She had not told him a word when the yearly cricket-match came on at Lord's between the public schools, though Sam had already gone back to Aldbrickham. Mrs Twycott felt stronger than usual: she went to the match with Randolph, and was able to leave her chair and walk about occasionally. The bright idea occurred to her that she could casually broach the subject while moving round among the spectators, when the boy's spirits were high with interest in the game, and he would weigh domestic matters as feathers in the scale beside the day's victory. They promenaded under the lurid July sun, this pair, so wide apart, yet so near, and Sophy saw the large proportion of boys like her own, in their broad white collars and dwarf hats, and all around the rows of great coaches under which was jumbled the *débris* of luxurious luncheons; bones, pie-crusts, champagne-bottles, glasses, plates, napkins, and the family silver; while on the coaches sat the proud fathers and mothers; but never a poor mother like her. If Randolph had not appertained to these, had not centred all his interests in them, had not cared exclusively for the class they belonged to, how happy would things have been! A great huzza at some small performance with the bat burst from the multitude of relatives, and Randolph jumped wildly into the air to see what had happened. Sophy fetched up the sentence that had been already shaped; but she could not get it out. The occasion was, perhaps, an inopportune one. The contrast between her story and the display of fashion to which Randolph had grown to regard himself as akin would be fatal. She awaited a better time.

It was on an evening when they were alone in their plain suburban residence, where life was not blue but brown, that she ultimately broke silence, qualifying her announcement of a probable second marriage by assuring him that it would not take place for a long time to come, when he would be living quite independently of her.

The boy thought the idea a very reasonable one, and asked if she had chosen anybody? She hesitated; and he seemed to have a misgiving. He hoped his stepfather would be a gentleman? he said.

'Not what you call a gentleman,' she answered timidly. 'He'll be much as I was before I knew your father'; and by degrees she acquainted him with the whole. The youth's face remained fixed for a moment; then he flushed, leant on the table, and burst into passionate tears.

His mother went up to him, kissed all of his face that she could get at, and patted his back as if he were still the baby he once had been, crying herself the while. When he had somewhat recovered from his paroxysm he went hastily to his own room and fastened the door.

Parleyings were attempted through the keyhole, outside which she waited and listened. It was long before he would reply, and when he did it was to say sternly at her from within: 'I am ashamed of you! It will ruin me! A miserable boor! a churl! a clown! It will degrade me in the eyes of all the gentlemen of England!'

'Say no more – perhaps I am wrong! I will struggle against it!' she cried miserably.

Before Randolph left her that summer a letter arrived from Sam to inform her that he had been unexpectedly fortunate in obtaining the shop. He was in possession; it was the largest in the town, combining fruit with vegetables, and he thought it would form a home worthy even of her some day. Might he not run up to town to see her?

She met him by stealth, and said he must still wait for her final answer. The autumn dragged on, and when Randolph was home at Christmas for the holidays she broached the matter again. But the young gentleman was inexorable.

It was dropped for months; renewed again; abandoned under his repugnance; again attempted; and thus the gentle creature reasoned and pleaded till four or five long years had passed. Then the faithful Sam revived his suit with some peremptoriness. Sophy's son, now an undergraduate, was down from Oxford one Easter, when she again opened the subject. As soon as he was ordained, she argued, he would have a home of his own, wherein she, with her bad grammar and her ignorance, would be an encumbrance to him. Better obliterate her as much as possible.

He showed a more manly anger now, but would not agree. She on her side was more persistent, and he had doubts whether she could be trusted in his absence. But by indignation and contempt for her taste he completely maintained his ascendency; and finally taking her before a little cross and altar that he had erected in his bedroom for his private devotions, there bade her kneel, and swear that she would not wed Samuel Hobson without his consent. 'I owe this to my father!' he said.

The poor woman swore, thinking he would soften as soon as he was ordained and in full swing of clerical work. But he did not. His education had by this time sufficiently ousted his humanity to keep him quite firm; though his mother might have led an idyllic life with her faithful fruiterer and greengrocer, and nobody have been anything the worse in the world.

Her lameness became more confirmed as time went on, and she seldom or never left the house in the long southern thoroughfare, where she seemed to be pining her heart away. 'Why mayn't I say to Sam that I'll marry him? Why mayn't I?' she would murmur plaintively to herself when nobody was near.

Some four years after this date a middle-aged man was standing at the door of the largest fruiterer's shop in Aldbrick-ham. He was the proprietor, but today, instead of his usual business attire, he wore a neat suit of black; and his window was partly shuttered. From the railway-station a funeral procession was seen approaching: it passed his door and went out of the town towards the village of Gaymead. The man, whose eyes were wet, held his hat in his hand as the vehicles moved by; while from the mourning coach a young smooth-shaven priest in a high waistcoat looked black as a cloud at the shopkeeper standing there.

The Fiddler of The Reels

'Talking of Exhibitions, World's Fairs, and what not,' said the old gentleman, 'I would not go round the corner to see a dozen of them nowadays. The only exhibition that ever made, or ever will make, any impression upon my imagination was the first of the series, the parent of them all, and now a thing of old times – the Great Exhibition of 1851, in Hyde Park, London. None of the younger generation can realize the sense of novelty it produced in us who were then in our prime. A noun substantive went so far as to become an adjective in honour of the occasion. It was "exhibition" hat, "exhibition" razor-strop, "exhibition" watch; nay, even "exhibition" weather, "exhibition" spirits, sweethearts, babies, wives – for the time.

'For South Wessex, the year formed in many ways an extra-ordinary chronological frontier or transit-line, at which there occurred what one might call a precipice in Time. As in a geological "fault", we had presented to us a sudden bringing of ancient and modern into absolute contact, such as probably in no other single year since the Conquest was ever witnessed in this part of the country.'

These observations led us onward to talk of the different personages, gentle and simple, who lived and moved within our narrow and peaceful horizon at that time; and of three people in particular, whose queer little history was oddly touched at points by the Exhibition, more concerned with it than that of anybody else who dwelt in those outlying shades of the world, Stickleford, Mellstock, and Egdon. First in prominence among these three came Wat Ollamoor – if that were his real name – whom the seniors in our party had known well.

He was a woman's man, they said, – supremely so – externally little else. To men he was not attractive; perhaps a little repulsive at times. Musician, dandy, and company-man in practice; veterinary surgeon in theory, he lodged awhile in Mellstock village, coming from nobody knew where; though some said his

first appearance in this neighbourhood had been as fiddle-player
in a show at Greenhill Fair.

Many a worthy villager envied him his power over unsophisti-
cated maidenhood – a power which seemed sometimes to have a
touch of the weird and wizardly in it. Personally he was not ill-
favoured, though rather un-English, his complexion being a rich
olive, his rank hair dark and rather clammy – made still
clammier by secret ointments, which, when he came fresh to a
party, caused him to smell like 'boys'-love' (southernwood)
steeped in lamp-oil. On occasion he wore curls – a double row –
running almost horizontally around his head. But as these were
sometimes noticeably absent, it was concluded that they were not
altogether of Nature's making. By girls whose love for him had
turned to hatred he had been nicknamed 'Mop', from this
abundance of hair, which was long enough to rest upon his
shoulders; as time passed the name more and more prevailed.

His fiddling possibly had the most to do with the fascination he
exercised, for, to speak fairly, it could claim for itself a most
peculiar and personal quality, like that in a moving preacher.
There were tones in it which bred the immediate conviction that
indolence and averseness to systematic application were all that
lay between 'Mop' and the career of a second Paganini.

While playing he invariably closed his eyes; using no notes,
and, as it were, allowing the violin to wander on at will into the
most plaintive passages ever heard by rustic man. There was a
certain lingual character in the supplicatory expressions he
produced, which would well-nigh have drawn an ache from the
heart of a gate-post. He could make any child in the parish, who
was at all sensitive to music, burst into tears in a few minutes by
simply fiddling one of the old dance-tunes he almost entirely
affected – country jigs, reels, and 'Favourite Quick Steps' of the
last century – some mutilated remains of which even now
reappear as nameless phantoms in new quadrilles and gallops,
where they are recognized only by the curious, or by such old-
fashioned and far-between people as have been thrown with men
like Wat Ollamoor in their early life.

His date was a little later than that of the old Mellstock quire-
band which comprised the Dewys, Mail, and the rest – in fact, he
did not rise above the horizon thereabout till those well-known
musicians were disbanded as ecclesiastical functionaries. In their

honest love of thoroughness they despised the new man's style.
Theophilus Dewy (Reuben the tranter's younger brother) used to
say there was no 'plumness' in it – no bowing, no solidity – it was
all fantastical. And probably this was true. Anyhow, Mop had,
very obviously, never bowed a note of church-music from his
birth; he never once sat in the gallery of Mellstock church where
the others had tuned their venerable psalmody so many
hundreds of times; had never, in all likelihood, entered a church
at all. All were devil's tunes in his repertory. 'He could no more
play the "Wold Hundredth" to his true time than he could play
the brazen serpent,' the tranter would say. (The brazen serpent
was supposed in Mellstock to be a musical instrument particularly hard to blow.)

Occasionally Mop could produce the aforesaid moving effect
upon the souls of grown-up persons, especially young women of
fragile and responsive organization. Such an one was Car'line
Aspent. Though she was already engaged to be married before
she met him, Car'line, of them all, was the most influenced by
Mop Ollamoor's heart-stealing melodies, to her discomfort, nay,
positive pain and ultimate injury. She was a pretty, invocating,
weak-mouthed girl, whose chief defect as a companion with her
sex was a tendency to peevishness now and then. At this time she
was not a resident in Mellstock parish where Mop lodged, but
lived some miles off at Stickleford, further down the river.

How and where she first made acquaintance with him and his
fiddling is not truly known, but the story was that it either began
or was developed on one spring evening, when, in passing
through Lower Mellstock, she chanced to pause on the bridge
near his house to rest herself, and languidly leaned over the
parapet. Mop was standing on his door-step, as was his custom,
spinning the insidious thread of semi- and demi-semiquavers
from the E string of his fiddle for the benefit of passers-by, and
laughing as the tears rolled down the cheeks of the little children
hanging around him. Car'line pretended to be engrossed with the
rippling of the stream under the arches, but in reality she was
listening, as he knew. Presently the aching of the heart seized her
simultaneously with a wild desire to glide airily in the mazes of
an infinite dance. To shake off the fascination she resolved to go
on, although it would be necessary to pass him as he played. On
stealthily glancing ahead at the performer, she found to her relief

that his eyes were closed in abandonment to instrumentation, and she strode on boldly. But when closer her step grew timid, her tread convulsed itself more and more accordantly with the time of the melody, till she very nearly danced along. Gaining another glance at him when immediately opposite, she saw that *one* of his eyes was open, quizzing her as he smiled at her emotional state. Her gait could not divest itself of its compelled capers till she had gone a long way past the house; and Car'line was unable to shake off the strange infatuation for hours.

After that day, whenever there was to be in the neighbourhood a dance to which she could get an invitation, and where Mop Ollamoor was to be the musician, Car'line contrived to be present, though it sometimes involved a walk of several miles; for he did not play so often in Stickleford as elsewhere.

The next evidences of his influence over her were singular enough, and it would require a neurologist to fully explain them. She would be sitting quietly, any evening after dark, in the house of her father, the parish-clerk, which stood in the middle of Stickleford village street, this being the highroad between Lower Mellstock and Moreford, five miles eastward. Here, without a moment's warning, and in the midst of a general conversation between her father, sister, and the young man before alluded to, who devotedly wooed her in ignorance of her infatuation, she would start from her seat in the chimney-corner as if she had received a galvanic shock, and spring convulsively towards the ceiling; then she would burst into tears, and it was not till some half-hour had passed that she grew calm as usual. Her father, knowing her hysterical tendencies, was always excessively anxious about this trait in his youngest girl, and feared the attack to be a species of epileptic fit. Not so her sister Julia. Julia had found out what was the cause. At the moment before the jumping, only an exceptionally sensitive ear situated in the chimney-nook could have caught from down the flue the beat of a man's footstep along the highway without. But it was in that footfall, for which she had been waiting, that the origin of Car'line's involuntary springing lay. The pedestrian was Mop Ollamoor, as the girl well knew; but his business that way was not to visit her; he sought another woman whom he spoke of as his Intended, and who lived at Moreford, two miles further on. On one, and only one, occasion did it happen that Car'line could not control her utterance; it was when her sister alone chanced to be present. 'O – O – O – !' she cried. 'He's going to *her*, and not coming to *me!*'

To do the fiddler justice he had not at first thought greatly of, or spoken much to, this girl of impressionable mould. But he had soon found out her secret, and could not resist a little by-play with her too easily hurt heart, as an interlude between his more serious love-makings at Moreford. The two became well acquainted, though only by stealth, hardly a soul in Stickleford except her sister, and her lover Ned Hipcroft, being aware of the attachment. Her father disapproved of her coldness to Ned; her sister, too, hoped she might get over this nervous passion for a man of whom so little was known. The ultimate result was that Car'line's manly and simple wooer Edward found his suit becoming practically hopeless. He was a respectable mechanic, in a far sounder position than Mop the nominal horse-doctor; but when, before leaving her, Ned put his flat and final question, would she marry him, then and there, now or never, it was with little expectation of obtaining more than the negative she gave him. Though her father supported him and her sister supported him, he could not play the fiddle so as to draw your soul out of your body like a spider's thread, as Mop did, till you felt as limp as withywind and yearned for something to cling to. Indeed, Hipcroft had not the slightest ear for music; could not sing two notes in tune, much less play them.

The No he had expected and got from her, in spite of a preliminary encouragement, gave Ned a new start in life. It had been uttered in such a tone of sad entreaty that he resolved to persecute her no more; she should not even be distressed by a sight of his form in the distant perspective of the street and lane. He left the place, and his natural course was to London.

The railway to South Wessex was in process of construction, but it was not as yet opened for traffic; and Hipcroft reached the capital by a six days' trudge on foot, as many a better man had done before him. He was one of the last of the artisan class who used that now extinct method of travel to the great centres of labour, so customary then from time immemorial.

In London he lived and worked regularly at his trade. More fortunate than many, his disinterested willingness recommended him from the first. During the ensuing four years he was never out of employment. He neither advanced nor receded in the modern sense; he improved as a workman, but he did not shift one jot in social position. About his love for Car'line he maintained a rigid silence. No doubt he often thought of her; but being always occupied, and having no relations at Stickleford, he held no communication with that part of the country, and showed no desire to return. In his quiet lodging in Lambeth he moved about after working-hours with the facility of a woman, doing his own cooking, attending to his stocking-heels, and shaping himself by degrees to a life-long bachelorhood. For this conduct one is bound to advance the canonical reason that time could not efface from his heart the image of little Car'line Aspent – and it may be in part true; but there was also the inference that his was a nature not greatly dependent upon the ministrations of the other sex for its comforts.

The fourth year of his residence as a mechanic in London was the year of the Hyde Park Exhibition already mentioned, and at the construction of this huge glass-house, then unexampled in the world's history, he worked daily. It was an era of great hope and activity among the nations and industries. Though Hipcroft was, in his small way, a central man in the movement, he plodded on with his usual outward placidity. Yet for him, too, the year was destined to have its surprises, for when the bustle of getting the building ready for the opening day was past, the ceremonies had been witnessed, and people were flocking thither from all parts of the globe, he received a letter from Car'line. Till that day the silence of four years between himself and Stickleford had never been broken.

She informed her old lover, in an uncertain penmanship which suggested a trembling hand, of the trouble she had been put to in ascertaining his address, and then broached the subject which had prompted her to write. Four years ago, she said with the greatest delicacy of which she was capable, she had been so foolish as to refuse him. Her wilful wrong-headedness had since been a grief to her many times, and of late particularly. As for Mr Ollamoor, he had been absent almost as long as Ned – she did not know where. She would gladly marry Ned now if he were to ask her again, and be a tender little wife to him till her life's end.

A tide of warm feeling must have surged through Ned Hipcroft's frame on receipt of this news, if we may judge by the

issue. Unquestionably he loved her still, even if not to the
exclusion of every other happiness. This from his Car'line, she
who had been dead to him these many years, alive to him again
as of old, was in itself a pleasant, gratifying thing. Ned had grown
so resigned to, or satisfied with, his lonely lot, that he probably
would not have shown much jubilation at anything. Still, a
certain ardour of preoccupation, after his first surprise, revealed
how deeply her confession of faith in him had stirred him.
Measured and methodical in his ways, he did not answer the
letter that day, nor the next, nor the next. He was having 'a good
think'. When he did answer it, there was a great deal of sound
reasoning mixed in with the unmistakable tenderness of his
reply; but the tenderness itself was sufficient to reveal that he was
pleased with her straightforward frankness; that the anchorage
she had once obtained in his heart was renewable, if it had not
been continuously firm.

He told her – and as he wrote his lips twitched humorously
over the few gentle words of raillery he indited among the rest of
his sentences – that it was all very well for her to come round at
this time of day. Why wouldn't she have him when he wanted
her? She had no doubt learned that he was not married, but
suppose his affections had since been fixed on another? She ought
to beg his pardon. Still, he was not the man to forget her. But
considering how he had been used, and what he had suffered,
she could not quite expect him to go down to Stickleford and
fetch her. But if she would come to him, and say she was sorry,
as was only fair; why, yes, he would marry her, knowing what a
good little woman she was at the core. He added that the request
for her to come to him was a less one to make than it would have
been when he first left Stickleford, or even a few months ago; for
the new railway into South Wessex was now open, and there had
just begun to be run wonderfully contrived special trains, called
excursion-trains, on account of the Great Exhibition; so that she
could come up easily alone.

She said in her reply how good it was of him to treat her so
generously, after her hot and cold treatment of him; that though
she felt frightened at the magnitude of the journey, and was
never as yet in a railway train, having only seen one pass at a
distance, she embraced his offer with all her heart; and would,

indeed, own to him how sorry she was, and beg his pardon, and try to be a good wife always, and make up for lost time.

The remaining details of when and where were soon settled, Car'line informing him, for her ready identification in the crowd, that she would be wearing 'my new sprigged-laylock cotton gown', and Ned gaily responding that, having married her the morning after her arrival, he would make a day of it by taking her to the Exhibition. One early summer afternoon, accordingly, he came from his place of work, and hastened towards Waterloo Station to meet her. It was as wet and chilly as an English June day can occasionally be, but as he waited on the platform in the drizzle he glowed inwardly, and seemed to have something to live for again.

The 'excursion-train' – an absolutely new departure in the history of travel – was still a novelty on the Wessex line, and probably everywhere. Crowds of people had flocked to all the stations on the way up to witness the unwonted sight of so long a train's passage, even where they did not take advantage of the opportunity it offered. The seats for the humbler class of travellers in these early experiments in steam-locomotion, were open trucks, without any protection whatever from the wind and rain; and damp weather having set in with the afternoon, the unfortunate occupants of these vehicles were, on the train drawing up at the London terminus, found to be in a pitiable condition from their long journey; blue-faced, stiff-necked, sneezing, rain-beaten, chilled to the marrow, many of the men being hatless; in fact, they resembled people who had been out all night in an open boat on a rough sea, rather than inland excursionists for pleasure. The women had in some degree protected themselves by turning up the skirts of their gowns over their heads, but as by this arrangement they were additionally exposed about the hips, they were all more or less in a sorry plight.

In the bustle and crush of alighting forms of both sexes which followed the entry of the huge concatenation into the station, Ned Hipcroft soon discerned the slim little figure his eye was in search of, in the sprigged lilac, as described. She came up to him with a frightened smile – still pretty, though so damp, weather-beaten, and shivering from long exposure to the wind.

'O Ned!' she sputtered, 'I – I – ' He clasped her in his arms and kissed her, whereupon she burst into a flood of tears.

'You are wet, my poor dear! I hope you'll not get cold,' he said. And surveying her and her multifarious surrounding packages, he noticed that by the hand she led a toddling child – a little girl of three or so – whose hood was as clammy and tender face as blue as those of the other travellers.

'Who is this – somebody you know?' asked Ned curiously.

'Yes, Ned. She's mine.'

'Yours?'

'Yes – my own.'

'Your own child?'

'Yes!'

'But who's the father?'

'The young man I had after you courted me.'

'Well – as God's in – '

'Ned, I didn't name it in my letter, because, you see, it would have been so hard to explain! I thought that when we met I could tell you how she happened to be born, so much better than in writing! I hope you'll excuse it this once, dear Ned, and not scold me, now I've come so many, many miles!'

'This means Mr Mop Ollamoor, I reckon!' said Hipcroft, gazing palely at them from the distance of the yard or two to which he had withdrawn with a start.

Car'line gasped. 'But he's been gone away for years!' she supplicated. 'And I never had a young man before! And I was so onlucky to be catched the first time he took advantage o'me, though some of the girls down there go on like anything!'

Ned remained in silence, pondering.

'You'll forgive me, dear Ned?' she added, beginning to sob outright. 'I haven't taken 'ee in after all, because – because you can pack us back again, if you want to; though 'tis hundreds o' miles, and so wet, and night a-coming on, and I with no money!'

'What the devil can I do!' Hipcroft groaned.

A more pitiable picture than the pair of helpless creatures presented was never seen on a rainy day, as they stood on the great, gaunt, puddled platform, a whiff of drizzle blowing under the roof upon them now and then; the pretty attire in which they had started from Stickleford in the early morning bemuddled and sodden, weariness on their faces, and fear of him in their eyes; for the child began to look as if she thought she too had done some wrong, remaining in an appalled silence till the tears rolled down her chubby cheeks.

'What's the matter, my little maid?' said Ned mechanically.

'I do want to go home!' she let out, in tones that told of a bursting heart. 'And my totties be cold, an' I shan't have no bread an' butter no more!'

'I don't know what to say to it all!' declared Ned, his own eye moist as he turned and walked a few steps with his head down; then regarded them again point-blank. From the child escaped troubled breaths and silently welling tears.

'Want some bread and butter, do 'ee?' he said, with factitious hardness.

'Ye – e – s!'

'Well, I dare say I can get 'ee a bit! Naturally, you must want some. And you, too, for that matter, Car'line.'

'I do feel a little hungered. But I can keep it off,' she murmured.

'Folk shouldn't do that,' he said gruffly.... 'There, come along!' He caught up the child, as he added, 'You must bide here tonight, anyhow, I s'pose! What can you do otherwise? I'll get 'ee some tea and victuals; and as for this job, I'm sure I don't know what to say! This is the way out.'

They pursued their way, without speaking, to Ned's lodgings, which were not far off. There he dried them and made them comfortable, and prepared tea; they thankfully sat down. The ready-made household of which he suddenly found himself the head imparted a cosy aspect to his room, and a paternal one to himself. Presently he turned to the child and kissed her now blooming cheeks; and, looking wistfully at Car'line, kissed her also.

'I don't see how I can send you back all them miles,' he growled, 'now you've come all the way o' purpose to join me. But you must trust me, Car'line, and show you've real faith in me. Well, do you feel better now, my little woman?'

The child nodded beamingly, her mouth being otherwise occupied.

'I did trust you, Ned, in coming; and I shall always!'

Thus, without any definite agreement to forgive her, he tacitly acquiesced in the fate that Heaven had sent him; and on the day of their marriage (which was not quite so soon as he had expected it could be, on account of the time necessary for banns) he took her to the Exhibition when they came back from church, as he had promised. While standing near a large mirror in one of the courts devoted to furniture, Car'line started, for in the glass appeared the reflection of a form exactly resembling Mop Ollamoor's – so exactly, that it seemed impossible to believe anybody but that artist in person to be the original. On passing round the objects which hemmed in Ned, her, and the child from a direct view, no Mop was to be seen. Whether he were really in London or not at that time was never known; and Car'line always stoutly denied that her readiness to go and meet Ned in town arose from any rumour that Mop had also gone thither; which denial there was no reasonable ground for doubting.

And then the year glided away, and the Exhibition folded itself up and became a thing of the past. The park trees that had been enclosed for six months were again exposed to the winds and storms, and the sod grew green anew. Ned found that Car'line resolved herself into a very good wife and companion, though she had made herself what is called cheap to him; but in that she was like another domestic article, a cheap tea-pot, which often brews better tea than a dear one. One autumn Hipcroft found himself with but little work to do, and a prospect of less for the winter. Both being country born and bred, they fancied they would like to live again in their natural atmosphere. It was accordingly decided between them that they should leave the pent-up London lodging, and that Ned should seek out employment near his native place, his wife and her daughter staying with Car'line's father during the search for occupation and an abode of their own.

Tinglings of pride pervaded Car'line's spasmodic little frame as she journeyed down with Ned to the place she had left two or three years before, in silence and under a cloud. To return to where she had once been despised, a smiling London wife with a distinct London accent, was a triumph which the world did not witness every day.

The train did not stop at the petty roadside station that lay nearest to Stickleford, and the trio went on to Casterbridge. Ned thought it a good opportunity to make a few preliminary inquiries for employment at workshops in the borough where he had been known; and feeling cold from her journey, and it being dry underfoot and only dusk as yet, with a moon on the point of rising, Car'line and her little girl walked on toward Stickleford, leaving Ned to follow at a quicker pace, and pick her up at a certain half-way house, widely known as an inn.

The woman and child pursued the well-remembered way comfortably enough, though they were both becoming wearied. In the course of three miles they had passed Heedless-William's Pond, the familiar landmark by Bloom's End, and were drawing near the Quiet Woman, a lone roadside hostel on the lower verge of the Egdon Heath, since and for many years abolished. In stepping up towards it Car'line heard more voices within than had formerly been customary at such an hour, and she learned that an auction of fat stock had been held near the spot that afternoon. The child would be the better for a rest as well as herself, she thought, and she entered.

The guests and customers overflowed into the passage, and Car'line had no sooner crossed the threshold than a man whom she remembered by sight came forward with a glass and mug in his hands towards a friend leaning against the wall; but, seeing her, very gallantly offered her a drink of the liquor, which was gin-and-beer hot, pouring her out a tumblerful and saying, in a moment or two: 'Surely, 'tis little Car'line Aspent that was – down at Stickleford?'

She assented, and, though she did not exactly want this beverage, she drank it since it was offered, and her entertainer begged her to come in further and sit down. Once within the room she found that all the persons present were seated close against the walls, and there being a chair vacant she did the same. An explanation of their position occurred the next moment. In the opposite corner stood Mop, rosining his bow and looking just the same as ever. The company had cleared the middle of the room for dancing, and they were about to dance again. As she wore a veil to keep off the wind she did not think he had recognized her, or could possibly guess the identity of the child; and to her satisfied surprise she found that she could confront him quite calmly – mistress of herself in the dignity her London life had given her. Before she had quite emptied her glass the dance was called, the dancers formed in two lines, the music sounded, and the figure began.

Then matters changed for Car'line. A tremor quickened itself to life in her, and her hand so shook that she could hardly set down her glass. It was not the dance nor the dancers, but the notes of that old violin which thrilled the London wife, these having still all the witchery that she had so well known of yore, and under which she had used to lose her power of independent will. How it all came back! There was the fiddling figure against the wall; the large, oily, mop-like head of him, and beneath the mop the face with closed eyes.

After the first moments of paralyzed reverie the familiar tune in the familiar rendering made her laugh and shed tears simultaneously. Then a man at the bottom of the dance, whose partner had dropped away, stretched out his hand and beckoned to her to take the place. She did not want to dance; she entreated by signs to be left where she was, but she was entreating of the tune and its player rather than of the dancing man. The saltatory tendency which the fiddler and his cunning instrument had ever been able to start in her was seizing Car'line just as it had done in earlier years, possibly assisted by the gin-and-beer hot. Tired as she was she grasped her little girl by the hand, and plunging in at the bottom of the figure, whirled about with the rest. She found that her companions were mostly people of the neighbouring hamlets and farms – Bloom's End, Mellstock, Lewgate, and elsewhere; and by degrees she was recognized as she convulsively danced on, wishing that Mop would cease and let her heart rest from the aching he caused, and her feet also.

After long and many minutes the dance ended, when she was urged to fortify herself with more gin-and-beer; which she did, feeling very weak and overpowered with hysteric emotion. She refrained from unveiling, to keep Mop in ignorance of her presence, if possible. Several of the guests having left, Car'line hastily wiped her lips and also turned to go; but, according to the account of some who remained, at that very moment a five-handed reel was proposed, in which two or three begged her to join.

She declined on the plea of being tired and having to walk to Stickleford, when Mop began aggressively tweedling 'My Fancy-Lad', in D major, as the air to which the reel was to be footed. He must have recognized her, though she did not know it, for it was the strain of all seductive strains which she was least able to resist – the one he had played when she was leaning over the bridge at the date of their first acquaintance. Car'line stepped despairingly into the middle of the room with the other four.

Reels were resorted to hereabouts at this time by the more robust spirits, for the reduction of superfluous energy which the ordinary figure-dances were not powerful enough to exhaust. As everybody knows, or does not know, the five reelers stood in the form of a cross, the reel being performed by each line of three alternately, the persons who successively came to the middle place dancing in both directions. Car'line soon found herself in this place, the axis of the whole performance, and could not get out of it, the tune turning into the first part without giving her opportunity. And now she began to suspect that Mop did know her, and was doing this on purpose, though whenever she stole a glance at him his closed eyes betokened obliviousness to everything outside his own brain. She continued to wend her way through the figure of 8 that was formed by her course, the fiddler introducing into his notes the wild and agonizing sweetness of a living voice in one too highly wrought; its pathos running high and running low in endless variation, projecting through her nerves excruciating spasms, a sort of blissful torture. The room swam, the tune was endless; and in about a quarter of an hour the only other woman in the figure dropped out exhausted, and sank panting on a bench.

The reel instantly resolved itself into a four-handed one. Car'line would have given anything to leave off; but she had, or fancied she had, no power, while Mop played such tunes; and thus another ten minutes slipped by, a haze of dust now clouding the candles, the floor being of stone, sanded. Then another dancer fell out – one of the men – and went into the passage in a frantic search for liquor. To turn the figure into a three-handed reel was the work of a second, Mop modulating at the same time into 'The Fairy Dance', as better suited to the contracted movement, and no less one of those foods of love which, as manufactured by his bow, had always intoxicated her.

In a reel for three there was no rest whatever, and four or five minutes were enough to make her remaining two partners, now thoroughly blown, stamp their last bar, and, like their predecessors, limp off into the next room to get something to drink. Car'line, half-stifled inside her veil, was left dancing alone, the apartment now being empty of everybody save herself, Mop, and their little girl.

She flung up the veil, and cast her eyes upon him, as if imploring him to withdraw himself and his acoustic magnetism from the atmosphere. Mop opened one of his own orbs, as though for the first time, fixed it peeringly upon her, and smiling dreamily, threw into his strains the reserve of expression which he could not afford to waste on a big and noisy dance. Crowds of little chromatic subtleties, capable of drawing tears from a statue, proceeded straightway from the ancient fiddle, as if it were dying of the emotion which had been pent up within it ever since its banishment from some Italian or German city where it first took shape and sound. There was that in the look of Mop's one dark eye which said: 'You cannot leave off, dear, whether you would or no!' and it bred in her a paroxysm of desperation that defied him to tire her down.

She thus continued to dance alone, defiantly as she thought, but in truth slavishly and abjectly, subject to every wave of the melody, and probed by the gimlet-like gaze of her fascinator's open eye; keeping up at the same time a feeble smile in his face, as a feint to signify it was still her own pleasure which led her on. A terrified embarrassment as to what she could say to him if she were to leave off, had its unrecognized share in keeping her going. The child, who was beginning to be distressed by the strange situation, came up and whimpered: 'Stop, mother, stop, and let's go home!' as she seized Car'line's hand.

Suddenly Car'line sank staggering to the floor; and rolling over on her face, prone she remained. Mop's fiddle thereupon emitted an elfin shriek of finality; stepping quickly down from the nine-gallon beer-cask which had formed his rostrum, he went to the little girl, who disconsolately bent over her mother.

The guests who had gone into the back-room for liquor and change of air, hearing something unusual, trooped back hither-ward, where they endeavoured to revive poor, weak Car'line by blowing her with the bellows and opening the window. Ned, her husband, who had been detained in Casterbridge, as aforesaid, came along the road at this juncture, and hearing excited voices through the open casement, and to his great surprise, the mention of his wife's name, he entered amid the rest upon the scene. Car'line was now in convulsions, weeping violently, and for a long time nothing could be done with her. While he was sending for a cart to take her onward to Stickleford Hipcroft anxiously inquired how it had all happened; and then the assembly explained that a fiddler formerly known in the locality had lately visited his old haunts, and had taken upon himself without invitation to play that evening at the inn and raise a dance.

Ned demanded the fiddler's name, and they said Ollamoor.

'Ah!' exclaimed Ned, looking round him. 'Where is he, and where – where's my little girl?'

Ollamoor had disappeared, and so had the child. Hipcroft was in ordinary a quiet and tractable fellow, but a determination which was to be feared settled in his face now. 'Blast him!' he cried. 'I'll beat his skull in for'n, if I swing for it tomorrow!'

He had rushed to the poker which lay on the hearth, and hastened down the passage, the people following. Outside the house, on the other side of the highway, a mass of dark heathland rose sullenly upward to its not easily accessible interior, a ravined plateau, whereon jutted into the sky, at the distance of a couple of miles, the fir-woods of Mistover backed by the Yalbury coppices – a place of Dantesque gloom at this hour, which would have afforded secure hiding for a battery of artillery, much less a man and a child.

Some other men plunged thitherward with him, and more went along the road. They were gone about twenty minutes altogether, returning without result to the inn. Ned sat down in the settle, and clasped his forehead with his hands.

'Well – what a fool the man is, and hev been all these years, if he thinks the child his, as a' do seem to!' they whispered. 'And everybody else knowing otherwise!'

'No, I don't think 'tis mine!' cried Ned hoarsely, as he looked up from his hands. 'But she *is* mine, all the same! Ha'n't I nussed her? Ha'n't I fed her and teached her? Ha'n't I played wi' her? O, little Carry – gone with that rogue – gone!'

'You ha'n't lost your mis'ess, anyhow,' they said to console him. 'She's throwed up the sperrits, and she is feeling better, and she's more to 'ee than a child that isn't yours.'

'She isn't! She's not so particular much to me, especially now she's lost the little maid! But Carry's the whole world to me!'

'Well, ver' like you'll find her tomorrow.'

'Ah – but shall I? Yet he *can't* hurt her – surely he can't! Well –
how's Car'line now? I am ready. Is the cart here?'

She was lifted into the vehicle, and they sadly lumbered on
toward Stickleford. Next day she was calmer; but the fits were
still upon her; and her will seemed shattered. For the child she
appeared to show singularly little anxiety, though Ned was
nearly distracted by his passionate paternal love for a child not
his own. It was nevertheless quite expected that the impish Mop
would restore the lost one after a freak of a day or two; but time
went on, and neither he nor she could be heard of, and Hipcroft
murmured that perhaps he was exercising upon her some unholy
musical charm, as he had done upon Car'line herself. Weeks
passed, and still they could obtain no clue either to the fiddler's
whereabouts or to the girl's; and how he could have induced her
to go with him remained a mystery.

Then Ned, who had obtained only temporary employment in
the neighbourhood, took a sudden hatred toward his native
district, and a rumour reaching his ears through the police that a
somewhat similar man and child had been seen at a fair near
London, he playing a violin, she dancing on stilts, a new interest
in the capital took possession of Hipcroft with an intensity which
would scarcely allow him time to pack before returning thither.
He did not, however, find the lost one, though he made it the
entire business of his over-hours to stand about in by-streets in
the hope of discovering her, and would start up in the night,
saying, 'That rascal's torturing her to maintain him!' To which
his wife would answer peevishly, 'Don't 'ee raft yourself so, Ned!
You prevent my getting a bit o' rest! He won't hurt her!' and fall
asleep again.

That Carry and her father had emigrated to America was the
general opinion; Mop, no doubt, finding the girl a highly
desirable companion when he had trained her to keep him by her
earnings as a dancer. There, for that matter, they may be
performing in some capacity now, though he must be an old
scamp verging on three-score-and-ten, and she a woman of four-
and-forty.

The Honourable Laura

It was a cold and gloomy Christmas Eve. The mass of cloud overhead was almost impervious to such daylight as still lingered; the snow lay several inches deep upon the ground, and the slanting downfall which still went on threatened to considerably increase its thickness before the morning. The Prospect Hotel, a building standing near the wild north coast of Lower Wessex, looked so lonely and so useless at such a time as this that a passing wayfarer would have been led to forget summer possibilities, and to wonder at the commercial courage which could invest capital, on the basis of the popular taste for the picturesque, in a country subject to such dreary phases. That the district was alive with visitors in August seemed but a dim tradition in weather so totally opposed to all that tempts mankind from home. However, there the hotel stood immovable; and the cliffs, creeks, and headlands which were the primary attractions of the spot, rising in full view on the opposite side of the valley, were now but stern angular outlines, while the townlet in front was tinged over with a grimy dirtiness rather than the pearly grey that in summer lent such beauty to its appearance.

Within the hotel commanding this outlook the landlord walked idly about with his hands in his pockets, not in the least expectant of a visitor, and yet unable to settle down to any occupation which should compensate in some degree for the losses that winter idleness entailed on his regular profession. So little, indeed, was anybody expected, that the coffee-room waiter – a genteel boy, whose plated buttons in summer were as close together upon the front of his short jacket as peas in a pod – now appeared in the back yard, metamorphosed into the unrecognizable shape of a rough country lad in corduroys and hobnailed boots, sweeping the snow away, and talking the local dialect in all its purity, quite oblivious of the new polite accent he had learned in the hot weather from the well-behaved visitors. The front door was closed, and, as if to express still more fully the sealed and chrysalis state of the establishment, a sand-bag was placed at the bottom to keep out the insidious snowdrift, the wind setting in directly from that quarter.

The landlord, entering his own parlour, walked to the large fire which it was absolutely necessary to keep up for his comfort, no such blaze burning in the coffee-room or elsewhere, and after giving it a stir returned to a table in the lobby, whereon lay the visitors' book – now closed and pushed back against the wall. He carelessly opened it; not a name had been entered there since the 19th of the previous November, and that was only the name of a man who had arrived on a tricycle, who, indeed, had not been asked to enter at all.

While he was engaged thus the evening grew darker; but before it was as yet too dark to distinguish objects upon the road winding round the back of the cliffs, the landlord perceived a black spot on the distant white, which speedily enlarged itself and drew near. The probabilities were that this vehicle – for a vehicle of some sort it seemed to be – would pass by and pursue its way to the nearest railway-town as others had done. But, contrary to the landlord's expectation, as he stood conning it through the yet unshuttered windows, the solitary object, on reaching the corner, turned into the hotel-front, and drove up to the door.

It was a conveyance particularly unsuited to such a season and weather, being nothing more substantial than an open basket-carriage drawn by a single horse. Within sat two persons, of different sexes, as could soon be discerned, in spite of their muffled attire. The man held the reins, and the lady had got some shelter from the storm by clinging close to his side. The landlord rang the hostler's bell to attract the attention of the stable-man, for the approach of the visitors had been deadened to noiseless- ness by the snow, and when the hostler had come to the horse's head the gentleman and lady alighted, the landlord meeting them in the hall.

The male stranger was a foreign-looking individual of about eight-and-twenty. He was close-shaven, excepting a moustache, his features being good, and even handsome. The lady, who stood timidly behind him, seemed to be much younger – possibly not more than eighteen, though it was difficult to judge either of her age or appearance in her present wrappings.

The gentleman expressed his wish to stay till the morning, explaining somewhat unnecessarily, considering that the house was an inn, that they had been unexpectedly benighted on their drive. Such a welcome being given them as landlords can give in dull times, the latter ordered fires in the drawing and coffee-rooms, and went to the boy in the yard, who soon scrubbed himself up, dragged his disused jacket from its box, polished the buttons with his sleeve, and appeared civilized in the hall. The lady was shown into a room where she could take off her snow-damped garments, which she sent down to be dried, her companion, meanwhile, putting a couple of sovereigns on the table, as if anxious to make everything smooth and comfortable at starting, and requesting that a private sitting-room might be got ready. The landlord assured him that the best upstairs parlour – usually public – should be kept private this evening, and sent the maid to light the candles. Dinner was prepared for them, and, at the gentleman's desire, served in the same apartment; where, the young lady having joined him, they were left to the rest and refreshment they seemed to need.

That something was peculiar in the relations of the pair had more than once struck the landlord, though wherein that peculiarity lay it was hard to decide. But that his guest was one who paid his way readily had been proved by his conduct, and dismissing conjectures he turned to practical affairs.

About nine o'clock he re-entered the hall, and, everything being done for the day, again walked up and down, occasionally gazing through the glass door at the prospect without, to ascertain how the weather was progressing. Contrary to prognos-tication, snow had ceased falling, and, with the rising of the moon, the sky had partially cleared, light fleeces of cloud drifting across the silvery disk. There was every sign that a frost was going to set in later on. For these reasons the distant rising road was even more distinct now between its high banks than it had been in the declining daylight. Not a track or rut broke the virgin surface of the white mantle that lay along it, all marks left by the lately arrived travellers having been speedily obliterated by the flakes falling at the time.

And now the landlord beheld by the light of the moon a sight very similar to that he had seen by the light of day. Again a black spot was advancing down the road that margined the coast. He was in a moment or two enabled to perceive that the present vehicle moved onward at a more headlong pace than the little carriage which had preceded it; next, that it was a brougham drawn by two powerful horses; next, that this carriage, like the former one, was bound for the hotel-door. This desirable feature of resemblance caused the landlord once more to withdraw the sand-bag and advance into the porch.

An old gentleman was the first to alight. He was followed by a young one, and both unhesitatingly came forward.

'Has a young lady, less than nineteen years of age, recently arrived here in the company of a man some years her senior?' asked the old gentleman, in haste. 'A man cleanly shaven for the most part, having the appearance of an opera-singer, and calling himself Signor Smittozzi?'

'We have had arrivals lately,' said the landlord, in the tone of having had twenty at least – not caring to acknowledge the attenuated state of business that afflicted Prospect Hotel in winter.

'And among them can your memory recall two persons such as those I describe? – the man a sort of baritone?'

'There certainly is or was a young couple staying in the hotel; but I could not pronounce on the compass of the gentleman's voice.'

'No, no; of course not. I am quite bewildered. They arrived in a basket-carriage, altogether badly provided?'

'They came in a carriage, I believe, as most of our visitors do.'

'Yes, yes. I must see them at once. Pardon my want of ceremony, and show us in to where they are.'

'But, sir, you forget. Suppose the lady and gentleman I mean are not the lady and gentleman you mean? It would be awkward to allow you to rush in upon them just now while they are at dinner, and might cause me to lose their future patronage.'

'True, true. They may not be the same persons. My anxiety, I perceive, makes me rash in my assumptions!'

'Upon the whole, I think they must be the same, Uncle Quantock,' said the young man, who had not till now spoken. And turning to the landlord: 'You possibly have not such a large assemblage of visitors here, on this somewhat forbidding evening, that you quite forget how this couple arrived, and what the lady wore?' His tone of addressing the landlord had in it a quiet frigidity that was not without irony.

'Ah! what she wore; that's it, James. What did she wear?'

'I don't usually take stock of my guests' clothing,' replied the landlord drily, for the ready money of the first arrival had decidedly biassed him in favour of that gentleman's cause. 'You can certainly see some of it if you want to,' he added carelessly, 'for it is drying by the kitchen fire.'

Before the words were half out of his mouth the old gentleman had exclaimed, 'Ah!' and precipitated himself along what seemed to be the passage to the kitchen; but as this turned out to be only the entrance to a dark china-closet, he hastily emerged again, after a collision with the inn-crockery had told him of his mistake.

'I beg your pardon, I'm sure; but if you only knew my feelings (which I cannot at present explain), you would make allowances. Anything I have broken I will willingly pay for.'

'Don't mention it, sir,' said the landlord. And showing the way, they adjourned to the kitchen without further parley. The eldest of the party instantly seized the lady's cloak, that hung upon a clothes-horse, exclaiming: 'Ah! yes, James, it is hers. I knew we were on their track.'

'Yes, it is hers,' answered the nephew quietly, for he was much less excited than his companion.

'Show us their room at once,' said the uncle.

'William, have the lady and gentleman in the front sitting-room finished dining?'

'Yes, sir, long ago,' said the hundred plated buttons.

'Then show up these gentlemen to them at once. You stay here tonight, gentlemen, I presume? Shall the horses be taken out?'

'Feed the horses and wash their mouths. Whether we stay or not depends upon circumstances,' said the placid younger man, as he followed his uncle and the waiter to the staircase.

'I think, Nephew James,' said the former, as he paused with his foot on the first step – 'I think we had better not be announced, but take them by surprise. She may go throwing herself out of the window, or do some equally desperate thing!'

'Yes, certainly, we'll enter unannounced.' And he called back the lad who preceded them.

'I cannot sufficiently thank you, James, for so effectually aiding me in this pursuit!' exclaimed the old gentleman, taking the other by the hand. 'My increasing infirmities would have hindered my overtaking her tonight, had it not been for your timely aid.'

'I am only too happy, uncle, to have been of service to you in this or any other matter. I only wish I could have accompanied you on a pleasanter journey. However, it is advisable to go up to them at once, or they may hear us.' And they softly ascended the stairs.

On the door being opened a room too large to be comfortable was disclosed, lit by the best branch-candlesticks of the hotel, before the fire of which apartment the truant couple were sitting, very innocently looking over the hotel scrap-book and the album containing views of the neighbourhood. No sooner had the old man entered than the young lady – who now showed herself to be quite as young as described, and remarkably prepossessing as to features – perceptibly turned pale. When the nephew entered she turned still paler, as if she were going to faint. The young man described as an opera-singer rose with grim civility, and placed chairs for his visitors.

'Caught you, thank God!' said the old gentleman breathlessly.

'Yes, worse luck, my lord!' murmured Signor Smittozzi, in native London-English, that distinguished Italian having, in fact, first seen the light as the baby of Mr and Mrs Smith in the vicinity of the City Road. 'She would have been mine tomorrow. And I think that under the peculiar circumstances it would be wiser – considering how soon the breath of scandal will tarnish a lady's fame – to let her be mine tomorrow, just the same.'

'Never!' said the old man. 'Here is a lady under age, without experience – child-like in her maiden innocence and virtue – whom you have plied by your vile arts, till this morning at dawn – '

'Lord Quantock, were I not bound to respect your grey hairs – '

'Till this morning at dawn you tempted her away from her father's roof. What blame can attach to her conduct that will not, on a full explanation of the matter, be readily passed over in her and thrown entirely on you? Laura, you return at once with me. I should not have arrived, after all, early enough to deliver you, if it had not been for the disinterestedness of your cousin, Captain Northbrook, who, on my discovering your flight this morning, offered with a promptitude for which I can never sufficiently thank him, to accompany me on my journey, as the only male

relative I have near me. Come, do you hear? Put on your things;
we are off at once.'

'I don't want to go!' pouted the young lady.

'I daresay you don't,' replied her father drily. 'But children
never know what's best for them. So come along, and trust to my
opinion.'

Laura was silent, and did not move, the opera gentleman
looking helplessly into the fire, and the lady's cousin sitting
meditatively calm, as the single one of the four whose position
enabled him to survey the whole escapade with the cool criticism
of a comparative outsider.

'I say to you, Laura, as the father of a daughter under age, that
you instantly come with me. What? Would you compel me to use
physical force to reclaim you?'

'I don't want to return!' again declared Laura.

'It is your duty to return nevertheless, and at once, I inform
you.'

'I don't want to!'

'Now, dear Laura, this is what I say: return with me and your
cousin James quietly, like a good and repentant girl, and nothing
will be said. Nobody knows what has happened as yet, and if we
start at once, we shall be home before it is light tomorrow
morning. Come.'

'I am not obliged to come at your bidding, father, and I would
rather not!'

Now James, the cousin, during this dialogue might have been
observed to grow somewhat restless, and even impatient. More
than once he had parted his lips to speak, but second thoughts
each time held him back. The moment had come, however, when
he could keep silence no longer.

'Come, madam!' he spoke out, 'this farce with your father has,
in my opinion, gone on long enough. Just make no more ado,
and step downstairs with us.'

She gave herself an intractable little twist, and did not reply.

'By the Lord Harry, Laura, I won't stand this!' he said angrily.
'Come, get on your things before I come and compel you. There is
a kind of compulsion to which this talk is child's play. Come,
madam – instantly, I say!'

The old nobleman turned to his nephew and said mildly:

'Leave me to insist, James. It doesn't become you. I can speak to her sharply enough, if I choose.'

James, however, did not heed his uncle, and went on to the troublesome young woman: 'You say you don't want to come, indeed! A pretty story to tell me, that! Come, march out of the room at once, and leave that hulking fellow for me to deal with afterward. Get on quickly – come!' and he advanced toward her as if to pull her by the hand.

'Nay, nay,' expostulated Laura's father, much surprised at his nephew's sudden demeanour. 'You take too much upon yourself. Leave her to me.'

'I won't leave her to you any longer!'

'You have no right, James, to address either me or her in this way; so just hold your tongue. Come, my dear.'

'I have every right!' insisted James.

'How do you make that out?'

'I have the right of a husband.'

'Whose husband?'

'Hers.'

'What?'

'She's my wife.'

'James!'

'Well, to cut a long story short, I may say that she secretly married me, in spite of your lordship's prohibition, about three months ago. And I must add that, though she cooled down rather quickly, everything went on smoothly enough between us for some time; in spite of the awkwardness of meeting only by stealth. We were only waiting for a convenient moment to break the news to you when this idle Adonis turned up, and after poisoning her mind against me, brought her into this disgrace.'

Here the operatic luminary, who had sat in rather an abstracted and nerveless attitude till the cousin made his declaration, fired up and cried: 'I declare before Heaven that till this moment I never knew she was a wife! I found her in her father's house an unhappy girl – unhappy, as I believe, because of the loneliness and dreariness of that establishment, and the want of society, and for nothing else whatever. What this statement about her being your wife means I am quite at a loss to understand. Are you indeed married to him, Laura?'

Laura nodded from within her tearful handkerchief. 'It was

because of my anomalous position in being privately married to him,' she sobbed, 'that I was unhappy at home – and – and I didn't like him so well as I did at first – and I wished I could get out of the mess I was in! And then I saw you a few times, and when you said, "We'll run off", I thought I saw a way out of it all, and then I agreed to come with you-oo-oo!'

'Well! well! well! And is this true?' murmured the bewildered old nobleman, staring from James to Laura, and from Laura to James, as if he fancied they might be figments of the imagination. 'Is this, then, James, the secret of your kindness to your old uncle in helping him to find his daughter? Good Heavens! What further depths of duplicity are there left for a man to learn!'

'I have married her, Uncle Quantock, as I said,' answered James coolly. 'The deed is done, and can't be undone by talking here.'

'Where were you married?'

'At St Mary's, Toneborough.'

'When?'

'On the 29th of September, during the time she was visiting there.'

'Who married you?'

'I don't know. One of the curates – we were quite strangers to the place. So, instead of my assisting you to recover her, you may as well assist me.'

'Never! never!' said Lord Quantock. 'Madam, and sir, I beg to tell you that I wash my hands of the whole affair. If you are man and wife, as it seems you are, get reconciled as best you may. I have no more to say or do with either of you. I leave you, Laura, in the hands of your husband, and much joy may you bring him; though the situation, I own, is not encouraging.'

Saying this, the indignant speaker pushed back his chair against the table with such force that the candlesticks rocked on their bases, and left the room.

Laura's wet eyes roved from one of the young men to the other, who now stood glaring face to face, and, being much frightened at their aspect, slipped out of the room after her father. Him, however, she could hear going out of the front door, and, not knowing where to take shelter, she crept into the darkness of an adjoining bedroom, and there awaited events with a palpitating heart.

Meanwhile the two men remaining in the sitting-room drew nearer to each other, and the opera-singer broke the silence by saying, 'How could you insult me in the way you did, calling me a fellow, and accusing me of poisoning her mind toward you, when you knew very well I was as ignorant of your relation to her as an unborn babe?'

'O yes, you were quite ignorant; I can believe that readily,' sneered Laura's husband.

'I here call Heaven to witness that I never knew!'

'Recitativo – the rhythm excellent, and the tone well sustained. Is it likely that any man could win the confidence of a young fool her age, and not get that out of her? Preposterous! Tell it to the most improved new pit-stalls.'

'Captain Northbrook, your insinuations are as despicable as your wretched person!' cried the baritone, losing all patience. And springing forward he slapped the captain in the face with the palm of his hand.

Northbrook flinched but slightly, and calmly using his handkerchief to learn if his nose was bleeding, said, 'I quite expected this insult, so I came prepared.' And he drew forth from a black valise which he carried in his hand a small case of pistols.

The baritone started at the unexpected sight, but recovering from his surprise said, 'Very well, as you will,' though perhaps his tone showed a slight want of confidence.

'Now,' continued the husband, quite confidingly, 'we want no parade, no nonsense, you know. Therefore we'll dispense with seconds?'

The signor slightly nodded.

'Do you know this part of the country well?' Cousin James went on, in the same cool and still manner. 'If you don't, I do. Quite at the bottom of the rocks out there, just beyond the stream which falls over them to the shore, is a smooth sandy space, not so much shut in as to be out of the moonlight; and the way down to it from this side is over steps cut in the cliff; and we can find our way down without trouble. We – we two – will find our way down; but only one of us will find his way up, you understand?'

'Quite.'

'Then suppose we start; the sooner it is over the better. We can order supper before we go out – supper for two; for though we are three at present – '

'Three?'

'Yes; you and I and she – '

'O yes.'

' – We shall be only two by and by; so that, as I say, we will order supper for two; for the lady and a gentleman. Whichever comes back alive will tap at her door, and call her in to share the repast with him – she's not off the premises. But we must not alarm her now; and above all things we must not let the inn-people see us go out; it would look so odd for two to go out, and only one come in. Ha! ha!'

'Ha! ha! exactly.'

'Are you ready?'

'Oh – quite.'

'Then I'll lead the way.'

He went softly to the door and downstairs, ordering supper to be ready in an hour, as he had said; then making a feint of returning to the room again, he beckoned to the singer, and together they slipped out of the house by a side door.

The sky was now quite clear, and the wheelmarks of the brougham which had borne away Laura's father, Lord Quantock, remained distinctly visible. Soon the verge of the down was reached, the captain leading the way, and the baritone following silently, casting furtive glances at his companion, and beyond him at the scene ahead. In due course they arrived at the chasm in the cliff which formed the waterfall. The outlook here was wild and picturesque in the extreme, and fully justified the many praises, paintings, and photographic views to which the spot had given birth. What in summer was charmingly green and grey, was now rendered weird and fantastic by the snow.

From their feet the cascade plunged downward almost verti-cally to a depth of eighty or a hundred feet before finally losing itself in the sand, and though the stream was but small, its impact upon jutting rocks in its descent divided it into a hundred spirts and splashes that sent up a mist into the upper air. A few marginal drippings had been frozen into icicles, but the centre flowed on unimpeded.

The operatic artist looked down as he halted, but his thoughts were plainly not of the beauty of the scene. His companion with the pistols was immediately in front of him, and there was no

handrail on the side of the path toward the chasm. Obeying a
quick impulse, he stretched out his arm, and with a superhuman
thrust sent Laura's husband reeling over. A whirling human
shape, diminishing downward in the moon's rays further and
further toward invisibility, a smack-smack upon the projecting
ledges of rock – at first louder and heavier than that of the brook,
and then scarcely to be distinguished from it – then a cessation,
then the splashing of the stream as before, and the accompanying murmur of the sea, were all the incidents that disturbed the
customary flow of the lofty waterfall.

The singer waited in a fixed attitude for a few minutes, then
turning, he rapidly retraced his steps over the intervening upland
toward the road, and in less than a quarter of an hour was at the
door of the hotel. Slipping quietly in as the clock struck ten, he
said to the landlord, over the bar hatchway –

'The bill as soon as you can let me have it, including charges
for the supper that was ordered, though we cannot stay to eat it,
I am sorry to say.' He added with forced gaiety, 'The lady's father
and cousin have thought better of intercepting the marriage, and
after quarrelling with each other have gone home independently.'

'Well done, sir!' said the landlord, who still sided with this
customer in preference to those who had given trouble and
barely paid for baiting the horses. '"Love will find out the way!"
as the saying is. Wish you joy, sir!'

Signor Smittozzi went upstairs, and on entering the sitting-
room found that Laura had crept out from the dark adjoining
chamber in his absence. She looked up at him with eyes red from
weeping, and with symptoms of alarm.

'What is it? – where is he?' she said apprehensively.

'Captain Northbrook has gone back. He says he will have no
more to do with you.'

'And I am quite abandoned by them! – and they'll forget me,
and nobody care about me any more!' She began to cry afresh.

'But it is the luckiest thing that could have happened. All is
just as it was before they came disturbing us. But, Laura, you
ought to have told me about that private marriage, though it is
all the same now; it will be dissolved, of course. You are a wid–
virtually a widow.'

'It is no use to reproach me for what is past. What am I to do now?'

'We go at once to Cliff-Martin. The horse has rested thoroughly these last three hours, and he will have no difficulty in doing an additional half-dozen miles. We shall be there before twelve, and there are late taverns in the place, no doubt. There we'll sell both horse and carriage tomorrow morning; and go by the coach to Downstaple. Once in the train we are safe.'

'I agree to anything,' she said listlessly.

In about ten minutes the horse was put in, the bill paid, the lady's dried wraps put round her, and the journey resumed.

When about a mile on their way they saw a glimmering light in advance of them. 'I wonder what that is?' said the baritone, whose manner had latterly become nervous, every sound and sight causing him to turn his head.

'It is only a turnpike,' said she. 'That light is the lamp kept burning over the door.'

'Of course, of course, dearest. How stupid I am!'

On reaching the gate they perceived that a man on foot had approached it, apparently by some more direct path than the roadway they pursued, and was, at the moment they drew up, standing in conversation with the gatekeeper.

'It is quite impossible that he could fall over the cliff by accident or the will of God on such a light night as this,' the pedestrian was saying. 'These two children I tell you of saw two men go along the path toward the waterfall, and ten minutes later only one of 'em came back, walking fast, like a man who wanted to get out of the way because he had done something queer. There is no manner of doubt that he pushed the other man over, and, mark me, it will soon cause a hue and cry for that man.'

The candle shone in the face of the Signor and showed that there had arisen upon it a film of ghastliness. Laura, glancing toward him for a few moments, observed it, till, the gatekeeper having mechanically swung open the gate, her companion drove through, and they were soon again enveloped in the white silence.

Her conductor had said to Laura, just before, that he meant to inquire the way at this turnpike; but he had certainly not done so.

As soon as they had gone a little further the omission, intentional or not, began to cause them some trouble. Beyond the secluded district which they now traversed ran the more frequented road, where progress would be easy, the snow being probably already beaten there to some extent by traffic; but they had not yet reached it, and having no one to guide them their journey began to appear less feasible than it had done before starting. When the little lane which they had entered ascended another hill, and seemed to wind round in a direction contrary to the expected route to Cliff-Martin, the question grew serious. Ever since overhearing the conversation at the turnpike, Laura had maintained a perfect silence, and had even shrunk somewhat away from the side of her lover.

'Why don't you talk, Laura,' he said with forced buoyancy, 'and suggest the way we should go?'

'O yes, I will,' she responded, a curious fearfulness being audible in her voice.

After this she uttered a few occasional sentences which seemed to persuade him that she suspected nothing. At last he drew rein, and the weary horse stood still.

'We are in a fix,' he said.

She answered eagerly: 'I'll hold the reins while you run forward to the top of the ridge, and see if the road takes a favourable turn beyond. It would give the horse a few minutes' rest, and if you find out no change in the direction, we will retrace this lane, and take the other turning.'

The expedient seemed a good one in the circumstances, especially when recommended by the singular eagerness of her voice; and placing the reins in her hands – a quite unnecessary precaution, considering the state of their hack – he stepped out and went forward through the snow till she could see no more of him.

No sooner was he gone than Laura, with a rapidity which contrasted strangely with her previous stillness, made fast the reins to the corner of the phaeton, and slipping out on the opposite side, ran back with all her might down the hill, till, coming to an opening in the fence, she scrambled through it, and plunged into the copse which bordered this portion of the lane. Here she stood in hiding under one of the large bushes, clinging so closely to its umbrage as to seem but a portion of its mass, and listening intently for the faintest sound of pursuit. But nothing disturbed the stillness save the occasional slipping of gathered snow from the boughs, or the rustle of some wild animal over the crisp flake-bespattered herbage. At length, apparently convinced that her former companion was either unable to find her, or not anxious to do so in the present strange state of affairs, she crept out from the bushes, and in less than an hour found herself again approaching the door of the Prospect Hotel.

As she drew near, Laura could see that, far from being wrapped in darkness, as she might have expected, there were ample signs that all the tenants were on the alert, lights moving about the open space in front. Satisfaction was expressed in her face when she discerned that no reappearance of her baritone and his pony-carriage was causing this sensation; but it speedily gave way to grief and dismay when she saw by the lights the form of a man borne on a stretcher by two others into the porch of the hotel.

'I have caused all this,' she murmured between her quivering lips. 'He has murdered him!' Running forward to the door, she hastily asked of the first person she met if the man on the stretcher was dead.

'No, miss,' said the labourer addressed, eyeing her up and down as an unexpected apparition. 'He is still alive, they say, but not sensible. He either fell or was pushed over the waterfall; 'tis thoughted he was pushed. He is the gentleman who came here just now with the old lord, and went out afterward (as is thoughted) with a stranger who had come a little earlier. Anyhow, that's as I had it.'

Laura entered the house, and acknowledging without the least reserve that she was the injured man's wife, had soon installed herself as head nurse by the bed on which he lay. When the two surgeons who had been sent for arrived, she learnt from them that his wounds were so severe as to leave but a slender hope of recovery, it being little short of miraculous that he was not killed on the spot, which his enemy had evidently reckoned to be the case. She knew who that enemy was, and shuddered.

Laura watched all night, but her husband knew nothing of her presence. During the next day he slightly recognized her, and in the evening was able to speak. He informed the surgeons that, as was surmised, he had been pushed over the cascade by Signor

Smittozzi; but he communicated nothing to her who nursed him, not even replying to her remarks; he nodded courteously at any act of attention she rendered, and that was all.

In a day or two it was declared that everything favoured his recovery, notwithstanding the severity of his injuries. Full search was made for Smittozzi, but as yet there was no intelligence of his whereabouts, though the repentant Laura communicated all she knew. As far as could be judged, he had come back to the carriage after searching out the way, and finding the young lady missing, had looked about for her till he was tired; then had driven on to Cliff-Martin, sold the horse and carriage next morning, and disappeared, probably by one of the departing coaches which ran thence to the nearest station, the only difference from his original programme being that he had gone alone.

During the days and weeks of that long and tedious recovery Laura watched by her husband's bedside with a zeal and assiduity which would have considerably extenuated any fault save one of such magnitude as hers. That her husband did not forgive her was soon obvious. Nothing that she could do in the way of smoothing pillows, easing his position, shifting bandages, or administering draughts, could win from him more than a few measured words of thankfulness, such as he would probably have uttered to any other woman on earth who had performed these particular services for him.

'Dear, dear James,' she said one day, bending her face upon the bed in an excess of emotion. 'How you have suffered! It has been too cruel. I am more glad you are getting better than I can say. I have prayed for it – and I am sorry for what I have done; I am innocent of the worst, and – I hope you will not think me so very bad, James!'

'O no. On the contrary, I shall think you very good – as a nurse,' he answered, the caustic severity of his tone being apparent through its weakness.

Laura let fall two or three silent tears, and said no more that day.

Somehow or other Signor Smittozzi seemed to be making good his escape. It transpired that he had not taken a passage in either of the suspected coaches, though he had certainly got out of the county; altogether, the chance of finding him was problematical.

Not only did Captain Northbrook survive his injuries, but it soon appeared that in the course of a few weeks he would find himself little if any the worse for the catastrophe. It could also be seen that Laura, while secretly hoping for her husband's forgiveness for a piece of folly of which she saw the enormity more clearly every day, was in great doubt as to what her future relations with him would be. Moreover, to add to the complication, whilst she, as a runaway wife, was unforgiven by her husband, she and her husband, as a runaway couple, were unforgiven by her father, who had never once communicated with either of them since his departure from the inn. But her immediate anxiety was to win the pardon of her husband, who possibly might be bearing in mind, as he lay upon his couch, the familiar words of Brabantio, 'She has deceived her father, and may thee.'

Matters went on thus till Captain Northbrook was able to walk about. He then removed with his wife to quiet apartments on the south coast, and here his recovery was rapid. Walking up the cliffs one day, supporting him by her arm as usual, she said to him, simply, 'James, if I go on as I am going now, and always attend to your smallest want, and never think of anything but devotion to you, will you – try to like me a little?'

'It is a thing I must carefully consider,' he said, with the same gloomy dryness which characterized all his words to her now. 'When I have considered, I will tell you.'

He did not tell her that evening, though she lingered long at her routine work of making his bedroom comfortable, putting the light so that it would not shine into his eyes, seeing him fall asleep, and then retiring noiselessly to her own chamber. When they met in the morning at breakfast, and she had asked him as usual how he had passed the night, she added timidly, in the silence which followed his reply, 'Have you considered?'

'No, I have not considered sufficiently to give you an answer.'

Laura sighed, but to no purpose; and the day wore on with intense heaviness to her, and the customary modicum of strength gained to him.

The next morning she put the same question, and looked up

despairingly in his face, as though her whole life hung upon his reply.

'Yes, I have considered,' he said.

'Ah!'

'We must part.'

'O James!'

'I cannot forgive you; no man would. Enough is settled upon you to keep you in comfort, whatever your father may do. I shall sell out, and disappear from this hemisphere.'

'You have absolutely decided?' she asked miserably. 'I have nobody now to c-c-care for – '

'I have absolutely decided,' he shortly returned. 'We had better part here. You will go back to your father. There is no reason why I should accompany you, since my presence would only stand in the way of the forgiveness he will probably grant you if you appear before him alone. We will say farewell to each other in three days from this time. I have calculated on being ready to go on that day.'

Bowed down with trouble she withdrew to her room, and the three days were passed by her husband in writing letters and attending to other business matters, saying hardly a word to her the while. The morning of departure came; but before the horses had been put in to take the severed twain in different directions, out of sight of each other, possibly for ever, the postman arrived with the morning letters.

There was one for the captain; none for her – there were never any for her. However, on this occasion something was enclosed for her in his, which he handed her. She read it and looked up helpless.

'My dear father – is dead!' she said. In a few moments she added, in a whisper, 'I must go to the Manor to bury him.... Will you go with me, James?'

He musingly looked out of the window. 'I suppose it is an awkward and melancholy undertaking for a woman alone,' he said coldly. 'Well, well – my poor uncle! – Yes, I'll go with you, and see you through the business.'

So they went off together instead of asunder, as planned. It is unnecessary to record the details of the journey, or of the sad week which followed it at her father's house. Lord Quantock's seat was a fine old mansion standing in its own park, and there were plenty of opportunities for husband and wife either to avoid each other, or to get reconciled if they were so minded, which one of them was at least. Captain Northbrook was not present at the reading of the will. She came to him afterward, and found him packing up his papers, intending to start next morning, now that he had seen her through the turmoil occasioned by her father's death.

'He has left me everything that he could!' she said to her husband. 'James, will you forgive me now, and stay?'

'I cannot stay.'

'Why not?'

'I cannot stay,' he repeated.

'But why?'

'I don't like you.'

He acted up to his word. When she came downstairs the next morning she was told that he had gone.

Laura bore her double bereavement as best she could. The vast mansion in which she had hitherto lived, with all its historic contents, had gone to her father's successor in the title; but her own was no unhandsome one. Around lay the undulating park, studded with trees a dozen times her own age; beyond it, the wood; beyond the wood, the farms. All this fair and quiet scene was hers. She nevertheless remained a lonely, repentant, depressed being, who would have given the greater part of everything she possessed to ensure the presence and affection of that husband whose very austerity and phlegm – qualities that had formerly led to the alienation between them – seemed now to be adorable features in his character.

She hoped and hoped again, but all to no purpose. Captain Northbrook did not alter his mind and return. He was quite a different sort of man from one who altered his mind; that she was at last despairingly forced to admit. And then she left off hoping, and settled down to a mechanical routine of existence which in some measure dulled her grief, but at the expense of all her natural animation and the sprightly wilfulness which had once charmed those who knew her, though it was perhaps all the while a factor in the production of her unhappiness.

To say that her beauty quite departed as the years rolled on would be to overstate the truth. Time is not a merciful master, as we all know, and he was not likely to act exceptionally in the case of a woman who had mental troubles to bear in addition to the ordinary weight of years. Be this as it may, eleven other winters came and went, and Laura Northbrook remained the lonely mistress of house and lands without once hearing of her husband. Every probability seemed to favour the assumption that he had died in some foreign land; and offers for her hand were not few as the probability verged on certainty with the long lapse of time. But the idea of remarriage seemed never to have entered her head for a moment. Whether she continued to hope even now for his return could not be distinctly ascertained; at all events she lived a life unmodified in the slightest degree from that of the first six months of his absence.

This twelfth year of Laura's loneliness, and the thirtieth of her life drew on apace, and the season approached that had seen the unhappy adventure for which she so long had suffered. Christmas promised to be rather wet than cold, and the trees on the outskirts of Laura's estate dripped monotonously from day to day upon the turnpike-road which bordered them. On an afternoon in this week between three and four o'clock a hired fly might have been seen driving along the highway at this point, and on reaching the top of the hill it stopped. A gentleman of middle age alighted from the vehicle.

'You need drive no further,' he said to the coachman. 'The rain seems to have nearly ceased. I'll stroll a little way, and return on foot to the inn by dinner time.'

The flyman touched his hat, turned the horse, and drove back as directed. When he was out of sight the gentleman walked on, but he had not gone far before the rain again came down pitilessly, though of this the pedestrian took little heed, going leisurely onward till he reached Laura's park gate, which he passed through. The clouds were thick and the days were short, so that by the time he stood in front of the mansion it was dark. In addition to this his appearance, which on alighting from the carriage had been untarnished, partook now of the character of a drenched wayfarer not too well blessed with this world's goods. He halted for no more than a moment at the front entrance, and going round to the servants' quarter, as if he had a preconceived purpose in so doing, there rang the bell. When a page came to him he inquired if they would kindly allow him to dry himself by the kitchen fire.

The page retired, and after a murmured colloquy returned with the cook, who informed the wet and muddy man that though it was not her custom to admit strangers, she should have no particular objection to his drying himself, the night being so damp and gloomy. Therefore the wayfarer entered and sat down by the fire.

'The owner of this house is a very rich gentleman, no doubt?' he asked, as he watched the meat turning on the spit.

''Tis not a gentleman, but a lady,' said the cook.

'A widow, I presume?'

'A sort of widow. Poor soul, her husband is gone abroad, and has never been heard of for many years.'

'She sees plenty of company, no doubt, to make up for his absence?'

'No, indeed – hardly a soul. Service here is as bad as being in a nunnery.'

In short, the wayfarer, who had at first been so coldly received, contrived by his frank and engaging manner to draw the ladies of the kitchen into a most confidential conversation, in which Laura's history was minutely detailed, from the day of her husband's departure to the present. The salient feature in all their discourse was her unflagging devotion to his memory.

Having apparently learned all that he wanted to know – among other things that she was at this moment, as always, alone – the traveller said he was quite dry; and thanking the servants for their kindness, departed as he had come. On emerging into the darkness he did not, however, go down the avenue by which he had arrived. He simply walked round to the front door. There he rang, and the door was opened to him by a manservant whom he had not seen during his sojourn at the other end of the house.

In answer to the servant's inquiry for his name, he said ceremoniously, 'Will you tell The Honourable Mrs Northbrook that the man she nursed many years ago, after a frightful accident, has called to thank her?'

The footman retreated, and it was rather a long time before any further signs of attention were apparent. Then he was shown into the drawing-room, and the door closed behind him.

On the couch was Laura, trembling and pale. She parted her lips and held out her hands to him, but could not speak. But he did not require speech, and in a moment they were in each other's arms.

Strange news circulated through that mansion and the neighbouring town on the next and following days. But the world has a way of getting used to things, and the intelligence of the return of The Honourable Mrs Northbrook's long-absent husband was soon received with comparative calm.

A few days more brought Christmas, and the forlorn home of Laura Northbrook blazed from basement to attic with light and cheerfulness. Not that the house was overcrowded with visitors, but many were present, and the apathy of a dozen years came at length to an end. The animation which set in thus at the close of the old year did not diminish on the arrival of the new; and by the time its twelve months had likewise run the course of its predecessors, a son had been added to the dwindled line of the Northbrook family.

A Few Crusted Characters

from Life's Little Ironies

Andrey Satchel and the Parson and Clerk

'It all arose, you must know, from Andrey being fond of a drop of
drink at that time – though he's a sober enough man now by all
account, so much the better for him. Jane, his bride, you see, was
somewhat older than Andrey; how much older I don't pretend to
say; she was not one of our parish, and the register alone may be
able to tell that. But, at any rate, her being a little ahead of her
young man in mortal years, coupled with other bodily circumstances owing to that young man – '

('Ah, poor thing!' sighed the women.)

' – made her very anxious to get the thing done before he
changed his mind; and 'twas with a joyful countenance (they
say) that she, with Andrey and his brother and sister-in-law,
marched off to church one November morning as soon as 'twas
day a'most to be made one with Andrey for the rest of her life. He
had left our place long before it was light, and the folks that were
up all waved their lanterns at him, and flung up their hats as he
went.

'The church of her parish was a mile and more from where she
lived, and, as it was a wonderful fine day for the time of year, the
plan was that as soon as they were married they would make out
a holiday by driving straight off to Port Bredy, to see the ships
and the sea and the sojers, instead of coming back to a meal at
the house of the distant relation she lived wi', and moping about
there all the afternoon.

'Well, some folks noticed that Andrey walked with rather
wambling steps to church that morning; the truth o't was that
his nearest neighbour's child had been christened the day before,
and Andrey, having stood godfather, had stayed all night keeping
up the christening, for he had said to himself, "Not if I live to be a
thousand shall I again be made a godfather one day, and a
husband the next, and perhaps a father the next, and therefore
I'll make the most of the blessing." So that when he started from

home in the morning he had not been in bed at all. The result was, as I say, that when he and his bride-to-be walked up the church to get married, the pa'son (who was a very strict man inside the church, whatever he was outside) looked hard at Andrey, and said, very sharp:

'"How's this, my man? You are in liquor. And so early, too. I'm ashamed of you!"

'"Well, that's true, sir," says Andrey. "But I can walk straight enough for practical purposes. I can walk a chalk line," he says (meaning no offence), "as well as some other folk: and" – (getting hotter) – "I reckon that if you, Pa'son Billy Toogood, had kept up a christening all night so thoroughly as I have done, you wouldn't be able to stand at all; d— me if you would!"

'This answer made Pa'son Billy – as they used to call him – rather spitish, not to say hot, for he was a warm-tempered man if provoked, and he said, very decidedly: "Well, I cannot marry you in this state; and I will not! Go home and get sober!" And he slapped the book together like a rat-trap.

'Then the bride burst out crying as if her heart would break, for very fear that she would lose Andrey after all her hard work to get him, and begged and implored the pa'son to go on with the ceremony. But no.

'"I won't be a party to your solemnizing matrimony with a tipsy man," says Mr Toogood. "It is not right and decent. I am sorry for you, my young woman, seeing the condition you are in, but you'd better go home again. I wonder how you could think of bringing him here drunk like this!"

'"But if – if he don't come drunk he won't come at all, sir!" she says, through her sobs.

'"I can't help that," says the pa'son; and plead as she might, it did not move him. Then she tried him another way.

'"Well, then, if you'll go home, sir, and leave us here, and come back to the church in an hour or two, I'll undertake to say that he shall be as sober as a judge," she cries. "We'll bide here, with your permission; for if he once goes out of this here church unmarried, all Van Amburgh's horses won't drag him back again!"

'"Very well," says the pa'son. "I'll give you two hours, and then I'll return."

'"And please, sir, lock the door, so that we can't escape!" says she.

'"Yes," says the pa'son.

'"And let nobody know that we are here."

'The pa'son then took off his clane white surplice, and went away; and the others consulted upon the best means for keeping the matter a secret, which it was not a very hard thing to do, the place being so lonely, and the hour so early. The witnesses, Andrey's brother and brother's wife, neither one o' which cared about Andrey's marrying Jane, and had come rather against their will, said they couldn't wait two hours in that hole of a place, wishing to get home to Longpuddle before dinner-time. They were altogether so crusty that the clerk said there was no difficulty in their doing as they wished. They could go home as if their brother's wedding had actually taken place and the married couple had gone onward for their day's pleasure jaunt to Port Bredy as intended. He, the clerk, and any casual passer-by would act as witnesses when the pa'son came back.

'This was agreed to, and away Andrey's relations went, nothing loath, and the clerk shut the church door and prepared to lock in the couple. The bride went up and whispered to him, with her eyes a-streaming still.

'"My dear good clerk," she says, "if we bide here in the church, folk may see us through the windows, and find out what has happened; and 'twould cause such a talk and scandal that I never should get over it: and perhaps, too, dear Andrey might try to get out and leave me! Will ye lock us up in the tower, my dear good clerk?" she says. "I'll tole him in there if you will."

'The clerk had no objection to do this to oblige the poor young woman, and they toled Andrey into the tower, and the clerk locked 'em both up straightway, and then went home, to return at the end of the two hours.

'Pa'son Toogood had not been long in his house after leaving the church when he saw a gentleman in pink and top-boots ride past his windows, and with a sudden flash of heat he called to mind that the hounds met that day just on the edge of his parish. The pa'son was one who dearly loved sport, and much he longed to be there.

'In short, except o' Sundays and at tide-times in the week, Pa'son Billy was the life o' the hunt. 'Tis true that he was poor, and that he rode all of a heap, and that his black mare was rat-tailed and old, and his tops older, and all over of one colour, whitey-brown, and full o' cracks. But he'd been in at the death of three thousand foxes. And – being a bachelor man – every time he went to bed in summer he used to open the bed at bottom and crawl up head foremost, to mind en of the coming winter and the good sport he'd have, and the foxes going to earth. And whenever there was a christening at the Squire's, and he had dinner there afterwards, as he always did, he never failed to christen the chiel over again in a bottle of port wine.

'Now the clerk was the pa'son's groom and gardener and general manager, and had just got back to his work in the garden when he, too, saw the hunting man pass, and presently saw lots more of 'em, noblemen and gentry, and then he saw the hounds, the huntsman, Jim Treadhedge, the whipper-in, and I don't know who besides. The clerk loved going to cover as frantical as the pa'son, so much so that whenever he saw or heard the pack he could no more rule his feelings than if they were the winds of heaven. He might be bedding, or he might be sowing – all was forgot. So he throws down his spade and rushes in to the pa'son, who was by this time as frantical to go as he.

'"That there mare of yours, sir, do want exercise bad, very bad, this morning!" the clerk says, all of a tremble. "Don't ye think I'd better trot her round the downs for an hour, sir?"

'"To be sure, she does want exercise badly. I'll trot her round myself," says the pa'son.

'"Oh – you'll trot her yerself? Well, there's the cob, sir. Really that cob is getting oncontrollable through biding in a stable so long! If you wouldn't mind my putting on the saddle – "

'"Very well. Take him out, certainly," says the pa'son, never caring what the clerk did so long as he himself could get off immediately. So, scrambling into his riding-boots and breeches as quick as he could, he rode off towards the meet, intending to be back in an hour. No sooner was he gone than the clerk mounted the cob, and was off after him. When the pa'son got to the meet he found a lot of friends, and was as jolly as he could be: the hounds found a'most as soon as they threw off, and there was great excitement. So, forgetting that he had meant to go back at once, away rides the pa'son with the rest o' the hunt, all across the fallow ground that lies between Lippet Wood and Green's Copse; and as he galloped he looked behind for a moment, and there was the clerk close to his heels.

'"Ha, ha, clerk – you here?" he says.

'"Yes, sir, here be I," says t'other.

'"Fine exercise for the horses!"

'"Ay, sir – hee, hee!" says the clerk.

'So they went on and on, into Green's Copse, then across to Higher Jirton; then on across this very turnpike-road to Waterston Ridge, then away towards Yalbury Wood: up hill and down dale, like the very wind, the clerk close to the pa'son, and the pa'son not far from the hounds. Never was there a finer run knowed with that pack than they had that day; and neither pa'son nor clerk thought one word about the unmarried couple locked up in the church tower waiting to get j'ined.

'"These hosses of yours, sir, will be much improved by this!" says the clerk as he rode along, just a neck behind the pa'son. "'Twas a happy thought of your reverent mind to bring 'em out today. Why, it may be frosty and slippery in a day or two, and then the poor things mid not be able to leave the stable for weeks."

'"They may not, they may not, it is true. A merciful man is merciful to his beast," says the pa'son.

'"Hee, hee!" says the clerk, glancing sly into the pa'son's eye.

'"Ha, ha!" says the pa'son, a-glancing back into the clerk's. "Halloo!" he shouts, as he sees the fox break cover at that moment.

'"Halloo!" cries the clerk. "There he goes! Why, dammy, there's two foxes –"

'"Hush, clerk, hush! Don't let me hear that word again! Remember our calling."

'"True, sir, true. But really, good sport do carry away a man so, that he's apt to forget his high persuasion!" And the next minute the corner of the clerk's eye shot again into the corner of the pa'son's, and the pa'son's back again to the clerk's. "Hee, hee!" said the clerk.

'"Ha, ha!" said Pa'son Toogood.

'"Ah, sir," says the clerk again, "this is better than crying Amen to your Ever-and-ever on a winter's morning!"

'"Yes, indeed, clerk! To everything there's a season," says Pa'son Toogood, quite pat, for he was a learned Christian man when he liked, and had chapter and ve'se at his tongue's end, as a pa'son should.

'At last, late in the day, the hunting came to an end by the fox running into a' old woman's cottage, under her table, and up the clock-case. The pa'son and clerk were among the first in at the death, their faces a-staring in at the old woman's winder, and the clock striking as he'd never been heard to strik' before. Then came the question of finding their way home.

'Neither the pa'son nor the clerk knowed how they were going to do this, for their beasts were wellnigh tired down to the ground. But they started back-along as well as they could, though they were so done up that they could only drag along at a' amble, and not much of that at a time.

'"We shall never, never get there!" groaned Mr Toogood, quite bowed down.

'"Never!" groans the clerk. "'Tis a judgment upon us for our iniquities!"

'"I fear it is," murmurs the pa'son.

'Well, 'twas quite dark afore they entered the pa'sonage gate, having crept into the parish as quiet as if they'd stole a hammer, little wishing their congregation to know what they'd been up to all day long. And as they were so dog-tired, and so anxious about the horses, never once did they think of the unmarried people. As soon as ever the horses had been stabled and fed, and the pa'son and clerk had had a bit and a sup theirselves, they went to bed.

'Next morning when Pa'son Toogood was at breakfast, thinking of the glorious sport he'd had the day before, the clerk came in a hurry to the door and asked to see him.

'"It has just come into my mind, sir, that we've forgot all about the couple that we was to have married yesterday!"

'The half-chawed victuals dropped from the pa'son's mouth as if he'd been shot. "Bless my soul," says he, "so we have! How very awkward!"

'"It is, sir; very. Perhaps we've ruined the 'ooman!"

'"Ah – to be sure – I remember! She ought to have been married before."

'"If anything has happened to her up in that there tower, and no doctor or nuss – "'

('Ah – poor thing!' sighed the women.)

'" – 'twill be a quarter-sessions matter for us, not to speak of the disgrace to the Church!"

'"Good God, clerk, don't drive me wild!" says the pa'son. "Why the hell didn't I marry 'em, drunk or sober!" (Pa'sons used to cuss in them days like plain honest men.) "Have you been to the church to see what happened to them, or inquired in the village?"

'"Not I, sir! It only came into my head a moment ago, and I always like to be second to you in church matters. You could have knocked me down with a sparrow's feather when I thought o't, sir; I assure 'ee you could!"

'Well, the pa'son jumped up from his breakfast, and together they went off to the church.

'"It is not at all likely that they are there now," says Mr Toogood, as they went; "and indeed I hope they are not. They be pretty sure to have escaped and gone home."

'However, they opened the church-hatch, entered the church-yard, and looking up at the tower there they seed a little small white face at the belfry-winder, and a little small hand waving. 'Twas the bride.

'"God my life, clerk," says Mr Toogood. "I don't know how to face 'em!" And he sank down upon a tombstone. "How I wish I hadn't been so cussed particular!"

'"Yes – 'twas a pity we didn't finish it when we'd begun," the clerk said. "Still, since the feelings of your holy priestcraft wouldn't let ye, the couple must put up with it."

'"True, clerk, true! Does she look as if anything premature had took place?"

'"I can't see her no lower down than her arm-pits, sir."

'"Well – how do her face look?"

'"It do look mighty white!"

'"Well, we must know the worst! Dear me, how the small of my back do ache from that ride yesterday! ... But to more godly business!"

'They went on into the church, and unlocked the tower stairs, and immediately poor Jane and Andrey busted out like starved mice from a cupboard, Andrey limp and sober enough now, and his bride pale and cold, but otherwise as usual.

'"What," says the pa'son with a great breath of relief, "you haven't been here ever since?"

'"Yes, we have, sir!" says the bride, sinking down upon a seat in her weakness. "Not a morsel, wet or dry, have we had since! It was impossible to get out without help, and here we've stayed!"

'"But why didn't you shout, good souls?" said the pa'son.

'"She wouldn't let me," says Andrey.

'"Because we were so ashamed at what had led to it," sobs Jane. "We felt that if it were noised abroad it would cling to us all our lives! Once or twice Andrey had a good mind to toll the bell, but then he said: 'No; I'll starve first. I won't bring disgrace on my name and yours, my dear.' And so we waited and waited, and walked round and round; but never did you come till now!"

'"To my regret!" says the pa'son. "Now, then, we will soon get it over."

'"I – I should like some victuals," said Andrey; "'twould gie me courage to do it, if it is only a crust o' bread and a' onion; for I am that leery that I can feel my stomach rubbing against my backbone."

'"I think we had better get it done," said the bride, a bit anxious in manner; "since we are all here convenient, too!"

'Andrey gave way about the victuals, and the clerk called in a second witness who wouldn't be likely to gossip about it, and soon the knot was tied, and the bride looked smiling and calm forthwith, and Andrey limper than ever.

'"Now," said Pa'son Toogood, "you two must come to my house, and have a good lining put to your insides before you go a step further."

'They were very glad of the offer, and went out of the churchyard by one path while the pa'son and clerk went out by the other, and so did not attract notice, it being still early. They entered the rectory as if they'd just come back from their trip to Port Bredy; and then they knocked in the victuals and drink till they could hold no more.

'It was a long while before the story of what they had gone through was known, but it was talked of in time, and they themselves laugh over it now; though what Jane got for her pains was no great bargain after all. 'Tis true she saved her name.'

Old Andrey's Experience as a Musician

'I was one of the quire-boys at that time, and we and the players were to appear at the manor-house as usual that Christmas week, to play and sing in the hall to the Squire's people and visitors (among 'em being the archdeacon, Lord and Lady Baxby, and I don't know who); afterwards going, as we always did, to have a good supper in the servants' hall. Andrew knew this was the custom, and meeting us when we were starting to go, he said to us: "Lord, how I should like to join in that meal of beef, and turkey, and plum-pudding, and ale, that you happy ones be going to just now! One more or less will make no difference to the Squire. I am too old to pass as a singing boy, and too bearded to pass as a singing girl; can ye lend me a fiddle, neighbours, that I may come with ye as a bandsman?"

'Well, we didn't like to be hard upon him, and lent him an old one, though Andrew knew no more of music than the Giant o' Cernel; and armed with the instrument he walked up to the Squire's house with the others of us at the time appointed, and went in boldly, his fiddle under his arm. He made himself as natural as he could in opening the music-books and moving the candles to the best points for throwing light upon the notes; and all went well till we had played and sung "While shepherds watch", and "Star, arise", and "Hark the glad sound". Then the Squire's mother, a tall gruff old lady, who was much interested in church-music, said quite unexpectedly to Andrew: "My man, I see you don't play your instrument with the rest. How is that?"

'Every one of the quire was ready to sink into the earth with concern at the fix Andrew was in. We could see that he had fallen into a cold sweat, and how he would get out of it we did not know.

'"I've had a misfortune, mem," he says, bowing as meek as a child. "Coming along the road I fell down and broke my bow."

'"O, I am sorry to hear that," says she. "Can't it be mended?"

'"O no, mem," says Andrew. "'Twas broke all to splinters."

'"I'll see what I can do for you," says she.

'And then it seemed all over, and we played "Rejoice, ye drowsy mortals all", in D and two sharps. But no sooner had we got through it than she says to Andrew: '"I've sent up into the attic, where we have some old musical instruments, and found a bow for you." And she hands the bow to poor wretched Andrew, who didn't even know which end to take hold of. "Now we shall have the full accompaniment," says she.

'Andrew's face looked as if it were made of rotten apple as he stood in the circle of players in front of his book; for if there was one person in the parish that everybody was afraid of, 'twas this hook-nosed old lady. However, by keeping a little behind the next man he managed to make pretence of beginning, sawing away with his bow without letting it touch the strings, so that it looked as if he were driving into the tune with heart and soul. 'Tis a question if he wouldn't have got through all right if one of the Squire's visitors (no other than the archdeacon) hadn't noticed that he held the fiddle upside down, the nut under his chin, and the tail-piece in his hand; and they began to crowd round him, thinking 'twas some new way of performing.

'This revealed everything; the Squire's mother had Andrew turned out of the house as a vile impostor, and there was great interruption to the harmony of the proceedings, the Squire declaring he should have notice to leave his cottage that day fortnight. However, when we got to the servants' hall there sat Andrew, who had been let in at the back door by the orders of the Squire's wife, after being turned out at the front by the orders of the Squire, and nothing more was heard about his leaving his cottage. But Andrew never performed in public as a musician after that night; and now he's dead and gone, poor man, as we all shall be!'

Absent-Mindedness in a Parish Choir

'It happened on Sunday after Christmas – the last Sunday ever they played in Longpuddle church gallery, as it turned out, though they didn't know it then. As you may know, sir, the players formed a very good band – almost as good as the Mellstock parish players that were led by the Dewys; and that's saying a great deal. There was Nicholas Puddingcome, the leader, with the first fiddle; there was Timothy Thomas, the bass-viol man; John Biles, the tenor fiddler, Dan'l Hornhead, with the serpent; Robert Dowdle, with the clarionet; and Mr Nicks, with the oboe – all sound and powerful musicians, and strong-winded men – they that blowed. For that reason they were much in demand Christmas week for little reels and dancing parties: for they could turn a jig or a hornpipe out of hand as well as ever they could turn out a psalm, and perhaps better, not to speak irreverent. In short, one half-hour they could be playing a Christmas carol in the Squire's hall to the ladies and gentlemen, and drinking tay and coffee with 'em as modest as saints; and the next, at The Tinker's Arms, blazing away like wild horses with the "Dashing White Sergeant" to nine couple of dancers and more, and swallowing rum-and-cider hot as flame.

'Well, this Christmas they'd been out to one rattling randy after another every night, and had got next to no sleep at all. Then came the Sunday after Christmas, their fatal day. 'Twas so mortal cold that year that they could hardly sit in the gallery; for though the congregation down in the body of the church had a stove to keep off the frost, the players in the gallery had nothing at all. So Nicholas said at morning service, when 'twas freezing an inch an hour, "Please the Lord I won't stand this numbing weather no longer: this afternoon we'll have something in our insides to make us warm, if it cost a king's ransom."

'So he brought a gallon of hot brandy and beer, ready mixed, to church with him in the afternoon, and by keeping the jar well wrapped up in Timothy Thomas's bass-viol bag it kept drinkably warm till they wanted it, which was just a thimbleful in the Absolution, and another after the Creed, and the remainder at the beginning o' the sermon. When they'd had the last pull they felt quite comfortable and warm, and as the sermon went on – most unfortunately for 'em it was a long one that afternoon – they fell asleep, every man jack of 'em; and there they slept on as sound as rocks.

''Twas a very dark afternoon, and by the end of the sermon all you could see of the inside of the church were the pa'son's two candles alongside of him in the pulpit, and his spaking face behind 'em. The sermon being ended at last, the pa'son gie'd out the Evening Hymn. But no quire set about sounding up the tune, and the people began to turn their heads to learn the reason why, and then Levi Limpet, a boy who sat in the gallery, nudged Timothy and Nicholas, and said, "Begin! begin!"

'"Hey? what?" says Nicholas, starting up; and the church being so dark and his head so muddled he thought he was at the party they had played at all the night before, and away he went, bow and fiddle, at "The Devil among the Tailors", the favourite jig of our neighbourhood at that time. The rest of the band, being in the same state of mind and nothing doubting, followed their leader with all their strength, according to custom. They poured out that there tune till the lower bass notes of "The Devil among the Tailors" made the cobwebs in the roof shiver like ghosts; then Nicholas, seeing nobody moved, shouted out as he scraped (in his usual commanding way at dances when the folk didn't know the figures), "Top couples cross hands! And when I make the fiddle squeak at the end, every man kiss his pardner under the mistletoe!"

'The boy Levi was so frightened that he bolted down the gallery stairs and out homeward like lightning. The pa'son's hair fairly stood on end when he heard the evil tune raging through the church, and thinking the quire had gone crazy he held up his hand and said: "Stop, stop, stop! Stop, stop! What's this?" But they didn't hear'n for the noise of their own playing, and the more he called the louder they played.

'Then the folks came out of their pews, wondering down to the ground, and saying: "What do they mean by such wickedness! We shall be consumed like Sodom and Gomorrah!"

'And the Squire, too, came out of his pew lined wi' green baize, where lots of lords and ladies visiting at the house were worshipping along with him, and went and stood in front of the gallery, and shook his fist in the musicians' faces, saying, "What! In this reverent edifice! What!"

'And at last they heard'n through their playing, and stopped.

'"Never such an insulting, disgraceful thing – never!" says the Squire, who couldn't rule his passion.

'"Never!" says the pa'son, who had come down and stood beside him.

'"Not if the Angels of Heaven," says the Squire (he was a wickedish man, the Squire was, though now for once he happened to be on the Lord's side) – "not if the Angels of Heaven come down," he says, "shall one of you villainous players ever sound a note in this church again; for the insult to me, and my family, and my visitors, and the pa'son, and God Almighty, that you've a-perpetrated this afternoon!"

'Then the unfortunate church band came to their senses, and remembered where they were; and 'twas a sight to see Nicholas Puddingcome and Timothy Thomas and John Biles creep down the gallery stairs with their fiddles under their arms, and poor Dan'l Hornhead with his serpent, and Robert Dowdle with his clarionet, all looking as little as ninepins; and out they went. The pa'son might have forgi'ed 'em when he learned the truth o't, but the Squire would not. That very week he sent for a barrel-organ that would play two-and-twenty new psalm-tunes, so exact and particular that, however sinful inclined you was, you could play nothing but psalm-tunes whatsomever. He had a really respectable man to turn the winch, as I said, and the old players played no more.'

Netty Sargent's Copyhold

'She continued to live with her uncle, in the lonely house by the copse, just as at the time you knew her; a tall spry young woman. Ah, how well one can remember her black hair and dancing eyes at that time, and her sly way of screwing up her mouth when she meant to tease ye! Well, she was hardly out of short frocks before the chaps were after her, and by long and by late she was courted by a young man whom perhaps you did not know – Jasper Cliff was his name – and, though she might have had many a better fellow, he so greatly took her fancy that 'twas Jasper or nobody for her. He was a selfish customer, always thinking less of what he was going to do than of what he was going to gain by his doings. Jasper's eyes might have been fixed upon Netty, but his mind was upon her uncle's house; though he was fond of her in his way – I admit that.

'This house, built by her great-great-grandfather, with its garden and little field, was copyhold – granted upon lives in the old way, and had been so granted for generations. Her uncle's was the last life upon the property; so that at his death, if there was no admittance of new lives, it would all fall into the hands of the lord of the manor. But 'twas easy to admit – a slight "fine", as 'twas called, of a few pounds, was enough to entitle him to a new deed o' grant by the custom of the manor; and the lord could not hinder it.

'Now there could be no better provision for his niece and only relative than a sure house over her head, and Netty's uncle should have seen to the renewal in time, owing to the peculiar custom of forfeiture by the dropping of the last life before the new fine was paid; for the Squire was very anxious to get hold of the house and land; and every Sunday when the old man came into the church and passed the Squire's pew, the Squire would say, "A little weaker in his knees, a little crookeder in his back – and the re-admittance not applied for: ha! ha! I shall be able to make a complete clearing of that corner of the manor some day!"

''Twas extraordinary, now we look back upon it, that old Sargent should have been so dilatory; yet some people are like it; and he put off calling at the Squire's agent's office with the fine week after week, saying to himself, "I shall have more time next market-day than I have now." One unfortunate hindrance was that he didn't very well like Jasper Cliff, and as Jasper kept urging Netty, and Netty on that account kept urging her uncle, the old man was inclined to postpone the reliving as long as he could, to spite the selfish young lover. At last old Mr Sargent fell ill, and then Jasper could bear it no longer: he produced the fine-money himself, and handed it to Netty, and spoke to her plainly.

'"You and your uncle ought to know better. You should press him more. There's the money. If you let the house and ground slip between ye, I won't marry; hang me if I will! For folks won't deserve a husband that can do such things."

'The worried girl took the money and went home, and told her uncle that it was no house no husband for her. Old Mr Sargent pooh-poohed the money, for the amount was not worth consideration, but he did now bestir himself, for he saw she was bent upon marrying Jasper, and he did not wish to make her unhappy, since she was so determined. It was much to the Squire's annoyance that he found Sargent had moved in the matter at last; but he could not gainsay it, and the documents were prepared (for on this manor the copyholders had writings with their holdings, though on some manors they had none). Old Sargent being now too feeble to go to the agent's house, the deed was to be brought to his house signed, and handed over as a receipt for the money; the counterpart to be signed by Sargent, and sent back to the Squire.

'The agent had promised to call on old Sargent for this purpose at five o'clock, and Netty put the money into her desk to have it close at hand. While doing this she heard a slight cry from her uncle, and turning round, saw that he had fallen forward in his chair. She went and lifted him, but he was unconscious; and unconscious he remained. Neither medicine nor stimulants would bring him to himself. She had been told that he might possibly go off in that way, and it seemed as if the end had come. Before she had started for the doctor his face and extremities grew quite cold and white, and she saw that help would be useless. He was stone-dead.

'Netty's situation rose upon her distracted mind in all its seriousness. The house, garden, and field were lost – by a few hours – and with them a home for herself and her lover. She would not think so meanly of Jasper as to suppose that he would adhere to the resolution declared in a moment of impatience; but she trembled, nevertheless. Why could not her uncle have lived a couple of hours longer, since he had lived so long? It was now past three o'clock; at five the agent was to call, and, if all had gone well, by ten minutes past five the house and holding would have been securely hers for her own and Jasper's lives, these being two of the three proposed to be added by paying the fine. How that wretched old Squire would rejoice at getting the little tenancy into his hands! He did not really require it, but constitutionally hated these tiny copyholds and leaseholds and freeholds, which made islands of independence in the fair, smooth ocean of his estates.

'Then an idea struck into the head of Netty how to accomplish her object in spite of her uncle's negligence. It was a dull December afternoon: and the first step in her scheme – so the story goes, and I see no reason to doubt it – '

''Tis true as the light,' affirmed Christopher Twink. 'I was just passing by.'

'The first step in her scheme was to fasten the outer door, to make sure of not being interrupted. Then she set to work by placing her uncle's small, heavy oak table before the fire; then she went to her uncle's corpse, sitting in the chair as he had died – a stuffed armchair, on casters, and rather high in the seat, so it was told me – and wheeled the chair, uncle and all, to the table, placing him with his back towards the window, in the attitude of bending over the said oak table, which I knew as a boy as well as I know any piece of furniture in my own house. On the table she laid the large family Bible open before him, and placed his forefinger on the page; and then she opened his eyelids a bit, and put on him his spectacles, so that from behind he appeared for all the world as if he were reading the Scriptures. Then she unfastened the door and sat down, and when it grew dark she lit a candle, and put it on the table beside her uncle's book.

'Folk may well guess how the time passed with her till the

agent came, and how, when his knock sounded upon the door,
she nearly started out of her skin – at least that's as it was told
me. Netty promptly went to the door.

'"I am sorry, sir," she says, under her breath; "my uncle is not
so well tonight, and I'm afraid he can't see you."

'"H'm! – that's a pretty tale," says the steward. "So I've come
all this way about this trumpery little job for nothing!"

'"O no, sir – I hope not," says Netty. "I suppose the business of
granting the new deed can be done just the same?"

'"Done? Certainly not. He must pay the renewal money, and
sign the parchment in my presence."

'She looked dubious. "Uncle is so dreadful nervous about law
business," says she, "that, as you know, he's put it off and put it
off for years; and now today really I've feared it would verily
drive him out of his mind. His poor three teeth quite chattered
when I said to him that you would be here soon with the
parchment writing. He always was afraid of agents, and folks
that come for rent, and such-like."

'"Poor old fellow – I'm sorry for him. Well, the thing can't be
done unless I see him and witness his signature."

'"Suppose, sir, that you see him sign, and he don't see you
looking at him! I'd soothe his nerves by saying you weren't strict
about the form of witnessing, and didn't wish to come in. So that
it was done in your bare presence it would be sufficient, would it
not? As he's such an old, shrinking, shivering man, it would be a
great considerateness on your part if that would do."

'"In my bare presence would do, of course – that's all I come
for. But how can I be a witness without his seeing me?"

'"Why, in this way, sir; if you'll oblige me by just stepping
here." She conducted him a few yards to the left, till they were
opposite the parlour window. The blind had been left up
purposely, and the candle-light shone out upon the garden
bushes. Within the agent could see, at the other end of the room,
the back and side of the old man's head, and his shoulders and
arm, sitting with the book and candle before him, and his
spectacles on his nose, as she had placed him.

'"He's reading his Bible, as you see, sir," she says, quite in her
meekest way.

'"Yes. I thought he was a careless sort of man in matters of
religion?"

'"He always was fond of his Bible," Netty assured him. "Though I think he's nodding over it just at this moment. However, that's natural in an old man, and unwell. Now you could stand here and see him sign, couldn't you, sir, as he's such an invalid?"

'"Very well," said the agent, lighting a cigar. "You have ready by you the merely nominal sum you'll have to pay for the admittance, of course?"

'"Yes," said Netty. "I'll bring it out." She fetched the cash, wrapped in paper, and handed it to him, and when he had counted it the steward took from his breast pocket the precious parchments and gave one to her to be signed.

'"Uncle's hand is a little paralyzed," she said. "And what with his being half asleep, too, really I don't know what sort of a signature he'll be able to make."

'"Doesn't matter, so that he signs."

'"Might I hold his hand?"

'"Ay, hold his hand, my young woman – that will be near enough."

'Netty re-entered the house, and the agent continued smoking outside the window. Now came the ticklish part of Netty's performance. The steward saw her put the inkhorn – "horn", says I in my old-fashioned way – the inkstand, before her uncle, and touch his elbow as if to arouse him, and speak to him, and spread out the deed; when she had pointed to show him where to sign she dipped the pen and put it into his hand. To hold his hand she artfully stepped behind him, so that the agent could only see a little bit of his head, and the hand she held; but he saw the old man's hand trace his name on the document. As soon as 'twas done she came out to the steward with the parchment in her hand, and the steward signed as witness by the light from the parlour window. Then he gave her the deed signed by the Squire, and left; and next morning Netty told the neighbours that her uncle was dead in his bed.'

'She must have undressed him and put him there.'

'She must. O, that girl had a nerve, I can tell ye! Well, to cut a long story short, that's how she got back the house and field that were, strictly speaking, gone from her; and by getting them, got her a husband.

'Every virtue has its reward, they say. Netty had hers for her

ingenious contrivance to gain Jasper. Two years after they were
married he took to beating her – not hard, you know; just a
smack or two, enough to set her in a temper, and let out to the
neighbours what she had done to win him, and how she repented
of her pains. When the old Squire was dead, and his son came
into the property, this confession of hers began to be whispered
about. But Netty was a pretty young woman, and the Squire's
son was a pretty young man at that time, and wider-minded than
his father, having no objection to little holdings; and he never
took any proceedings against her.'

The Withered Arm

A Lorn Milkmaid

It was an eighty-cow dairy, and the troop of milkers, regular and supernumerary, were all at work; for, though the time of year was as yet but early April, the feed lay entirely in water-meadows, and the cows were 'in full pail'. The hour was about six in the evening, and three-fourths of the large, red, rectangular animals having been finished off, there was opportunity for a little conversation.

'He do bring home his bride tomorrow, I hear. They've come as far as Anglebury today.'

The voice seemed to proceed from the belly of the cow called Cherry, but the speaker was a milking-woman, whose face was buried in the flank of that motionless beast.

'Hav' anybody seen her?' said another.

There was a negative response from the first. 'Though they say she's a rosy-cheeked, tisty-tosty little body enough,' she added; and as the milkmaid spoke she turned her face so that she could glance past her cow's tail to the other side of the barton, where a thin, fading woman of thirty milked somewhat apart from the rest.

'Years younger than he, they say,' continued the second, with also a glance of reflectiveness in the same direction.

'How old do you call him, then?'

'Thirty or so.'

'More like forty,' broke in an old milkman near, in a long white pinafore or 'wrapper', and with the brim of his hat tied down, so that he looked like a woman. ''A was born before our Great Weir was builded, and I hadn't man's wages when I laved water there.'

The discussion waxed so warm that the purr of the milk streams became jerky, till a voice from another cow's belly cried with authority, 'Now then, what the Turk do it matter to us about Farmer Lodge's age, or Farmer Lodge's new mis'ess? I shall have to pay him nine pound a year for the rent of every one of these milchers, whatever his age or hers. Get on with your work, or 'twill be dark afore we have done. The evening is pinking in a'ready.' This speaker was the dairyman himself, by whom the milkmaids and men were employed.

Nothing more was said publicly about Farmer Lodge's wedding, but the first woman murmured under her cow to her next neighbour, ''Tis hard for *she*,' signifying the thin worn milkmaid aforesaid.

'O no,' said the second. 'He ha'n't spoke to Rhoda Brook for years.'

When the milking was done they washed their pails and hung them on a many-forked stand made as usual of the peeled limb of an oak-tree, set upright in the earth, and resembling a colossal antlered horn. The majority then dispersed in various directions homeward. The thin woman who had not spoken was joined by a boy of twelve or thereabout, and the twain went away up the field also.

Their course lay apart from that of the others, to a lonely spot high above the water-meads, and not far from the border of Egdon Heath, whose dark countenance was visible in the distance as they drew nigh to their home.

'They've just been saying down in barton that your father brings his young wife home from Anglebury tomorrow,' the woman observed. 'I shall want to send you for a few things to market, and you'll be pretty sure to meet 'em.'

'Yes, mother,' said the boy. 'Is father married then?'

'Yes.... You can give her a look, and tell me what she's like, if you do see her.'

'Yes, mother.'

'If she's dark or fair, and if she's tall – as tall as I. And if she seems like a woman who has ever worked for a living, or one that has been always well off, and has never done anything, and shows marks of the lady on her, as I expect she do.'

'Yes.'

They crept up the hill in the twilight and entered the cottage. It was built of mud-walls, the surface of which had been washed by many rains into channels and depressions that left none of the original flat face visible; while here and there in the thatch above a rafter showed like a bone protruding through the skin.

She was kneeling down in the chimney-corner, before two pieces of turf laid together with the heather inwards, blowing at the red-hot ashes with her breath till the turves flamed. The radiance lit her pale cheek, and made her dark eyes, that had once been handsome, seem handsome anew. 'Yes,' she resumed, 'see if she is dark or fair, and if you can, notice if her hands be white; if not, see if they look as though she had ever done housework, or are milker's hands like mine.'

The boy again promised, inattentively this time, his mother not observing that he was cutting a notch with his pocket-knife in the beech-backed chair.

The Young Wife

The road from Anglebury to Holmstoke is in general level; but there is one place where a sharp ascent breaks its monotony. Farmers homeward-bound from the former market-town, who trot all the rest of the way, walk their horses up this short incline.

The next evening while the sun was yet bright a handsome new gig, with a lemon-coloured body and red wheels, was spinning westward along the level highway at the heels of a powerful mare. The driver was a yeoman in the prime of life, cleanly shaven like an actor, his face being toned to that bluish-vermilion hue which so often graces a thriving farmer's features when returning home after successful dealings in the town. Beside him sat a woman, many years his junior – almost, indeed, a girl. Her face too was fresh in colour, but it was of a totally different quality – soft and evanescent, like the light under a heap of rose-petals.

Few people travelled this way, for it was not a main road; and the long white riband of gravel that stretched before them was empty, save of one small scarce-moving speck, which presently resolved itself into the figure of a boy, who was creeping on at a snail's pace, and continually looking behind him – the heavy bundle he carried being some excuse for, if not the reason of, his dilatoriness. When the bouncing gig-party slowed at the bottom of the incline above mentioned, the pedestrian was only a few yards in front. Supporting the large bundle by putting one hand on his hip, he turned and looked straight at the farmer's wife as though he would read her through and through, pacing along abreast of the horse.

The low sun was full in her face, rendering every feature, shade, and contour distinct, from the curve of her little nostril to the colour of her eyes. The farmer, though he seemed annoyed at the boy's persistent presence, did not order him to get out of the way; and thus the lad preceded them, his hard gaze never leaving her, till they reached the top of the ascent, when the farmer trotted on with relief in his lineaments – having taken no outward notice of the boy whatever.

'How that poor lad stared at me!' said the young wife.

'Yes, dear; I saw that he did.'

'He is one of the village, I suppose?'

'One of the neighbourhood. I think he lives with his mother a mile or two off.'

'He knows who we are, no doubt?'

'O yes. You must expect to be stared at just at first, my pretty Gertrude.'

'I do – though I think the poor boy may have looked at us in the hope we might relieve him of his heavy load, rather than from curiosity.'

'O no,' said her husband off-handedly. 'These country lads will carry a hundredweight once they get it on their backs; besides his pack had more size than weight in it. Now, then, another mile and I shall be able to show you our house in the distance – if it is not too dark before we get there.' The wheels spun round, and particles flew from their periphery as before, till a white house of ample dimensions revealed itself, with farm-buildings and ricks at the back.

Meanwhile the boy had quickened his pace, and turning up a by-lane some mile and half short of the white farmstead, ascended towards the leaner pastures, and so on to the cottage of his mother.

She had reached home after her day's milking at the outlying dairy, and was washing cabbage at the doorway in the declining light. 'Hold up the net a moment,' she said, without preface, as the boy came up.

He flung down his bundle, held the edge of the cabbage-net, and as she filled its meshes with the dripping leaves she went on, 'Well, did you see her?'

'Yes; quite plain.'

'Is she ladylike?'

'Yes; and more. A lady complete.'

'Is she young?'

'Well, she's growed up, and her ways be quite a woman's.'

'Of course. What colour is her hair and face?'

'Her hair is lightish, and her face as comely as a live doll's.'

'Her eyes, then, are not dark like mine?'

'No – of a bluish turn, and her mouth is very nice and red; and when she smiles, her teeth show white.'

'Is she tall?' said the woman sharply.

'I couldn't see. She was sitting down.'

'Then do you go to Holmstoke church tomorrow morning: she's sure to be there. Go early and notice her walking in, and come home and tell me if she's taller than I.'

'Very well, mother. But why don't you go and see for yourself?'

'*I* go to see her! I wouldn't look up at her if she were to pass my window this instant. She was with Mr Lodge, of course. What did he say or do?'

'Just the same as usual.'

'Took no notice of you?'

'None.'

Next day the mother put a clean shirt on the boy, and started him off for Holmstoke church. He reached the ancient little pile when the door was just being opened, and he was the first to enter. Taking his seat by the font, he watched all the parishioners file in. The well-to-do Farmer Lodge came nearly last; and his young wife, who accompanied him, walked up the aisle with the shyness natural to a modest woman who had appeared thus for the first time. As all other eyes were fixed upon her, the youth's stare was not noticed now.

When he reached home his mother said, 'Well?' before he had entered the room.

'She is not tall. She is rather short,' he replied.

'Ah!' said his mother, with satisfaction.

'But she's very pretty – very. In fact, she's lovely.' The youthful freshness of the yeoman's wife had evidently made an impression even on the somewhat hard nature of the boy.

'That's all I want to hear,' said his mother quickly. 'Now, spread the table-cloth. The hare you wired is very tender; but mind that nobody catches you. – You've never told me what sort of hands she had.'

'I have never seen 'em. She never took off her gloves.'

'What did she wear this morning?'

'A white bonnet and a silver-coloured gownd. It whewed and whistled so loud when it rubbed against the pews that the lady coloured up more than ever for very shame at the noise, and pulled it in to keep it from touching; but when she pushed into her seat, it whewed more than ever. Mr Lodge, he seemed pleased, and his waistcoat stuck out, and his great golden seals hung like a lord's; but she seemed to wish her noisy gownd anywhere but on her.'

'Not she! However, that will do now.'

These descriptions of the newly-married couple were continued from time to time by the boy at his mother's request, after any chance encounter he had had with them. But Rhoda Brook, though she might easily have seen young Mrs Lodge for herself by walking a couple of miles, would never attempt an excursion towards the quarter where the farmhouse lay. Neither did she, at the daily milking in the dairyman's yard on Lodge's outlying second farm, ever speak on the subject of the recent marriage. The dairyman, who rented the cows of Lodge, and knew perfectly the tall milkmaid's history, with manly kindliness always kept the gossip in the cow-barton from annoying Rhoda. But the atmosphere thereabout was full of the subject during the first days of Mrs Lodge's arrival; and from her boy's description and the casual words of the other milkers, Rhoda Brook could raise a mental image of the unconscious Mrs Lodge that was realistic as a photograph.

A Vision

One night, two or three weeks after the bridal return, when the boy was gone to bed, Rhoda sat a long time over the turf ashes that she had raked out in front of her to extinguish them. She contemplated so intently the new wife, as presented to her in her mind's eye over the embers, that she forgot the lapse of time. At last, wearied with her day's work, she too retired.

But the figure which had occupied her so much during this and the previous days was not to be banished at night. For the first time Gertrude Lodge visited the supplanted woman in her dreams. Rhoda Brook dreamed – since her assertion that she really saw, before falling asleep, was not to be believed – that the young wife, in the pale silk dress and white bonnet, but with features shockingly distorted, and wrinkled as by age, was sitting upon her chest as she lay. The pressure of Mrs Lodge's person grew heavier; the blue eyes peered cruelly into her face; and then the figure thrust forward its left hand mockingly, so as to make the wedding-ring it wore glitter in Rhoda's eyes. Maddened mentally, and nearly suffocated by pressure, the sleeper struggled; the incubus, still regarding her, withdrew to the foot of the bed, only, however, to come forward by degrees, resume her seat, and flash her left hand as before.

Gasping for breath, Rhoda, in a last desperate effort, swung out her right hand, seized the confronting spectre by its obtrusive left arm, and whirled it backward to the floor, starting up herself as she did so with a low cry.

'O, merciful heaven!' she cried, sitting on the edge of the bed in a cold sweat; 'that was not a dream – she was here!'

She could feel her antagonist's arm within her grasp even now – the very flesh and bone of it, as it seemed. She looked on the floor whither she had whirled the spectre, but there was nothing to be seen.

Rhoda Brook slept no more that night, and when she went milking at the next dawn they noticed how pale and haggard she looked. The milk that she drew quivered into the pail; her hand had not calmed even yet, and still retained the feel of the arm. She came home to breakfast as wearily as if it had been suppertime.

'What was that noise in your chimmer, mother, last night?' said her son. 'You fell off the bed, surely?'

'Did you hear anything fall? At what time?'

'Just when the clock struck two.'

She could not explain, and when the meal was done went silently about her household work, the boy assisting her, for he hated going afield on the farms, and she indulged his reluctance. Between eleven and twelve the garden-gate clicked, and she lifted her eyes to the window. At the bottom of the garden, within the gate, stood the woman of her vision. Rhoda seemed transfixed.

'Ah, she said she would come!' exclaimed the boy, also observing her.

'Said so – when? How does she know us?'

'I have seen and spoken to her. I talked to her yesterday.'

'I told you,' said the mother, flushing indignantly, 'never to speak to anybody in that house, or go near the place.'

'I did not speak to her till she spoke to me. And I did not go near the place. I met her in the road.'

'What did you tell her?'

'Nothing. She said, "Are you the poor boy who had to bring the heavy load from market?" And she looked at my boots, and said they would not keep my feet dry if it came on wet, because they were so cracked. I told her I lived with my mother, and we had enough to do to keep ourselves, and that's how it was; and she said then, "I'll come and bring you some better boots, and see your mother." She gives away things to other folks in the meads besides us.'

Mrs Lodge was by this time close to the door – not in her silk, as Rhoda had dreamt of in the bed-chamber, but in a morning hat, and gown of common light material, which became her better than silk. On her arm she carried a basket.

The impression remaining from the night's experience was still strong. Brook had almost expected to see the wrinkles, the scorn, and the cruelty on her visitor's face. She would have escaped an interview, had escape been possible. There was, however, no backdoor to the cottage, and in an instant the boy had lifted the latch to Mrs Lodge's gentle knock.

'I see I have come to the right house,' said she, glancing at the lad, and smiling. 'But I was not sure till you opened the door.'

The figure and action were those of the phantom; but her voice was so indescribably sweet, her glance so winning, her smile so tender, so unlike that of Rhoda's midnight visitant, that the latter could hardly believe the evidence of her senses. She was truly glad that she had not hidden away in sheer aversion, as she had been inclined to do. In her basket Mrs Lodge brought the pair of boots that she had promised to the boy, and other useful articles.

At these proofs of a kindly feeling towards her and hers Rhoda's heart reproached her bitterly. This innocent young thing should have her blessing and not her curse. When she left them a light seemed gone from the dwelling. Two days later she came again to know if the boots fitted; and less than a fortnight after that paid Rhoda another call. On this occasion the boy was absent.

'I walk a good deal,' said Mrs Lodge, 'and your house is the nearest outside our own parish. I hope you are well. You don't look quite well.'

Rhoda said she was well enough; and, indeed, though the paler of the two, there was more of the strength that endures in her well-defined features and large frame than in the soft-cheeked young woman before her. The conversation became quite confidential as regarded their powers and weaknesses; and when Mrs Lodge was leaving, Rhoda said, 'I hope you will find this air agree with you, ma'am, and not suffer from the damp of the water-meads.'

The younger one replied that there was not much doubt of it, her general health being usually good. 'Though, now you remind me,' she added, 'I have one little ailment which puzzles me. It is nothing serious, but I cannot make it out.'

She uncovered her left hand and arm; and their outline confronted Rhoda's gaze as the exact original of the limb she had beheld and seized in her dream. Upon the pink round surface of the arm were faint marks of an unhealthy colour, as if produced by a rough grasp. Rhoda's eyes became riveted on the discolorations; she fancied that she discerned in them the shape of her own four fingers.

'How did it happen?' she said mechanically.

'I cannot tell,' replied Mrs Lodge, shaking her head. 'One night when I was sound asleep, dreaming I was away in some strange place, a pain suddenly shot into my arm there, and was so keen as to awaken me. I must have struck it in the daytime, I suppose, though I don't remember doing so.' She added, laughing, 'I tell my dear husband that it looks just as if he had flown into a rage and struck me there. O, I daresay it will soon disappear.'

'Ha, ha! Yes.... On what night did it come?'

Mrs Lodge considered, and said it would be a fortnight ago on the morrow. 'When I awoke I could not remember where I was,' she added, 'till the clock striking two reminded me.'

She had named the night and the hour of Rhoda's spectral encounter, and Brook felt like a guilty thing. The artless disclosure startled her; she did not reason on the freaks of coincidence; and all the scenery of that ghastly night returned with double vividness to her mind.

'O, can it be,' she said to herself, when her visitor had departed, 'that I exercise a malignant power over people against my own will?' She knew that she had been slyly called a witch since her fall; but never having understood why that particular stigma had been attached to her, it had passed disregarded. Could this be the explanation, and had such things as this ever happened before?

A Suggestion

The summer drew on, and Rhoda Brook almost dreaded to meet Mrs Lodge again, notwithstanding that her feeling for the young wife amounted well-nigh to affection. Something in her own individuality seemed to convict Rhoda of crime. Yet a fatality sometimes would direct the steps of the latter to the outskirts of Holmstoke whenever she left her house for any other purpose than her daily work; and hence it happened that their next encounter was out of doors. Rhoda could not avoid the subject which had so mystified her, and after the first few words she stammered, 'I hope your – arm is well again, ma'am?' She had perceived with consternation that Gertrude Lodge carried her left arm stiffly.

'No; it is not quite well. Indeed it is no better at all; it is rather worse. It pains me dreadfully sometimes.'

'Perhaps you had better go to a doctor, ma'am.'

She replied that she had already seen a doctor. Her husband had insisted upon her going to one. But the surgeon had not seemed to understand the afflicted limb at all; he had told her to bathe it in hot water, and she had bathed it, but the treatment had done no good.

'Will you let me see it?' said the milkwoman.

Mrs Lodge pushed up her sleeve and disclosed the place, which was a few inches above the wrist. As soon as Rhoda Brook saw it, she could hardly preserve her composure. There was nothing of the nature of a wound, but the arm at that point had a shrivelled look, and the outline of the four fingers appeared more distinct than at the former time. Moreover, she fancied that they were imprinted in precisely the relative position of her clutch upon the

arm in the trance; the first finger towards Gertrude's wrist, and
the fourth towards her elbow.

What the impress resembled seemed to have struck Gertrude
herself since their last meeting. 'It looks almost like finger-marks,'
she said; adding with a faint laugh, 'my husband says it is as if
some witch, or the devil himself, had taken hold of me there, and
blasted the flesh.'

Rhoda shivered. 'That's fancy,' she said hurriedly. 'I wouldn't
mind it, if I were you.'

'I shouldn't so much mind it,' said the younger, with
hesitation, 'if – if I hadn't a notion that it makes my husband –
dislike me – no, love me less. Men think so much of personal
appearance.'

'Some do – he for one.'

'Yes; and he was very proud of mine, at first.'

'Keep your arm covered from his sight.'

'Ah – he knows the disfigurement is there!' She tried to hide
the tears that filled her eyes.

'Well, ma'am, I earnestly hope it will go away soon.'

And so the milkwoman's mind was chained anew to the
subject by a horrid sort of spell as she returned home. The sense
of having been guilty of an act of malignity increased, affect as
she might to ridicule her superstition. In her secret heart Rhoda
did not altogether object to a slight diminution of her successor's
beauty, by whatever means it had come about; but she did not
wish to inflict upon her physical pain. For though this pretty
young woman had rendered impossible any reparation which
Lodge might have made Rhoda for his past conduct, everything
like resentment at the unconscious usurpation had quite passed
away from the elder's mind.

If the sweet and kindly Gertrude Lodge only knew of the
dream-scene in the bed-chamber, what would she think? Not to
inform her of it seemed treachery in the presence of her
friendliness; but tell she could not of her own accord – neither
could she devise a remedy.

She mused upon the matter the greater part of the night; and
the next day, after the morning milking, set out to obtain another
glimpse of Gertrude Lodge if she could, being held to her by a
gruesome fascination. By watching the house from a distance the
milkmaid was presently able to discern the farmer's wife in a ride

she was taking alone – probably to join her husband in some distant field. Mrs Lodge perceived her, and cantered in her direction.

'Good morning, Rhoda!' Gertrude said, when she had come up. 'I was going to call.'

Rhoda noticed that Mrs Lodge held the reins with some difficulty.

'I hope – the bad arm,' said Rhoda.

'They tell me there is possibly one way by which I might be able to find out the cause, and so perhaps the cure, of it,' replied the other anxiously. 'It is by going to some clever man over in Egdon Heath. They did not know if he was still alive – and I cannot remember his name at this moment; but they said that you knew more of his movements than anybody else hereabout, and could tell me if he were still to be consulted. Dear me – what was his name? But you know.'

'Not Conjuror Trendle?' said her thin companion, turning pale.

'Trendle – yes. Is he alive?'

'I believe so,' said Rhoda, with reluctance.

'Why do you call him conjuror?'

'Well – they say – they used to say he was a – he had powers other folks have not.'

'O, how could my people be so superstitious as to recommend a man of that sort! I thought they meant some medical man. I shall think no more of him.'

Rhoda looked relieved, and Mrs Lodge rode on. The milk-woman had inwardly seen, from the moment she heard of her having been mentioned as a reference for this man, that there must exist a sarcastic feeling among the work-folk that a sorceress would know the whereabouts of the exorcist. They suspected her, then. A short time ago this would have given no concern to a woman of her common sense. But she had a haunting reason to be superstitious now; and she had been seized with sudden dread that this Conjuror Trendle might name her as the malignant influence which was blasting the fair person of Gertrude, and so lead her friend to hate her for ever, and to treat her as some fiend in human shape.

But all was not over. Two days after, a shadow intruded into the window-pattern thrown on Rhoda Brook's floor by the afternoon sun. The woman opened the door at once, almost breathlessly.

'Are you alone?' said Gertrude. She seemed to be no less harassed and anxious than Brook herself.

'Yes,' said Rhoda.

'The place on my arm seems worse, and troubles me!' the young farmer's wife went on. 'It is so mysterious! I do hope it will not be an incurable wound. I have again been thinking of what they said about Conjuror Trendle. I don't really believe in such men, but I should not mind just visiting him, from curiosity – though on no account must my husband know. Is it far to where he lives?'

'Yes – five miles,' said Rhoda backwardly. 'In the heart of Egdon.'

'Well, I should have to walk. Could not you go with me to show me the way – say tomorrow afternoon?'

'O, not I; that is – ,' the milkwoman murmured, with a start of dismay. Again the dread seized her that something to do with her fierce act in the dream might be revealed, and her character in the eyes of the most useful friend she had ever had be ruined irretrievably.

Mrs Lodge urged, and Rhoda finally assented, though with much misgiving. Sad as the journey would be to her, she could not conscientiously stand in the way of a possible remedy for her patron's strange affliction. It was agreed that, to escape suspicion of their mystic intent, they should meet at the edge of the heath at the corner of a plantation which was visible from the spot where they now stood.

Conjuror Trendle

By the next afternoon Rhoda would have done anything to escape this inquiry. But she had promised to go. Moreover, there was a horrid fascination at times in becoming instrumental in throwing such possible light on her own character as would reveal her to be something greater in the occult world than she had ever herself suspected.

She started just before the time of day mentioned between them, and half-an-hour's brisk walking brought her to the south-eastern extension of the Egdon tract of country, where the fir plantation was. A slight figure, cloaked and veiled, was already there. Rhoda recognized, almost with a shudder, that Mrs Lodge bore her left arm in a sling.

They hardly spoke to each other, and immediately set out on their climb into the interior of this solemn country, which stood high above the rich alluvial soil they had left half-an-hour before. It was a long walk; thick clouds made the atmosphere dark, though it was as yet only early afternoon; and the wind howled dismally over the slopes of the heath – not improbably the same heath which had witnessed the agony of the Wessex King Ina, presented to after-ages as Lear. Gertrude Lodge talked most, Rhoda replying with monosyllabic preoccupation. She had a strange dislike to walking on the side of her companion where hung the afflicted arm, moving round to the other when inadvertently near it. Much heather had been brushed by their feet when they descended upon a cart-track, beside which stood the house of the man they sought.

He did not profess his remedial practices openly, or care anything about their continuance, his direct interests being those of a dealer in furze, turf, 'sharp sand', and other local products. Indeed, he affected not to believe largely in his own powers, and when warts that had been shown him for cure miraculously disappeared – which it must be owned they infallibly did – he would say lightly, 'O, I only drink a glass of grog upon 'em at your expense – perhaps it's all chance,' and immediately turn the subject.

He was at home when they arrived, having in fact seen them descending into his valley. He was a grey-bearded man, with a reddish face, and he looked singularly at Rhoda the first moment he beheld her. Mrs Lodge told him her errand; and then with words of self-disparagement he examined her arm.

'Medicine can't cure it,' he said promptly. ''Tis the work of an enemy.'

Rhoda shrank into herself, and drew back.

'An enemy? What enemy?' asked Mrs Lodge.

He shook his head. 'That's best known to yourself,' he said. 'If you like, I can show the person to you, though I shall not myself know who it is. I can do no more; and don't wish to do that.'

She pressed him; on which he told Rhoda to wait outside where she stood, and took Mrs Lodge into the room. It opened

immediately from the door; and, as the latter remained ajar,
Rhoda Brook could see the proceedings without taking part in
them. He brought a tumbler from the dresser, nearly filled it with
water, and fetching an egg, prepared it in some private way; after
which he broke it on the edge of the glass so that the white went
in and the yolk remained. As it was getting gloomy, he took the
glass and its contents to the window, and told Gertrude to watch
the mixture closely. They leant over the table together, and the
milkwoman could see the opaline hue of the egg-fluid changing
form as it sank in the water, but she was not near enough to
define the shape that it assumed.

'Do you catch the likeness of any face or figure as you look?'
demanded the conjuror of the young woman.

She murmured a reply, in tones so low as to be inaudible to
Rhoda, and continued to gaze intently into the glass. Rhoda
turned, and walked a few steps away.

When Mrs Lodge came out, and her face was met by the light,
it appeared exceedingly pale – as pale as Rhoda's – against the
sad dun shades of the upland's garniture. Trendle shut the door
behind her, and they at once started homeward together. But
Rhoda perceived that her companion had quite changed.

'Did he charge much?' she asked tentatively.

'O no – nothing. He would not take a farthing,' said Gertrude.

'And what did you see?' inquired Rhoda.

'Nothing I – care to speak of.' The constraint in her manner
was remarkable; her face was so rigid as to wear an oldened
aspect, faintly suggestive of the face in Rhoda's bed-chamber.

'Was it you who first proposed coming here?' Mrs Lodge
suddenly inquired, after a long pause. 'How very odd, if you did!'

'No. But I am not sorry we have come, all things considered,'
she replied. For the first time a sense of triumph possessed her,
and she did not altogether deplore that the young thing at her
side should learn that their lives had been antagonized by other
influences than their own.

The subject was no more alluded to during the long and dreary
walk home. But in some way or other a story was whispered
about the many-dairied lowland that winter that Mrs Lodge's
gradual loss of the use of her left arm was owing to her being
'overlooked' by Rhoda Brook. The latter kept her own counsel
about the incubus, but her face grew sadder and thinner; and in

the spring she and her boy disappeared from the neighbourhood of Holmstoke.

A Second Attempt

Half a dozen years passed away, and Mr and Mrs Lodge's married experience sank into prosiness, and worse. The farmer was usually gloomy and silent: the woman whom he had wooed for her grace and beauty was contorted and disfigured in the left limb; moreover, she had brought him no child, which rendered it likely that he would be the last of a family who had occupied that valley for some two hundred years. He thought of Rhoda Brook and her son; and feared this might be a judgment from heaven upon him.

The once blithe-hearted and enlightened Gertrude was changing into an irritable, superstitious woman, whose whole time was given to experimenting upon her ailment with every quack remedy she came across. She was honestly attached to her husband, and was ever secretly hoping against hope to win back his heart again by regaining some at least of her personal beauty. Hence it arose that her closet was lined with bottles, packets, and ointment-pots of every description – nay, bunches of mystic herbs, charms, and books of necromancy, which in her schoolgirl time she would have ridiculed as folly.

'Damned if you won't poison yourself with these apothecary messes and witch mixtures some time or other,' said her husband, when his eye chanced to fall upon the multitudinous array.

She did not reply, but turned her sad, soft glance upon him in such heart-swollen reproach that he looked sorry for his words, and added, 'I only meant it for your good, you know, Gertrude.'

'I'll clear out the whole lot, and destroy them,' said she huskily, 'and try such remedies no more!'

'You want somebody to cheer you,' he observed. 'I once thought of adopting a boy; but he is too old now. And he is gone away I don't know where.'

She guessed to whom he alluded; for Rhoda Brook's story had in the course of years become known to her; though not a word had ever passed between her husband and herself on the subject.

Neither had she ever spoken to him of her visit to Conjuror Trendle, and of what was revealed to her, or she thought was revealed to her, by that solitary heathman.

She was now five-and-twenty; but she seemed older. 'Six years of marriage, and only a few months of love,' she sometimes whispered to herself. And then she thought of the apparent cause, and said, with a tragic glance at her withering limb, 'If I could only again be as I was when he first saw me!'

She obediently destroyed her nostrums and charms; but there remained a hankering wish to try something else – some other sort of cure altogether. She had never revisited Trendle since she had been conducted to the house of the solitary by Rhoda against her will; but it now suddenly occurred to Gertrude that she would, in a last desperate effort at deliverance from this seeming curse, again seek out the man, if he yet lived. He was entitled to a certain credence, for the indistinct form he had raised in the glass had undoubtedly resembled the only woman in the world who – as she now knew, though not then – could have a reason for bearing her ill-will. The visit should be paid.

This time she went alone, though she nearly got lost on the heath, and roamed a considerable distance out of her way. Trendle's house was reached at last, however: he was not indoors, and instead of waiting at the cottage, she went to where his bent figure was pointed out to her at work a long way off. Trendle remembered her, and laying down the handful of furze-roots which he was gathering and throwing into a heap, he offered to accompany her in her homeward direction, as the distance was considerable and the days were short. So they walked together, his head bowed nearly to the earth, and his form of a colour with it.

'You can send away warts and other excrescences, I know,' she said; 'why can't you send away this?' And the arm was uncovered.

'You think too much of my powers!' said Trendle; 'and I am old and weak now, too. No, no; it is too much for me to attempt in my own person. What have ye tried?'

She named to him some of the hundred medicaments and counterspells which she had adopted from time to time. He shook his head.

'Some were good enough,' he said approvingly; 'but not many of them for such as this. This is of the nature of a blight, not of the nature of a wound; and if you ever do throw it off, it will be all at once.'

'If I only could!'

'There is only one chance of doing it known to me. It has never failed in kindred afflictions, – that I can declare. But it is hard to carry out, and especially for a woman.'

'Tell me!' said she.

'You must touch with the limb the neck of a man who's been hanged.'

She started a little at the image he had raised.

'Before he's cold – just after he's cut down,' continued the conjuror impassively.

'How can that do good?'

'It will turn the blood and change the constitution. But, as I say, to do it is hard. You must go to the jail when there's a hanging, and wait for him when he's brought off the gallows. Lots have done it, though perhaps not such pretty women as you. I used to send dozens for skin complaints. But that was in former times. The last I sent was in '13 – near twelve years ago.'

He had no more to tell her; and, when he had put her into a straight track homeward, turned and left her, refusing all money as at first.

A Ride

The communication sank deep into Gertrude's mind. Her nature was rather a timid one; and probably of all remedies that the white wizard could have suggested there was not one which would have filled her with so much aversion as this, not to speak of the immense obstacles in the way of its adoption.

Casterbridge, the county-town, was a dozen or fifteen miles off; and though in those days, when men were executed for horse-stealing, arson, and burglary, an assize seldom passed without a hanging, it was not likely that she could get access to the body of the criminal unaided. And the fear of her husband's anger made her reluctant to breathe a word of Trendle's suggestion to him or to anybody about him.

She did nothing for months, and patiently bore her disfigurement as before. But her woman's nature, craving for renewed love, through the medium of renewed beauty (she was but twenty-five), was ever stimulating her to try what, at any rate, could hardly do her any harm. 'What came by a spell will go by a spell surely,' she would say. Whenever her imagination pictured the act she shrank in terror from the possibility of it: then the words of the conjuror, 'It will turn your blood,' were seen to be capable of a scientific no less than a ghastly interpretation; the mastering desire returned, and urged her on again.

There was at this time but one county paper, and that her husband only occasionally borrowed. But old-fashioned days had old-fashioned means, and news was extensively conveyed by word of mouth from market to market, or from fair to fair, so that, whenever such an event as an execution was about to take place, few within a radius of twenty miles were ignorant of the coming sight; and, so far as Holmstoke was concerned, some enthusiasts had been known to walk all the way to Casterbridge and back in one day, solely to witness the spectacle. The next assizes were in March; and when Gertrude Lodge heard that they had been held, she inquired stealthily at the inn as to the result, as soon as she could find opportunity.

She was, however, too late. The time at which the sentences were to be carried out had arrived, and to make the journey and obtain admission at such short notice required at least her husband's assistance. She dared not tell him, for she had found by delicate experiment that these smouldering village beliefs made him furious if mentioned, partly because he half entertained them himself. It was therefore necessary to wait for another opportunity.

Her determination received a fillip from learning that two epileptic children had attended from this very village of Holmstoke many years before with beneficial results, though the experiment had been strongly condemned by the neighbouring clergy. April, May, June, passed; and it is no overstatement to say that by the end of the last-named month Gertrude well-nigh longed for the death of a fellow-creature. Instead of her formal prayers each night, her unconscious prayer was, 'O Lord, hang some guilty or innocent person soon!'

This time she made earlier inquiries, and was altogether more systematic in her proceedings. Moreover, the season was summer, between the haymaking and the harvest, and in the leisure thus afforded him her husband had been holiday-taking away from home.

The assizes were in July, and she went to the inn as before. There was to be one execution – only one – for arson.

Her greatest problem was not how to get to Casterbridge, but what means she should adopt for obtaining admission to the jail. Though access for such purposes had formerly never been denied, the custom had fallen into desuetude; and in contemplating her possible difficulties, she was again almost driven to fall back upon her husband. But, on sounding him about the assizes, he was so uncommunicative, so more than usually cold, that she did not proceed, and decided that whatever she did she would do alone.

Fortune, obdurate hitherto, showed her unexpected favour. On the Thursday before the Saturday fixed for the execution, Lodge remarked to her that he was going away from home for another day or two on business at a fair, and that he was sorry he could not take her with him.

She exhibited on this occasion so much readiness to stay at home that he looked at her in surprise. Time had been when she would have shown deep disappointment at the loss of such a jaunt. However, he lapsed into his usual taciturnity, and on the day named left Holmstoke.

It was now her turn. She at first had thought of driving, but on reflection held that driving would not do, since it would necessitate her keeping to the turnpike-road, and so increase by tenfold the risk of her ghastly errand being found out. She decided to ride, and avoid the beaten track, notwithstanding that in her husband's stables there was no animal just at present which by any stretch of imagination could be considered a lady's mount, in spite of his promise before marriage to always keep a mare for her. He had, however, many cart-horses, fine ones of their kind; and among the rest was a serviceable creature, an equine Amazon, with a back as broad as a sofa, on which Gertrude had occasionally taken an airing when unwell. This horse she chose.

On Friday afternoon one of the men brought it round. She was dressed, and before going down looked at her shrivelled arm. 'Ah!' she said to it, 'if it had not been for you this terrible ordeal would have been saved me!'

When strapping up the bundle in which she carried a few articles of clothing, she took occasion to say to the servant, 'I take these in case I should not get back tonight from the person I am going to visit. Don't be alarmed if I am not in by ten, and close up the house as usual. I shall be at home tomorrow for certain.' She meant then to tell her husband privately: the deed accomplished was not like the deed projected. He would almost certainly forgive her.

And then the pretty palpitating Gertrude Lodge went from her husband's homestead; but though her goal was Casterbridge she did not take the direct route thither through Stickleford. Her cunning course at first was in precisely the opposite direction. As soon as she was out of sight, however, she turned to the left, by a road which led into Egdon, and on entering the heath wheeled round, and set out in the true course, due westerly. A more private way down the county could not be imagined; and as to direction, she had merely to keep her horse's head to a point a little to the right of the sun. She knew that she would light upon a furze-cutter or cottager of some sort from time to time, from whom she might correct her bearing.

Though the date was comparatively recent, Egdon was much less fragmentary in character than now. The attempts – successful and otherwise – at cultivation on the lower slopes, which intrude and break up the original heath into small detached heaths, had not been carried far; Enclosure Acts had not taken effect, and the banks and fences which now exclude the cattle of those villagers who formerly enjoyed rights of commonage thereon, and the carts of those who had turbary privileges which kept them in firing all the year round, were not erected. Gertrude, therefore, rode along with no other obstacles than the prickly furze-bushes, the mats of heather, the white water-courses, and the natural steeps and declivities of the ground.

Her horse was sure, if heavy-footed and slow, and though a draught animal, was easy-paced; had it been otherwise, she was not a woman who could have ventured to ride over such a bit of country with a half-dead arm. It was therefore nearly eight o'clock when she drew rein to breathe her bearer on the last outlying high point of heath-land towards Casterbridge, previous to leaving Egdon for the cultivated valleys.

She halted before a pool called Rushy-pond, flanked by the ends of two hedges; a railing ran through the centre of the pond, dividing it in half. Over the railing she saw the low green country; over the green trees the roofs of the town; over the roofs a white flat façade, denoting the entrance to the county jail. On the roof of this front specks were moving about; they seemed to be workmen erecting something. Her flesh crept. She descended slowly, and was soon amid cornfields and pastures. In another half-hour, when it was almost dusk, Gertrude reached the White Hart, the first inn of the town on that side.

Little surprise was excited by her arrival; farmers' wives rode on horseback then more than they do now; though, for that matter, Mrs Lodge was not imagined to be a wife at all; the innkeeper supposed her some harum-skarum young woman who had come to attend 'hang-fair' next day. Neither her husband nor herself ever dealt in Casterbridge market, so that she was unknown. While dismounting she beheld a crowd of boys standing at the door of a harness-maker's shop just above the inn, looking inside it with deep interest.

'What is going on there?' she asked of the ostler.

'Making the rope for tomorrow.'

She throbbed responsively, and contracted her arm.

''Tis sold by the inch afterwards,' the man continued. 'I could get you a bit, miss, for nothing, if you'd like?'

She hastily repudiated any such wish, all the more from a curious creeping feeling that the condemned wretch's destiny was becoming interwoven with her own; and having engaged a room for the night, sat down to think.

Up to this time she had formed but the vaguest notions about her means of obtaining access to the prison. The words of the cunning-man returned to her mind. He had implied that she should use her beauty, impaired though it was, as a pass-key. In her inexperience she knew little about jail functionaries; she had heard of a high-sheriff and an under-sheriff, but dimly only. She knew, however, that there must be a hangman, and to the hangman she determined to apply.

A Water-Side Hermit

At this date, and for several years after, there was a hangman to almost every jail. Gertrude found, on inquiry, that the Caster-bridge official dwelt in a lonely cottage by a deep slow river flowing under the cliff on which the prison buildings were situate – the stream being the self-same one, though she did not know it, which watered the Stickleford and Holmstoke meads lower down in its course.

Having changed her dress, and before she had eaten or drunk – for she could not take her ease till she had ascertained some particulars – Gertrude pursued her way by a path along the water-side to the cottage indicated. Passing thus the outskirts of the jail, she discerned on the level roof over the gateway three rectangular lines against the sky, where the specks had been moving in her distant view; she recognized what the erection was, and passed quickly on. Another hundred yards brought her to the executioner's house, which a boy pointed out. It stood close to the same stream, and was hard by a weir, the waters of which emitted a steady roar.

While she stood hesitating the door opened, and an old man came forth shading a candle with one hand. Locking the door on the outside, he turned to a flight of wooden steps fixed against the end of the cottage, and began to ascend them, this being evidently the staircase to his bedroom. Gertrude hastened forward, but by the time she reached the foot of the ladder he was at the top. She called to him loudly enough to be heard above the roar of the weir; he looked down and said, 'What d'ye want here?'

'To speak to you a minute.'

The candlelight, such as it was, fell upon her imploring, pale, upturned face, and Davies (as the hangman was called) backed down the ladder. 'I was just going to bed,' he said; '"Early to bed and early to rise," but I don't mind stopping a minute for such a one as you. Come into house.' He reopened the door, and preceded her to the room within.

The implements of his daily work, which was that of a jobbing gardener, stood in a corner, and seeing probably that she looked rural, he said, 'If you want me to undertake country work I can't come, for I never leave Casterbridge for gentle nor simple – not I. My real calling is officer of justice,' he added formally.

'Yes, yes! That's it. Tomorrow!'

'Ah! I thought so. Well, what's the matter about that? 'Tis no use to come here about the knot – folks do come continually, but I tell 'em one knot is as merciful as another if ye keep it under the ear. Is the unfortunate man a relation; or, I should say, perhaps' (looking at her dress) 'a person who's been in your employ?'

'No. What time is the execution?'

'The same as usual – twelve o'clock, or as soon after as the London mail-coach gets in. We always wait for that, in case of a reprieve.'

'O – a reprieve – I hope not!' she said involuntarily.

'Well, – hee, hee! – as a matter of business, so do I! But still, if ever a young fellow deserved to be let off, this one does; only just turned eighteen, and only present by chance when the rick was fired. Howsomever, there's not much risk of it, as they are obliged to make an example of him, there having been so much destruction of property that way lately.'

'I mean,' she explained, 'that I want to touch him for a charm, a cure of an affliction, by the advice of a man who has proved the virtue of the remedy.'

'O yes, miss! Now I understand. I've had such people come in past years. But it didn't strike me that you looked of a sort to require blood-turning. What's the complaint? The wrong kind for this, I'll be bound.'

'My arm.' She reluctantly showed the withered skin.

'Ah! – 'tis all a-scram!' said the hangman, examining it.

'Yes,' said she.

'Well,' he continued, with interest, 'that *is* the class o' subject, I'm bound to admit! I like the look of the wownd; it is truly as suitable for the cure as any I ever saw. 'Twas a knowing-man that sent 'ee, whoever he was.'

'You can contrive for me all that's necessary?' she said breathlessly.

'You should really have gone to the governor of the jail, and your doctor with 'ee, and given your name and address – that's how it used to be done, if I recollect. Still, perhaps, I can manage it for a trifling fee.'

'O, thank you! I would rather do it this way, as I should like it kept private.'

'Lover not to know, eh?'

'No – husband.'

'Aha! Very well. I'll get 'ee a touch of the corpse.'

'Where is it now?' she said, shuddering.

'It? – *he*, you mean; he's living yet. Just inside that little small winder up there in the glum.' He signified the jail on the cliff above.

She thought of her husband and her friends. 'Yes, of course,' she said; 'and how am I to proceed?'

He took her to the door. 'Now, do you be waiting at the little wicket in the wall, that you'll find up there in the lane, not later than one o'clock. I will open it from the inside, as I shan't come home to dinner till he's cut down. Good-night. Be punctual; and if you don't want anybody to know 'ee, wear a veil. Ah – once I had such a daughter as you!'

She went away, and climbed the path above, to assure herself that she would be able to find the wicket next day. Its outline was soon visible to her – a narrow opening in the outer wall of the prison precincts. The steep was so great that, having reached the wicket, she stopped a moment to breathe; and, looking back upon the water-side cot, saw the hangman again ascending his outdoor staircase. He entered the loft or chamber to which it led, and in a few minutes extinguished his light.

The town clock struck ten, and she returned to the White Hart as she had come.

A Rencounter

It was one o'clock on Saturday. Gertrude Lodge, having been admitted to the jail as above described, was sitting in a waiting-room within the second gate, which stood under a classic archway of ashlar, then comparatively modern, and bearing the inscription, 'COVNTY JAIL: 1793'. This had been the façade she saw from the heath the day before. Near at hand was a passage to the roof on which the gallows stood.

The town was thronged, and the market suspended; but Gertrude had seen scarcely a soul. Having kept her room till the hour of the appointment, she had proceeded to the spot by a way which avoided the open space below the cliff where the spectators had gathered; but she could, even now, hear the multitudinous babble of their voices, out of which rose at intervals the hoarse croak of a single voice uttering the words, 'Last dying speech and confession!' There had been no reprieve, and the execution was over; but the crowd still waited to see the body taken down.

Soon the persistent woman heard a trampling overhead, then a hand beckoned to her, and, following directions, she went out and crossed the inner paved court beyond the gatehouse, her knees trembling so that she could scarcely walk. One of her arms was out of its sleeve, and only covered by her shawl.

On the spot at which she had now arrived were two trestles, and before she could think of their purpose she heard heavy feet descending stairs somewhere at her back. Turn her head she would not, or could not, and, rigid in this position, she was conscious of a rough coffin passing her shoulder, borne by four men. It was open, and in it lay the body of a young man, wearing the smockfrock of a rustic, and fustian breeches. The corpse had been thrown into the coffin so hastily that the skirt of the smockfrock was hanging over. The burden was temporarily deposited on the trestles.

By this time the young woman's state was such that a grey mist seemed to float before her eyes, on account of which, and the veil she wore, she could scarcely discern anything: it was as though she had nearly died, but was held up by a sort of galvanism.

'Now!' said a voice close at hand, and she was just conscious that the word had been addressed to her.

By a last strenuous effort she advanced, at the same time hearing persons approaching behind her. She bared her poor curst arm; and Davies, uncovering the face of the corpse, took Gertrude's hand, and held it so that her arm lay across the dead man's neck, upon a line the colour of an unripe blackberry, which surrounded it.

Gertrude shrieked: 'the turn o' the blood,' predicted by the conjuror, had taken place. But at that moment a second shriek rent the air of the enclosure: it was not Gertrude's, and its effect upon her was to make her start round.

Immediately behind her stood Rhoda Brook, her face drawn, and her eyes red with weeping. Behind Rhoda stood Gertrude's own husband; his countenance lined, his eyes dim, but without a tear.

'D—n you! what are you doing here?' he said hoarsely.

'Hussy – to come between us and our child now!' cried Rhoda. 'This is the meaning of what Satan showed me in the vision! You are like her at last!' And clutching the bare arm of the younger woman, she pulled her unresistingly back against the wall. Immediately Brook had loosened her hold the fragile young Gertrude slid down against the feet of her husband. When he lifted her up she was unconscious.

The mere sight of the twain had been enough to suggest to her that the dead young man was Rhoda's son. At that time the relatives of an executed convict had the privilege of claiming the body for burial, if they chose to do so; and it was for this purpose that Lodge was awaiting the inquest with Rhoda. He had been summoned by her as soon as the young man was taken in the crime, and at different times since; and he had attended in court during the trial. This was the 'holiday' he had been indulging in of late. The two wretched parents had wished to avoid exposure; and hence had come themselves for the body, a waggon and sheet for its conveyance and covering being in waiting outside.

Gertrude's case was so serious that it was deemed advisable to call to her the surgeon who was at hand. She was taken out of the jail into the town; but she never reached home alive. Her delicate vitality, sapped perhaps by the paralyzed arm, collapsed under the double shock that followed the severe strain, physical and mental, to which she had subjected herself during the previous twenty-four hours. Her blood had been 'turned' indeed – too far. Her death took place in the town three days after.

Her husband was never seen in Casterbridge again; once only in the old market-place at Anglebury, which he had so much frequented, and very seldom in public anywhere. Burdened at first with moodiness and remorse, he eventually changed for the better, and appeared as a chastened and thoughtful man. Soon after attending the funeral of his poor young wife he took steps towards giving up the farms in Holmstoke and the adjoining parish, and, having sold every head of his stock, he went away to Port-Bredy, at the other end of the county, living there in solitary lodgings till his death two years later of a painless decline. It was then found that he had bequeathed the whole of his not inconsiderable property to a reformatory for boys, subject to the payment of a small annuity to Rhoda Brook, if she could be found to claim it.

For some time she could not be found; but eventually she reappeared in her old parish, – absolutely refusing, however, to have anything to do with the provision made for her. Her monotonous milking at the dairy was resumed, and followed for many long years, till her form became bent, and her once abundant dark hair white and worn away at the forehead – perhaps by long pressure against the cows. Here, sometimes, those who knew her experiences would stand and observe her, and wonder what sombre thoughts were beating inside that impassive, wrinkled brow, to the rhythm of the alternating milk-streams.

A Tryst at an Ancient Earthwork

At one's every step forward it rises higher against the south sky, with an obtrusive personality that compels the senses to regard it and consider. The eyes may bend in another direction, but never without the consciousness of its heavy, high-shouldered presence at its point of vantage. Across the intervening levels the gale races in a straight line from the fort, as if breathed out of it hitherward. With the shifting of the clouds the faces of the steeps vary in colour and in shade, broad lights appearing where mist and vagueness had prevailed, dissolving in their turn into melancholy grey, which spreads over and eclipses the luminous bluffs. In this so-thought immutable spectacle all is change.

Out of the invisible marine region on the other side birds soar suddenly into the air, and hang over the summits of the heights with the indifference of long familiarity. Their forms are white against the tawny concave of cloud, and the curves they exhibit in their floating signify that they are seagulls which have journeyed inland from expected stress of weather. As the birds rise behind the fort, so do the clouds rise behind the birds, almost, as it seems, stroking with their bagging bosoms the uppermost flyers.

The profile of the whole stupendous ruin, as seen at a distance of a mile eastward, is cleanly cut as that of a marble inlay. It is varied with protuberances, which from hereabouts have the animal aspect of warts, wens, knuckles, and hips. It may indeed be likened to an enormous many-limbed organism of an antediluvian time partaking of the cephalopod in shape – lying lifeless, and covered with a thin green cloth, which hides its substance, while revealing its contour. This dull green mantle of herbage stretches down towards the levels, where the ploughs have essayed for centuries to creep up near and yet nearer to the base of the castle, but have always stopped short before reaching it. The furrows of these environing attempts show themselves distinctly, bending to the incline as they trench upon it; mounting in steeper curves, till the steepness baffles them, and their parallel threads show like the striae of waves pausing on the curl. The peculiar place of which these are some of the features is 'Mai-Dun', 'The Castle of the Great Hill', said to be the Dunium of Ptolemy, the capital of the Durotriges, which eventually came into Roman occupation, and was finally deserted on their withdrawal from the island.

The evening is followed by a night on which an invisible moon bestows a subdued, yet pervasive light – without radiance, as without blackness. From the spot whereon I am ensconced in a cottage, a mile away, the fort has now ceased to be visible; yet, as by day, to anybody whose thoughts have been engaged with it and its barbarous grandeurs of past time the form asserts its existence behind the night gauzes as persistently as if it had a voice. Moreover, the south-west wind continues to feed the intervening arable flats with vapours brought directly from its sides.

The midnight hour for which there has been occasion to wait at length arrives, and I journey towards the stronghold in obedience to a request urged earlier in the day. It concerns an appointment, which I rather regret my decision to keep now that night is come. The route thither is hedgeless and treeless – I need not add deserted. The moonlight is sufficient to disclose the pale riband-like surface of the way as it trails along between the expanses of darker fallow. Though the road passes near the fortress it does not conduct directly to its fronts. As the place is without an inhabitant, so it is without a trackway. So presently leaving the macadamized road to pursue its course elsewhither, I step off upon the fallow, and plod stumblingly across it. The castle looms out of the shade by degrees, like a thing waking up and asking what I want there. It is now so enlarged by nearness that its whole shape cannot be taken in at one view. The ploughed ground ends as the rise sharpens, the sloping basement of grass begins, and I climb upward to invade Mai-Dun.

Impressive by day as this largest Ancient-British work in the kingdom undoubtedly is, its impressiveness is increased now. After standing still and spending a few minutes in adding its age to its size, and its size to its solitude, it becomes appallingly mournful in its growing closeness. A squally wind blows in the face with an impact which proclaims that the vapours of the air sail low tonight. The slope that I so laboriously clamber up the wind skips sportively down. Its track can be discerned even in this light by the undulations of the withered grass-bents – the only produce of this upland summit except moss. Four minutes of ascent, and a vantage-ground of some sort is gained. It is only the crest of the outer rampart. Immediately within this a chasm gapes; its bottom is imperceptible, but the counterscarp slopes not too steeply to admit of a sliding descent if cautiously performed. The shady bottom, dank and chilly, is thus gained, and reveals itself as a kind of winding lane, wide enough for a waggon to pass along, floored with rank herbage, and trending away, right and left, into obscurity, between the concentric walls of earth. The towering closeness of these on each hand, their impenetrability, and their ponderousness, are felt as a physical pressure. The way is now up the second of them, which stands steeper and higher than the first. To turn aside, as did Christian's companion, from such a Hill Difficulty, is the more natural tendency; but the way to the interior is upward. There is, of course, an entrance to the fortress; but that lies far off on the other side. It might possibly have been the wiser course to seek for easier ingress there.

However, being here, I ascend the second acclivity. The grass stems – the grey beard of the hill – sway in a mass close to my stooping face. The dead heads of these various grasses – fescues, fox-tails, and ryes – bob and twitch as if pulled by a string underground. From a few thistles a whistling proceeds; and even the moss speaks, in its humble way, under the stress of the blast.

That the summit of the second line of defence has been gained is suddenly made known by a contrasting wind from a new quarter, coming over with the curve of a cascade. These novel gusts raise a sound from the whole camp or castle, playing upon it bodily as upon a harp. It is with some difficulty that a foothold can be preserved under their sweep. Looking aloft for a moment I perceive that the sky is much more overcast than it has been hitherto, and in a few instants a dead lull in what is now a gale ensues with almost preternatural abruptness. I take advantage of this to sidle down the second counterscarp, but by the time the ditch is reached the lull reveals itself to be but the precursor of a storm. It begins with a heave of the whole atmosphere, like the sigh of a weary strong man on turning to recommence unusual exertion, just as I stand here in the second fosse. That which now radiates from the sky upon the scene is not so much light as vaporous phosphorescence.

The wind, quickening, abandons the natural direction it has pursued on the open upland, and takes the course of the gorge's length, rushing along therein helter-skelter, and carrying thick rain upon its back. The rain is followed by hailstones which fly through the defile in battalions – rolling, hopping, ricochetting, snapping, clattering down the shelving banks in an undefinable haze of confusion. The earthen sides of the fosse seem to quiver under the drenching onset, though it is practically no more to them than the blows of Thor upon the giant of Jotun-land. It is impossible to proceed further till the storm somewhat abates, and I draw up behind a spur of the inner scarp, where possibly a barricade stood two thousand years ago; and thus await events.

The roar of the storm can be heard travelling the complete circuit of the castle – a measured mile – coming round at intervals like a circumambulating column of infantry. Doubtless such a column has passed this way in its time, but the only columns which enter in these latter days are the columns of sheep and oxen that are sometimes seen here now; while the only semblance of heroic voices heard are the utterances of such, and of the many winds which make their passage through the ravines.

The expected lightning radiates round, and a rumbling as from its subterranean vaults – if there are any – fills the castle. The lightning repeats itself, and, coming after the aforesaid thoughts of martial men, it bears a fanciful resemblance to swords moving in combat. It has the very brassy hue of the ancient weapons that here were used. The so sudden entry upon the scene of this metallic flame is as the entry of a presiding exhibitor who unrolls the maps, uncurtains the pictures, unlocks the cabinets, and effects a transformation by merely exposing the materials of his science, unintelligibly cloaked till then. The abrupt configuration of the bluffs and mounds is now for the first time clearly revealed – mounds whereon, doubtless, spears and shields have frequently lain while their owners loosened their sandals and yawned and stretched their arms in the sun. For the first time, too, a glimpse is obtainable of the true entrance used by its occupants of old, some way ahead.

There, where all passage has seemed to be inviolably barred by an almost vertical façade, the ramparts are found to overlap each other like loosely clasped fingers, between which a zigzag path may be followed – a cunning construction that puzzles the uninformed eye. But its cunning, even where not obscured by dilapidation, is now wasted on the solitary forms of a few wild badgers, rabbits, and hares. Men must have often gone out by those gates in the morning to battle with the Roman legions under Vespasian; some to return no more, others to come back at evening, bringing with them the noise of their heroic deeds. But not a page, not a stone, has preserved their fame.

Acoustic perceptions multiply tonight. We can almost hear the stream of years that have borne those deeds away from us. Strange articulations seem to float on the air from that point, the gateway, where the animation in past times must frequently have concentrated itself at hours of coming and going, and general excitement. There arises an ineradicable fancy that they are human voices; if so, they must be the lingering air-borne vibrations of conversations uttered at least fifteen hundred years ago. The attention is attracted from mere nebulous imaginings about yonder spot by a real moving of something close at hand.

I recognize by the now moderate flashes of lightning, which are sheet-like and nearly continuous, that it is the gradual elevation of a small mound of earth. At first no larger than a man's fist it reaches the dimensions of a hat, then sinks a little and is still. It is but the heaving of a mole who chooses such weather as this to work in from some instinct that there will be nobody abroad to molest him. As the fine earth lifts and lifts and falls loosely aside fragments of burnt clay roll out of it – clay that once formed part of cups or other vessels used by the inhabitants of the fortress.

The violence of the storm has been counterbalanced by its transitoriness. From being immersed in well-nigh solid media of cloud and hail shot with lightning, I find myself uncovered of the humid investiture and left bare to the mild gaze of the moon, which sparkles now on every wet grass-blade and frond of moss.

But I am not yet inside the fort, and the delayed ascent of the third and last escarpment is now made. It is steeper than either. The first was a surface to walk up, the second to stagger up, the third can only be ascended on the hands and toes. On the summit obtrudes the first evidence which has been met with in these precincts that the time is really the nineteenth century; it is in the form of a white notice-board on a post, and the wording can just be discerned by the rays of the setting moon:

> CAUTION. – Any Person found removing Relics, Skeletons, Stones, Pottery, Tiles, or other Material from this Earthwork, or cutting up the Ground, will be Prosecuted as the Law directs.

Here one observes a difference underfoot from what has gone before: scraps of Roman tile and stone chippings protrude through the grass in meagre quantity, but sufficient to suggest that masonry stood on the spot. Before the eye stretches under the moonlight the interior of the fort. So open and so large is it as to be practically an upland plateau, and yet its area lies wholly within the walls of what may be designated as one building. It is a long-violated retreat; all its corner-stones, plinths, and architraves were carried away to build neighbouring villages even before mediaeval or modern history began. Many a block which once may have helped to form a bastion here rests now in broken and diminished shape as part of the chimney-corner of some shepherd's cottage within the distant horizon, and the cornerstones of this heathen altar may form the base-course of some adjoining village church.

Yet the very bareness of these inner courts and wards, their condition of mere pasturage, protects what remains of them as no defences could do. Nothing is left visible that the hands can seize on or the weather overturn, and a permanence of general outline at least results, which no other condition could ensure.

The position of the castle on this isolated hill bespeaks deliberate and strategic choice exercised by some remote mind capable of prospective reasoning to a far extent. The natural configuration of the surrounding country and its bearing upon such a stronghold were obviously long considered and viewed mentally before its extensive design was carried into execution. Who was the man that said, 'Let it be built here!' – not on that hill yonder, or on that ridge behind, but on this best spot of all? Whether he were some great one of the Belgae, or of the Durotriges, or the travelling engineer of Britain's united tribes, must for ever remain time's secret; his form cannot be realized, nor his countenance, nor the tongue that he spoke, when he set down his foot with a thud and said, 'Let it be here!'

Within the innermost enclosure, though it is so wide that at a superficial glance the beholder has only a sense of standing on a breezy down, the solitude is rendered yet more solitary by the knowledge that between the benighted sojourner herein and all kindred humanity are those three concentric walls of earth which no being would think of scaling on such a night as this, even were he to hear the most pathetic cries issuing hence that could be uttered by a spectre-chased soul. I reach a central mound or platform – the crown and axis of the whole structure. The view from here by day must be of almost limitless extent. On this raised floor, daïs, or rostrum, harps have probably twanged more or less tuneful notes in celebration of daring, strength, or cruelty; of worship, superstition, love, birth, and death; of simple loving-kindness perhaps never. Many a time must the king or leader have directed his keen eyes hence across the open lands towards the ancient road, the Icening Way, still visible in the distance, on the watch for armed companies approaching either to succour or to attack.

I am startled by a voice pronouncing my name. Past and present have become so confusedly mingled under the associations of the spot that for a time it has escaped my memory that this mound was the place agreed on for the aforesaid appointment. I turn and behold my friend. He stands with a dark lantern in his hand and a spade and light pickaxe over his shoulder. He expresses both delight and surprise that I have come. I tell him I had set out before the bad weather began.

He, to whom neither weather, darkness, nor difficulty seems to have any relation or significance, so entirely is his soul wrapt up in his own deep intentions, asks me to take the lantern and accompany him. I take it and walk by his side. He is a man about sixty, small in figure, with grey old-fashioned whiskers cut to the shape of a pair of crumb-brushes. He is entirely in black broadcloth – or rather, at present, black and brown, for he is bespattered with mud from his heels to the crown of his low hat. He has no consciousness of this – no sense of anything but his purpose, his ardour for which causes his eyes to shine like those of a lynx, and gives his motions all the elasticity of an athlete's.

'Nobody to interrupt us at this time of night!' he chuckles with fierce enjoyment.

We retreat a little way and find a sort of angle, an elevation in the sod, a suggested squareness amid the mass of irregularities around. Here, he tells me, if anywhere, the king's house stood. Three months of measurement and calculation have confirmed him in this conclusion.

He requests me now to open the lantern, which I do, and the light streams out upon the wet sod. At last divining his proceedings I say that I had no idea, in keeping the tryst, that he was going to do more at such an unusual time than meet me for a meditative ramble through the stronghold. I ask him why, having a practicable object, he should have minded interruptions and not have chosen the day? He informs me, quietly pointing to his spade, that it was because his purpose is to dig, then signifying with a grim nod the gaunt notice-post against the sky beyond. I inquire why, as a professed and well-known antiquary with capital letters at the tail of his name, he did not obtain the necessary authority, considering the stringent penalties for this sort of thing; and he chuckles fiercely again with suppressed delight, and says, 'Because they wouldn't have given it!'

He at once begins cutting up the sod, and, as he takes the pickaxe to follow on with, assures me that, penalty or no penalty, honest men or marauders, he is sure of one thing, that we shall not be disturbed at our work till after dawn.

I remember to have heard of men who, in their enthusiasm for some special science, art, or hobby, have quite lost the moral sense which would restrain them from indulging it illegitimately; and I conjecture that here, at last, is an instance of such an one. He probably guesses the way my thoughts travel, for he stands up and solemnly asserts that he has a distinctly justifiable intention in this matter; namely, to uncover, to search, to verify a theory or displace it, and to cover up again. He means to take away nothing – not a grain of sand. In this he says he sees no such monstrous sin. I inquire if this is really a promise to me? He repeats that it is a promise, and resumes digging. My contribution to the labour is that of directing the light constantly upon the hole. When he has reached something more than a foot deep he digs more cautiously, saying that, be it much or little there, it will not lie far below the surface; such things never are deep. A few minutes later the point of the pickaxe clicks upon a stony substance. He draws the implement out as feelingly as if it had entered a man's body. Taking up the spade he shovels with care, and a surface, level as an altar, is presently disclosed. His eyes flash anew; he pulls handfuls of grass and mops the surface clean, finally rubbing it with his handkerchief. Grasping the lantern from my hand he holds it close to the ground, when the rays reveal a complete mosaic – a pavement of minute tesserae of many colours, of intricate pattern, a work of much art, of much time, and of much industry. He exclaims in a shout that he knew it always – that it is not a Celtic stronghold exclusively, but also a Roman; the former people having probably contributed little more than the original framework which the latter took and adapted till it became the present imposing structure.

I ask, What if it is Roman?

A great deal, according to him. That it proves all the world to be wrong in this great argument, and himself alone to be right! Can I wait while he digs further?

I agree – reluctantly; but he does not notice my reluctance. At an adjoining spot he begins flourishing the tools anew with the skill of a navvy, this venerable scholar with letters after his name. Sometimes he falls on his knees, burrowing with his hands in the manner of a hare, and where his old-fashioned broadcloth touches the sides of the hole it gets plastered with the damp earth. He continually murmurs to himself how important, how very important, this discovery is! He draws out an object; we wash it in the same primitive way by rubbing it with the wet grass, and it proves to be a semi-transparent bottle of iridescent beauty, the sight of which draws groans of luxurious sensibility from the digger. Further and further search brings out a piece of a weapon. It is strange indeed that by merely peeling off a wrapper of modern accumulations we have lowered ourselves into an ancient world. Finally a skeleton is uncovered, fairly perfect. He lays it out on the grass, bone to its bone.

My friend says the man must have fallen fighting here, as this is no place of burial. He turns again to the trench, scrapes, feels, till from a corner he draws out a heavy lump – a small image four or five inches high. We clean it as before. It is a statuette, apparently of gold, or more probably, of bronze-gilt – a figure of Mercury, obviously, its head being surmounted with the petasus or winged hat, the usual accessory of that deity. Further inspection reveals the workmanship to be of good finish and detail, and, preserved by the limy earth, to be as fresh in every line as on the day it left the hands of its artificer.

We seem to be standing in the Roman Forum and not on a hill in Wessex. Intent upon this truly valuable relic of the old empire of which even this remote spot was a component part, we do not notice what is going on in the present world till reminded of it by the sudden renewal of the storm. Looking up I perceive that the wide extinguisher of cloud has again settled down upon the fortress-town, as if resting upon the edge of the inner rampart, and shutting out the moon. I turn my back to the tempest, still directing the light across the hole. My companion digs on unconcernedly; he is living two thousand years ago, and despises things of the moment as dreams. But at last he is fairly beaten, and standing up beside me looks round on what he has done. The rays of the lantern pass over the trench to the tall skeleton stretched upon the grass on the other side. The beating rain has washed the bones clean and smooth, and the forehead, cheek-bones, and two-and-thirty teeth of the skull glisten in the candle-shine as they lie.

This storm, like the first, is of the nature of a squall, and it ends as abruptly as the other. We dig no further. My friend says that it is enough – he has proved his point. He turns to replace the bones in the trench and covers them. But they fall to pieces under his touch: the air has disintegrated them, and he can only sweep in the fragments. The next act of his plan is more than difficult, but is carried out. The treasures are inhumed again in their respective holes: they are not ours. Each deposition seems to cost him a twinge; and at one moment I fancied I saw him slip his hand into his coat pocket.

'We must re-bury them *all*,' say I.

'O yes,' he answers with integrity. 'I was wiping my hand.'

The beauties of the tesselated floor of the governor's house are once again consigned to darkness; the trench is filled up; the sod laid smoothly down; he wipes the perspiration from his forehead with the same handkerchief he had used to mop the skeleton and tesserae clean; and we make for the eastern gate of the fortress.

Dawn bursts upon us suddenly as we reach the opening. It comes by the lifting and thinning of the clouds that way till we are bathed in a pink light. The direction of his homeward journey is not the same as mine, and we part under the outer slope.

Walking along quickly to restore warmth I muse upon my eccentric friend, and cannot help asking myself this question: Did he really replace the gilded image of the god Mercurius with the rest of the treasures? He seemed to do so; and yet I could not testify to the fact. Probably, however, he was as good as his word.

It was thus I spoke to myself, and so the adventure ended. But one thing remains to be told, and that is concerned with seven years after. Among the effects of my friend, at that time just deceased, was found, carefully preserved, a gilt statuette representing Mercury, labelled 'Debased Roman'. No record was attached to explain how it came into his possession. The figure was bequeathed to the Casterbridge Museum.

Fellow-Townsmen

The shepherd on the east hill could shout out lambing intelligence to the shepherd on the west hill, over the intervening town chimneys, without great inconvenience to his voice, so nearly did the steep pastures encroach upon the burghers' backyards. And at night it was possible to stand in the very midst of the town and hear from their native paddocks on the lower levels of greensward the mild lowing of the farmer's heifers, and the profound, warm blowings of breath in which those creatures indulge. But the community which had jammed itself in the valley thus flanked formed a veritable town, with a real mayor and corporation, and a staple manufacture.

During a certain damp evening five-and-thirty years ago, before the twilight was far advanced, a pedestrian of professional appearance, carrying a small bag in his hand and an elevated umbrella, was descending one of these hills by the turnpike-road when he was overtaken by a phaeton.

'Hullo, Downe – is that you?' said the driver of the vehicle, a young man of pale and refined appearance. 'Jump up here with me, and ride down to your door.'

The other turned a plump, cheery, rather self-indulgent face over his shoulder towards the hailer.

'O, good evening, Mr Barnet – thanks,' he said, and mounted beside his acquaintance.

They were fellow-burgesses of the town which lay beneath them, but though old and very good friends they were differently circumstanced. Barnet was a richer man than the struggling young lawyer Downe, a fact which was to some extent perceptible in Downe's manner towards his companion, though nothing of it ever showed in Barnet's manner towards the solicitor. Barnet's position in the town was none of his own making; his father had been a very successful flax-merchant in the same place, where the trade was still carried on as briskly as the small capacities of its quarters would allow. Having acquired a fair fortune, old Mr Barnet had retired from business, bringing up his son as a gentleman-burgher, and, it must be added, as a well-educated, liberal-minded young man.

'How is Mrs Barnet?' asked Downe.

'Mrs Barnet was very well when I left home,' the other answered constrainedly, exchanging his meditative regard of the horse for one of self-consciousness.

Mr Downe seemed to regret his inquiry, and immediately took up another thread of conversation. He congratulated his friend on his election as a councilman; he thought he had not seen him since that event took place; Mrs Downe had meant to call and congratulate Mrs Barnet, but he feared that she had failed to do so as yet.

Barnet seemed hampered in his replies. 'We should have been glad to see you. I – my wife would welcome Mrs Downe at any time, as you know.... Yes, I am a member of the corporation – rather an inexperienced member, some of them say. It is quite true; and I should have declined the honour as premature – having other things on my hands just now, too – if it had not been pressed upon me so very heartily.'

'There is one thing you have on your hands which I can never quite see the necessity for,' said Downe, with good-humoured freedom. 'What the deuce do you want to build that new mansion for, when you have already got such an excellent house as the one you live in?'

Barnet's face acquired a warmer shade of colour; but as the question had been idly asked by the solicitor while regarding the surrounding flocks and fields, he answered after a moment with no apparent embarrassment –

'Well, we wanted to get out of the town, you know; the house I am living in is rather old and inconvenient.'

Mr Downe declared that he had chosen a pretty site for the new building. They would be able to see for miles and miles from the windows. Was he going to give it a name? He supposed so.

Barnet thought not. There was no other house near that was likely to be mistaken for it. And he did not care for a name.

'But I think it has a name!' Downe observed: 'I went past – when was it? – this morning; and I saw something – "Château Ringdale", I think it was, stuck up on a board!'

'It was an idea she – we had for a short time,' said Barnet hastily. 'But we have decided finally to do without a name – at any rate such a name as that. It must have been a week ago that you saw it. It was taken down last Saturday.... Upon that matter I am firm!' he added grimly.

Downe murmured in an unconvinced tone that he thought he had seen it yesterday.

Talking thus they drove into the town. The street was unusually still for the hour of seven in the evening; an increasing drizzle from the sea had prevailed since the afternoon, and now formed a gauze across the yellow lamps, and trickled with a gentle rattle down the heavy roofs of stone tile, that bent the house-ridges hollow-backed with its weight, and in some instances caused the walls to bulge outwards in the upper story. Their route took them past the little town-hall, the Black-Bull Hotel, and onward to the junction of a small street on the right, consisting of a row of those two-and-two windowed brick residences of no particular age, which are exactly alike wherever found, except in the people they contain.

'Wait – I'll drive you up to your door,' said Barnet, when Downe prepared to alight at the corner. He thereupon turned into the narrow street, when the faces of three little girls could be discerned close to the panes of a lighted window a few yards ahead, surmounted by that of a young matron, the gaze of all four being directed eagerly up the empty street. 'You are a fortunate fellow, Downe,' Barnet continued, as mother and children disappeared from the window to run to the door. 'You must be happy if any man is. I would give a hundred such houses as my new one to have a home like yours.'

'Well – yes, we get along pretty comfortably,' replied Downe complacently.

'That house, Downe, is none of my ordering,' Barnet broke out, revealing a bitterness hitherto suppressed, and checking the horse a moment to finish his speech before delivering up his passenger. 'The house I have already is good enough for me, as you supposed. It is my own freehold; it was built by my grandfather, and is stout enough for a castle. My father was born there, lived there, and died there. I was born there, and have always lived there; yet I must needs build a new one.'

'Why do you?' said Downe.

'Why do I? To preserve peace in the household. I do anything for that; but I don't succeed. I was firm in resisting "Château

Ringdale", however; not that I would not have put up with the absurdity of the name, but it was too much to have your house christened after Lord Ringdale, because your wife once had a fancy for him. If you only knew everything, you would think all attempt at reconciliation hopeless. In your happy home you have had no such experiences; and God forbid that you ever should. See, here they are all ready to receive you!'

'Of course! And so will your wife be waiting to receive you,' said Downe. 'Take my word for it she will! And with a dinner prepared for you far better than mine.'

'I hope so,' Barnet replied dubiously.

He moved on to Downe's door, which the solicitor's family had already opened. Downe descended, but being encumbered with his bag and umbrella, his foot slipped, and he fell upon his knees in the gutter.

'O, my dear Charles!' said his wife, running down the steps; and, quite ignoring the presence of Barnet, she seized hold of her husband, pulled him to his feet, and kissed him, exclaiming, 'I hope you are not hurt, darling!' The children crowded round, chiming in piteously, 'Poor papa!'

'He's all right,' said Barnet, perceiving that Downe was only a little muddy, and looking more at the wife than at the husband. Almost at any other time – certainly during his fastidious bachelor years – he would have thought her a too demonstrative woman; but those recent circumstances of his own life to which he had just alluded made Mrs Downe's solicitude so affecting that his eye grew damp as he witnessed it. Bidding the lawyer and his family good-night he left them, and drove slowly into the main street towards his own house.

The heart of Barnet was sufficiently impressionable to be influenced by Downe's parting prophecy that he might not be so unwelcome home as he imagined: the dreary night might, at least on this one occasion, make Downe's forecast true. Hence it was in a suspense that he could hardly have believed possible that he halted at his door. On entering his wife was nowhere to be seen, and he inquired for her. The servant informed him that her mistress had the dressmaker with her, and would be engaged for some time.

'Dressmaker at this time of day!'

'She dined early, sir, and hopes you will excuse her joining you
this evening.'

'But she knew I was coming tonight?'

'O yes, sir.'

'Go up and tell her I am come.'

The servant did so; but the mistress of the house merely
transmitted her former words.

Barnet said nothing more, and presently sat down to his lonely
meal, which was eaten abstractedly, the domestic scene he had
lately witnessed still impressing him by its contrast with the
situation here. His mind fell back into past years upon a certain
pleasing and gentle being whose face would loom out of their
shades at such times as these. Barnet turned in his chair, and
looked with unfocused eyes in a direction southward from where
he sat, as if he saw not the room but a long way beyond. 'I
wonder if she lives there still!' he said.

He rose with a sudden rebelliousness, put on his hat and coat,
and went out of the house, pursuing his way along the glistening
pavement while eight o'clock was striking from St Mary's tower,
and the apprentices and shopmen were slamming up the shutters
from end to end of the town. In two minutes only those shops
which could boast of no attendant save the master or the mistress
remained with open eyes. These were ever somewhat less prompt
to exclude customers than the others: for their owners' ears the
closing hour had scarcely the cheerfulness that it possessed for
the hired servants of the rest. Yet the night being dreary the delay
was not for long, and their windows, too, blinked together one by
one.

During this time Barnet had proceeded with decided step in a
direction at right angles to the broad main thoroughfare of the
town, by a long street leading due southward. Here, though his
family had no more to do with the flax manufacture, his own
name occasionally greeted him on gates and warehouses, being
used allusively by small rising tradesmen as a recommendation,
in such words as 'Smith, from Barnet & Co.' – 'Robinson, late
manager at Barnet's'. The sight led him to reflect upon his
father's busy life, and he questioned if it had not been far happier
than his own.

The houses along the road became fewer, and presently open

ground appeared between them on either side, the track on the right hand rising to a higher level till it merged in a knoll. On the summit a row of builders' scaffold-poles probed the indistinct sky like spears, and at their bases could be discerned the lower courses of a building lately begun. Barnet slackened his pace and stood for a few moments without leaving the centre of the road, apparently not much interested in the sight, till suddenly his eye was caught by a post in the fore part of the ground bearing a white board at the top. He went to the rails, vaulted over, and walked in far enough to discern painted upon the board 'Château Ringdale'.

A dismal irony seemed to lie in the words, and its effect was to irritate him. Downe, then, had spoken truly. He stuck his umbrella into the sod, and seized the post with both hands, as if intending to loosen and throw it down. Then, like one bewildered by an opposition which would exist none the less though its manifestations were removed, he allowed his arms to sink to his side.

'Let it be,' he said to himself. 'I have declared there shall be peace – if possible.'

Taking up his umbrella he quietly left the enclosure, and went on his way, still keeping his back to the town. He had advanced with more decision since passing the new building, and soon a hoarse murmur rose upon the gloom; it was the sound of the sea. The road led to the harbour, at a distance of a mile from the town, from which the trade of the district was fed. After seeing the obnoxious nameboard Barnet had forgotten to open his umbrella, and the rain tapped smartly on his hat, and occasionally stroked his face as he went on.

Though the lamps were still continued at the roadside they stood at wider intervals than before, and the pavement had given place to rough gravel. Every time he came to a lamp an increasing shine made itself visible upon his shoulders, till at last they quite glistened with wet. The murmur from the shore grew stronger, but it was still some distance off when he paused before one of the smallest of the detached houses by the wayside, standing in its own garden, the latter being divided from the road by a row of wooden palings. Scrutinizing the spot to ensure that he was not mistaken, he opened the gate and gently knocked at the cottage door.

When he had patiently waited minutes enough to lead any man in ordinary cases to knock again, the door was heard to open, though it was impossible to see by whose hand, there being no light in the passage. Barnet said at random, 'Does Miss Savile live here?'

A youthful voice assured him that she did live there, and by a sudden afterthought asked him to come in. It would soon get a light, it said: but the night being wet, mother had not thought it worth while to trim the passage lamp.

'Don't trouble yourself to get a light for me,' said Barnet hastily; 'it is not necessary at all. Which is Miss Savile's sitting-room?'

The young person, whose white pinafore could just be discerned, signified a door in the side of the passage, and Barnet went forward at the same moment, so that no light should fall upon his face. On entering the room he closed the door behind him, pausing till he heard the retreating footsteps of the child.

He found himself in an apartment which was simply and neatly, though not poorly furnished; everything, from the miniature chiffonnier to the shining little daguerreotype which formed the central ornament of the mantelpiece, being in scrupulous order. The picture was enclosed by a frame of embroidered card-board – evidently the work of feminine hands – and it was the portrait of a thin faced, elderly lieutenant in the navy. From behind the lamp on the table a female form now rose into view, that of a young girl, and a resemblance between her and the portrait was early discoverable. She had been so absorbed in some occupation on the other side of the lamp as to have barely found time to realize her visitor's presence.

They both remained standing for a few seconds without speaking. The face that confronted Barnet had a beautiful outline; the Raffaelesque oval of its contour was remarkable for an English countenance, and that countenance housed in a remote country-road to an unheard-of harbour. But her features did not do justice to this splendid beginning: Nature had recollected that she was not in Italy; and the young lady's lineaments, though not so inconsistent as to make her plain, would have been accepted rather as pleasing than as correct. The preoccupied expression which, like images on the retina, remained with her for a moment after the state that caused it had ceased, now changed into a reserved, half-proud, and slightly indignant look, in which the blood diffused itself quickly across her cheek, and additional brightness broke the shade of her rather heavy eyes.

'I know I have no business here,' he said, answering the look. 'But I had a great wish to see you, and inquire how you were. You can give your hand to me, seeing how often I have held it in past days?'

'I would rather forget than remember all that, Mr Barnet,' she answered, as she coldly complied with the request. 'When I think of the circumstances of our last meeting, I can hardly consider it kind of you to allude to such a thing as our past – or, indeed, to come here at all.'

'There was no harm in it surely? I don't trouble you often, Lucy.'

'I have not had the honour of a visit from you for a very long time, certainly, and I did not expect it now,' she said, with the same stiffness in her air. 'I hope Mrs Barnet is very well?'

'Yes, yes!' he impatiently returned. 'At least I suppose so – though I only speak from inference!'

'But she is your wife, sir,' said the young girl tremulously.

The unwonted tones of a man's voice in that feminine chamber had startled a canary that was roosting in its cage by the window; the bird awoke hastily, and fluttered against the bars. She went and stilled it by laying her face against the cage and murmuring a coaxing sound. It might partly have been done to still herself.

'I didn't come to talk of Mrs Barnet,' he pursued; 'I came to talk of you, of yourself alone; to inquire how you are getting on since your great loss.' And he turned towards the portrait of her father.

'I am getting on fairly well, thank you.'

The force of her utterance was scarcely borne out by her look; but Barnet courteously reproached himself for not having guessed a thing so natural; and to dissipate all embarrassment added, as he bent over the table, 'What were you doing when I came? – painting flowers, and by candlelight?'

'O no,' she said, 'not painting them – only sketching the outlines. I do that at night to save time – I have to get three dozen done by the end of the month.'

Barnet looked as if he regretted it deeply. 'You will wear your poor eyes out,' he said, with more sentiment than he had hitherto shown. 'You ought not to do it. There was a time when I should have said you must not. Well – I almost wish I had never seen light with my own eyes when I think of that!'

'Is this a time or place for recalling such matters?' she asked, with dignity. 'You used to have a gentlemanly respect for me, and for yourself. Don't speak any more as you have spoken, and don't come again. I cannot think that this visit is serious, or was closely considered by you.'

'Considered: well, I came to see you as an old and good friend – not to mince matters, to visit a woman I loved. Don't be angry! I could not help doing it, so many things brought you into my mind.... This evening I fell in with an acquaintance, and when I saw how happy he was with his wife and family welcoming him home, though with only one-tenth of my income and chances, and thought what might have been in my case, it fairly broke down my discretion, and off I came here. Now I am here I feel that I am wrong to some extent. But the feeling that I should like to see you, and talk of those we used to know in common, was very strong.'

'Before that can be the case a little more time must pass,' said Miss Savile quietly; 'a time long enough for me to regard with some calmness what at present I remember far too impatiently – though it may be you almost forget it. Indeed you must have forgotten it long before you acted as you did.' Her voice grew stronger and more vivacious as she added: 'But I am doing my best to forget it too, and I know I shall succeed from the progress I have made already!'

She had remained standing till now, when she turned and sat down, facing half away from him.

Barnet watched her moodily. 'Yes, it is only what I deserve,' he said. 'Ambition pricked me on – no, it was not ambition, it was wrongheadedness! Had I but reflected....' He broke out vehemently: 'But always remember this, Lucy: if you had written to me only one little line after that misunderstanding, I declare I should have come back to you. That ruined me!' He slowly walked as far as the little room would allow him to go, and remained with his eyes on the skirting.

'But, Mr Barnet, how could I write to you? There was no opening for my doing so.'

'Then there ought to have been,' said Barnet, turning. 'That was my fault!'

'Well, I don't know anything about that; but as there had been nothing said by me which required any explanation by letter, I did not send one. Everything was so indefinite, and feeling your position to be so much wealthier than mine, I fancied I might have mistaken your meaning. And when I heard of the other lady – a woman of whose family even you might be proud – I thought how foolish I had been, and said nothing.'

'Then I suppose it was destiny – accident – I don't know what, that separated us, dear Lucy. Anyhow you were the woman I ought to have made my wife – and I let you slip, like the foolish man that I was!'

'O, Mr Barnet,' she said, almost in tears, 'don't revive the subject to me; I am the wrong one to console you – think, sir, – you should not be here – it would be so bad for me if it were known!'

'It would – it would, indeed,' he said hastily. 'I am not right in doing this, and I won't do it again.'

'It is a very common folly of human nature, you know, to think the course you did *not* adopt must have been the best,' she continued with gentle solicitude, as she followed him to the door of the room. 'And you don't know that I should have accepted you, even if you had asked me to be your wife.' At this his eye met hers, and she dropped her gaze. She knew that her voice belied her. There was a silence till she looked up to add, in a voice of soothing playfulness, 'My family was so much poorer than yours, even before I lost my dear father, that – perhaps your companions would have made it unpleasant for us on account of my deficiencies.'

'Your disposition would soon have won them round,' said Barnet.

She archly expostulated: 'Now, never mind my disposition; try to make it up with your wife! Those are my commands to you. And now you are to leave me at once.'

'I will. I must make the best of it all, I suppose,' he replied, more cheerfully than he had as yet spoken. 'But I shall never again meet with such a dear girl as you!' And he suddenly opened the door, and left her alone. When his glance again fell on the lamps that were sparsely ranged along the dreary level road, his eyes were in a state which showed straw-like motes of light radiating from each flame into the surrounding air.

On the other side of the way Barnet observed a man under an umbrella, walking parallel with himself. Presently this man left the footway, and gradually converged on Barnet's course. The latter then saw that it was Charlson, a surgeon of the town, who owed him money. Charlson was a man not without ability; yet he did not prosper. Sundry circumstances stood in his way as a medical practitioner: he was needy; he was not a coddle; he gossiped with men instead of with women; he had married a stranger instead of one of the town young ladies; and he was given to conversational buffoonery. Moreover, his look was quite erroneous. Those only proper features in the family doctor, the quiet eye, and the thin straight passionless lips which never curl in public either for laughter or for scorn, were not his; he had a full-curved mouth, and a bold black eye that made timid people nervous. His companions were what in old times would have been called boon companions – an expression which, though of irreproachable root, suggests fraternization carried to the point of unscrupulousness. All this was against him in the little town of his adoption.

Charlson had been in difficulties, and to oblige him Barnet had put his name to a bill; and, as he had expected, was called upon to meet it when it fell due. It had been only a matter of fifty pounds, which Barnet could well afford to lose, and he bore no ill-will to the thriftless surgeon on account of it. But Charlson had a little too much brazen indifferentism in his composition to be altogether a desirable acquaintance.

'I hope to be able to make that little bill-business right with you in the course of three weeks, Mr Barnet,' said Charlson with hail-fellow friendliness.

Barnet replied good-naturedly that there was no hurry.

This particular three weeks had moved on in advance of Charlson's present with the precision of a shadow for some considerable time.

'I've had a dream,' Charlson continued. Barnet knew from his tone that the surgeon was going to begin his characteristic nonsense, and did not encourage him. 'I've had a dream,' repeated Charlson, who required no encouragement. 'I dreamed that a gentleman, who has been very kind to me, married a haughty lady in haste, before he had quite forgotten a nice little girl he knew before, and that one wet evening, like the present, as I was walking up the harbour-road, I saw him come out of that dear little girl's present abode.'

Barnet glanced towards the speaker. The rays from a neighbouring lamp struck through the drizzle under Charlson's umbrella, so as just to illumine his face against the shade behind, and show that his eye was turned up under the outer corner of its lid, whence it leered with impish jocoseness as he thrust his tongue into his cheek.

'Come,' said Barnet gravely, 'we'll have no more of that.'

'No, no – of course not,' Charlson hastily answered, seeing that his humour had carried him too far, as it had done many times before. He was profuse in his apologies, but Barnet did not reply. Of one thing he was certain – that scandal was a plant of quick root, and that he was bound to obey Lucy's injunction for Lucy's own sake.

He did so, to the letter; and though, as the crocus followed the snowdrop and the daffodil the crocus in Lucy's garden, the harbour-road was a not unpleasant place to walk in, Barnet's feet never trod its stones, much less approached her door. He avoided a saunter that way as he would have avoided a dangerous dram, and took his airings a long distance northward, among severely square and brown ploughed fields, where no other townsman came. Sometimes he went round by the lower lanes of the borough, where the rope-walks stretched in which his family formerly had share, and looked at the rope-makers walking backwards, overhung by apple-trees and bushes, and intruded on by cows and calves, as if trade had established itself there at considerable inconvenience to Nature.

One morning, when the sun was so warm as to raise a steam from the south-eastern slopes of those flanking hills that looked so lovely above the old roofs, but made every low-chimneyed house in the town as smoky as Tophet, Barnet glanced from the windows of the town-council room for lack of interest in what was proceeding within. Several members of the corporation were present, but there was not much business doing, and in a few minutes Downe came leisurely across to him, saying that he seldom saw Barnet now.

Barnet owned that he was not often present.

Downe looked at the crimson curtain which hung down beside the panes, reflecting its hot hues into their faces, and then out of the window. At that moment there passed along the street a tall commanding lady, in whom the solicitor recognized Barnet's wife. Barnet had done the same thing, and turned away.

'It will be all right some day,' said Downe, with cheering sympathy.

'You have heard, then, of her last outbreak?'

Downe depressed his cheerfulness to its very reverse in a moment. 'No, I have not heard of anything serious,' he said, with as long a face as one naturally round could be turned into at short notice. 'I only hear vague reports of such things.'

'You may think it will be all right,' said Barnet drily. 'But I have a different opinion.... No, Downe, we must look the thing in the face. Not poppy nor mandragora – however, how are your wife and children?'

Downe said that they were all well, thanks; they were out that morning somewhere; he was just looking to see if they were walking that way. Ah, there they were, just coming down the street; and Downe pointed to the figures of two children with a nursemaid, and a lady walking behind them.

'You will come out and speak to her?' he asked.

'Not this morning. The fact is I don't care to speak to anybody just now.'

'You are too sensitive, Mr Barnet. At school I remember you used to get as red as a rose if anybody uttered a word that hurt your feelings.'

Barnet mused. 'Yes,' he admitted, 'there is a grain of truth in that. It is because of that I often try to make peace at home. Life would be tolerable then at any rate, even if not particularly bright.'

'I have thought more than once of proposing a little plan to you,' said Downe with some hesitation. 'I don't know whether it will meet your views, but take it or leave it, as you choose. In fact, it was my wife who suggested it: that she would be very glad to call on Mrs Barnet and get into her confidence. She seems to think that Mrs Barnet is rather alone in the town, and without advisers. Her impression is that your wife will listen to reason.

Emily has a wonderful way of winning the hearts of people of her own sex.'

'And of the other sex too, I think. She is a charming woman, and you were a lucky fellow to find her.'

'Well, perhaps I was,' simpered Downe, trying to wear an aspect of being the last man in the world to feel pride. 'However, she will be likely to find out what ruffles Mrs Barnet. Perhaps it is some misunderstanding, you know – something that she is too proud to ask you to explain, or some little thing in your conduct that irritates her because she does not fully comprehend you. The truth is, Emily would have been more ready to make advances if she had been quite sure of her fitness for Mrs Barnet's society, who has of course been accustomed to London people of good position, which made Emily fearful of intruding.'

Barnet expressed his warmest thanks for the well-intentioned proposition. There was reason in Mrs Downe's fear – that he owned. 'But do let her call,' he said. 'There is no woman in England I would so soon trust on such an errand. I am afraid there will not be any brilliant result; still I shall take it as the kindest and nicest thing if she will try it, and not be frightened at a repulse.'

When Barnet and Downe had parted, the former went to the Town Savings-Bank, of which he was a trustee, and endeavoured to forget his troubles in the contemplation of low sums of money, and figures in a network of red and blue lines. He sat and watched the working people making their deposits, to which at intervals he signed his name. Before he left in the afternoon Downe put his head inside the door.

'Emily has seen Mrs Barnet,' he said, in a low voice. 'She has got Mrs Barnet's promise to take her for a drive down to the shore tomorrow, if it is fine. Good afternoon!'

Barnet shook Downe by the hand without speaking, and Downe went away.

The next day was as fine as the arrangement could possibly require. As the sun passed the meridian and declined westward, the tall shadows from the scaffold-poles of Barnet's rising residence streaked the ground as far as to the middle of the highway. Barnet himself was there inspecting the progress of the works for the first time during several weeks. A building in an

old-fashioned town five-and-thirty years ago did not, as in the
modern fashion, rise from the sod like a booth at a fair. The
foundations and lower courses were put in and allowed to settle
for many weeks before the superstructure was built up, and a
whole summer of drying was hardly sufficient to do justice to the
important issues involved. Barnet stood within a window-niche
which had as yet received no frame, and thence looked down a
slope into the road. The wheels of a chaise were heard, and then
his handsome Xantippe, in the company of Mrs Downe, drove
past on their way to the shore. They were driving slowly; there
was a pleasing light in Mrs Downe's face, which seemed faintly to
reflect itself upon the countenance of her companion – that
politesse du coeur which was so natural to her having possibly
begun already to work results. But whatever the situation, Barnet
resolved not to interfere, or do anything to hazard the promise of
the day. He might well afford to trust the issue to another when
he could never direct it but to ill himself. His wife's clenched rein-
hand in its lemon-coloured glove, her stiff erect figure, clad in
velvet and lace, and her boldly-outlined face, passed on, exhibiting their owner as one fixed for ever above the level of her
companion – socially by her early breeding, and materially by
her higher cushion.

Barnet decided to allow them a proper time to themselves, and
then stroll down to the shore and drive them home. After
lingering on at the house for another hour he started with this
intention. A few hundred yards below 'Château Ringdale' stood
the cottage in which the late lieutenant's daughter had her
lodging. Barnet had not been so far that way for a long time, and
as he approached the forbidden ground a curious warmth passed
into him, which led him to perceive that, unless he were careful,
he might have to fight the battle with himself about Lucy over
again. A tenth of his present excuse would, however, have
justified him in travelling by that road today.

He came opposite the dwelling, and turned his eyes for a
momentary glance into the little garden that stretched from the
palings to the door. Lucy was in the enclosure; she was walking
and stooping to gather some flowers, possibly for the purpose of
painting them, for she moved about quickly, as if anxious to save
time. She did not see him; he might have passed unnoticed; but a
sensation which was not in strict unison with his previous

sentiments that day led him to pause in his walk and watch her. She went nimbly round and round the beds of anemones, tulips, jonquils, polyanthuses, and other old-fashioned flowers, looking a very charming figure in her half-mourning bonnet, and with an incomplete nosegay in her left hand. Raising herself to pull down a lilac blossom she observed him.

'Mr Barnet!' she said, innocently smiling. 'Why, I have been thinking of you many times since Mrs Barnet went by in the pony-carriage, and now here you are!'

'Yes, Lucy,' he said.

Then she seemed to recall particulars of their last meeting, and he believed that she flushed, though it might have been only the fancy of his own super-sensitiveness.

'I am going to the harbour,' he added.

'Are you?' Lucy remarked simply. 'A great many people begin to go there now the summer is drawing on.'

Her face had come more into his view as she spoke, and he noticed how much thinner and paler it was than when he had seen it last. 'Lucy, how weary you look! tell me, can I help you?' he was going to cry out. – 'If I do,' he thought, 'it will be the ruin of us both!' He merely said that the afternoon was fine, and went on his way.

As he went a sudden blast of air came over the hill as if in contradiction to his words, and spoilt the previous quiet of the scene. The wind had already shifted violently, and now smelt of the sea.

The harbour-road soon began to justify its name. A gap appeared in the rampart of hills which shut out the sea, and on the left of the opening rose a vertical cliff, coloured a burning orange by the sunlight, the companion cliff on the right being livid in shade. Between these cliffs, like the Libyan bay which sheltered the shipwrecked Trojans, was a little haven, seemingly a beginning made by Nature herself of a perfect harbour, which appealed to the passer-by as only requiring a little human industry to finish it and make it famous, the ground on each side as far back as the daisied slopes that bounded the interior valley being a mere layer of blown sand. But the Port-Bredy burgesses a mile inland had, in the course of ten centuries, responded many times to that mute appeal, with the result that the tides had invariably choked up their works with sand and shingle as soon as completed. There were but few houses here: a rough pier, a few boats, some stores, an inn, a residence or two, a ketch unloading in the harbour, were the chief features of the settlement. On the open ground by the shore stood his wife's pony-carriage, empty, the boy in attendance holding the horse.

When Barnet drew nearer, he saw an indigo-coloured spot moving swiftly along beneath the radiant base of the eastern cliff, which proved to be a man in a jersey, running with all his might. He held up his hand to Barnet, as it seemed, and they approached each other. The man was local, but a stranger to him.

'What is it, my man?' said Barnet.

'A terrible calamity!' the boatman hastily explained. Two ladies had been capsized in a boat – they were Mrs Downe and Mrs Barnet of the old town; they had driven down there that afternoon – they had alighted, and it was so fine, that, after walking about a little while, they had been tempted to go out for a short sail round the cliff. Just as they were putting in to the shore, the wind shifted with a sudden gust, the boat listed over, and it was thought they were both drowned. How it could have happened was beyond his mind to fathom, for John Green knew how to sail a boat as well as any man there.

'Which is the way to the place?' said Barnet.

It was just round the cliff.

'Run to the carriage and tell the boy to bring it to the place as soon as you can. Then go to the Harbour Inn and tell them to ride to town for a doctor. Have they been got out of the water?'

'One lady has.'

'Which?'

'Mrs Barnet. Mrs Downe, it is feared, has fleeted out to sea.'

Barnet ran on to that part of the shore which the cliff had hitherto obscured from his view, and there discerned, a long way ahead, a group of fishermen standing. As soon as he came up one or two recognized him, and, not liking to meet his eye, turned aside with misgiving. He went amidst them and saw a small sailing-boat lying draggled at the water's edge; and, on the sloping shingle beside it, a soaked and sandy woman's form in the velvet dress and yellow gloves of his wife.

All had been done that could be done. Mrs Barnet was in her own house under medical hands, but the result was still uncertain.

Barnet had acted as if devotion to his wife were the dominant passion of his existence. There had been much to decide – whether to attempt restoration of the apparently lifeless body as it lay on the shore – whether to carry her to the Harbour Inn – whether to drive with her at once to his own house. The first course, with no skilled help or appliances near at hand, had seemed hopeless. The second course would have occupied nearly as much time as a drive to the town, owing to the intervening ridges of shingle, and the necessity of crossing the harbour by boat to get to the house, added to which much time must have elapsed before a doctor could have arrived down there. By bringing her home in the carriage some precious moments had slipped by; but she had been laid in her own bed in seven minutes, a doctor called to her side, and every possible restorative brought to bear upon her.

At what a tearing pace he had driven up that road, through the yellow evening sunlight, the shadows flapping irksomely into his eyes as each wayside object rushed past between him and the west! Tired workmen with their baskets at their backs had turned on their homeward journey to wonder at his speed. Halfway between the shore and Port-Bredy town he had met Charlson, who had been the first surgeon to hear of the accident. He was accompanied by his assistant in a gig. Barnet had sent on the latter to the coast in case that Downe's poor wife should by that time have been reclaimed from the waves, and had brought Charlson back with him to the house.

Barnet's presence was not needed here, and he felt it to be his next duty to set off at once and find Downe, that no other than himself might break the news to him.

He was quite sure that no chance had been lost for Mrs Downe by his leaving the shore. By the time that Mrs Barnet had been laid in the carriage a much larger group had assembled to lend assistance in finding her friend, rendering his own help superfluous. But the duty of breaking the news was made doubly painful by the circumstance that the catastrophe which had befallen Mrs Downe was solely the result of her own and her husband's loving-kindness towards himself.

He found Downe in his office. When the solicitor comprehended the intelligence he turned pale, stood up, and remained for a moment perfectly still, as if bereft of his faculties; then his shoulders heaved, he pulled out his handkerchief and began to cry like a child. His sobs might have been heard in the next room. He seemed to have no idea of going to the shore, or of doing anything; but when Barnet took him gently by the hand and proposed to start at once, he quietly acquiesced, neither uttering any further word nor making any effort to repress his tears.

Barnet accompanied him to the shore, where, finding that no trace had as yet been seen of Mrs Downe, and that his stay would be of no avail, he left Downe with his friends and the young doctor, and once more hastened back to his own house.

At the door he met Charlson. 'Well!' Barnet said.

'I have just come down,' said the doctor; 'we have done everything, but without result. I sympathize with you in your bereavement.'

Barnet did not much appreciate Charlson's sympathy, which sounded to his ears as something of a mockery from the lips of a man who knew what Charlson knew about his domestic relations. Indeed there seemed an odd spark in Charlson's full black eye as he said the words; but that might have been imaginary.

'And, Mr Barnet,' Charlson resumed, 'that little matter between us – I hope to settle it finally in three weeks at least.'

'Never mind that now,' said Barnet abruptly. He directed the surgeon to go to the harbour in case his services might even now be necessary there: and himself entered the house.

The servants were coming from his wife's chamber, looking helplessly at each other and at him. He passed them by and entered the room, where he stood regarding the shape on the bed for a few minutes, after which he walked into his own dressing-room adjoining, and there paced up and down. In a minute or two he noticed what a strange and total silence had come over the upper part of the house; his own movements, muffled as they were by the carpet, seemed noisy, and his thoughts to disturb the air like articulate utterances. His eye glanced through the window. Far down the road to the harbour a roof detained his gaze: out of it rose a red chimney, and out of the red chimney a curl of smoke, as from a fire newly kindled. He had often seen such a sight before. In that house lived Lucy Savile; and the smoke was from the fire which was regularly lighted at this time to make her tea.

After that he went back to the bedroom, and stood there some time regarding his wife's silent form. She was a woman some years older than himself, but had not by any means overpassed the maturity of good looks and vigour. Her passionate features, well-defined, firm, and statuesque in life, were doubly so now: her mouth and brow, beneath her purplish black hair, showed only too clearly that the turbulency of character which had made a bear-garden of his house had been no temporary phase of her existence. While he reflected, he suddenly said to himself, I wonder if all has been done?

The thought was led up to by his having fancied that his wife's features lacked in its completeness the expression which he had been accustomed to associate with the faces of those whose spirits have fled for ever. The effacement of life was not so marked but that, entering uninformed, he might have supposed her sleeping. Her complexion was that seen in the numerous faded portraits by Sir Joshua Reynolds; it was pallid in comparison with life, but there was visible on a close inspection the remnant of what had once been a flush; the keeping between the cheeks and the hollows of the face being thus preserved, although positive colour was gone. Long orange rays of evening sun stole in through chinks in the blind, striking on the large mirror, and being thence reflected upon the crimson hangings and woodwork of the heavy bedstead, so that the general tone of light was remarkably warm; and it was probable that something might be due to this circumstance. Still the fact impressed him as strange. Charlson had been gone more than a quarter of an hour: could it be possible that he had left too soon, and that his attempts to restore her had operated so sluggishly as only now to have made themselves felt? Barnet laid his hand upon her chest, and fancied that ever and anon a faint flutter of palpitation, gentle as that of a butterfly's wing, disturbed the stillness there – ceasing for a time, then struggling to go on, then breaking down in weakness and ceasing again.

Barnet's mother had been an active practitioner of the healing art among her poorer neighbours, and her inspirations had all been derived from an octavo volume of Domestic Medicine, which at this moment was lying, as it had lain for many years, on a shelf in Barnet's dressing-room. He hastily fetched it, and there read under the head 'Drowning': –

> Exertions for the recovery of any person who has not been
> immersed for a longer period than half-an-hour should be
> continued for at least four hours, as there have been many cases in
> which returning life has made itself visible even after a longer
> interval.
>
> Should, however, a weak action of any of the organs show itself
> when the case seems almost hopeless, our efforts must be redoubled;
> the feeble spark in this case requires to be solicited; it will certainly
> disappear under a relaxation of labour.

Barnet looked at his watch; it was now barely two hours and a
half from the time when he had first heard of the accident. He
threw aside the book and turned quickly to reach a stimulant
which had previously been used. Pulling up the blind for more
light, his eye glanced out of the window. There he saw that red
chimney still smoking cheerily, and that roof, and through the
roof that somebody. His mechanical movements stopped, his
hand remained on the blind-cord, and he seemed to become
breathless, as if he had suddenly found himself treading a high
rope.

While he stood a sparrow lighted on the window-sill, saw him,
and flew away. Next a man and a dog walked over one of the
green hills which bulged above the roofs of the town. But Barnet
took no notice.

We may wonder what were the exact images that passed
through his mind during those minutes of gazing upon Lucy
Savile's house, the sparrow, the man and the dog, and Lucy
Savile's house again. There are honest men who will not admit to
their thoughts, even as idle hypotheses, views of the future that
assume as done a deed which they would recoil from doing; and
there are other honest men for whom morality ends at the
surface of their own heads, who will deliberate what the first will
not so much as suppose. Barnet had a wife whose presence
distracted his home; she now lay as in death; by merely doing
nothing – by letting the intelligence which had gone forth to the
world lie undisturbed – he would effect such a deliverance for
himself as he had never hoped for, and open up an opportunity of
which till now he had never dreamed. Whether the conjuncture
had arisen through any unscrupulous, ill-considered impulse of
Charlson to help out of a strait the friend who was so kind as

never to press him for what was due could not be told; there was
nothing to prove it; and it was a question which could never be
asked. The triangular situation – himself – his wife – Lucy Savile
– was the one clear thing.

From Barnet's actions we may infer that he *supposed* such and
such a result, for a moment, but did not deliberate. He withdrew
his hazel eyes from the scene without, calmly turned, rang the
bell for assistance, and vigorously exerted himself to learn if life
still lingered in that motionless frame. In a short time another
surgeon was in attendance; and then Barnet's surmise proved to
be true. The slow life timidly heaved again; but much care and
patience were needed to catch and retain it, and a considerable
period elapsed before it could be said with certainty that Mrs
Barnet lived. When this was the case, and there was no further
room for doubt, Barnet left the chamber. The blue evening smoke
from Lucy's chimney had died down to an imperceptible stream,
and as he walked about downstairs he murmured to himself, 'My
wife was dead, and she is alive again.'

It was not so with Downe. After three hours' immersion his
wife's body had been recovered, life, of course, being quite
extinct. Barnet on descending, went straight to his friend's house,
and there learned the result. Downe was helpless in his wild grief,
occasionally even hysterical. Barnet said little, but finding that
some guiding hand was necessary in the sorrow-stricken household, took upon him to supervise and manage till Downe should
be in a state of mind to do so for himself.

One September evening, four months later, when Mrs Barnet was
in perfect health, and Mrs Downe but a weakening memory, an
errand-boy paused to rest himself in front of Mr Barnet's old
house, depositing his basket on one of the window-sills. The
street was not yet lighted, but there were lights in the house, and
at intervals a flitting shadow fell upon the blind at his elbow.
Words also were audible from the same apartment, and they
seemed to be those of persons in violent altercation. But the boy
could not gather their purport, and he went on his way.

Ten minutes afterwards the door of Barnet's house opened, and
a tall closely-veiled lady in a travelling-dress came out and
descended the freestone steps. The servant stood in the doorway
watching her as she went with a measured tread down the street.

When she had been out of sight for some minutes Barnet appeared at the door from within.

'Did your mistress leave word where she was going?' he asked.

'No, sir.'

'Is the carriage ordered to meet her anywhere?'

'No, sir.'

'Did she take a latch-key?'

'No, sir.'

Barnet went in again, sat down in his chair, and leaned back. Then in solitude and silence he brooded over the bitter emotions that filled his heart. It was for this that he had gratuitously restored her to life, and made his union with another impossible! The evening drew on, and nobody came to disturb him. At bedtime he told the servants to retire, that he would sit up for Mrs Barnet himself; and when they were gone he leaned his head upon his hand and mused for hours.

The clock struck one, two; still his wife came not, and, with impatience added to depression, he went from room to room till another weary hour had passed. This was not altogether a new experience for Barnet; but she had never before so prolonged her absence. At last he sat down again and fell asleep.

He awoke at six o'clock to find that she had not returned. In searching about the rooms he discovered that she had taken a case of jewels which had been hers before her marriage. At eight a note was brought him; it was from his wife, in which she stated that she had gone by the coach to the house of a distant relative near London, and expressed a wish that certain boxes, articles of clothing, and so on, might be sent to her forthwith. The note was brought to him by a waiter at the Black-Bull Hotel, and had been written by Mrs Barnet immediately before she took her place in the stage.

By the evening this order was carried out, and Barnet, with a sense of relief, walked out into the town. A fair had been held during the day, and the large clear moon which rose over the most prominent hill flung its light upon the booths and standings that still remained in the street, mixing its rays curiously with those from the flaring naphtha lamps. The town was full of country-people who had come in to enjoy themselves, and on this account Barnet strolled through the streets unobserved. With a certain recklessness he made for the harbour-road, and presently found himself by the shore, where he walked on till he came to the spot near which his friend the kindly Mrs Downe had lost her life, and his own wife's life had been preserved. A tremulous pathway of bright moonshine now stretched over the water which had engulfed them, and not a living soul was near.

Here he ruminated on their characters, and next on the young girl in whom he now took a more sensitive interest than at the time when he had been free to marry her. Nothing, so far as he was aware, had ever appeared in his own conduct to show that such an interest existed. He had made it a point of the utmost strictness to hinder that feeling from influencing in the faintest degree his attitude towards his wife; and this was made all the more easy for him by the small demand Mrs Barnet made upon his attentions, for which she ever evinced the greatest contempt; thus unwittingly giving him the satisfaction of knowing that their severance owed nothing to jealousy, or, indeed, to any personal behaviour of his at all. Her concern was not with him or his feelings, as she frequently told him; but that she had, in a moment of weakness, thrown herself away upon a common burgher when she might have aimed at, and possibly brought down, a peer of the realm. Her frequent depreciation of Barnet in these terms had at times been so intense that he was sorely tempted to retaliate on her egotism by owning that he loved at the same low level on which he lived; but prudence had prevailed, for which he was now thankful.

Something seemed to sound upon the shingle behind him over and above the raking of the wave. He looked round, and a slight girlish shape appeared quite close to him. He could not see her face because it was in the direction of the moon.

'Mr Barnet?' the rambler said, in timid surprise. The voice was the voice of Lucy Savile.

'Yes,' said Barnet. 'How can I repay you for this pleasure?'

'I only came because the night was so clear. I am now on my way home.'

'I am glad we have met. I want to know if you will let me do something for you, to give me an occupation, as an idle man? I am sure I ought to help you, for I know you are almost without friends.'

She hesitated. 'Why should you tell me that?' she said.

'In the hope that you will be frank with me.'

'I am not altogether without friends here. But I am going to make a little change in my life – to go out as a teacher of freehand drawing and practical perspective, of course I mean on a comparatively humble scale, because I have not been specially educated for that profession. But I am sure I shall like it much.'

'You have an opening?'

'I have not exactly got it, but I have advertised for one.'

'Lucy, you must let me help you!'

'Not at all.'

'You need not think it would compromise you, or that I am indifferent to delicacy. I bear in mind how we stand. It is very unlikely that you will succeed as teacher of the class you mention, so let me do something of a different kind for you. Say what you would like, and it shall be done.'

'No; if I can't be a drawing-mistress or governess, or something of that sort, I shall go to India and join my brother.'

'I wish I could go abroad, anywhere, everywhere with you, Lucy, and leave this place and its associations for ever!'

She played with the end of her bonnet-string, and hastily turned aside. 'Don't ever touch upon that kind of topic again,' she said, with a quick severity not free from anger. 'It simply makes it impossible for me to see you, much less receive any guidance from you. No, thank you, Mr Barnet; you can do nothing for me at present; and as I suppose my uncertainty will end in my leaving for India, I fear you never will. If ever I think you *can* do anything, I will take the trouble to ask you. Till then, good-bye.'

The tone of her latter words was equivocal, and while he remained in doubt whether a gentle irony was or was not inwrought with their sound, she swept lightly round and left him alone. He saw her form get smaller and smaller along the damp belt of sea-sand between ebb and flood; and when she had vanished round the cliff into the harbour-road he himself followed in the same direction.

That her hopes from an advertisement should be the single thread which held Lucy Savile in England was too much for Barnet. On reaching the town he went straight to the residence of Downe, now a widower with four children. The young motherless brood had been sent to bed about a quarter of an hour earlier, and when Barnet entered he found Downe sitting alone.

It was the same room as that from which the family had been looking out for Downe at the beginning of the year, when Downe had slipped into the gutter and his wife had been so enviably tender towards him. The old neatness had gone from the house; articles lay in places which could show no reason for their presence, as if momentarily deposited there some months ago, and forgotten ever since; there were no flowers; things were jumbled together on the furniture which should have been in cupboards; and the place in general had that stagnant, unrenovated air which usually pervades the maimed home of the widower.

Downe soon renewed his customary full-worded lament over his wife, and even when he had worked himself up to tears, went on volubly, as if a listener were a luxury to be enjoyed whenever he could be caught.

'She was a treasure beyond compare, Mr Barnet! I shall never see such another. Nobody now to nurse me – nobody to console me in those daily troubles, you know, Barnet, which makes consolation so necessary to a nature like mine. It would be unbecoming to repine, for her spirit's home was elsewhere – the tender light in her eyes always showed it; but it is a long dreary time that I have before me, and nobody else can ever fill the void left in my heart by her loss – nobody – nobody!' And Downe wiped his eyes again.

'She was a good woman in the highest sense,' gravely answered Barnet, who, though Downe's words drew genuine compassion from his heart, could not help feeling that a tender reticence would have been a finer tribute to Mrs Downe's really sterling virtues than such a second-class lament as this.

'I have something to show you,' Downe resumed, producing from a drawer a sheet of paper on which was an elaborate design for a canopied tomb. 'This has been sent me by the architect, but it is not exactly what I want.'

'You have got Jones to do it, I see, the man who is carrying out my house,' said Barnet, as he glanced at the signature to the drawing.

'Yes, but it is not quite what I want. I want something more striking – more like a tomb I have seen in St Paul's Cathedral. Nothing less will do justice to my feelings, and how far short of them that will fall!'

Barnet privately thought the design a sufficiently imposing one
as it stood, even extravagantly ornate; but, feeling that he had no
right to criticize, he said gently, 'Downe, should you not live
more in your children's lives at the present time, and soften the
sharpness of regret for your own past by thinking of their future?'

'Yes, yes; but what can I do more?' asked Downe, wrinkling his
forehead hopelessly.

It was with anxious slowness that Barnet produced his reply –
the secret object of his visit tonight. 'Did you not say one day that
you ought by rights to get a governess for the children?'

Downe admitted that he had said so, but that he could not see
his way to it. 'The kind of woman I should like to have,' he said,
'would be rather beyond my means. No; I think I shall send them
to school in the town when they are old enough to go out alone.'

'Now, I know of something better than that. The late
Lieutenant Savile's daughter, Lucy, wants to do something for
herself in the way of teaching. She would be inexpensive, and
would answer your purpose as well as anybody for six or twelve
months. She would probably come daily if you were to ask her,
and so your housekeeping arrangements would not be much
affected.'

'I thought she had gone away,' said the solicitor, musing.
'Where does she live?'

Barnet told him, and added that, if Downe should think of her
as suitable, he would do well to call as soon as possible, or she
might be on the wing. 'If you do see her,' he said, 'it would be
advisable not to mention my name. She is rather stiff in her ideas
of me, and it might prejudice her against a course if she knew
that I recommended it.'

Downe promised to give the subject his consideration, and
nothing more was said about it just then. But when Barnet rose
to go, which was not till nearly bedtime, he reminded Downe of
the suggestion and went up the street to his own solitary home
with a sense of satisfaction at his promising diplomacy in a
charitable cause.

The walls of his new house were carried up nearly to their full
height. By a curious though not infrequent reaction, Barnet's
feelings about that unnecessary structure had undergone a
change; he took considerable interest in its progress as a long-

neglected thing, his wife before her departure having grown quite weary of it as a hobby. Moreover, it was an excellent distraction for a man in the unhappy position of having to live in a provincial town with nothing to do. He was probably the first of his line who had ever passed a day without toil, and perhaps something like an inherited instinct disqualifies such men for a life of pleasant inaction, such as lies in the power of those whose leisure is not a personal accident, but a vast historical accretion which has become part of their natures.

Thus Barnet got into a way of spending many of his leisure hours on the site of the new building, and he might have been seen on most days at this time trying the temper of the mortar by punching the joints with his stick, looking at the grain of a floor-board, and meditating where it grew, or picturing under what circumstances the last fire would be kindled in the at present sootless chimneys. One day when thus occupied he saw three children pass by in the company of a fair young woman, whose sudden appearance caused him to flush perceptibly.

'Ah, she is there,' he thought. 'That's a blessed thing.'

Casting an interested glance over the rising building and the busy workmen, Lucy Savile and the little Downes passed by; and after that time it became a regular though almost unconscious custom of Barnet to stand in the half-completed house and look from the ungarnished windows at the governess as she tripped towards the sea-shore with her young charges, which she was in the habit of doing on most fine afternoons. It was on one of these occasions, when he had been loitering on the first-floor landing, near the hole left for the staircase, not yet erected, that there appeared above the edge of the floor a little hat, followed by a little head.

Barnet withdrew through a doorway, and the child came to the top of the ladder, stepping on to the floor and crying to her sisters and Miss Savile to follow. Another head rose above the floor, and another, and then Lucy herself came into view. The troop ran hither and thither through the empty, shaving-strewn rooms, and Barnet came forward.

Lucy uttered a small exclamation: she was very sorry that she had intruded; she had not the least idea that Mr Barnet was there: the children had come up, and she had followed.

Barnet replied that he was only too glad to see them there. 'And now, let me show you the rooms,' he said.

She passively assented, and he took her round. There was not much to show in such a bare skeleton of a house, but he made the most of it, and explained the different ornamental fittings that were soon to be fixed here and there. Lucy made but few remarks in reply, though she seemed pleased with her visit, and stole away down the ladder, followed by her companions.

After this the new residence became yet more of a hobby for Barnet. Downe's children did not forget their first visit, and when the windows were glazed, and the handsome staircase spread its broad low steps into the hall, they came again, prancing in unwearied succession through every room from ground-floor to attics, while Lucy stood waiting for them at the door. Barnet, who rarely missed a day in coming to inspect progress, stepped out from the drawing-room.

'I could not keep them out,' she said, with an apologetic blush. 'I tried to do so very much: but they are rather wilful, and we are directed to walk this way for the sea air.'

'Do let them make the house their regular playground, and you yours,' said Barnet. 'There is no better place for children to romp and take their exercise in than an empty house, particularly in muddy or damp weather such as we shall get a good deal of now; and this place will not be furnished for a long long time – perhaps never. I am not at all decided about it.'

'O, but it must!' replied Lucy, looking round at the hall. 'The rooms are excellent, twice as high as ours; and the views from the windows are so lovely.'

'I daresay, I daresay,' he said absently.

'Will all the furniture be new?' she asked.

'All the furniture be new – that's a thing I have not thought of. In fact I only come here and look on. My father's house would have been large enough for me, but another person had a voice in the matter, and it was settled that we should build. However, the place grows upon me; its recent associations are cheerful, and I am getting to like it fast.'

A certain uneasiness in Lucy's manner showed that the conversation was taking too personal a turn for her. 'Still, as modern tastes develop, people require more room to gratify them in,' she said, withdrawing to call the children; and serenely bidding him good afternoon she went on her way.

Barnet's life at this period was singularly lonely, and yet he was happier than he could have expected. His wife's estrangement and absence, which promised to be permanent, left him free as a boy in his movements, and the solitary walks that he took gave him ample opportunity for chastened reflection on what might have been his lot if he had only shown wisdom enough to claim Lucy Savile when there was no bar between their lives, and she was to be had for the asking. He would occasionally call at the house of his friend Downe; but there was scarcely enough in common between their two natures to make them more than friends of that excellent sort whose personal knowledge of each other's history and character is always in excess of intimacy, whereby they are not so likely to be severed by a clash of sentiment as in cases where intimacy springs up in excess of knowledge. Lucy was never visible at these times, being either engaged in the school-room, or in taking an airing out of doors; but, knowing that she was now comfortable, and had given up the, to him, depressing idea of going off to the other side of the globe, he was quite content.

The new house had so far progressed that the gardeners were beginning to grass down the front. During an afternoon which he was passing in marking the curve for the carriage-drive, he beheld her coming in boldly towards him from the road. Hitherto Barnet had only caught her on the premises by stealth; and this advance seemed to show that at last her reserve had broken down.

A smile gained strength upon her face as she approached, and it was quite radiant when she came up, and said, without a trace of embarrassment, 'I find I owe you a hundred thanks – and it comes to me quite as a surprise! It was through your kindness that I was engaged by Mr Downe. Believe me, Mr Barnet, I did not know it until yesterday, or I should have thanked you long and long ago!'

'I had offended you – just a trifle – at the time, I think?' said Barnet, smiling, 'and it was best that you should not know.'

'Yes, yes,' she returned hastily. 'Don't allude to that; it is past and over, and we will let it be. The house is finished almost, is it not? How beautiful it will look when the evergreens are grown! Do you call the style Palladian, Mr Barnet?'

'I – really don't quite know what it is. Yes, it must be Palladian, certainly. But I'll ask Jones, the architect; for, to tell the truth, I had not thought much about the style: I had nothing to do with choosing it, I am sorry to say.'

She would not let him harp on this gloomy refrain, and talked on bright matters till she said, producing a small roll of paper which he had noticed in her hand all the while, 'Mr Downe wished me to bring you this revised drawing of the late Mrs Downe's tomb, which the architect has just sent him. He would like you to look it over.'

The children came up with their hoops, and she went off with them down the harbour-road as usual. Barnet had been glad to get those words of thanks; he had been thinking for many months that he would like her to know of his share in finding her a home such as it was; and what he could not do for himself, Downe had now kindly done for him. He returned to his desolate house with a lighter tread; though in reason he hardly knew why his tread should be light.

On examining the drawing, Barnet found that, instead of the vast altar-tomb and canopy Downe had determined on at their last meeting, it was to be a more modest memorial even than had been suggested by the architect; a coped tomb of good solid construction, with no useless elaboration at all. Barnet was truly glad to see that Downe had come to reason of his own accord; and he returned the drawing with a note of approval.

He followed up the house-work as before, and as he walked up and down the rooms, occasionally gazing from the windows over the bulging green hills and the quiet harbour that lay between them, he murmured words and fragments of words, which, if listened to, would have revealed all the secrets of his existence. Whatever his reason in going there, Lucy did not call again: the walk to the shore seemed to be abandoned: he must have thought it as well for both that it should be so, for he did not go anywhere out of his accustomed ways to endeavour to discover her.

The winter and the spring had passed, and the house was complete. It was a fine morning in the early part of June, and

Barnet, though not in the habit of rising early, had taken a long walk before breakfast; returning by way of the new building. A sufficiently exciting cause of his restlessness today might have been the intelligence which had reached him the night before, that Lucy Savile was going to India after all, and notwithstanding the representations of her friends that such a journey was unadvisable in many ways for an unpractised girl, unless some more definite advantage lay at the end of it than she could show to be the case. Barnet's walk up the slope to the building betrayed that he was in a dissatisfied mood. He hardly saw that the dewy time of day lent an unusual freshness to the bushes and trees which had so recently put on their summer habit of heavy leafage, and made his newly-laid lawn look as well established as an old manorial meadow. The house had been so adroitly placed between six tall elms which were growing on the site beforehand, that they seemed like real ancestral trees; and the rooks, young and old, cawed melodiously to their visitor.

The door was not locked, and he entered. No workmen appeared to be present, and he walked from sunny window to sunny window of the empty rooms, with a sense of seclusion which might have been very pleasant but for the antecedent knowledge that his almost paternal care of Lucy Savile was to be thrown away by her wilfulness. Footsteps echoed through an adjoining room; and bending his eyes in that direction, he perceived Mr Jones, the architect. He had come to look over the building before giving the contractor his final certificate. They walked over the house together. Everything was finished except the papering: there were the latest improvements of the period in bell-hanging, ventilating, smoke-jacks, fire-grates, and French windows. The business was soon ended, and Jones, having directed Barnet's attention to a book of wall-paper patterns which lay on a bench for his choice, was leaving to keep another engagement, when Barnet said, 'Is the tomb finished yet for Mrs Downe?'

'Well – yes: it is at last,' said the architect, coming back and speaking as if he were in a mood to make a confidence. 'I have had no end of trouble in the matter, and, to tell the truth, I am heartily glad it is over.'

Barnet expressed his surprise. 'I thought poor Downe had given up those extravagant notions of his? Then he has gone

back to the altar and canopy after all? Well, he is to be excused,
poor fellow!'

'O no – he has not at all gone back to them – quite the reverse,'
Jones hastened to say. 'He has so reduced design after design,
that the whole thing has been nothing but waste labour for me;
till in the end it has become a common headstone, which a
mason put up in half a day.'

'A common headstone?' said Barnet.

'Yes. I held out for some time for the addition of a footstone at
least. But he said, "O no – he couldn't afford it."'

'Ah, well – his family is growing up, poor fellow, and his
expenses are getting serious.'

'Yes, exactly,' said Jones, as if the subject were none of his. And
again directing Barnet's attention to the wall-papers, the bustling
architect left him to keep some other engagement.

'A common headstone,' murmured Barnet, left again to
himself. He mused a minute or two, and next began looking over
and selecting from the patterns; but had not long been engaged
in the work when he heard another footstep on the gravel
without, and somebody enter the open porch.

Barnet went to the door – it was his manservant in search of
him.

'I have been trying for some time to find you, sir,' he said. 'This
letter has come by the post, and it is marked immediate. And
there's this one from Mr Downe, who called just now wanting to
see you.' He searched his pocket for the second.

Barnet took the first letter – it had a black border, and bore the
London postmark. It was not in his wife's handwriting, or in that
of any person he knew; but conjecture soon ceased as he read the
page, wherein he was briefly informed that Mrs Barnet had died
suddenly on the previous day, at the furnished villa she had
occupied near London.

Barnet looked vaguely round the empty hall, at the blank
walls, out of the doorway. Drawing a long palpitating breath, and
with eyes downcast, he turned and climbed the stairs slowly, like
a man who doubted their stability. The fact of his wife having, as
it were, died once already, and lived on again, had entirely
dislodged the possibility of her actual death from his conjecture.
He went to the landing, leant over the balusters, and after a
reverie, of whose duration he had but the faintest notion, turned

to the window and stretched his gaze to the cottage further down the road, which was visible from his landing, and from which Lucy still walked to the solicitor's house by a cross path. The faint words that came from his moving lips were simply, 'At last!'

Then, almost involuntarily, Barnet fell down on his knees and murmured some incoherent words of thanksgiving. Surely his virtue in restoring his wife to life had been rewarded! But, as if the impulse struck uneasily on his conscience, he quickly rose, brushed the dust from his trousers, and set himself to think of his next movements. He could not start for London for some hours; and as he had no preparations to make that could not be made in half-an-hour, he mechanically descended and resumed his occupation of turning over the wall-papers. They had all got brighter for him, those papers. It was all changed – who would sit in the rooms that they were to line? He went on to muse upon Lucy's conduct in so frequently coming to the house with the children; her occasional blush in speaking to him; her evident interest in him. What woman can in the long run avoid being interested in a man whom she knows to be devoted to her? If human solicitation could ever effect anything, there should be no going to India for Lucy now. All the papers previously chosen seemed wrong in their shades, and he began from the beginning to choose again.

While entering on the task he heard a forced 'Ahem!' from without the porch, evidently uttered to attract his attention, and footsteps again advancing to the door. His man, whom he had quite forgotten in his mental turmoil, was still waiting there.

'I beg your pardon, sir,' the man said from round the doorway; 'but here's the note from Mr Downe that you didn't take. He called just after you went out, and as he couldn't wait, he wrote this on your study-table.'

He handed in the letter – no black-bordered one now, but a practical-looking note in the well-known writing of the solicitor.

Dear Barnet – it ran – Perhaps you will be prepared for the information I am about to give – that Lucy Savile and myself are going to be married this morning. I have hitherto said nothing as to my intention to any of my friends, for reasons which I am sure you will fully appreciate. The crisis has been brought about by her expressing

her intention to join her brother in India. I then discovered that I
could not do without her.

It is to be quite a private wedding; but it is my particular wish that
you come down here quietly at ten, and go to church with us; it will
add greatly to the pleasure I shall experience in the ceremony, and, I
believe, to Lucy's also. I have called on you very early to make the
request, in the belief that I should find you at home; but you are
beforehand with me in your early rising. – Yours sincerely,

C. DOWNE.

'Need I wait, sir?' said the servant after a dead silence.

'That will do, William. No answer,' said Barnet calmly.

When the man had gone Barnet re-read the letter. Turning
eventually to the wall-papers, which he had been at such pains
to select, he deliberately tore them into halves and quarters, and
threw them into the empty fireplace. Then he went out of the
house, locked the door, and stood in the front awhile. Instead of
returning into the town he went down the harbour-road and
thoughtfully lingered about by the sea, near the spot where the
body of Downe's late wife had been found and brought ashore.

Barnet was a man with a rich capacity for misery, and there is
no doubt that he exercised it to its fullest extent now. The events
that had, as it were, dashed themselves together into one half-
hour of this day showed that curious refinement of cruelty in
their arrangement which often proceeds from the bosom of the
whimsical god at other times known as blind Circumstance. That
his few minutes of hope, between the reading of the first and
second letters, had carried him to extraordinary heights of
rapture was proved by the immensity of his suffering now. The
sun blazing into his face would have shown a close watcher that
a horizontal line, which had never been seen before, but which
was never to be gone thereafter, was somehow gradually forming
itself in the smooth of his forehead. His eyes, of a light hazel, had
a curious look which can only be described by the word bruised;
the sorrow that looked from them being largely mixed with the
surprise of a man taken unawares.

The secondary particulars of his present position, too, were odd
enough, though for some time they appeared to engage little of
his attention. Not a soul in the town knew, as yet, of his wife's
death; and he almost owed Downe the kindness of not publishing

it till the day was over: the conjuncture, taken with that which
had accompanied the death of Mrs Downe, being so singular as to
be quite sufficient to darken the pleasure of the impressionable
solicitor to a cruel extent, if made known to him. But as Barnet
could not set out on his journey to London, where his wife lay,
for some hours (there being at this date no railway within a
distance of many miles), no great reason existed why he should
leave the town.

Impulse in all its forms characterized Barnet, and when he
heard the distant clock strike the hour of ten his feet began to
carry him up the harbour-road with the manner of a man who
must do something to bring himself to life. He passed Lucy
Savile's old house, his own new one, and came in view of the
church. Now he gave a perceptible start, and his mechanical
condition went away. Before the church-gate were a couple of
carriages, and Barnet then could perceive that the marriage
between Downe and Lucy was at that moment being solemnized
within. A feeling of sudden, proud self-confidence, an indocile
wish to walk unmoved in spite of grim environments, plainly
possessed him, and when he reached the wicket-gate he turned
in without apparent effort. Pacing up the paved footway he
entered the church and stood for a while in the nave passage. A
group of people was standing round the vestry door; Barnet
advanced through these and stepped into the vestry.

There they were, busily signing their names. Seeing Downe
about to look round Barnet averted his somewhat disturbed face
for a second or two; when he turned again front to front he was
calm and quite smiling; it was a creditable triumph over himself,
and deserved to be remembered in his native town. He greeted
Downe heartily, offering his congratulations.

It seemed as if Barnet expected a half-guilty look upon Lucy's
face; but no; save the natural flush and flurry engendered by the
service just performed, there was nothing whatever in her
bearing which showed a disturbed mind: her grey-brown eyes
carried in them now as at other times the well-known expression
of common-sensed rectitude which never went so far as to touch
on hardness. She shook hands with him, and Downe said
warmly, 'I wish you could have come sooner: I called on purpose
to ask you. You'll drive back with us now?'

'No, no,' said Barnet; 'I am not at all prepared; but I thought I would look in upon you for a moment, even though I had not time to go home and dress. I'll stand back and see you pass out, and observe the effect of the spectacle upon myself as one of the public.'

Then Lucy and her husband laughed, and Barnet laughed and retired; and the quiet little party went gliding down the nave and towards the porch, Lucy's new silk dress sweeping with a smart rustle round the base-mouldings of the ancient font, and Downe's little daughters following in a state of round-eyed interest in their position, and that of Lucy, their teacher and friend.

So Downe was comforted after his Emily's death, which had taken place twelve months, two weeks, and three days before that time.

When the two flys had driven off and the spectators had vanished, Barnet followed to the door, and went out into the sun. He took no more trouble to preserve a spruce exterior; his step was unequal, hesitating, almost convulsive; and the slight changes of colour which went on in his face seemed refracted from some inward flame. In the churchyard he became pale as a summer cloud, and finding it not easy to proceed he sat down on one of the tombstones and supported his head with his hand.

Hard by was a sexton filling up a grave which he had not found time to finish on the previous evening. Observing Barnet, he went up to him, and recognizing him, said, 'Shall I help you home, sir?'

'O no, thank you,' said Barnet, rousing himself and standing up. The sexton returned to his grave, followed by Barnet, who, after watching him awhile, stepped into the grave, now nearly filled, and helped to tread in the earth.

The sexton apparently thought his conduct a little singular, but he made no observation, and when the grave was full, Barnet suddenly stopped, looked far away, and with a decided step proceeded to the gate and vanished. The sexton rested on his shovel and looked after him for a few moments, and then began banking up the mound.

In those short minutes of treading in the dead man Barnet had formed a design, but what it was the inhabitants of that town did not for some long time imagine. He went home, wrote several letters of business, called on his lawyer, an old man of the same place who had been the legal adviser of Barnet's father before

him, and during the evening overhauled a large quantity of
letters and other documents in his possession. By eleven o'clock
the heap of papers in and before Barnet's grate had reached
formidable dimensions, and he began to burn them. This, owing
to their quantity, it was not so easy to do as he had expected, and
he sat long into the night to complete the task.

The next morning Barnet departed for London, leaving a note
for Downe to inform him of Mrs Barnet's sudden death, and that
he was gone to bury her; but when a thrice-sufficient time for
that purpose had elapsed, he was not seen again in his
accustomed walks, or in his new house, or in his old one. He was
gone for good, nobody knew whither. It was soon discovered that
he had empowered his lawyer to dispose of all his property, real
and personal, in the borough, and pay in the proceeds to the
account of an unknown person at one of the large London banks.
The person was by some supposed to be himself under an
assumed name; but few, if any, had certain knowledge of that
fact.

The elegant new residence was sold with the rest of his
possessions; and its purchaser was no other than Downe, now a
thriving man in the borough, and one whose growing family and
new wife required more roomy accommodation than was
afforded by the little house up the narrow side street. Barnet's old
habitation was bought by the trustees of the Congregational
Baptist body in that town, who pulled down the time-honoured
dwelling and built a new chapel on its site. By the time the last
hour of that, to Barnet, eventful year had chimed, every vestige
of him had disappeared from the precincts of his native place, and
the name became extinct in the borough of Port-Bredy, after
having been a living force therein for more than two hundred
years.

Twenty-one years and six months do not pass without setting a
mark even upon durable stone and triple brass; upon humanity
such a period works nothing less than transformation. In
Barnet's old birthplace vivacious young children with bones like
India-rubber had grown up to be stable men and women, men
and women had dried in the skin, stiffened, withered, and sunk
into decrepitude; while selections from every class had been
consigned to the outlying cemetery. Of inorganic differences the

greatest was that a railway had invaded the town, tying it on to a
main line at a junction a dozen miles off. Barnet's house on the
harbour-road, once so insistently new, had acquired a respectable
mellowness, with ivy, Virginia creepers, lichens, damp patches,
and even constitutional infirmities of its own like its elder fellows.
Its architecture, once so very improved and modern, had already
become stale in style, without having reached the dignity of
being old-fashioned. Trees about the harbour-road had increased
in circumference or disappeared under the saw; while the church
had had such a tremendous practical joke played upon it by some
facetious restorer or other as to be scarce recognizable by its
dearest old friends.

During this long interval George Barnet had never once been
seen or heard of in the town of his fathers.

It was the evening of a market-day, and some half-dozen
middle-aged farmers and dairymen were lounging round the bar
of the Black-Bull Hotel, occasionally dropping a remark to each
other, and less frequently to the two barmaids who stood within
the pewter-topped counter in a perfunctory attitude of attention,
these latter sighing and making a private observation to one
another at odd intervals, on more interesting experiences than
the present.

'Days get shorter,' said one of the dairymen, as he looked
towards the street, and noticed that the lamplighter was passing
by.

The farmers merely acknowledged by their countenances the
propriety of this remark, and finding that nobody else spoke, one
of the barmaids said 'yes' in a tone of painful duty.

'Come fair-day we shall have to light up before we start for
home-along.'

'That's true,' his neighbour conceded, with a gaze of blank-
ness.

'And after that we shan't see much further difference all's
winter.'

The rest were not unwilling to go even so far as this.

The barmaid sighed again, and raised one of her hands from
the counter on which they rested to scratch the smallest surface
of her face with the smallest of her fingers. She looked towards
the door, and presently remarked, 'I think I hear the bus coming
in from station.'

The eyes of the dairymen and farmers turned to the glass door dividing the hall from the porch, and in a minute or two the omnibus drew up outside. Then there was a lumbering down of luggage, and then a man came into the hall, followed by a porter with a portmanteau on his poll, which he deposited on a bench.

The stranger was an elderly person, with curly ashen-white hair, a deeply-creviced outer corner to each eyelid, and a countenance baked by innumerable suns to the colour of terracotta, its hue and that of his hair contrasting like heat and cold respectively. He walked meditatively and gently, like one who was fearful of disturbing his own mental equilibrium. But whatever lay at the bottom of his breast had evidently made him so accustomed to its situation there that it caused him little practical inconvenience.

He paused in silence while, with his dubious eyes fixed on the barmaids, he seemed to consider himself. In a moment or two he addressed them, and asked to be accommodated for the night. As he waited he looked curiously round the hall, but said nothing. As soon as invited he disappeared up the staircase, preceded by a chambermaid and candle, and followed by a lad with his trunk. Not a soul had recognized him.

A quarter of an hour later, when the farmers and dairymen had driven off to their homesteads in the country, he came downstairs, took a biscuit and one glass of wine, and walked out into the town, where the radiance from the shop-windows had grown so in volume of late years as to flood with cheerfulness every standing cart, barrow, stall, and idler that occupied the wayside, whether shabby or genteel. His chief interest at present seemed to lie in the names painted over the shop-fronts and on doorways, as far as they were visible; these now differed to an ominous extent from what they had been one-and-twenty years before.

The traveller passed on till he came to the bookseller's, where he looked in through the glass door. A fresh-faced young man was standing behind the counter, otherwise the shop was empty. The grey-haired observer entered, asked for some periodical by way of paying for admission, and with his elbow on the counter began to turn over the pages he had bought, though that he read nothing was obvious.

At length he said, 'Is old Mr Watkins still alive?' in a voice which had a curious youthful cadence in it even now.

'My father is dead, sir,' said the young man.

'Ah, I am sorry to hear it,' said the stranger. 'But it is so many years since I last visited this town that I could hardly expect it should be otherwise.' After a short silence he continued – 'And is the firm of Barnet, Browse, and Company still in existence? – they used to be large flax-merchants and twine-spinners here?'

'The firm is still going on, sir, but they have dropped the name of Barnet. I believe that was a sort of fancy name – at least, I never knew of any living Barnet. 'Tis now Browse and Co.'

'And does Andrew Jones still keep on as architect?'

'He's dead, sir.'

'And the vicar of St Mary's – Mr Melrose?'

'He's been dead a great many years.'

'Dear me!' He paused yet longer, and cleared his voice. 'Is Mr Downe, the solicitor, still in practice?'

'No, sir, he's dead. He died about seven years ago.'

Here it was a longer silence still; and an attentive observer would have noticed that the paper in the stranger's hand increased its imperceptible tremor to a visible shake. That grey-haired gentleman noticed it himself, and rested the paper on the counter. 'Is *Mrs* Downe still alive?' he asked, closing his lips firmly as soon as the words were out of his mouth, and dropping his eyes.

'Yes, sir, she's alive and well. She's living at the old place.'

'In East Street?'

'O no; at Château Ringdale. I believe it has been in the family for some generations.'

'She lives with her children, perhaps?'

'No; she has no children of her own. There were some Miss Downes; I think they were Mr Downe's daughters by a former wife; but they are married and living in other parts of the town. Mrs Downe lives alone.'

'Quite alone?'

'Yes, sir; quite alone.'

The newly-arrived gentleman went back to the hotel and dined; after which he made some change in his dress, shaved back his beard to the fashion that had prevailed twenty years earlier, when he was young and interesting, and once more emerging, bent his steps in the direction of the harbour-road. Just before getting to the point where the pavement ceased and the houses isolated themselves, he overtook a shambling, stooping, unshaven man, who at first sight appeared like a professional tramp, his shoulders having a perceptible greasiness as they passed under the gaslight. Each pedestrian momentarily turned and regarded the other, and the tramp-like gentleman started back.

'Good – why – is that Mr Barnet? 'Tis Mr Barnet, surely!'

'Yes; and you are Charlson?'

'Yes – ah – you notice my appearance. The Fates have rather ill-used me. By the bye, that fifty pounds. I never paid it, did I? ... But I was not ungrateful!' Here the stooping man laid one hand emphatically on the palm of the other. 'I gave you a chance, Mr George Barnet, which many men would have thought full value received – the chance to marry your Lucy. As far as the world was concerned, your wife was a *drowned woman*, hey?'

'Heaven forbid all that, Charlson!'

'Well, well, 'twas a wrong way of showing gratitude, I suppose. And now a drop of something to drink for old acquaintance' sake! And Mr Barnet, she's again free – there's a chance now if you care for it – ha, ha!' And the speaker pushed his tongue into his hollow cheek and slanted his eye in the old fashion.

'I know all,' said Barnet quickly; and slipping a small present into the hands of the needy, saddening man, he stepped ahead and was soon in the outskirts of the town.

He reached the harbour-road, and paused before the entrance to a well-known house. It was so highly bosomed in trees and shrubs planted since the erection of the building that one would scarcely have recognized the spot as that which had been a mere neglected slope till chosen as a site for a dwelling. He opened the swing-gate, closed it noiselessly, and gently moved into the semicircular drive, which remained exactly as it had been marked out by Barnet on the morning when Lucy Savile ran in to thank him for procuring her the post of governess to Downe's children. But the growth of trees and bushes which revealed itself at every step was beyond all expectation; sun-proof and moon-proof bowers vaulted the walks, and the walls of the house were uniformly bearded with creeping plants as high as the first-floor windows.

After lingering for a few minutes in the dusk of the bending boughs, the visitor rang the door-bell, and on the servant appearing, he announced himself as 'an old friend of Mrs Downe's'.

The hall was lighted, but not brightly, the gas being turned low, as if visitors were rare. There was a stagnation in the dwelling; it seemed to be waiting. Could it really be waiting for him? The partitions which had been probed by Barnet's walking-stick when the mortar was green, were now quite brown with the antiquity of their varnish, and the ornamental woodwork of the staircase, which had glistened with a pale yellow newness when first erected, was now of a rich wine-colour. During the servant's absence the following colloquy could be dimly heard through the nearly closed door of the drawing-room.

'He didn't give his name?'

'He only said "an old friend", ma'am.'

'What kind of gentleman is he?'

'A staidish gentleman, with grey hair.'

The voice of the second speaker seemed to affect the listener greatly. After a pause, the lady said, 'Very well, I will see him.'

And the stranger was shown in face to face with the Lucy who had once been Lucy Savile. The round cheek of that formerly young lady had, of course, alarmingly flattened its curve in her modern representative; a pervasive greyness overspread her once dark-brown hair, like morning rime on heather. The parting down the middle was wide and jagged; once it had been a thin white line, a narrow crevice between two high banks of shade. But there was still enough left to form a handsome knob behind, and some curls beneath inwrought with a few hairs like silver wires were very becoming. In her eyes the only modification was that their originally mild rectitude of expression had become a little more stringent than heretofore. Yet she was still girlish – a girl who had been gratuitously weighted by destiny with a burden of five-and-forty years instead of her proper twenty.

'Lucy, don't you know me?' he said, when the servant had closed the door.

'I knew you the instant I saw you!' she returned cheerfully. 'I don't know why, but I always thought you would come back to your old town again.'

She gave him her hand, and then sat down. 'They said you

were dead,' continued Lucy, 'but I never thought so. We should have heard of it for certain if you had been.'

'It is a very long time since we met.'

'Yes; what you must have seen, Mr Barnet, in all these roving years, in comparison with what I have seen in this quiet place!' Her face grew more serious. 'You know my husband has been dead a long time? I am a lonely old woman now, considering what I have been; though Mr Downe's daughters – all married – manage to keep me pretty cheerful.'

'And I am a lonely old man, and have been any time these twenty years.'

'But where have you kept yourself? And why did you go off so mysteriously?'

'Well, Lucy, I have kept myself a little in America, and a little in Australia, a little in India, a little at the Cape, and so on; I have not stayed in any place for a long time, as it seems to me, and yet more than twenty years have flown. But when people get to my age two years go like one! – Your second question, why did I go away so mysteriously, is surely not necessary. You guessed why, didn't you?'

'No, I never once guessed,' she said simply; 'nor did Charles, nor did anybody as far as I know.'

'Well, indeed! Now think it over again, and then look at me, and say if you can't guess?'

She looked him in the face with an inquiring smile. 'Surely not because of me?' she said, pausing at the commencement of surprise.

Barnet nodded, and smiled again; but his smile was sadder than hers.

'Because I married Charles?' she asked.

'Yes; solely because you married him on the day I was free to ask you to marry me. My wife died four-and-twenty hours before you went to church with Downe. The fixing of my journey at that particular moment was because of her funeral; but once away I knew I should have no inducement to come back, and took my steps accordingly.'

Her face assumed an aspect of gentle reflection, and she looked up and down his form with great interest in her eyes. 'I never thought of it!' she said. 'I knew, of course, that you had once implied some warmth of feeling towards me, but I concluded that it passed off. And I have always been under the impression that your wife was alive at the time of my marriage. Was it not stupid of me! – But you will have some tea or something? I have never dined late, you know, since my husband's death. I have got into the way of making a regular meal of tea. You will have some tea with me, will you not?'

The travelled man assented quite readily, and tea was brought in. They sat and chatted over the tray, regardless of the flying hour. 'Well, well!' said Barnet presently, as for the first time he leisurely surveyed the room; 'how like it all is, and yet how different! Just where your piano stands was a board on a couple of trestles, bearing the patterns of wall-papers, when I was last here. I was choosing them – standing in this way, as it might be. Then my servant came in at the door, and handed me a note, so. It was from Downe, and announced that you were just going to be married to him. I chose no more wall-papers – tore up all those I had selected, and left the house. I never entered it again till now.'

'Ah, at last I understand it all,' she murmured.

They had both risen and gone to the fireplace. The mantel came almost on a level with her shoulder, which gently rested against it, and Barnet laid his hand upon the shelf close beside her shoulder. 'Lucy,' he said, 'better late than never. Will you marry me now?'

She started back, and the surprise which was so obvious in her wrought even greater surprise in him that it should be so. It was difficult to believe that she had been quite blind to the situation, and yet all reason and common sense went to prove that she was not acting.

'You take me quite unawares by such a question!' she said, with a forced laugh of uneasiness. It was the first time she had shown any embarrassment at all. 'Why,' she added, 'I couldn't marry you for the world.'

'Not after all this! Why not?'

'It is – I would – I really think I may say it – I would upon the whole rather marry you, Mr Barnet, than any other man I have ever met, if I ever dreamed of marriage again. But I don't dream of it – it is quite out of my thoughts; I have not the least intention of marrying again.'

'But – on my account – couldn't you alter your plans a little? Come!'

'Dear Mr Barnet,' she said with a little flutter, 'I would on your account if on anybody's in existence. But you don't know in the least what it is you are asking – such an impracticable thing – I won't say ridiculous, of course, because I see that you are really in earnest, and earnestness is never ridiculous to my mind.'

'Well, yes,' said Barnet more slowly, dropping her hand, which he had taken at the moment of pleading, 'I am in earnest. The resolve, two months ago, at the Cape, to come back once more was, it is true, rather sudden, and as I see now, not well considered. But I am in earnest in asking.'

'And I in declining. With all good feeling and all kindness, let me say that I am quite opposed to the idea of marrying a second time.'

'Well, no harm has been done,' he answered, with the same subdued and tender humorousness that he had shown on such occasions in early life. 'If you really won't accept me, I must put up with it, I suppose.' His eye fell on the clock as he spoke. 'Had you any notion that it was so late?' he asked. 'How absorbed I have been!'

She accompanied him to the hall, helped him to put on his overcoat, and let him out of the house herself.

'Good-night,' said Barnet, on the doorstep, as the lamp shone in his face. 'You are not offended with me?'

'Certainly not. Nor you with me?'

'I'll consider whether I am or not,' he pleasantly replied. 'Good-night.'

She watched him safely through the gate; and when his footsteps had died away upon the road, closed the door softly and returned to the room. Here the modest widow long pondered his speeches, with eyes dropped to an unusually low level. Barnet's urbanity under the blow of her refusal greatly impressed her. After having his long period of probation rendered useless by her decision, he had shown no anger, and had philosophically taken her words as if he deserved no better ones. It was very gentlemanly of him, certainly; it was more than gentlemanly; it was heroic and grand. The more she meditated, the more she questioned the virtue of her conduct in checking him so peremptorily; and went to her bedroom in a mood of dissatisfaction. On looking in the glass she was reminded that there was not so much remaining of her former beauty as to make his frank declaration an impulsive natural homage to her cheeks and eyes; it must undoubtedly have arisen from an old staunch feeling of his, deserving tenderest consideration. She recalled to her mind with much pleasure that he had told her he was staying at the Black-Bull Hotel; so that if, after waiting a day or two, he should not, in his modesty, call again, she might then send him a nice little note. To alter her views for the present was far from her intention; but she would allow herself to be induced to reconsider the case, as any generous woman ought to do.

The morrow came and passed, and Mr Barnet did not drop in. At every knock, light youthful hues flew across her cheek; and she was abstracted in the presence of her other visitors. In the evening she walked about the house, not knowing what to do with herself; the conditions of existence seemed totally different from those which ruled only four-and-twenty short hours ago. What had been at first a tantalizing elusive sentiment was getting acclimatized within her as a definite hope, and her person was so informed by that emotion that she might almost have stood as its emblematical representative by the time the clock struck ten. In short, an interest in Barnet precisely resembling that of her early youth led her present heart to belie her yesterday's words to him, and she longed to see him again.

The next day she walked out early, thinking she might meet him in the street. The growing beauty of her romance absorbed her, and she went from the street to the fields, and from the fields to the shore, without any consciousness of distance, till reminded by her weariness that she could go no further. He had nowhere appeared. In the evening she took a step which under the circumstances seemed justifiable; she wrote a note to him at the hotel, inviting him to tea with her at six precisely, and signing her note 'Lucy'.

In a quarter of an hour the messenger came back. Mr Barnet had left the hotel early in the morning of the day before, but he had stated that he would probably return in the course of the week.

The note was sent back, to be given to him immediately on his arrival.

There was no sign from the inn that this desired event had occurred, either on the next day or the day following. On both nights she had been restless, and had scarcely slept half-an-hour.

On the Saturday, putting off all diffidence, Lucy went herself to the Black-Bull, and questioned the staff closely.

Mr Barnet had cursorily remarked when leaving that he might return on the Thursday or Friday, but they were directed not to reserve a room for him unless he should write.

He had left no address.

Lucy sorrowfully took back her note, went home, and resolved to wait.

She did wait – years and years – but Barnet never reappeared.

The Melancholy Hussar of the
German Legion

I

Here stretch the downs, high and breezy and green, absolutely
unchanged since those eventful days. A plough has never
disturbed the turf, and the sod that was uppermost then is
uppermost now. Here stood the camp; here are distinct traces of
the banks thrown up for the horses of the cavalry, and spots
where the midden-heaps lay are still to be observed. At night,
when I walk across the lonely place, it is impossible to avoid
hearing, amid the scourings of the wind over the grass-bents and
thistles, the old trumpet and bugle calls, the rattle of the halters;
to help seeing rows of spectral tents and the *impedimenta* of the
soldiery. From within the canvases come guttural syllables of
foreign tongues, and broken songs of the fatherland; for they
were mainly regiments of the King's German Legion that slept
round the tent-poles hereabouts at that time.

It was nearly ninety years ago. The British uniform of the
period, with its immense epaulettes, queer cocked-hat, breeches,
gaiters, ponderous cartridge-box, buckled shoes, and what not,
would look strange and barbarous now. Ideas have changed;
invention has followed invention. Soldiers were monumental
objects then. A divinity still hedged kings here and there; and
war was considered a glorious thing.

Secluded old manor-houses and hamlets lie in the ravines and
hollows among these hills, where a stranger had hardly ever
been seen till the King chose to take the baths yearly at the sea-
side watering-place a few miles to the south; as a consequence of
which battalions descended in a cloud upon the open country
around. Is it necessary to add that the echoes of many
characteristic tales, dating from that picturesque time, still linger
about here in more or less fragmentary form, to be caught by the
attentive ear? Some of them I have repeated; most of them I have
forgotten; one I have never repeated, and assuredly can never
forget.

Phyllis told me the story with her own lips. She was then an old lady of seventy-five, and her auditor a lad of fifteen. She enjoined silence as to her share in the incident, till she should be 'dead, buried, and forgotten'. Her life was prolonged twelve years after the day of her narration, and she has now been dead nearly twenty. The oblivion which in her modesty and humility she courted for herself has only partially fallen on her, with the unfortunate result of inflicting an injustice upon her memory; since such fragments of her story as got abroad at the time, and have been kept alive ever since, are precisely those which are most unfavourable to her character.

It all began with the arrival of the York Hussars, one of the foreign regiments above alluded to. Before that day scarcely a soul had been seen near her father's house for weeks. When a noise like the brushing skirt of a visitor was heard on the doorstep, it proved to be a scudding leaf; when a carriage seemed to be nearing the door, it was her father grinding his sickle on the stone in the garden for his favourite relaxation of trimming the box-tree borders to the plots. A sound like luggage thrown down from the coach was a gun far away at sea; and what looked like a tall man by the gate at dusk was a yew bush cut into a quaint and attenuated shape. There is no such solitude in country places now as there was in those old days.

Yet all the while King George and his Court were at his favourite sea-side resort, not more than five miles off.

The daughter's seclusion was great, but beyond the seclusion of the girl lay the seclusion of the father. If her social condition was twilight, his was darkness. Yet he enjoyed his darkness, while her twilight oppressed her. Dr Grove had been a professional man whose taste for lonely meditation over metaphysical questions had diminished his practice till it no longer paid him to keep it going; after which he had relinquished it and hired at a nominal rent the small, dilapidated, half farm, half manor-house of this obscure inland nook, to make a sufficiency of an income which in a town would have been inadequate for their maintenance. He stayed in his garden the greater part of the day, growing more and more irritable with the lapse of time, and the increasing perception that he had wasted his life in the pursuit of illusions. He saw his friends less and less frequently. Phyllis became so shy that if she met a stranger anywhere in her short rambles she felt ashamed at his gaze, walked awkwardly, and blushed to her shoulders.

Yet Phyllis was discovered even here by an admirer, and her hand most unexpectedly asked in marriage.

The King, as aforesaid, was at the neighbouring town, where he had taken up his abode at Gloucester Lodge; and his presence in the town naturally brought many county people thither. Among these idlers – many of whom professed to have connections and interests with the Court – was one Humphrey Gould, a bachelor; a personage neither young nor old; neither good-looking nor positively plain. Too steady-going to be 'a buck' (as fast and unmarried men were then called), he was an approximately fashionable man of a mild type. This bachelor of thirty found his way to the village on the down: beheld Phyllis; made her father's acquaintance in order to make hers; and by some means or other she sufficiently inflamed his heart to lead him in that direction almost daily; till he became engaged to marry her.

As he was of an old local family, some of whose members were held in respect in the county, Phyllis, in bringing him to her feet, had accomplished what was considered a brilliant move for one in her constrained position. How she had done it was not quite known to Phyllis herself. In those days unequal marriages were regarded rather as a violation of the laws of nature than as a mere infringement of convention, the more modern view, and hence when Phyllis, of the watering-place *bourgeoisie*, was chosen by such a gentlemanly fellow, it was as if she were going to be taken to heaven, though perhaps the uninformed would have seen no great difference in the respective positions of the pair, the said Gould being as poor as a crow.

This pecuniary condition was his excuse – probably a true one – for postponing their union, and as the winter drew nearer, and the King departed for the season, Mr Humphrey Gould set out for Bath, promising to return to Phyllis in a few weeks. The winter arrived, the date of his promise passed, yet Gould postponed his coming, on the ground that he could not very easily leave his father in the city of their sojourn, the elder having no other relative near him. Phyllis, though lonely in the extreme, was content. The man who had asked her in marriage was a desirable husband for her in many ways; her father highly approved of his suit; but this neglect of her was awkward, if not painful, for

Phyllis. Love him in the true sense of the word she assured me she never did, but she had a genuine regard for him; admired a certain methodical and dogged way in which he sometimes took his pleasure; valued his knowledge of what the Court was doing, had done, or was about to do; and she was not without a feeling of pride that he had chosen her when he might have exercised a more ambitious choice.

But he did not come; and the spring developed. His letters were regular though formal; and it is not to be wondered that the uncertainty of her position, linked with the fact that there was not much passion in her thoughts of Humphrey, bred an indescribable dreariness in the heart of Phyllis Grove. The spring was soon summer, and the summer brought the King; but still no Humphrey Gould. All this while the engagement by letter was maintained intact.

At this point of time a golden radiance flashed in upon the lives of people here, and charged all youthful thought with emotional interest. This radiance was the aforesaid York Hussars.

II

The present generation has probably but a very dim notion of the celebrated York Hussars of ninety years ago. They were one of the regiments of the King's German Legion, and (though they somewhat degenerated later on) their brilliant uniform, their splendid horses, and above all, their foreign air and mustachios (rare appendages then), drew crowds of admirers of both sexes wherever they went. These with other regiments had come to encamp on the downs and pastures, because of the presence of the King in the neighbouring town.

The spot was high and airy, and the view extensive, commanding Portland – the Isle of Slingers – in front, and reaching to St Aldhelm's Head eastward, and almost to the Start on the west.

Phyllis, though not precisely a girl of the village, was as interested as any of them in this military investment. Her father's home stood somewhat apart, and on the highest point of ground to which the lane ascended, so that it was almost level with the top of the church tower in the lower part of the parish. Immediately from the outside of the garden-wall the grass spread away to a great distance, and it was crossed by a path which

came close to the wall. Ever since her childhood it had been
Phyllis's pleasure to clamber up this fence and sit on the top – a
feat not so difficult as it may seem, the walls in this district being
built of rubble, without mortar, so that there were plenty of
crevices for small toes.

She was sitting up here one day, listlessly surveying the
pasture without, when her attention was arrested by a solitary
figure walking along the path. It was one of the renowned
German Hussars, and he moved onward with his eyes on the
ground, and with the manner of one who wished to escape
company. His head would probably have been bent like his eyes
but for his stiff neck-gear. On nearer view she perceived that his
face was marked with deep sadness. Without observing her, he
advanced by the footpath till it brought him almost immediately
under the wall.

Phyllis was much surprised to see a fine, tall soldier in such a
mood as this. Her theory of the military, and of the York Hussars
in particular (derived entirely from hearsay, for she had never
talked to a soldier in her life), was that their hearts were as gay as
their accoutrements.

At this moment the Hussar lifted his eyes and noticed her on
her perch, the white muslin neckerchief which covered her
shoulders and neck where left bare by her low gown, and her
white raiment in general, showing conspicuously in the bright
sunlight of this summer day. He blushed a little at the suddenness
of the encounter, and without halting a moment from his pace
passed on.

All that day the foreigner's face haunted Phyllis; its aspect was
so striking, so handsome, and his eyes were so blue, and sad, and
abstracted. It was perhaps only natural that on some following
day at the same hour she should look over that wall again, and
wait till he had passed a second time. On this occasion he was
reading a letter, and at the sight of her his manner was that of
one who had half expected or hoped to discover her. He almost
stopped, smiled, and made a courteous salute. The end of the
meeting was that they exchanged a few words. She asked him
what he was reading, and he readily informed her that he was re-
perusing letters from his mother in Germany; he did not get them
often, he said, and was forced to read the old ones a great many

times. This was all that passed at the present interview, but others of the same kind followed.

Phyllis used to say that his English, though not good, was quite intelligible to her, so that their acquaintance was never hindered by difficulties of speech. Whenever the subject became too delicate, subtle, or tender, for such words of English as were at his command, the eyes no doubt helped out the tongue, and – though this was later on – the lips helped out the eyes. In short, this acquaintance, unguardedly made, and rash enough on her part, developed and ripened. Like Desdemona, she pitied him, and learnt his history.

His name was Matthäus Tina, and Saarbrück his native town, where his mother was still living. His age was twenty-two, and he had already risen to the grade of corporal, though he had not long been in the army. Phyllis used to assert that no such refined or well-educated young man could have been found in the ranks of the purely English regiments, some of these foreign soldiers having rather the graceful manner and presence of our native officers than of our rank and file.

She by degrees learnt from her foreign friend a circumstance about himself and his comrades which Phyllis would least have expected from the York Hussars. So far from being as gay as its uniform, the regiment was pervaded by a dreadful melancholy, a chronic home-sickness, which depressed many of the men to such an extent that they could hardly attend to their drill. The worst sufferers were the younger soldiers who had not been over here long. They hated England and English life; they took no interest whatever in King George and his island kingdom, and they only wished to be out of it and never to see it any more. Their bodies were here, but their hearts and minds were always far away in their dear fatherland, of which – brave men and stoical as they were in many ways – they would speak with tears in their eyes. One of the worst of the sufferers from his home-woe, as he called it in his own tongue, was Matthäus Tina, whose dreamy musing nature felt the gloom of exile still more intensely from the fact that he had left a lonely mother at home with nobody to cheer her.

Though Phyllis, touched by all this, and interested in his history, did not disdain her soldier's acquaintance, she declined (according to her own account, at least) to permit the young man to overstep the line of mere friendship for a long while – as long, indeed, as she considered herself likely to become the possession of another; though it is probable that she had lost her heart to Matthäus before she was herself aware. The stone wall of necessity made anything like intimacy difficult; and he had never ventured to come, or to ask to come, inside the garden, so that all their conversation had been overtly conducted across this boundary.

III

But news reached the village from a friend of Phyllis's father concerning Mr Humphrey Gould, her remarkably cool and patient betrothed. This gentleman had been heard to say in Bath that he considered his overtures to Miss Phyllis Grove to have reached only the stage of a half-understanding; and in view of his enforced absence on his father's account, who was too great an invalid now to attend to his affairs, he thought it best that there should be no definite promise as yet on either side. He was not sure, indeed, that he might not cast his eyes elsewhere.

This account – though only a piece of hearsay, and as such entitled to no absolute credit – tallied so well with the infrequency of his letters and their lack of warmth, that Phyllis did not doubt its truth for one moment; and from that hour she felt herself free to bestow her heart as she should choose. Not so her father; he declared the whole story to be a fabrication. He had known Mr Gould's family from his boyhood; and if there was one proverb which expressed the matrimonial aspect of that family well, it was 'Love me little, love me long'. Humphrey was an honourable man, who would not think of treating his engagement so lightly. 'Do you wait in patience,' he said; 'all will be right enough in time.'

From these words Phyllis at first imagined that her father was in correspondence with Mr Gould; and her heart sank within her; for in spite of her original intentions she had been relieved to hear that her engagement had come to nothing. But she presently learnt that her father had heard no more of Humphrey Gould than she herself had done; while he would not write and address her affianced directly on the subject, lest it should be deemed an imputation on that bachelor's honour.

'You want an excuse for encouraging one or other of those foreign fellows to flatter you with his unmeaning attentions,' her father exclaimed, his mood having of late been a very unkind one towards her. 'I see more than I say. Don't you ever set foot outside that garden-fence without my permission. If you want to see the camp I'll take you myself some Sunday afternoon.'

Phyllis had not the smallest intention of disobeying him in her actions, but she assumed herself to be independent with respect to her feelings. She no longer checked her fancy for the Hussar, though she was far from regarding him as her lover in the serious sense in which an Englishman might have been regarded as such. The young foreign soldier was almost an ideal being to her, with none of the appurtenances of an ordinary house-dweller; one who had descended she knew not whence, and would disappear she knew not whither; the subject of a fascinating dream – no more.

They met continually now – mostly at dusk – during the brief interval between the going down of the sun and the minute at which the last trumpet-call summoned him to his tent. Perhaps her manner had become less restrained latterly; at any rate that of the Hussar was so; he had grown more tender every day, and at parting after these hurried interviews she reached down her hand from the top of the wall that he might press it. One evening he held it such a while that she exclaimed, 'The wall is white, and somebody in the field may see your shape against it!'

He lingered so long that night that it was with the greatest difficulty that he could run across the intervening stretch of ground and enter the camp in time. On the next occasion of his awaiting her she did not appear in her usual place at the usual hour. His disappointment was unspeakably keen; he remained staring blankly at the spot, like a man in a trance. The trumpets and tattoo sounded, and still he did not go.

She had been delayed purely by an accident. When she arrived she was anxious because of the lateness of the hour, having heard as well as he the sounds denoting the closing of the camp. She implored him to leave immediately.

'No,' he said gloomily. 'I shall not go in yet – the moment you come – I have thought of your coming all day.'

'But you may be disgraced at being after time?'

'I don't mind that. I should have disappeared from the world some time ago if it had not been for two persons – my beloved, here, and my mother in Saarbrück. I hate the army. I care more for a minute of your company than for all the promotion in the world.'

Thus he stayed and talked to her, and told her interesting details of his native place, and incidents of his childhood, till she was in a simmer of distress at his recklessness in remaining. It was only because she insisted on bidding him good-night, and leaving the wall, that he returned to his quarters.

The next time that she saw him he was without the stripes that had adorned his sleeve. He had been broken to the level of private for his lateness that night; and as Phyllis considered herself to be the cause of his disgrace her sorrow was great. But the position was now reversed; it was his turn to cheer her.

'Don't grieve, meine Liebliche!' he said. 'I have got a remedy for whatever comes. First, even supposing I regain my stripes, would your father allow you to marry a non-commissioned officer in the York Hussars?'

She flushed. This practical step had not been in her mind in relation to such an unrealistic person as he was; and a moment's reflection was enough for it. 'My father would not – certainly would not,' she answered unflinchingly. 'It cannot be thought of! My dear friend, please do forget me: I fear I am ruining you and your prospects!'

'Not at all!' said he. 'You are giving this country of yours just sufficient interest to me to make me care to keep alive in it. If my dear land were here also, and my old parent, with you, I could be happy as I am, and would do my best as a soldier. But it is not so. And now listen. This is my plan. That you go with me to my own country, and be my wife there, and live there with my mother and me. I am not a Hanoverian, as you know, though I entered the army as such; my country is by the Saar, and is at peace with France, and if I were once in it I should be free.'

'But how get there?' she asked. Phyllis had been rather amazed than shocked at his proposition. Her position in her father's house was growing irksome and painful in the extreme; his parental affection seemed to be quite dried up. She was not a native of the village, like all the joyous girls around her; and in some way Matthäus Tina had infected her with his own passionate longing for his country, and mother, and home.

'But how?' she repeated, finding that he did not answer. 'Will you buy your discharge?'

'Ah, no,' he said. 'That's impossible in these times. No; I came here against my will; why should I not escape? Now is the time, as we shall soon be striking camp, and I might see you no more. This is my scheme. I will ask you to meet me on the highway two miles off, on some calm night next week that may be appointed. There will be nothing unbecoming in it, or to cause you shame; you will not fly alone with me, for I will bring with me my devoted young friend, Christoph, an Alsatian, who has lately joined the regiment, and who has agreed to assist in this enterprise. We shall have come from yonder harbour, where we shall have examined the boats, and found one suited to our purpose. Christoph has already a chart of the Channel, and we will then go to the harbour, and at midnight cut the boat from her moorings, and row away round the point out of sight; and by the next morning we are on the coast of France, near Cherbourg. The rest is easy, for I have saved money for the land journey, and can get a change of clothes. I will write to my mother, who will meet us on the way.'

He added details in reply to her inquiries, which left no doubt in Phyllis's mind of the feasibility of the undertaking. But its magnitude almost appalled her; and it is questionable if she would ever have gone further in the wild adventure if, on entering the house that night, her father had not accosted her in the most significant terms.

'How about the York Hussars?' he said.

'They are still at the camp; but they are soon going away, I believe.'

'It is useless for you to attempt to cloak your actions in that way. You have been meeting one of those fellows; you have been seen walking with him – foreign barbarians, not much better than the French themselves! I have made up my mind – don't speak a word till I have done, please! – I have made up my mind that you shall stay here no longer while they are on the spot. You shall go to your aunt's.'

It was useless for her to protest that she had never taken a walk with any soldier or man under the sun except himself. Her protestations were feeble, too, for though he was not literally correct in his assertion, he was virtually only half in error.

The house of her father's sister was a prison to Phyllis. She had quite recently undergone experience of its gloom; and when her father went on to direct her to pack what would be necessary for her to take, her heart died within her. In afteryears she never attempted to excuse her conduct during this week of agitation; but the result of her self-communing was that she decided to join in the scheme of her lover and his friend, and fly to the country which he had coloured with such lovely hues in her imagination. She always said that the one feature in his proposal which overcame her hesitation was the obvious purity and straightforwardness of his intentions. He showed himself to be so virtuous and kind; he treated her with a respect to which she had never before been accustomed; and she was braced to the obvious risks of the voyage by her confidence in him.

IV

It was on a soft, dark evening of the following week that they engaged in the adventure. Tina was to meet her at a point in the highway at which the lane to the village branched off. Christoph was to go ahead of them to the harbour where the boat lay, row it round the Nothe – or Look-out as it was called in those days – and pick them up on the other side of the promontory, which they were to reach by crossing the harbour-bridge on foot, and climbing over the Look-out hill.

As soon as her father had ascended to his room she left the house, and, bundle in hand, proceeded at a trot along the lane. At such an hour not a soul was afoot anywhere in the village, and she reached the junction of the lane with the highway unobserved. Here she took up her position in the obscurity formed by the angle of a fence, whence she could discern every one who approached along the turnpike-road, without being herself seen.

She had not remained thus waiting for her lover longer than a minute – though from the tension of her nerves the lapse of even that short time was trying – when, instead of the expected footsteps, the stage-coach could be heard descending the hill. She knew that Tina would not show himself till the road was clear, and waited impatiently for the coach to pass. Nearing the corner where she was it slackened speed, and, instead of going by as usual, drew up within a few yards of her. A passenger alighted, and she heard his voice. It was Humphrey Gould's.

He had brought a friend with him, and luggage. The luggage was deposited on the grass, and the coach went on its route to the royal watering-place.

'I wonder where that young man is with the horse and trap?' said her former admirer to his companion. 'I hope we shan't have to wait here long. I told him half-past nine o'clock precisely.'

'Have you got her present safe?'

'Phyllis's? O, yes. It is in this trunk. I hope it will please her.'

'Of course it will. What woman would not be pleased with such a handsome peace-offering?'

'Well – she deserves it. I've treated her rather badly. But she has been in my mind these last two days much more than I should care to confess to everybody. Ah, well; I'll say no more about that. It cannot be that she is so bad as they make out. I am quite sure that a girl of her good wit would know better than to get entangled with any of those Hanoverian soldiers. I won't believe it of her, and there's an end on't.'

More words in the same strain were casually dropped as the two men waited; words which revealed to her, as by a sudden illumination, the enormity of her conduct. The conversation was at length cut off by the arrival of the man with the vehicle. The luggage was placed in it, and they mounted, and were driven on in the direction from which she had just come.

Phyllis was so conscience-stricken that she was at first inclined to follow them; but a moment's reflection led her to feel that it would only be bare justice to Matthäus to wait till he arrived, and explain candidly that she had changed her mind – difficult as the struggle would be when she stood face to face with him. She bitterly reproached herself for having believed reports which represented Humphrey Gould as false to his engagement, when, from what she now heard from his own lips, she gathered that he had been living full of trust in her. But she knew well enough who had won her love. Without him her life seemed a dreary prospect, yet the more she looked at his proposal the more she feared to accept it – so wild as it was, so vague, so venturesome. She had promised Humphrey Gould, and it was only his assumed faithlessness which had led her to treat that promise as nought. His solicitude in bringing her these gifts touched her; her promise must be kept, and esteem must take the place of love. She would preserve her self-respect. She would stay at home, and marry him, and suffer.

Phyllis had thus braced herself to an exceptional fortitude when, a few minutes later, the outline of Matthäus Tina appeared behind a field-gate, over which he lightly leapt as she stepped forward. There was no evading it, he pressed her to his breast.

'It is the first and last time!' she wildly thought as she stood encircled by his arms.

How Phyllis got through the terrible ordeal of that night she could never clearly recollect. She always attributed her success in carrying out her resolve to her lover's honour, for as soon as she declared to him in feeble words that she had changed her mind, and felt that she could not, dared not, fly with him, he forbore to urge her, grieved as he was at her decision. Unscrupulous pressure on his part, seeing how romantically she had become attached to him, would no doubt have turned the balance in his favour. But he did nothing to tempt her unduly or unfairly.

On her side, fearing for his safety, she begged him to remain. This, he declared, could not be. 'I cannot break faith with my friend,' said he. Had he stood alone he would have abandoned his plan. But Christoph, with the boat and compass and chart, was waiting on the shore; the tide would soon turn; his mother had been warned of his coming; go he must.

Many precious minutes were lost while he tarried, unable to tear himself away. Phyllis held to her resolve, though it cost her many a bitter pang. At last they parted, and he went down the hill. Before his footsteps had quite died away she felt a desire to behold at least his outline once more, and running noiselessly after him regained view of his diminishing figure. For one moment she was sufficiently excited to be on the point of rushing forward and linking her fate with his. But she could not. The courage which at the critical instant failed Cleopatra of Egypt could scarcely be expected of Phyllis Grove.

A dark shape, similar to his own, joined him in the highway. It was Christoph, his friend. She could see no more; they had hastened on in the direction of the town and harbour, four miles ahead. With a feeling akin to despair she turned and slowly pursued her way homeward.

Tattoo sounded in the camp; but there was no camp for her

now. It was as dead as the camp of the Assyrians after the passage of the Destroying Angel.

She noiselessly entered the house, seeing nobody, and went to bed. Grief, which kept her awake at first, ultimately wrapped her in a heavy sleep. The next morning her father met her at the foot of the stairs.

'Mr Gould is come!' he said triumphantly.

Humphrey was staying at the inn, and had already called to inquire for her. He had brought her a present of a very handsome looking-glass in a frame of *repoussé* silverwork, which her father held in his hand. He had promised to call again in the course of an hour, to ask Phyllis to walk with him.

Pretty mirrors were rarer in country-houses at that day than they are now, and the one before her won Phyllis's admiration. She looked into it, saw how heavy her eyes were, and endeavoured to brighten them. She was in that wretched state of mind which leads a woman to move mechanically onward in what she conceives to be her allotted path. Mr Humphrey had, in his undemonstrative way, been adhering all along to the old understanding; it was for her to do the same, and to say not a word of her own lapse. She put on her bonnet and tippet, and when he arrived at the hour named she was at the door awaiting him.

V

Phyllis thanked him for his beautiful gift; but the talking was soon entirely on Humphrey's side as they walked along. He told her of the latest movements of the world of fashion – a subject which she willingly discussed to the exclusion of anything more personal – and his measured language helped to still her disquieted heart and brain. Had not her own sadness been what it was she must have observed his embarrassment. At last he abruptly changed the subject.

'I am glad you are pleased with my little present,' he said. 'The truth is that I brought it to propitiate 'ee, and to get you to help me out of a mighty difficulty.'

It was inconceivable to Phyllis that this independent bachelor – whom she admired in some respects – could have a difficulty.

'Phyllis – I'll tell you my secret at once; for I have a monstrous secret to confide before I can ask your counsel. The case is, then, that I am married: yes, I have privately married a dear young belle; and if you knew her, and I hope you will, you would say everything in her praise. But she is not quite the one that my father would have chose for me – you know the paternal idea as well as I – and I have kept it secret. There will be a terrible noise, no doubt; but I think that with your help I may get over it. If you would only do me this good turn – when I have told my father, I mean – say that you never could have married me, you know, or something of that sort – 'pon my life it will help to smooth the way vastly. I am so anxious to win him round to my point of view, and not to cause any estrangement.'

What Phyllis replied she scarcely knew, or how she counselled him as to his unexpected situation. Yet the relief that his announcement brought her was perceptible. To have confided her trouble in return was what her aching heart longed to do; and had Humphrey been a woman she would instantly have poured out her tale. But to him she feared to confess; and there was a real reason for silence, till a sufficient time had elapsed to allow her lover and his comrade to get out of harm's way.

As soon as she reached home again she sought a solitary place, and spent the time in half regretting that she had not gone away, and in dreaming over the meetings with Matthäus Tina from their beginning to their end. In his own country, amongst his own countrywomen, he would possibly soon forget her, even to her very name.

Her listlessness was such that she did not go out of the house for several days. There came a morning which broke in fog and mist, behind which the dawn could be discerned in greenish grey; and the outlines of the tents, and the rows of horses at the ropes. The smoke from the canteen fires drooped heavily.

The spot at the bottom of the garden where she had been accustomed to climb the wall to meet Matthäus was the only inch of English ground in which she took any interest; and in spite of the disagreeable haze prevailing she walked out there till she reached the well-known corner. Every blade of grass was weighted with little liquid globes, and slugs and snails had crept out upon the plots. She could hear the usual faint noises from the camp, and in the other direction the trot of farmers on the road to the town, for it was market-day. She observed that her frequent visits to this corner had quite trodden down the grass in the angle of the wall, and left marks of garden soil on the stepping-stones by which she had mounted to look over the top. Seldom having gone there till dusk, she had not considered that her traces might be visible by day. Perhaps it was these which had revealed her trysts to her father.

While she paused in melancholy regard, she fancied that the customary sounds from the tents were changing their character. Indifferent as Phyllis was to camp doings now, she mounted by the steps to the old place. What she beheld at first awed and perplexed her; then she stood rigid, her fingers hooked to the wall, her eyes staring out of her head, and her face as if hardened to stone.

On the open green stretching before her all the regiments in the camp were drawn up in line, in the mid-front of which two empty coffins lay on the ground. The unwonted sounds which she had noticed came from an advancing procession. It consisted of the band of the York Hussars playing a dead march; next two soldiers of that regiment in a mourning coach, guarded on each side, and accompanied by two priests. Behind came a crowd of rustics who had been attracted by the event. The melancholy procession marched along the front of the line, returned to the centre, and halted beside the coffins, where the two condemned men were blindfolded, and each placed kneeling on his coffin; a few minutes' pause was now given while they prayed.

A firing-party of twenty-four men stood ready with levelled carbines. The commanding officer, who had his sword drawn, waved it through some cuts of the sword-exercise till he reached the downward stroke, whereat the firing-party discharged their volley. The two victims fell, one upon his face across his coffin, the other backwards.

As the volley resounded there arose a shriek from the wall of Dr Grove's garden, and some one fell down inside; but nobody among the spectators without noticed it at the time. The two executed Hussars were Matthäus Tina and his friend Christoph. The soldiers on guard placed the bodies in the coffins almost instantly; but the colonel of the regiment, an Englishman, rode up and exclaimed in a stern voice: 'Turn them out – as an example to the men!'

The coffins were lifted endwise, and the dead Germans flung

out upon their faces on the grass. Then all the regiments wheeled in sections, and marched past the spot in slow time. When the survey was over the corpses were again coffined, and borne away.

Meanwhile Dr Grove, attracted by the noise of the volley, had rushed out into his garden, where he saw his wretched daughter lying motionless against the wall. She was taken indoors, but it was long before she recovered consciousness; and for weeks they despaired for her reason.

It transpired that the luckless deserters from the York Hussars had cut the boat from her moorings in the adjacent harbour, according to their plan, and with two other comrades who were smarting under ill-treatment from their colonel, had sailed in safety across the Channel. But mistaking their bearings they steered into Jersey, thinking that island the French coast. Here they were perceived to be deserters, and delivered up to the authorities. Matthäus and Christoph interceded for the other two at the court-martial, saying that it was entirely by the former's representations that these were induced to go. Their sentence was accordingly commuted to flogging, the death punishment being reserved for their leaders.

The visitor to the well-known old Georgian watering-place who may care to ramble to the neighbouring village under the hills and examine the register of burials, will there find two entries in these words: –

'Matth: Tina (Corpl) in His Majesty's Regmt of York Hussars, and Shot for Desertion, was Buried 30 June 1801, aged 22 years. Born in the town of Sarrbruk, Germany.

'Christoph Bless, belonging to His Majesty's Regmt of York Hussars, who was Shot for Desertion, was Buried 30 June 1801, aged 22 years. Born at Lothaargen, Alsatia.'

Their graves were dug at the back of the little church, near the wall. There is no memorial to mark the spot, but Phyllis pointed it out to me. While she lived she used to keep their mounds neat; but now they are overgrown with nettles, and sunk nearly flat. The older villagers, however, who know of the episode from their parents, still recollect the place where the soldiers lie. Phyllis lies near.

On The Western Circuit

The man who played the disturbing part in the two quiet feminine lives hereunder depicted – no great man, in any sense, by the way – first had knowledge of them on an October evening, in the city of Melchester. He had been standing in the Close, vainly endeavouring to gain amid the darkness a glimpse of the most homogeneous pile of mediaeval architecture in England, which towered and tapered from the damp and level sward in front of him. While he stood the presence of the Cathedral walls was revealed rather by the ear than by the eyes; he could not see them, but they reflected sharply a roar of sound which entered the Close by a street leading from the city square, and, falling upon the building, was flung back upon him.

He postponed till the morrow his attempt to examine the deserted edifice, and turned his attention to the noise. It was compounded of steam barrel-organs, the clanging of gongs, the ringing of hand-bells, the clack of rattles, and the undistinguishable shouts of men. A lurid light hung in the air in the direction of the tumult. Thitherward he went, passing under the arched gateway, along a straight street, and into the square.

He might have searched Europe over for a greater contrast between juxtaposed scenes. The spectacle was that of the eighth chasm of the Inferno as to colour and flame, and, as to mirth, a development of the Homeric heaven. A smoky glare, of the complexion of brass-filings, ascended from the fiery tongues of innumerable naphtha lamps affixed to booths, stalls, and other temporary erections which crowded the spacious market-square. In front of this irradiation scores of human figures, more or less in profile, were darting athwart and across, up, down, and around, like gnats against a sunset.

Their motions were so rhythmical that they seemed to be moved by machinery. And it presently appeared that they were moved by machinery indeed; the figures being those of the patrons of swings, see-saws, flying-leaps, above all of the three

steam roundabouts which occupied the centre of the position. It
was from the latter that the din of steam-organs came.

Throbbing humanity in full light was, on second thoughts,
better than architecture in the dark. The young man, lighting a
short pipe, and putting his hat on one side and one hand in his
pocket, to throw himself into harmony with his new environment, drew near to the largest and most patronized of the steam
circuses, as the roundabouts were called by their owners. This
was one of brilliant finish, and it was now in full revolution. The
musical instrument around which and to whose tones the riders
revolved, directed its trumpet-mouths of brass upon the young
man, and the long plate-glass mirrors set at angles, which
revolved with the machine, flashed the gyrating personages and
hobby-horses kaleidoscopically into his eyes.

It could now be seen that he was unlike the majority of the
crowd. A gentlemanly young fellow, one of the species found in
large towns only, and London particularly, built on delicate lines,
well, though not fashionably dressed, he appeared to belong to
the professional class; he had nothing square or practical about
his look, much that was curvilinear and sensuous. Indeed, some
would have called him a man not altogether typical of the
middle-class male of a century wherein sordid ambition is the
master-passion that seems to be taking the time-honoured place
of love.

The revolving figures passed before his eyes with an unexpected and quiet grace in a throng whose natural movements did
not suggest gracefulness or quietude as a rule. By some
contrivance there was imparted to each of the hobby-horses a
motion which was really the triumph and perfection of roundabout inventiveness – a galloping rise and fall, so timed that, of
each pair of steeds, one was on the spring while the other was on
the pitch. The riders were quite fascinated by these equine
undulations in this most delightful holiday-game of our times.
There were riders as young as six, and as old as sixty years, with
every age between. At first it was difficult to catch a personality,
but by and by the observer's eyes centred on the prettiest girl out
of the several pretty ones revolving.

It was not that one with the light frock and light hat whom he
had been at first attracted by; no, it was the one with the black
cape, grey skirt, light gloves and – no, not even she, but the one

behind her; she with the crimson skirt, dark jacket, brown hat and brown gloves. Unmistakably that was the prettiest girl.

Having finally selected her, this idle spectator studied her as well as he was able during each of her brief transits across his visual field. She was absolutely unconscious of everything save the act of riding: her features were rapt in an ecstatic dreaminess; for the moment she did not know her age or her history or her lineaments, much less her troubles. He himself was full of vague latter-day glooms and popular melancholies, and it was a refreshing sensation to behold this young thing then and there, absolutely as happy as if she were in a Paradise.

Dreading the moment when the inexorable stoker, grimily lurking behind the glittering rococo-work, should decide that this set of riders had had their pennyworth, and bring the whole concern of steam-engine, horses, mirrors, trumpets, drums, cymbals, and such-like to pause and silence, he waited for her every reappearance, glancing indifferently over the intervening forms, including the two plainer girls, the old woman and child, the two youngsters, the newly-married couple, the old man with a clay pipe, the sparkish youth with a ring, the young ladies in the chariot, the pair of journeyman-carpenters, and others, till his select country beauty followed on again in her place. He had never seen a fairer product of nature, and at each round she made a deeper mark in his sentiments. The stoppage then came, and the sighs of the riders were audible.

He moved round to the place at which he reckoned she would alight; but she retained her seat. The empty saddles began to refill, and she plainly was deciding to have another turn. The young man drew up to the side of her steed, and pleasantly asked her if she had enjoyed her ride.

'O yes!' she said, with dancing eyes. 'It has been quite unlike anything I have ever felt in my life before!'

It was not difficult to fall into conversation with her. Unreserved – too unreserved – by nature, she was not experienced enough to be reserved by art, and after a little coaxing she answered his remarks readily. She had come to live in Melchester from a village on the Great Plain, and this was the first time that she had ever seen a steam-circus; she could not understand how such wonderful machines were made. She had come to the city on the invitation of Mrs Harnham, who had taken her into her household to train her as a servant, if she showed any aptitude. Mrs Harnham was a young lady who before she married had been Miss Edith White, living in the country near the speaker's cottage; she was now very kind to her through knowing her in childhood so well. She was even taking the trouble to educate her. Mrs Harnham was the only friend she had in the world, and being without children had wished to have her near her in preference to anybody else, though she had only lately come; allowed her to do almost as she liked, and to have a holiday whenever she asked for it. The husband of this kind young lady was a rich wine-merchant of the town, but Mrs Harnham did not care much about him. In the daytime you could see the house from where they were talking. She, the speaker, liked Melchester better than the lonely country, and she was going to have a new hat for next Sunday that was to cost fifteen and ninepence.

Then she inquired of her acquaintance where he lived, and he told her in London, that ancient and smoky city, where everybody lived who lived at all, and died because they could not live there. He came into Wessex two or three times a year for professional reasons; he had arrived from Wintoncester yesterday, and was going on into the next county in a day or two. For one thing he did like the country better than the town, and it was because it contained such girls as herself.

Then the pleasure-machine started again, and, to the light-hearted girl, the figure of the handsome young man, the market-square with its lights and crowd, the houses beyond, and the world at large, began moving round as before, countermoving in the revolving mirrors on her right hand, she being as it were the fixed point in an undulating, dazzling, lurid universe, in which loomed forward most prominently of all the form of her late interlocutor. Each time that she approached the half of her orbit that lay nearest him they gazed at each other with smiles, and with that unmistakable expression which means so little at the moment, yet so often leads up to passion, heart-ache, union, disunion, devotion, overpopulation, drudgery, content, resignation, despair.

When the horses slowed anew he stepped to her side and proposed another heat. 'Hang the expense for once,' he said. 'I'll pay!'

She laughed till the tears came.

'Why do you laugh, dear?' said he.

'Because – you are so genteel that you must have plenty of money, and only say that for fun!' she returned.

'Ha-ha!' laughed the young man in unison, and gallantly producing his money she was enabled to whirl on again.

As he stood smiling there in the motley crowd, with his pipe in his hand, and clad in the rough pea-jacket and wideawake that he had put on for his stroll, who would have supposed him to be Charles Bradford Raye, Esquire, stuff-gownsman, educated at Wintoncester, called to the Bar at Lincoln's-Inn, now going the Western Circuit, merely detained in Melchester by a small arbitration after his brethren had moved on to the next county-town?

The square was overlooked from its remoter corner by the house of which the young girl had spoken, a dignified residence of considerable size, having several windows on each floor. Inside one of these, on the first floor, the apartment being a large drawing-room, sat a lady, in appearance from twenty-eight to thirty years of age. The blinds were still undrawn, and the lady was absently surveying the weird scene without, her cheek resting on her hand. The room was unlit from within, but enough of the glare from the market-place entered it to reveal the lady's face. She was what is called an interesting creature rather than a handsome woman; dark-eyed, thoughtful, and with sensitive lips.

A man sauntered into the room from behind and came forward.

'O, Edith, I didn't see you,' he said. 'Why are you sitting here in the dark?'

'I am looking at the fair,' replied the lady in a languid voice.

'Oh? Horrid nuisance every year! I wish it could be put a stop to.'

'I like it.'

'H'm. There's no accounting for taste.'

For a moment he gazed from the window with her, for politeness' sake, and then went out again.

In a few minutes she rang.

'Hasn't Anna come in?' asked Mrs Harnham.

'No m'm.'

'She ought to be in by this time. I meant her to go for ten minutes only.'

'Shall I go and look for her, m'm?' said the housemaid alertly.

'No. It is not necessary: she is a good girl and will come soon.'

However, when the servant had gone Mrs Harnham arose, went up to her room, cloaked and bonneted herself, and proceeded downstairs, where she found her husband.

'I want to see the fair,' she said; 'and I am going to look for Anna. I have made myself responsible for her, and must see she comes to no harm. She ought to be indoors. Will you come with me?'

'Oh, she's all right. I saw her on one of those whirligig things, talking to her young man as I came in. But I'll go if you wish, though I'd rather go a hundred miles the other way.'

'Then please do so. I shall come to no harm alone.'

She left the house and entered the crowd which thronged the market-place, where she soon discovered Anna, seated on the revolving horse. As soon as it stopped Mrs Harnham advanced and said severely, 'Anna, how can you be such a wild girl? You were only to be out for ten minutes.'

Anna looked blank, and the young man, who had dropped into the background, came to help her alight.

'Please don't blame her,' he said politely. 'It is my fault that she has stayed. She looked so graceful on the horse that I induced her to go round again. I assure you that she has been quite safe.'

'In that case I'll leave her in your hands,' said Mrs Harnham, turning to retrace her steps.

But this for the moment it was not so easy to do. Something had attracted the crowd to a spot in their rear, and the wine-merchant's wife, caught by its sway, found herself pressed against Anna's acquaintance without power to move away. Their faces were within a few inches of each other, his breath fanned her cheek as well as Anna's. They could do no other than smile at the accident; but neither spoke, and each waited passively. Mrs Harnham then felt a man's hand clasping her fingers, and from the look of consciousness on the young fellow's face she knew the hand to be his: she also knew that from the position of the girl he had no other thought than that the imprisoned hand was Anna's. What prompted her to refrain from undeceiving him she could hardly tell. Not content with holding the hand, he playfully slipped two of his fingers inside her glove, against her palm. Thus matters continued till the pressure lessened; but several minutes passed before the crowd thinned sufficiently to allow Mrs Harnham to withdraw.

'How did they get to know each other, I wonder?' she mused as she retreated. 'Anna is really very forward – and he very wicked and nice.'

She was so gently stirred with the stranger's manner and voice, with the tenderness of his idle touch, that instead of re-entering the house she turned back again and observed the pair from a screened nook. Really she argued (being little less impulsive than Anna herself) it was very excusable in Anna to encourage him, however she might have contrived to make his acquaintance; he was so gentlemanly, so fascinating, had such beautiful eyes. The thought that he was several years her junior produced a reasonless sigh.

At length the couple turned from the roundabout towards the door of Mrs Harnham's house, and the young man could be heard saying that he would accompany her home. Anna, then, had found a lover, apparently a very devoted one. Mrs Harnham was quite interested in him. When they drew near the door of the wine-merchant's house, a comparatively deserted spot by this time, they stood invisible for a little while in the shadow of a wall, where they separated, Anna going on to the entrance, and her acquaintance returning across the square.

'Anna,' said Mrs Harnham, coming up. 'I've been looking at you! That young man kissed you at parting, I am almost sure.'

'Well,' stammered Anna; 'he said, if I didn't mind – it would do me no harm, and, and, him a great deal of good!'

'Ah, I thought so! And he was a stranger till to night?'

'Yes ma'am.'

'Yet I warrant you told him your name and everything about yourself?'

'He asked me.'

'But he didn't tell you his?'

'Yes ma'am, he did!' cried Anna victoriously. 'It is Charles Bradford, of London.'

'Well, if he's respectable, of course I've nothing to say against your knowing him,' remarked her mistress, prepossessed, in spite of general principles, in the young man's favour. 'But I must reconsider all that, if he attempts to renew your acquaintance. A country-bred girl like you, who has never lived in Melchester till this month, who had hardly ever seen a black-coated man till you came here, to be so sharp as to capture a young Londoner like him!'

'I didn't capture him. I didn't do anything,' said Anna, in confusion.

When she was indoors and alone Mrs Harnham thought what a well-bred and chivalrous young man Anna's companion had seemed. There had been a magic in his wooing touch of her hand; and she wondered how he had come to be attracted by the girl.

The next morning the emotional Edith Harnham went to the usual weekday service in Melchester cathedral. In crossing the Close through the fog she again perceived him who had interested her the previous evening, gazing up thoughtfully at the high-piled architecture of the nave: and as soon as she had taken her seat he entered and sat down in a stall opposite hers.

He did not particularly heed her; but Mrs Harnham was continually occupying her eyes with him, and wondered more than ever what had attracted him in her unfledged maidservant. The mistress was almost as unaccustomed as the maiden herself to the end-of-the-age young man, or she might have wondered less. Raye, having looked about him awhile, left abruptly, without regard to the service that was proceeding; and Mrs Harnham – lonely, impressionable creature that she was – took no further interest in praising the Lord. She wished she had married a London man who knew the subtleties of love-making as they were evidently known to him who had mistakenly caressed her hand.

The calendar at Melchester had been light, occupying the court only a few hours; and the assizes at Casterbridge, the next county-town on the Western Circuit, having no business for Raye, he had not gone thither. At the next town after that they did not open till the following Monday, trials to begin on Tuesday morning. In the natural order of things Raye would have arrived at the latter place on Monday afternoon; but it was not till the middle of Wednesday that his gown and grey wig, curled in tiers, in the best fashion of Assyrian bas-reliefs, were seen blowing and bobbing behind him as he hastily walked up the High Street from his lodgings. But though he entered the assize building there was nothing for him to do, and sitting at the blue baize table in the well of the court, he mended pens with a mind far away from the case in progress. Thoughts of unpremeditated conduct, of which a week earlier he would not have believed himself capable, threw him into a mood of dissatisfied depression.

He had contrived to see again the pretty rural maiden Anna, the day after the fair, had walked out of the city with her to the earthworks of Old Melchester, and feeling a violent fancy for her, had remained in Melchester all Sunday, Monday, and Tuesday; by persuasion obtaining walks and meetings with the girl six or seven times during the interval; had in brief won her, body and soul.

He supposed it must have been owing to the seclusion in which he had lived of late in town that he had given way so unrestrainedly to a passion for an artless creature whose inexperience had, from the first, led her to place herself unreservedly in his hands. Much he deplored trifling with her feelings for the sake of a passing desire; and he could only hope that she might not live to suffer on his account.

She had begged him to come to her again; entreated him; wept. He had promised that he would do so, and he meant to carry out that promise. He could not desert her now. Awkward as such unintentional connections were, the interspace of a hundred miles – which to a girl of her limited capabilities was like a thousand – would effectually hinder this summer fancy from greatly encumbering his life; while thought of her simple love might do him the negative good of keeping him from idle pleasures in town when he wished to work hard. His circuit journeys would take him to Melchester three or four times a year; and then he could always see her.

The pseudonym, or rather partial name, that he had given her as his before knowing how far the acquaintance was going to carry him, had been spoken on the spur of the moment, without any ulterior intention whatever. He had not afterwards disturbed Anna's error, but on leaving her he had felt bound to give her an address at a stationer's not far from his chambers, at which she might write to him under the initials 'C. B.'

In due time Raye returned to his London abode, having called at Melchester on his way and spent a few additional hours with his fascinating child of nature. In town he lived monotonously every day. Often he and his rooms were enclosed by a tawny fog from all the world besides, and when he lighted the gas to read or write by, his situation seemed so unnatural that he would look into the fire and think of that trusting girl at Melchester again and again. Often, oppressed by absurd fondness for her, he would enter the dim religious nave of the Law Courts by the north door, elbow other juniors habited like himself, and like him unretained; edge himself into this or that crowded court where a sensational case was going on, just as if he were in it, though the police officers at the door knew as well as he knew himself that he had no more concern with the business in hand than the patient idlers at the gallery-door outside, who had waited to enter since eight in the morning because, like him, they belonged to the classes that live on expectation. But he would do these things to no purpose, and think how greatly the characters in such scenes contrasted with the pink and breezy Anna.

An unexpected feature in that peasant maiden's conduct was that she had not as yet written to him, though he had told her she might do so if she wished. Surely a young creature had never before been so reticent in such circumstances. At length he sent her a brief line, positively requesting her to write. There was no answer by the return post, but the day after a letter in a neat feminine hand, and bearing the Melchester postmark, was handed to him by the stationer.

The fact alone of its arrival was sufficient to satisfy his imaginative sentiment. He was not anxious to open the epistle, and in truth did not begin to read it for nearly half-an-hour, anticipating readily its terms of passionate retrospect and tender adjuration. When at last he turned his feet to the fireplace and unfolded the sheet, he was surprised and pleased to find that neither extravagance nor vulgarity was there. It was the most charming little missive he had ever received from woman. To be sure the language was simple and the ideas were slight; but it was so self-possessed; so purely that of a young girl who felt her womanhood to be enough for her dignity that he read it through twice. Four sides were filled, and a few lines written across, after the fashion of former days; the paper, too, was common, and not of the latest shade and surface. But what of those things? He had received letters from women who were fairly called ladies, but never so sensible, so human a letter as this. He could not single out any one sentence and say it was at all remarkable or clever; the *ensemble* of the letter it was which won him, and beyond the one request that he would write or come to her again soon there was nothing to show her sense of a claim upon him.

To write again and develop a correspondence was the last thing Raye would have preconceived as his conduct in such a situation; yet he did send a short, encouraging line or two, signed with his pseudonym, in which he asked for another letter, and cheeringly promised that he would try to see her again on some near day, and would never forget how much they had been to each other during their short acquaintance.

To return now to the moment at which Anna, at Melchester, had received Raye's letter.

It had been put into her own hand by the postman on his morning rounds. She flushed down to her neck on receipt of it, and turned it over and over. 'It is mine?' she said.

'Why, yes, can't you see it is?' said the postman, smiling as he guessed the nature of the document and the cause of the confusion.

'O yes, of course!' replied Anna, looking at the letter, forcedly tittering, and blushing still more.

Her look of embarrassment did not leave her with the postman's departure. She opened the envelope, kissed its contents, put away the letter in her pocket, and remained musing till her eyes filled with tears.

A few minutes later she carried up a cup of tea to Mrs Harnham in her bed-chamber. Anna's mistress looked at her, and said: 'How dismal you seem this morning, Anna. What's the matter?'

'I'm not dismal, I'm glad; only I – ' She stopped to stifle a sob.

'Well?'

'I've got a letter – and what good is it to me, if I can't read a word in it!'

'Why, I'll read it, child, if necessary.'

'But this is from somebody – I don't want anybody to read it but myself!' Anna murmured.

'I shall not tell anybody. Is it from that young man?'

'I think so.' Anna slowly produced the letter, saying: 'Then will you read it to me, ma'am?'

This was the secret of Anna's embarrassment and fluttering. She could neither read nor write. She had grown up under the care of an aunt by marriage, at one of the lonely hamlets on the Great Mid-Wessex Plain where, even in days of national education, there had been no school within a distance of two miles. Her aunt was an ignorant woman; there had been nobody to investigate Anna's circumstances, nobody to care about her learning the rudiments; though, as often in such cases, she had been well fed and clothed and not unkindly treated. Since she had come to live at Melchester with Mrs Harnham, the latter, who took a kindly interest in the girl, had taught her to speak correctly, in which accomplishment Anna showed considerable readiness, as is not unusual with the illiterate; and soon became quite fluent in the use of her mistress's phraseology. Mrs Harnham also insisted upon her getting a spelling and copy book, and beginning to practise in these. Anna was slower in this branch of her education, and meanwhile here was the letter.

Edith Harnham's large dark eyes expressed some interest in the contents, though, in her character of mere interpreter, she threw into her tone as much as she could of mechanical passiveness. She read the short epistle on to its concluding sentence, which idly requested Anna to send him a tender answer.

'Now – you'll do it for me, won't you, dear mistress?' said Anna eagerly. 'And you'll do it as well as ever you can, please? Because I couldn't bear him to think I am not able to do it myself. I should sink into the earth with shame if he knew that!'

From some words in the letter Mrs Harnham was led to ask questions, and the answers she received confirmed her suspicions. Deep concern filled Edith's heart at perceiving how the girl had committed her happiness to the issue of this new-sprung attachment. She blamed herself for not interfering in a flirtation which had resulted so seriously for the poor little creature in her charge; though at the time of seeing the pair together she had a feeling that it was hardly within her province to nip young affection in the bud. However, what was done could not be undone, and it behoved her now, as Anna's only protector, to help her as much as she could. To Anna's eager request that she, Mrs Harnham, should compose and write the answer to this young London man's letter, she felt bound to accede, to keep alive his attachment to the girl if possible; though in other circumstances she might have suggested the cook as an amanuensis.

A tender reply was thereupon concocted, and set down in Edith Harnham's hand. This letter it had been which Raye had received and delighted in. Written in the presence of Anna it certainly was, and on Anna's humble note-paper, and in a measure indited by the young girl; but the life, the spirit, the individuality, were Edith Harnham's.

'Won't you at least put your name yourself?' she said. 'You can manage to write that by this time?'

'No, no,' said Anna, shrinking back. 'I should do it so bad. He'd be ashamed of me, and never see me again!'

The note, so prettily requesting another from him, had, as we have seen, power enough in its pages to bring one. He declared it to be such a pleasure to hear from her that she must write every week. The same process of manufacture was accordingly repeated by Anna and her mistress, and continued for several weeks in succession; each letter being penned and suggested by Edith, the girl standing by; the answer read and commented on by Edith, Anna standing by and listening again.

Late on a winter evening, after the dispatch of the sixth letter, Mrs Harnham was sitting alone by the remains of her fire. Her husband had retired to bed and she had fallen into that fixity of musing which takes no count of hour or temperature. The state of mind had been brought about in Edith by a strange thing which she had done that day. For the first time since Raye's visit Anna had gone to stay over a night or two with her cottage friends on the Plain, and in her absence had arrived, out of its time, a letter from Raye. To this Edith had replied on her own responsibility, from the depths of her own heart, without waiting for her maid's collaboration. The luxury of writing to him what would be known to no consciousness but his was great, and she had indulged herself therein.

Why was it a luxury?

Edith Harnham led a lonely life. Influenced by the belief of the British parent that a bad marriage with its aversions is better than free womanhood with its interests, dignity, and leisure, she had consented to marry the elderly wine-merchant as a *pis aller*, at the age of seven-and-twenty – some three years before this date – to find afterwards that she had made a mistake. That contract had left her still a woman whose deeper nature had never been stirred.

She was now clearly realizing that she had become possessed to the bottom of her soul with the image of a man to whom she was hardly so much as a name. From the first he had attracted her by his looks and voice; by his tender touch; and, with these as generators, the writing of letter after letter and the reading of their soft answers had insensibly developed on her side an emotion which fanned his; till there had resulted a magnetic reciprocity between the correspondents, notwithstanding that one of them wrote in a character not her own. That he had been able to seduce another woman in two days was his crowning though unrecognized fascination for her as the she-animal.

They were her own impassioned and pent-up ideas – lowered to monosyllabic phraseology in order to keep up the disguise – that Edith put into letters signed with another name, much to the shallow Anna's delight, who, unassisted, could not for the world have conceived such pretty fancies for winning him, even had she been able to write them. Edith found that it was these, her own foisted-in sentiments, to which the young barrister mainly responded. The few sentences occasionally added from Anna's own lips made apparently no impression upon him.

The letter-writing in her absence Anna never discovered; but on her return the next morning she declared she wished to see her lover about something at once, and begged Mrs Harnham to ask him to come.

There was a strange anxiety in her manner which did not escape Mrs Harnham, and ultimately resolved itself into a flood of tears. Sinking down at Edith's knees, she made confession that the result of her relations with her lover it would soon become necessary to disclose.

Edith Harnham was generous enough to be very far from inclined to cast Anna adrift at this conjuncture. No true woman ever is so inclined from her own personal point of view, however prompt she may be in taking such steps to safeguard those dear to her. Although she had written to Raye so short a time previously, she instantly penned another Anna-note hinting clearly though delicately the state of affairs.

Raye replied by a hasty line to say how much he was concerned at her news: he felt that he must run down to see her almost immediately.

But a week later the girl came to her mistress's room with another note, which on being read informed her that after all he could not find time for the journey. Anna was broken with grief; but by Mrs Harnham's counsel strictly refrained from hurling at him the reproaches and bitterness customary from young women so situated. One thing was imperative: to keep the young man's romantic interest in her alive. Rather therefore did Edith, in the name of her *protégée*, request him on no account to be distressed about the looming event, and not to inconvenience himself to hasten down. She desired above everything to be no weight upon him in his career, no clog upon his high activities. She had wished him to know what had befallen: he was to dismiss it again from his mind. Only he must write tenderly as ever, and when he should come again on the spring circuit it would be soon enough to discuss what had better be done.

It may well be supposed that Anna's own feelings had not been quite in accord with these generous expressions; but the mistress's judgment had ruled, and Anna had acquiesced. 'All I want is that *niceness* you can so well put into your letters, my dear, dear mistress, and that I can't for the life o' me make up out of my own head; though I mean the same thing and feel it exactly when you've written it down!'

When the letter had been sent off, and Edith Harnham was left alone, she bowed herself on the back of her chair and wept.

'I wish his child was mine – I wish it was!' she murmured. 'Yet how can I say such a wicked thing!'

The letter moved Raye considerably when it reached him. The intelligence itself had affected him less than her unexpected manner of treating him in relation to it. The absence of any word of reproach, the devotion to his interests, the self-sacrifice apparent in every line, all made up a nobility of character that he had never dreamt of finding in womankind.

'God forgive me!' he said tremulously. 'I have been a wicked wretch. I did not know she was such a treasure as this!'

He reassured her instantly; declaring that he would not of course desert her, that he would provide a home for her somewhere. Meanwhile she was to stay where she was as long as her mistress would allow her.

But a misfortune supervened in this direction. Whether an inkling of Anna's circumstances reached the knowledge of Mrs Harnham's husband or not cannot be said, but the girl was compelled, in spite of Edith's entreaties, to leave the house. By her own choice she decided to go back for a while to the cottage on the Plain. This arrangement led to a consultation as to how the correspondence should be carried on; and in the girl's inability to continue personally what had been begun in her name, and in the difficulty of their acting in concert as heretofore, she requested Mrs Harnham – the only well-to-do friend she had in the world – to receive the letters and reply to them off-hand, sending them on afterwards to herself on the Plain, where she might at least get some neighbour to read them to her, if a trustworthy one could be met with. Anna and her box then departed for the Plain.

Thus it befell that Edith Harnham found herself in the strange position of having to correspond, under no supervision by the real woman, with a man not her husband, in terms which were virtually those of a wife, concerning a corporeal condition that was not Edith's at all; the man being one for whom, mainly through the sympathies involved in playing this part, she secretly cherished a predilection, subtle and imaginative truly, but strong and absorbing. She opened each letter, read it as if intended for herself, and replied from the promptings of her own heart and no other.

Throughout this correspondence, carried on in the girl's absence, the high-strung Edith Harnham lived in the ecstasy of fancy; the vicarious intimacy engendered such a flow of passionateness as was never exceeded. For conscience' sake Edith at first sent on each of his letters to Anna, and even rough copies of her replies; but later on these so-called copies were much abridged, and many letters on both sides were not sent on at all.

Though sensuous, and, superficially at least, infested with the self-indulgent vices of artificial society, there was a substratum of honesty and fairness in Raye's character. He had really a tender regard for the country girl, and it grew more tender than ever when he found her apparently capable of expressing the deepest sensibilities in the simplest words. He meditated, he wavered; and finally resolved to consult his sister, a maiden lady much older than himself, of lively sympathies and good intent. In making this confidence he showed her some of the letters.

'She seems fairly educated,' Miss Raye observed. 'And bright in ideas. She expresses herself with a taste that must be innate.'

'Yes. She writes very prettily, doesn't she, thanks to these elementary schools?'

'One is drawn out towards her, in spite of one's self, poor thing.'

The upshot of the discussion was that though he had not been directly advised to do it, Raye wrote, in his real name, what he would never have decided to write on his own responsibility; namely that he could not live without her, and would come down in the spring and shelve her looming difficulty by marrying her.

This bold acceptance of the situation was made known to Anna by Mrs Harnham driving out immediately to the cottage on the Plain. Anna jumped for joy like a little child. And poor, crude directions for answering appropriately were given to Edith Harnham, who on her return to the city carried them out with warm intensifications.

'O!' she groaned, as she threw down the pen. 'Anna – poor good little fool – hasn't intelligence enough to appreciate him! How should she? While I – don't bear his child!'

It was now February. The correspondence had continued altogether for four months; and the next letter from Raye contained incidentally a statement of his position and prospects. He said that in offering to wed her he had, at first, contemplated the step of retiring from a profession which hitherto had brought him very slight emolument, and which, to speak plainly, he had thought might be difficult of practice after his union with her. But the unexpected mines of brightness and warmth that her letters had disclosed to be lurking in her sweet nature had led him to abandon that somewhat sad prospect. He felt sure that, with her powers of development, after a little private training in the social forms of London under his supervision, and a little help from a governess if necessary, she would make as good a professional man's wife as could be desired, even if he should rise to the woolsack. Many a Lord Chancellor's wife had been less intuitively a lady than she had shown herself to be in her lines to him.

'O – poor fellow, poor fellow!' mourned Edith Harnham.

Her distress now raged as high as her infatuation. It was she who had wrought him to this pitch – to a marriage which meant his ruin; yet she could not, in mercy to her maid, do anything to hinder his plan. Anna was coming to Melchester that week, but she could hardly show the girl this last reply from the young man; it told too much of the second individuality that had usurped the place of the first.

Anna came, and her mistress took her into her own room for privacy. Anna began by saying with some anxiety that she was glad the wedding was so near.

'O Anna!' replied Mrs Harnham. 'I think we must tell him all – that I have been doing your writing for you? – lest he should not know it till after you become his wife, and it might lead to dissension and recriminations – '

'O mis'ess, dear mis'ess – please don't tell him now!' cried Anna in distress. 'If you were to do it, perhaps he would not marry me; and what should I do then? It would be terrible what would come to me! And I am getting on with my writing, too. I have brought with me the copybook you were so good as to give me, and I practise every day, and though it is so, so hard, I shall do it well at last, I believe, if I keep on trying.'

Edith looked at the copybook. The copies had been set by herself, and such progress as the girl had made was in the way of grotesque facsimile of her mistress's hand. But even if Edith's flowing caligraphy were reproduced the inspiration would be another thing.

'You do it so beautifully,' continued Anna, 'and say all that I want to say so much better than I could say it, that I do hope you won't leave me in the lurch just now!'

'Very well,' replied the other. 'But I – but I thought I ought not to go on!'

'Why?'

Her strong desire to confide her sentiments led Edith to answer truly:

'Because of its effect upon me.'

'But it *can't* have any!'

'Why, child?'

'Because you are married already!' said Anna with lucid simplicity.

'Of course it can't,' said her mistress hastily; yet glad, despite her conscience, that two or three outpourings still remained to her. 'But you must concentrate your attention on writing your name as I write it here.'

Soon Raye wrote about the wedding. Having decided to make the best of what he feared was a piece of romantic folly, he had acquired more zest for the grand experiment. He wished the ceremony to be in London, for greater privacy. Edith Harnham would have preferred it at Melchester; Anna was passive. His reasoning prevailed, and Mrs Harnham threw herself with mournful zeal into the preparations for Anna's departure. In a last desperate feeling that she must at every hazard be in at the death of her dream, and see once again the man who by a species of telepathy had exercised such an influence on her, she offered to go up with Anna and be with her through the ceremony – 'to see the end of her,' as her mistress put it with forced gaiety; an offer which the girl gratefully accepted; for she had no other friend capable of playing the part of companion and witness, in the presence of a gentlemanly bridegroom, in such a way as not to hasten an opinion that he had made an irremediable social blunder.

It was a muddy morning in March when Raye alighted from a four-wheel cab at the door of a registry office in the S. W. district of London, and carefully handed down Anna and her companion Mrs Harnham. Anna looked attractive in the somewhat fashionable clothes which Mrs Harnham had helped her to buy, though not quite so attractive as, an innocent child, she had appeared in her country gown on the back of the wooden horse at Melchester Fair.

Mrs Harnham had come up this morning by an early train, and a young man – a friend of Raye's – having met them at the door, all four entered the registry office together. Till an hour before this time Raye had never known the wine-merchant's wife, except at that first casual encounter, and in the flutter of the performance before them he had little opportunity for more than a brief acquaintance. The contract of marriage at a registry is soon got through; but somehow, during its progress, Raye discovered a strange and secret gravitation between himself and Anna's friend.

The formalities of the wedding – or rather ratification of a previous union – being concluded, the four went in one cab to Raye's lodgings, newly taken in a new suburb in preference to a house, the rent of which he could ill afford just then. Here Anna cut the little cake which Raye had bought at a pastrycook's on his way home from Lincoln's Inn the night before. But she did not do much besides. Raye's friend was obliged to depart almost immediately, and when he had left the only ones virtually present were Edith and Raye, who exchanged ideas with much animation. The conversation was indeed theirs only, Anna being as a domestic animal who humbly heard but understood not. Raye seemed startled in awakening to this fact, and began to feel dissatisfied with her inadequacy.

At last, more disappointed than he cared to own, he said, 'Mrs Harnham, my darling is so flurried that she doesn't know what she is doing or saying. I see that after this event a little quietude will be necessary before she gives tongue to that tender philosophy which she used to treat me to in her letters.'

They had planned to start early that afternoon for Knollsea, to spend the few opening days of their married life there, and as the hour for departure was drawing near Raye asked his wife if she would go to the writing-desk in the next room and scribble a little note to his sister, who had been unable to attend through indisposition, informing her that the ceremony was over, thanking her for her little present, and hoping to know her well now that she was the writer's sister as well as Charles's.

'Say it in the pretty poetical way you know so well how to adopt,' he added, 'for I want you particularly to win her, and both of you to be dear friends.'

Anna looked uneasy, but departed to her task, Raye remaining to talk to their guest. Anna was a long while absent, and her husband suddenly rose and went to her.

He found her still bending over the writing-table, with tears brimming up in her eyes; and he looked down upon the sheet of note-paper with some interest, to discover with what tact she had expressed her goodwill in the delicate circumstances. To his surprise she had progressed but a few lines, in the characters and spelling of a child of eight, and with the ideas of a goose.

'Anna,' he said, staring; 'what's this?'

'It only means – that I can't do it any better!' she answered, through her tears.

'Eh? Nonsense!'

'I can't!' she insisted, with miserable, sobbing hardihood. 'I – I – didn't write those letters, Charles! I only told *her* what to write! And not always that! But I am learning, O so fast, my dear, dear husband! And you'll forgive me, won't you, for not telling you before?' She slid to her knees, abjectly clasped his waist and laid her face against him.

He stood a few moments, raised her, abruptly turned, and shut the door upon her, rejoining Edith in the drawing-room. She saw that something untoward had been discovered, and their eyes remained fixed on each other.

'Do I guess rightly?' he asked, with wan quietude. '*You* were her scribe through all this?'

'It was necessary,' said Edith.

'Did she dictate every word you ever wrote to me?'

'Not every word.'

'In fact, very little?'

'Very little.'

'You wrote a great part of those pages every week from your own conceptions, though in her name!'

'Yes.'

'Perhaps you wrote many of the letters when you were alone, without communication with her?'

'I did.'

He turned to the bookcase, and leant with his hand over his face; and Edith, seeing his distress, became white as a sheet.

'You have deceived me – ruined me!' he murmured.

'O, don't say it!' she cried in her anguish, jumping up and putting her hand on his shoulder. 'I can't bear that!'

'Delighting me deceptively! Why did you do it – *why* did you!'

'I began doing it in kindness to her! How could I do otherwise than try to save such a simple girl from misery? But I admit that I continued it for pleasure to myself.'

Raye looked up. 'Why did it give you pleasure?' he asked.

'I must not tell,' said she.

He continued to regard her, and saw that her lips suddenly began to quiver under his scrutiny, and her eyes to fill and droop.

She started aside, and said that she must go to the station to catch the return train: could a cab be called immediately?

But Raye went up to her, and took her unresisting hand. 'Well, to think of such a thing as this!' he said. 'Why, you and I are friends – lovers – devoted lovers – by correspondence!'

'Yes; I suppose.'

'More.'

'More?'

'Plainly more. It is no use blinking that. Legally I have married her – God help us both! – in soul and spirit I have married you, and no other woman in the world!'

'Hush!'

'But I will not hush! Why should you try to disguise the full truth, when you have already owned half of it? Yes, it is between you and me that the bond is – not between me and her! Now I'll say no more. But, O my cruel one, I think I have one claim upon you!'

She did not say what, and he drew her towards him, and bent over her. 'If it was all pure invention in those letters,' he said emphatically, 'give me your cheek only. If you meant what you said, let it be lips. It is for the first and last time, remember!'

She put up her mouth, and he kissed her long. 'You forgive me?' she said, crying.

'Yes.'

'But you are ruined!'

'What matter!' he said, shrugging his shoulders. 'It serves me right!'

She withdrew, wiped her eyes, entered and bade good-bye to Anna, who had not expected her to go so soon, and was still wrestling with the letter. Raye followed Edith downstairs, and in three minutes she was in a hansom driving to the Waterloo station.

He went back to his wife. 'Never mind the letter, Anna, today,' he said gently. 'Put on your things. We, too, must be off shortly.'

The simple girl, upheld by the sense that she was indeed married, showed her delight at finding that he was as kind as ever after the disclosure. She did not know that before his eyes he beheld as it were a galley, in which he, the fastidious urban, was chained to work for the remainder of his life, with her, the unlettered peasant, chained to his side.

Edith travelled back to Melchester that day with a face that showed the very stupor of grief, her lips still tingling from the desperate pressure of his kiss. The end of her impassioned dream had come. When at dusk she reached the Melchester station her husband was there to meet her, but in his perfunctoriness and her preoccupation they did not see each other, and she went out of the station alone.

She walked mechanically homewards without calling a fly. Entering, she could not bear the silence of the house, and went up in the dark to where Anna had slept, where she remained thinking awhile. She then returned to the drawing-room, and not knowing what she did, crouched down upon the floor.

'I have ruined him!' she kept repeating. 'I have ruined him; because I would not deal treacherously towards her!'

In the course of half-an-hour a figure opened the door of the apartment.

'Ah – who's that?' she said, starting up, for it was dark.

'Your husband – who should it be?' said the worthy merchant.

'Ah – my husband! – I forgot I had a husband!' she whispered to herself.

'I missed you at the station,' he continued. 'Did you see Anna safely tied up? I hope so, for 'twas time.'

'Yes – Anna is married.'

Simultaneously with Edith's journey home Anna and her husband were sitting at the opposite windows of a second-class carriage which sped along to Knollsea. In his hand was a pocket-book full of creased sheets closely written over. Unfolding them one after another he read them in silence, and sighed.

'What are you doing, dear Charles?' she said timidly from the other window, and drew nearer to him as if he were a god.

'Reading over all those sweet letters to me signed "Anna",' he replied with dreary resignation.

An Imaginative Woman

When William Marchmill had finished his inquiries for lodgings at the well-known watering-place of Solentsea in Upper Wessex, he returned to the hotel to find his wife. She, with the children, had rambled along the shore, and Marchmill followed in the direction indicated by the military-looking hall-porter.

'By Jove, how far you've gone! I am quite out of breath,' Marchmill said, rather impatiently, when he came up with his wife, who was reading as she walked, the three children being considerably further ahead with the nurse.

Mrs Marchmill started out of the reverie into which the book had thrown her. 'Yes,' she said, 'you've been such a long time. I was tired of staying in that dreary hotel. But I am sorry if you have wanted me, Will?'

'Well, I have had trouble to suit myself. When you see the airy and comfortable rooms heard of, you find they are stuffy and uncomfortable. Will you come and see if what I've fixed on will do? There is not much room, I am afraid; but I can light on nothing better. The town is rather full.'

The pair left the children and nurse to continue their ramble, and went back together.

In age well-balanced, in personal appearance fairly matched, and in domestic requirements conformable, in temper this couple differed, though even here they did not often clash, he being equable, if not lymphatic, and she decidedly nervous and sanguine. It was to their tastes and fancies, those smallest, greatest particulars, that no common denominator could be applied. Marchmill considered his wife's likes and inclinations somewhat silly; she considered his sordid and material. The husband's business was that of a gunmaker in a thriving city northwards, and his soul was in that business always; the lady was best characterized by that superannuated phrase of elegance 'a votary of the muse'. An impressionable, palpitating creature was Ella, shrinking humanely from detailed knowledge of her husband's trade whenever she reflected that everything he manufactured had for its purpose the destruction of life. She could only recover her equanimity by assuring herself that some, at least, of his weapons were sooner or later used for the extermination of horrid vermin and animals almost as cruel to their inferiors in species as human beings were to theirs.

She had never antecedently regarded this occupation of his as any objection to having him for a husband. Indeed, the necessity of getting life-leased at all cost, a cardinal virtue which all good mothers teach, kept her from thinking of it at all till she had closed with William, had passed the honeymoon, and reached the reflecting stage. Then, like a person who has stumbled upon some object in the dark, she wondered what she had got; mentally walked round it, estimated it; whether it were rare or common; contained gold, silver, or lead; were a clog or a pedestal, everything to her or nothing.

She came to some vague conclusions, and since then had kept her heart alive by pitying her proprietor's obtuseness and want of refinement, pitying herself, and letting off her delicate and ethereal emotions in imaginative occupations, day-dreams, and night-sighs, which perhaps would not much have disturbed William if he had known of them.

Her figure was small, elegant, and slight in build, tripping, or rather bounding, in movement. She was dark-eyed, and had that marvellously bright and liquid sparkle in each pupil which characterizes persons of Ella's cast of soul, and is too often a cause of heartache to the possessor's male friends, ultimately sometimes to herself. Her husband was a tall, long-featured man, with a brown beard; he had a pondering regard; and was, it must be added, usually kind and tolerant to her. He spoke in squarely shaped sentences, and was supremely satisfied with a condition of sublunary things which made weapons a necessity.

Husband and wife walked till they had reached the house they were in search of, which stood in a terrace facing the sea, and was fronted by a small garden of wind-proof and salt-proof evergreens, stone steps leading up to the porch. It had its number in the row, but, being rather larger than the rest, was in addition sedulously distinguished as Coburg House by its landlady, though everybody else called it 'Thirteen, New Parade'. The spot was bright and lively now; but in winter it became necessary to place sandbags against the door, and to stuff up the keyhole against the

wind and rain, which had worn the paint so thin that the
priming and knotting showed through.

The householder, who had been watching for the gentleman's
return, met them in the passage, and showed the rooms. She
informed them that she was a professional man's widow, left in
needy circumstances by the rather sudden death of her husband,
and she spoke anxiously of the conveniences of the establishment.

Mrs Marchmill said that she liked the situation and the house;
but, it being small, there would not be accommodation enough,
unless she could have all the rooms.

The landlady mused with an air of disappointment. She
wanted the visitors to be her tenants very badly, she said, with
obvious honesty. But unfortunately two of the rooms were
occupied permanently by a bachelor gentleman. He did not pay
season prices, it was true; but as he kept on his apartments all the
year round, and was an extremely nice and interesting young
man, who gave no trouble, she did not like to turn him out for a
month's 'let', even at a high figure. 'Perhaps, however,' she
added, 'he might offer to go for a time.'

They would not hear of this, and went back to the hotel,
intending to proceed to the agent's to inquire further. Hardly had
they sat down to tea when the landlady called. Her gentleman,
she said, had been so obliging as to offer to give up his rooms for
three or four weeks rather than drive the newcomers away.

'It is very kind, but we won't inconvenience him in that way,'
said the Marchmills.

'O, it won't inconvenience him, I assure you!' said the landlady
eloquently. 'You see, he's a different sort of young man from
most – dreamy, solitary, rather melancholy – and he cares more
to be here when the south-westerly gales are beating against the
door, and the sea washes over the Parade, and there's not a soul
in the place, than he does now in the season. He'd just as soon be
where, in fact, he's going temporarily, to a little cottage on the
Island opposite, for a change.' She hoped therefore that they
would come.

The Marchmill family accordingly took possession of the house
next day, and it seemed to suit them very well. After luncheon
Mr Marchmill strolled out towards the pier, and Mrs Marchmill,
having despatched the children to their outdoor amusements on

the sands, settled herself in more completely, examining this and that article; and testing the reflecting powers of the mirror in the wardrobe door.

In the small back sitting-room, which had been the young bachelor's, she found furniture of a more personal nature than in the rest. Shabby books, of correct rather than rare editions, were piled up in a queerly reserved manner in corners, as if the previous occupant had not conceived the possibility that any incoming person of the season's bringing could care to look inside them. The landlady hovered on the threshold to rectify anything that Mrs Marchmill might not find to her satisfaction.

'I'll make this my own little room,' said the latter, 'because the books are here. By the way, the person who has left seems to have a good many. He won't mind my reading some of them, Mrs Hooper, I hope?'

'O dear no, ma'am. Yes, he has a good many. You see, he is in the literary line himself somewhat. He is a poet – yes, really a poet – and he has a little income of his own, which is enough to write verses on, but not enough for cutting a figure, even if he cared to.'

'A poet! O, I did not know that.'

Mrs Marchmill opened one of the books, and saw the owner's name written on the title-page. 'Dear me!' she continued; 'I know his name very well – Robert Trewe – of course I do; and his writings! And it is *his* rooms we have taken, and *him* we have turned out of his home?'

Ella Marchmill, sitting down alone a few minutes later, thought with interested surprise of Robert Trewe. Her own latter history will best explain that interest. Herself the only daughter of a struggling man of letters, she had during the last year or two taken to writing poems, in an endeavour to find a congenial channel in which to let flow her painfully embayed emotions, whose former limpidity and sparkle seemed departing in the stagnation caused by the routine of a practical household and the gloom of bearing children to a commonplace father. These poems, subscribed with a masculine pseudonym, had appeared in various obscure magazines, and in two cases in rather prominent ones. In the second of the latter the page which bore her effusion at the bottom, in smallish print, bore at the top, in large print, a few verses on the same subject by this very man, Robert Trewe.

Both of them had, in fact, been struck by a tragic incident reported in the daily papers, and had used it simultaneously as an inspiration, the editor remarking in a note upon the coincidence, and that the excellence of both poems prompted him to give them together.

After that event Ella, otherwise 'John Ivy', had watched with much attention the appearance anywhere in print of verse bearing the signature of Robert Trewe, who, with a man's unsusceptibility on the question of sex, had never once thought of passing himself off as a woman. To be sure, Mrs Marchmill had satisfied herself with a sort of reason for doing the contrary in her case; since nobody might believe in her inspiration if they found that the sentiments came from a pushing tradesman's wife, from the mother of three children by a matter-of-fact small-arms manufacturer.

Trewe's verse contrasted with that of the rank and file of recent minor poets in being impassioned rather than ingenious, luxuriant rather than finished. Neither *symboliste* nor *décadent*, he was a pessimist in so far as that character applies to a man who looks at the worst contingencies as well as the best in the human condition. Being little attracted by excellences of form and rhythm apart from content, he sometimes, when feeling outran his artistic speed, perpetrated sonnets in the loosely rhymed Elizabethan fashion, which every right-minded reviewer said he ought not to have done.

With sad and hopeless envy Ella Marchmill had often and often scanned the rival poet's work, so much stronger as it always was than her own feeble lines. She had imitated him, and her inability to touch his level would send her into fits of despondency. Months passed away thus, till she observed from the publishers' list that Trewe had collected his fugitive pieces into a volume, which was duly issued, and was much or little praised according to chance, and had a sale quite sufficient to pay for the printing.

This step onward had suggested to John Ivy the idea of collecting her pieces also, or at any rate of making up a book of her rhymes by adding many in manuscript to the few that had seen the light, for she had been able to get no great number into print. A ruinous charge was made for costs of publication; a few reviews noticed her poor little volume; but nobody talked of it, nobody bought it, and it fell dead in a fortnight – if it had ever been alive.

The author's thoughts were diverted to another groove just then by the discovery that she was going to have a third child, and the collapse of her poetical venture had perhaps less effect upon her mind than it might have done if she had been domestically unoccupied. Her husband had paid the publisher's bill with the doctor's, and there it all had ended for the time. But, though less than a poet of her century, Ella was more than a mere multiplier of her kind, and latterly she had begun to feel the old afflatus once more. And now by an odd conjunction she found herself in the rooms of Robert Trewe.

She thoughtfully rose from her chair and searched the apartment with the interest of a fellow-tradesman. Yes, the volume of his own verse was among the rest. Though quite familiar with its contents, she read it here as if it spoke aloud to her, then called up Mrs Hooper, the landlady, for some trivial service, and inquired again about the young man.

'Well, I'm sure you'd be interested in him, ma'am, if you could see him, only he's so shy that I don't suppose you will.' Mrs Hooper seemed nothing loth to minister to her tenant's curiosity about her predecessor. 'Lived here long? Yes, nearly two years. He keeps on his rooms even when he's not here: the soft air of this place suits his chest, and he likes to be able to come back at any time. He is mostly writing or reading, and doesn't see many people, though, for the matter of that, he is such a good, kind young fellow that folks would only be too glad to be friendly with him if they knew him. You don't meet kind-hearted people every day.'

'Ah, he's kind-hearted ... and good.'

'Yes; he'll oblige me in anything if I ask him. "Mr Trewe," I say to him sometimes, "you are rather out of spirits." "Well, I am, Mrs Hooper," he'll say, "though I don't know how you should find it out." "Why not take a little change?" I ask. Then in a day or two he'll say that he will take a trip to Paris, or Norway, or somewhere; and I assure you he comes back all the better for it.'

'Ah, indeed! His is a sensitive nature, no doubt.'

'Yes. Still he's odd in some things. Once when he had finished a poem of his composition late at night he walked up and down the room rehearsing it; and the floors being so thin – jerry-built houses, you know, though I say it myself – he kept me awake up above him till I wished him further.... But we get on very well.'

This was but the beginning of a series of conversations about the rising poet as the days went on. On one of these occasions Mrs Hooper drew Ella's attention to what she had not noticed before: minute scribblings in pencil on the wall-paper behind the curtains at the head of the bed.

'O! let me look,' said Mrs Marchmill, unable to conceal a rush of tender curiosity as she bent her pretty face close to the wall.

'These,' said Mrs Hooper, with the manner of a woman who knew things, 'are the very beginnings and first thoughts of his verses. He has tried to rub most of them out, but you can read them still. My belief is that he wakes up in the night, you know, with some rhyme in his head, and jots it down there on the wall lest he should forget it by the morning. Some of these very lines you see here I have seen afterwards in print in the magazines. Some are newer; indeed, I have not seen that one before. It must have been done only a few days ago.'

'O yes! ...'

Ella Marchmill flushed without knowing why, and suddenly wished her companion would go away, now that the information was imparted. An indescribable consciousness of personal interest rather than literary made her anxious to read the inscription alone; and she accordingly waited till she could do so, with a sense that a great store of emotion would be enjoyed in the act.

Perhaps because the sea was choppy outside the Island, Ella's husband found it much pleasanter to go sailing and steaming about without his wife, who was a bad sailor, than with her. He did not disdain to go thus alone on board the steamboats of the cheap-trippers, where there was dancing by moonlight, and where the couples would come suddenly down with a lurch into each other's arms; for, as he blandly told her, the company was too mixed for him to take her amid such scenes. Thus, while this thriving manufacturer got a great deal of change and sea-air out of his sojourn here, the life, external at least, of Ella was monotonous enough, and mainly consisted in passing a certain number of hours each day in bathing and walking up and down a stretch of shore. But the poetic impulse having again waxed strong, she was possessed by an inner flame which left her hardly conscious of what was proceeding around her.

She had read till she knew by heart Trewe's last little volume of verses, and spent a great deal of time in vainly attempting to rival some of them, till, in her failure, she burst into tears. The personal element in the magnetic attraction exercised by this circumambient, unapproachable master of hers was so much stronger than the intellectual and abstract that she could not understand it. To be sure, she was surrounded noon and night by his customary environment, which literally whispered of him to her at every moment; but he was a man she had never seen, and that all that moved her was the instinct to specialize a waiting emotion on the first fit thing that came to hand did not, of course, suggest itself to Ella.

In the natural way of passion under too practical conditions which civilization has devised for its fruition, her husband's love for her had not survived, except in the form of fitful friendship, any more than, or even so much as, her own for him; and, being a woman of very living ardours, that required sustenance of some sort, they were beginning to feed on this chancing material, which was, indeed, of a quality far better than chance usually offers.

One day the children had been playing hide-and-seek in a closet, whence, in their excitement, they pulled out some clothing. Mrs Hooper explained that it belonged to Mr Trewe, and hung it up in the closet again. Possessed of her fantasy, Ella went later in the afternoon, when nobody was in that part of the house, opened the closet, unhitched one of the articles, a mackintosh, and put it on, with the waterproof cap belonging to it.

'The mantle of Elijah!' she said. 'Would it might inspire me to rival him, glorious genius that he is!'

Her eyes always grew wet when she thought like that, and she turned to look at herself in the glass. *His* heart had beat inside that coat, and *his* brain had worked under that hat at levels of thought she would never reach. The consciousness of her weakness beside him made her feel quite sick. Before she had got the things off her the door opened, and her husband entered the room.

'What the devil – '

She blushed, and removed them.

'I found them in the closet here,' she said, 'and put them on in a freak. What have I else to do? You are always away!'

'Always away? Well ...'

That evening she had a further talk with the landlady, who might herself have nourished a half-tender regard for the poet, so ready was she to discourse ardently about him.

'You are interested in Mr Trewe, I know, ma'am,' she said; 'and he has just sent to say that he is going to call tomorrow afternoon to look up some books of his that he wants, if I'll be in, and he may select them from your room?'

'O yes!'

'You could very well meet Mr Trewe then, if you'd like to be in the way!'

She promised with secret delight, and went to bed musing of him.

Next morning her husband observed: 'I've been thinking of what you said, Ell: that I have gone about a good deal and left you without much to amuse you. Perhaps it's true. Today, as there's not much sea, I'll take you with me on board the yacht.'

For the first time in her experience of such an offer Ella was not glad. But she accepted it for the moment. The time for setting out drew near, and she went to get ready. She stood reflecting. The longing to see the poet she was now distinctly in love with overpowered all other considerations.

'I don't want to go,' she said to herself. 'I can't bear to be away! And I won't go.'

She told her husband that she had changed her mind about wishing to sail. He was indifferent, and went his way.

For the rest of the day the house was quiet, the children having gone out upon the sands. The blinds waved in the sunshine to the soft, steady stroke of the sea beyond the wall; and the notes of the Green Silesian band, a troop of foreign gentlemen hired for the season, had drawn almost all the residents and promenaders away from the vicinity of Coburg House. A knock was audible at the door.

Mrs Marchmill did not hear any servant go to answer it, and she became impatient. The books were in the room where she sat; but nobody came up. She rang the bell.

'There is some person waiting at the door,' she said.

'O no, ma'am! He's gone long ago. I answered it,' the servant replied, and Mrs Hooper came in herself.

'So disappointing!' she said. 'Mr Trewe not coming after all!'

'But I heard him knock, I fancy!'

'No; that was somebody inquiring for lodgings who came to the wrong house. I forgot to tell you that Mr Trewe sent a note just before lunch to say I needn't get any tea for him, as he should not require the books, and wouldn't come to select them.'

Ella was miserable, and for a long time could not even re-read his mournful ballad on 'Severed Lives', so aching was her erratic little heart, and so tearful her eyes. When the children came in with wet stockings, and ran up to her to tell her of their adventures, she could not feel that she cared about them half as much as usual.

'Mrs Hooper, have you a photograph of – the gentleman who lived here?' She was getting to be curiously shy in mentioning his name.

'Why, yes. It's in the ornamental frame on the mantelpiece in your own bedroom, ma'am.'

'No; the Royal Duke and Duchess are in that.'

'Yes, so they are; but he's behind them. He belongs rightly to that frame, which I bought on purpose; but as he went away he said: "Cover me up from those strangers that are coming, for God's sake. I don't want them staring at me, and I am sure they won't want me staring at them." So I slipped in the Duke and Duchess temporarily in front of him, as they had no frame, and Royalties are more suitable for letting furnished than a private young man. If you take 'em out you'll see him under. Lord, ma'am, he wouldn't mind if he knew it! He didn't think the next tenant would be such an attractive lady as you, or he wouldn't have thought of hiding himself, perhaps.'

'Is he handsome?' she asked timidly.

'*I* call him so. Some, perhaps, wouldn't.'

'Should I?' she asked, with eagerness.

'I think you would, though some would say he's more striking than handsome; a large-eyed thoughtful fellow, you know, with a very electric flash in his eye when he looks round quickly, such as you'd expect a poet to be who doesn't get his living by it.'

'How old is he?'

'Several years older than yourself, ma'am; about thirty-one or two, I think.'

Ella was, as a matter of fact, a few months over thirty herself; but she did not look nearly so much. Though so immature in nature, she was entering on that tract of life in which emotional women begin to suspect that last love may be stronger than first love; and she would soon, alas, enter on the still more melancholy tract when at least the vainer ones of her sex shrink from receiving a male visitor otherwise than with their backs to the window or the blinds half down. She reflected on Mrs Hooper's remark, and said no more about age.

Just then a telegram was brought up. It came from her husband, who had gone down the Channel as far as Budmouth with his friends in the yacht, and would not be able to get back till next day.

After her light dinner Ella idled about the shore with the children till dusk, thinking of the yet uncovered photograph in her room, with a serene sense of something ecstatic to come. For, with the subtle luxuriousness of fancy in which this young woman was an adept, on learning that her husband was to be absent that night she had refrained from incontinently rushing upstairs and opening the picture-frame, preferring to reserve the inspection till she could be alone, and a more romantic tinge be imparted to the occasion by silence, candles, solemn sea and stars outside, than was afforded by the garish afternoon sunlight.

The children had been sent to bed, and Ella soon followed, though it was not yet ten o'clock. To gratify her passionate curiosity she now made her preparations, first getting rid of superfluous garments and putting on her dressing-gown, then arranging a chair in front of the table and reading several pages of Trewe's tenderest utterances. Next she fetched the portrait-frame to the light, opened the back, took out the likeness, and set it up before her.

It was a striking countenance to look upon. The poet wore a luxuriant black moustache and imperial, and a slouched hat which shaded the forehead. The large dark eyes described by the landlady showed an unlimited capacity for misery; they looked out from beneath well-shaped brows as if they were reading the universe in the microcosm of the confronter's face, and were not altogether overjoyed at what the spectacle portended.

Ella murmured in her lowest, richest, tenderest tone: 'And it's *you* who've so cruelly eclipsed me these many times!'

As she gazed long at the portrait she fell into thought, till her eyes filled with tears, and she touched the cardboard with her lips. Then she laughed with a nervous lightness, and wiped her eyes.

She thought how wicked she was, a woman having a husband and three children, to let her mind stray to a stranger in this unconscionable manner. No, he was not a stranger! She knew his thoughts and feelings as well as she knew her own; they were, in fact, the self-same thoughts and feelings as hers, which her husband distinctly lacked; perhaps luckily for himself, considering that he had to provide for family expenses.

'He's nearer my real self, he's more intimate with the real me than Will is, after all, even though I've never seen him,' she said.

She laid his book and picture on the table at the bedside, and when she was reclining on the pillow she re-read those of Robert Trewe's verses which she had marked from time to time as most touching and true. Putting these aside she set up the photograph on its edge upon the coverlet, and contemplated it as she lay. Then she scanned again by the light of the candle the half-obliterated pencillings on the wallpaper beside her head. There they were – phrases, couplets, *bouts-rimés*, beginnings and middles of lines, ideas in the rough, like Shelley's scraps, and the least of them so intense, so sweet, so palpitating, that it seemed as if his very breath, warm and loving, fanned her cheeks from those walls, walls that had surrounded his head times and times as they surrounded her own now. He must often have put up his hand so – with the pencil in it. Yes, the writing was sideways, as it would be if executed by one who extended his arm thus.

These inscribed shapes of the poet's world,

> Forms more real than living man,
> Nurslings of immortality,

were, no doubt, the thoughts and spirit-strivings which had come to him in the dead of night, when he could let himself go and have no fear of the frost of criticism. No doubt they had often been written up hastily by the light of the moon, the rays of the lamp, in the blue-grey dawn, in full daylight perhaps never. And now her hair was dragging where his arm had lain when he secured the fugitive fancies; she was sleeping on a poet's lips, immersed in the very essence of him, permeated by his spirit as by an ether.

While she was dreaming the minutes away thus, a footstep came upon the stairs, and in a moment she heard her husband's heavy step on the landing immediately without.

'Ell, where are you?'

What possessed her she could not have described, but, with an instinctive objection to let her husband know what she had been doing, she slipped the photograph under the pillow just as he flung open the door with the air of a man who had dined not badly.

'O, I beg pardon,' said William Marchmill. 'Have you a headache? I am afraid I have disturbed you.'

'No, I've not got a headache,' said she. 'How is it you've come?'

'Well, we found we could get back in very good time after all, and I didn't want to make another day of it, because of going somewhere else tomorrow.'

'Shall I come down again?'

'O no. I'm as tired as a dog. I've had a good feed, and I shall turn in straight off. I want to get out at six o'clock tomorrow if I can.... I shan't disturb you by my getting up; it will be long before you are awake.' And he came forward into the room.

While her eyes followed his movements, Ella softly pushed the photograph further out of sight.

'Sure you're not ill?' he asked, bending over her.

'No, only wicked!'

'Never mind that.' And he stooped and kissed her. 'I wanted to be with you tonight.'

Next morning Marchmill was called at six o'clock; and in waking and yawning she heard him muttering to himself: 'What the deuce is this that's been crackling under me so?' Imagining her asleep he searched round him and withdrew something. Through her half-opened eyes she perceived it to be Mr Trewe.

'Well, I'm damned!' her husband exclaimed.

'What, dear?' said she.

'O, you are awake? Ha! ha!'

'What *do* you mean?'

'Some bloke's photograph – a friend of our landlady's, I

suppose. I wonder how it came here; whisked off the mantelpiece by accident perhaps when they were making the bed.'

'I was looking at it yesterday, and it must have dropped in then.'

'O, he's a friend of yours? Bless his picturesque heart!'

Ella's loyalty to the object of her admiration could not endure to hear him ridiculed. 'He's a clever man!' she said, with a tremor in her gentle voice which she herself felt to be absurdly uncalled for. 'He is a rising poet – the gentleman who occupied two of these rooms before we came, though I've never seen him.'

'How do you know, if you've never seen him?'

'Mrs Hooper told me when she showed me the photograph.'

'O, well, I must up and be off. I shall be home rather early. Sorry I can't take you today, dear. Mind the children don't go getting drowned.'

That day Mrs Marchmill inquired if Mr Trewe were likely to call at any other time.

'Yes,' said Mrs Hooper. 'He's coming this day week to stay with a friend near here till you leave. He'll be sure to call.'

Marchmill did return quite early in the afternoon; and, opening some letters which had arrived in his absence, declared suddenly that he and his family would have to leave a week earlier than they had expected to do – in short, in three days.

'Surely we can stay a week longer?' she pleaded. 'I like it here.'

'I don't. It is getting rather slow.'

'Then you might leave me and the children!'

'How perverse you are, Ell! What's the use? And have to come to fetch you! No: we'll all return together; and we'll make out our time in North Wales or Brighton a little later on. Besides, you've three days longer yet.'

It seemed to be her doom not to meet the man for whose rival talent she had a despairing admiration, and to whose person she was now absolutely attached. Yet she determined to make a last effort; and having gathered from her landlady that Trewe was living in a lonely spot not far from the fashionable town on the Island opposite, she crossed over in the packet from the neighbouring pier the following afternoon.

What a useless journey it was! Ella knew but vaguely where the house stood, and when she fancied she had found it, and ventured to inquire of a pedestrian if he lived there, the answer returned by the man was that he did not know. And if he did live there, how could she call upon him? Some women might have the assurance to do it, but she had not. How crazy he would think her. She might have asked him to call upon her, perhaps; but she had not the courage for that, either. She lingered mournfully about the picturesque seaside eminence till it was time to return to the town and enter the steamer for recrossing, reaching home for dinner without having been greatly missed.

At the last moment, unexpectedly enough, her husband said that he should have no objection to letting her and the children stay on till the end of the week, since she wished to do so, if she felt herself able to get home without him. She concealed the pleasure this extension of time gave her; and Marchmill went off the next morning alone.

But the week passed, and Trewe did not call.

On Saturday morning the remaining members of the March-mill family departed from the place which had been productive of so much fervour in her. The dreary, dreary train; the sun shining in moted beams upon the hot cushions; the dusty permanent way; the mean rows of wire – these things were her accompaniment: while out of the window the deep blue sea-levels disappeared from her gaze, and with them her poet's home. Heavy-hearted, she tried to read, and wept instead.

Mr Marchmill was in a thriving way of business, and he and his family lived in a large new house, which stood in rather extensive grounds a few miles outside the midland city wherein he carried on his trade. Ella's life was lonely here, as the suburban life is apt to be, particularly at certain seasons; and she had ample time to indulge her taste for lyric and elegiac composition. She had hardly got back when she encountered a piece by Robert Trewe in the new number of her favourite magazine, which must have been written almost immediately before her visit to Solentsea, for it contained the very couplet she had seen pencilled on the wall-paper by the bed, and Mrs Hooper had declared to be recent. Ella could resist no longer, but seizing a pen impulsively, wrote to him as a brother-poet, using the name of John Ivy, congratulating him in her letter on his triumphant executions in metre and rhythm of thoughts that moved his soul, as compared with her own brow-beaten efforts in the same pathetic trade.

To this address there came a response in a few days, little as she had dared to hope for it – a civil and brief note, in which the young poet stated that, though he was not well acquainted with Mr Ivy's verse, he recalled the name as being one he had seen attached to some very promising pieces; that he was glad to gain Mr Ivy's acquaintance by letter, and should certainly look with much interest for his productions in the future.

There must have been something juvenile or timid in her own epistle, as one ostensibly coming from a man, she declared to herself; for Trewe quite adopted the tone of an elder and superior in this reply. But what did it matter? He had replied; he had written to her with his own hand from that very room she knew so well, for he was now back again in his quarters.

The correspondence thus begun was continued for two months or more, Ella Marchmill sending him from time to time some that she considered to be the best of her pieces, which he very kindly accepted, though he did not say he sedulously read them, nor did he send her any of his own in return. Ella would have been more hurt at this than she was if she had not known that Trewe laboured under the impression that she was one of his own sex.

Yet the situation was unsatisfactory. A flattering little voice told her that, were he only to see her, matters would be otherwise. No doubt she would have helped on this by making a frank confession of womanhood, to begin with, if something had not happened, to her delight, to render it unnecessary. A friend of her husband's, the editor of the most important newspaper in their city and county, who was dining with them one day, observed during their conversation about the poet that his (the editor's) brother the landscape-painter was a friend of Mr Trewe's, and that the two men were at that very moment in Wales together.

Ella was slightly acquainted with the editor's brother. The next morning down she sat and wrote, inviting him to stay at her house for a short time on his way back, and requesting him to bring with him, if practicable, his companion Mr Trewe, whose acquaintance she was anxious to make. The answer arrived after some few days. Her correspondent and his friend Trewe would have much satisfaction in accepting her invitation on their way southward, which would be on such and such a day in the following week.

Ella was blithe and buoyant. Her scheme had succeeded; her beloved though as yet unseen one was coming. 'Behold, he standeth behind our wall; he looked forth at the windows, showing himself through the lattice,' she thought ecstatically. 'And, lo, the winter is past, the rain is over and gone, the flowers appear on the earth, the time of the singing of birds is come, and the voice of the turtle is heard in our land.'

But it was necessary to consider the details of lodging and feeding him. This she did most solicitously, and awaited the pregnant day and hour.

It was about five in the afternoon when she heard a ring at the door and the editor's brother's voice in the hall. Poetess as she was, or as she thought herself, she had not been too sublime that day to dress with infinite trouble in a fashionable robe of rich material, having a faint resemblance to the *chiton* of the Greeks, a style just then in vogue among ladies of an artistic and romantic turn, which had been obtained by Ella of her Bond Street dressmaker when she was last in London. Her visitor entered the drawing-room. She looked towards his rear; nobody else came through the door. Where, in the name of the God of Love, was Robert Trewe?

'O, I'm sorry,' said the painter, after their introductory words had been spoken. 'Trewe is a curious fellow, you know, Mrs Marchmill. He said he'd come; then he said he couldn't. He's rather dusty. We've been doing a few miles with knapsacks, you know; and he wanted to get on home.'

'He – he's not coming?'

'He's not; and he asked me to make his apologies.'

'When did you p-p-part from him?' she asked, her nether lip starting off quivering so much that it was like a *tremolo*-stop opened in her speech. She longed to run away from this dreadful bore and cry her eyes out.

'Just now, in the turnpike-road yonder there.'

'What! he has actually gone past my gates?'

'Yes. When we got to them – handsome gates they are, too, the finest bit of modern wrought-iron work I have seen – when we came to them we stopped, talking there a little while, and then he wished me good-bye and went on. The truth is, he's a little bit depressed just now, and doesn't want to see anybody. He's a very good fellow, and a warm friend, but a little uncertain and gloomy sometimes; he thinks too much of things. His poetry is rather too erotic and passionate, you know, for some tastes; and he has just come in for a terrible slating from the —— *Review* that was published yesterday; he saw a copy of it at the station by accident. Perhaps you've read it?'

'No.'

'So much the better. O, it is not worth thinking of; just one of those articles written to order, to please the narrow-minded set of subscribers upon whom the circulation depends. But he's upset by it. He says it is the misrepresentation that hurts him so; that, though he can stand a fair attack, he can't stand lies that he's powerless to refute and stop from spreading. That's just Trewe's weak point. He lives so much by himself that these things affect him much more than they would if he were in the bustle of fashionable or commercial life. So he wouldn't come here, making the excuse that it all looked so new and monied – if you'll pardon – '

'But – he must have known – there was sympathy here! Has he never said anything about getting letters from this address?'

'Yes, yes, he has, from John Ivy – perhaps a relative of yours, he thought, visiting here at the time?'

'Did he – like Ivy, did he say?'

'Well, I don't know that he took any great interest in Ivy.'

'Or in his poems?'

'Or in his poems – so far as I know, that is.'

Robert Trewe took no interest in her house, in her poems, or in their writer. As soon as she could get away she went into the nursery and tried to let off her emotion by unnecessarily kissing the children, till she had a sudden sense of disgust at being reminded how plain-looking they were, like their father.

The obtuse and single-minded landscape-painter never once perceived from her conversation that it was only Trewe she wanted, and not himself. He made the best of his visit, seeming to enjoy the society of Ella's husband, who also took a great fancy to him, and showed him everywhere about the neighbourhood, neither of them noticing Ella's mood.

The painter had been gone only a day or two when, while sitting upstairs alone one morning, she glanced over the London paper just arrived, and read the following paragraph:–

SUICIDE OF A POET

Mr Robert Trewe, who has been favourably known for some years as one of our rising lyrists, committed suicide at his lodgings at Solentsea on Saturday evening last by shooting himself in the right temple with a revolver. Readers hardly need to be reminded that Mr Trewe has recently attracted the attention of a much wider public than had hitherto known him, by his new volume of verse, mostly of an impassioned kind, entitled 'Lyrics to a Woman Unknown', which has been already favourably noticed in these pages for the extraordinary gamut of feeling it traverses, and which has been made the subject of a severe, if not ferocious, criticism in the —— Review. It is supposed, though not certainly known, that the article may have partially conduced to the sad act, as a copy of the review in question was found on his writing-table; and he has been observed to be in a somewhat depressed state of mind since the critique appeared.

Then came the report of the inquest, at which the following letter was read, it having been addressed to a friend at a distance: –

Dear ——, – Before these lines reach your hands I shall be delivered from the inconveniences of seeing, hearing, and knowing more of the things around me. I will not trouble you by giving my reasons for the step I have taken, though I can assure you they were sound and logical. Perhaps had I been blessed with a mother, or a sister, or a female friend of another sort tenderly devoted to me, I might have thought it worth while to continue my present existence. I have long dreamt of such an unattainable creature, as you know; and she, this undiscoverable, elusive one, inspired my last volume; the imaginary woman alone, for, in spite of what has been said in some quarters, there is no real woman behind the title. She has continued to the last unrevealed, unmet, unwon. I think it desirable to mention this in order that no blame may attach to any real woman as having been the cause of my decease by cruel or cavalier treatment of me. Tell my landlady that I am sorry to have caused her this unpleasantness; but my occupancy of the rooms will soon be forgotten. There are ample funds in my name at the bank to pay all expenses.

R. TREWE

Ella sat for a while as if stunned, then rushed into the adjoining chamber and flung herself upon her face on the bed.

Her grief and distraction shook her to pieces; and she lay in this frenzy of sorrow for more than an hour. Broken words came every now and then from her quivering lips: 'O, if he had only known of me – known of me – me! ... O, if I had only once met him – only once; and put my hand upon his hot forehead – kissed him – let him know how I loved him – that I would have suffered shame and scorn, would have lived and died, for him! Perhaps it would have saved his dear life! ... But no – it was not allowed! God is a jealous God; and that happiness was not for him and me!'

All possibilities were over; the meeting was stultified. Yet it was almost visible to her in her fantasy even now, though it could never be substantiated –

> The hour which might have been, yet might not be,
> Which man's and woman's heart conceived and bore,
> Yet whereof life was barren.

She wrote to the landlady at Solentsea in the third person, in as subdued a style as she could command, enclosing a postal order for a sovereign, and informing Mrs Hooper that Mrs Marchmill had seen in the papers the sad account of the poet's death, and having been, as Mrs Hooper was aware, much interested in Mr Trewe during her stay at Coburg House, she would be obliged if Mrs Hooper could obtain a small portion of his hair before his coffin was closed down, and send it her as a memorial of him, as also the photograph that was in the frame.

By the return-post a letter arrived containing what had been requested. Ella wept over the portrait and secured it in her private drawer; the lock of hair she tied with white ribbon and put in her bosom, whence she drew it and kissed it every now and then in some unobserved nook.

'What's the matter?' said her husband, looking up from his newspaper on one of these occasions. 'Crying over something? A lock of hair? Whose is it?'

'He's dead!' she murmured.

'Who?'

'I don't want to tell you, Will, just now, unless you insist!' she said, a sob hanging heavy in her voice.

'O, all right.'

'Do you mind my refusing? I will tell you some day.'

'It doesn't matter in the least, of course.'

He walked away whistling a few bars of no tune in particular; and when he had got down to his factory in the city the subject came into Marchmill's head again.

He, too, was aware that a suicide had taken place recently at the house they had occupied at Solentsea. Having seen the volume of poems in his wife's hand of late, and heard fragments of the landlady's conversation about Trewe when they were her tenants, he all at once said to himself, 'Why of course it's he! ... How the devil did she get to know him? What sly animals women are!'

Then he placidly dismissed the matter, and went on with his daily affairs. By this time Ella at home had come to a determination. Mrs Hooper, in sending the hair and photograph, had informed her of the day of the funeral; and as the morning and noon wore on an overpowering wish to know where they were laying him took possession of the sympathetic woman. Caring very little now what her husband or any one else might think of her eccentricities, she wrote Marchmill a brief note, stating that she was called away for the afternoon and evening, but would return on the following morning. This she left on his desk, and having given the same information to the servants, went out of the house on foot.

When Mr Marchmill reached home early in the afternoon the servants looked anxious. The nurse took him privately aside, and hinted that her mistress's sadness during the past few days had been such that she feared she had gone out to drown herself. Marchmill reflected. Upon the whole he thought that she had not done that. Without saying whither he was bound he also started off, telling them not to sit up for him. He drove to the railway-station, and took a ticket for Solentsea.

It was dark when he reached the place, though he had come by a fast train, and he knew that if his wife had preceded him thither it could only have been by a slower train, arriving not a great while before his own. The season at Solentsea was now past: the parade was gloomy, and the flys were few and cheap. He asked the way to the Cemetery, and soon reached it. The gate was locked, but the keeper let him in, declaring, however, that there was nobody within the precincts. Although it was not late, the autumnal darkness had now become intense; and he found some difficulty in keeping to the serpentine path which led to the quarter where, as the man had told him, the one or two interments for the day had taken place. He stepped upon the grass, and, stumbling over some pegs, stooped now and then to discern if possible a figure against the sky. He could see none; but lighting on a spot where the soil was trodden, beheld a crouching object beside a newly made grave. She heard him, and sprang up.

'Ell, how silly this is!' he said indignantly. 'Running away from home – I never heard such a thing! Of course I am not jealous of this unfortunate man; but it is too ridiculous that you, a married woman with three children and a fourth coming, should go losing your head like this over a dead lover! ... Do you know you were locked in? You might not have been able to get out all night.'

She did not answer.

'I hope it didn't go far between you and him, for your own sake.'

'Don't insult me, Will.'

'Mind, I won't have any more of this sort of thing; do you hear?'

'Very well,' she said.

He drew her arm within his own, and conducted her out of the Cemetery. It was impossible to get back that night; and not wishing to be recognized in their present sorry condition he took her to a miserable little coffee-house close to the station, whence they departed early in the morning, travelling almost without speaking, under the sense that it was one of those dreary situations occurring in married life which words could not mend, and reaching their own door at noon.

The months passed, and neither of the twain ever ventured to start a conversation upon this episode. Ella seemed to be only too frequently in a sad and listless mood, which might almost have been called pining. The time was approaching when she would have to undergo the stress of childbirth for a fourth time, and that apparently did not tend to raise her spirits.

'I don't think I shall get over it this time!' she said one day.

'Pooh! what childish foreboding! Why shouldn't it be as well now as ever?'

She shook her head. 'I feel almost sure I am going to die; and I should be glad, if it were not for Nelly, and Frank, and Tiny.'

'And me!'

'You'll soon find somebody to fill my place,' she murmured, with a sad smile. 'And you'll have a perfect right to; I assure you of that.'

'Ell, you are not thinking still about that – poetical friend of yours?'

She neither admitted nor denied the charge. 'I am not going to get over my illness this time,' she reiterated. 'Something tells me I shan't.'

This view of things was rather a bad beginning, as it usually is; and, in fact, six weeks later, in the month of May, she was lying in her room, pulseless and bloodless, with hardly strength enough left to follow up one feeble breath with another, the infant for whose unnecessary life she was slowly parting with her own being fat and well. Just before her death she spoke to Marchmill softly:

'Will, I want to confess to you the entire circumstances of that – about you know what – that time we visited Solentsea. I can't tell what possessed me – how I could forget you so, my husband! But I had got into a morbid state: I thought you had been unkind; that you had neglected me; that you weren't up to my intellectual level, while he was, and far above it. I wanted a fuller appreciator, perhaps, rather than another lover – '

She could get no further then for very exhaustion; and she went off in sudden collapse a few hours later, without having said anything more to her husband on the subject of her love for the poet. William Marchmill, in truth, like most husbands of several years' standing, was little disturbed by retrospective jealousies, and had not shown the least anxiety to press her for confessions concerning a man dead and gone beyond any power of inconveniencing him more.

But when she had been buried a couple of years it chanced one day that, in turning over some forgotten papers that he wished to destroy before his second wife entered the house, he lighted on a lock of hair in an envelope, with the photograph of the deceased poet, a date being written on the back in his late wife's hand. It was that of the time they spent at Solentsea.

Marchmill looked long and musingly at the hair and portrait, for something struck him. Fetching the little boy who had been the death of his mother, now a noisy toddler, he took him on his knee, held the lock of hair against the child's head, and set up the photograph on the table behind, so that he could closely compare the features each countenance presented. By a known but inexplicable trick of Nature there were undoubtedly strong traces of resemblance to the man Ella had never seen; the dreamy and peculiar expression of the poet's face sat, as the transmitted idea, upon the child's, and the hair was of the same hue.

'I'm damned if I didn't think so!' murmured Marchmill. 'Then she *did* play me false with that fellow at the lodgings! Let me see: the dates – the second week in August ... the third week in May.... Yes ... yes.... Get away, you poor little brat! You are nothing to me!'